Danny Wallace is a *Sunday Times*-bestselling author who lives in London. He has written six non-fiction books including *Yes Man* which became a hugely successful film with Jim Carrey in the lead role. In 2012 Danny's first novel *Charlotte Street* was published to great acclaim and has been described as 'brilliantly funny' by the *Daily Mail* and one of the year's 'coolest must-reads' by *Stylist*.

Danny has a weekly column in *ShortList* magazine and in 2012 was the host of the 'Xfm Breakfast Show with Danny Wallace', for which he won three Sony Radio Academy Awards and Arqiva Radio Presenter of the Year.

Find out more at: www.dannywallace.com

KT-163-656

Also by Danny Wallace:

Charlotte Street

Non-fiction:
Awkward Situations for Men
More Awkward Situations for Men
Friends Like These
Yes Man
Danny Wallace and the Centre of the Universe
Join Me
Random Acts of Kindness
Are You Dave Gorman?

'T...
a...
stealthily profound.'
William Boyd

'*Who is Tom Ditto?* is Danny Wallace at his very best:
..., assured and relentlessly clever. A brilliant novel.'
John Niven

'An air of mystery and of a past being reconstructed,
with a booster shot of comedy ... As you would
...ect from the author of *Awkward Situations for Men*,
the toe-curling embarrassment of much of
Tom's life is well realised.'
Observer

'Wallace has scored another hit with this quirky novel...
Packed full of gags, this is also a tender and
touching story.'
Sunday Mirror

'This is a terrific novel ... The plot is wild and
unexpected, with a dash of sinister,
and it's incredibly funny.'
The Times

'The brilliant author is back with this hilarious,
sharp new novel.'
The Sun on Sunday

'...is mystery, written by TV funny man Danny Wallace,
will leave you completely mesmerised.'
Now

'Wallace is adept at capturing the nuances of
the mundane and the ridiculous,
while being incredibly funny.'
Stylist

'Danny is as hilarious as ever.'
Shortlist

'Danny Wallace's beguiling second novel seduces the
reader by stealth with some laugh-out-loud throwaway
pieces of astute observational comedy … It's the
kind of book you have to ration to avoid it
being over too quickly.'
Daily Mail

'A funny, clever novel.'
Marie Claire

'Chortlesome.'
Bella

'A deep story with a consistently grounded humour.'
Emerald Street

'Wallace's observational skills and attention to detail are
superb…A hilarious and fresh take on modern life.
Brilliantly written.'
Heat

DANNY WALLACE

WHO IS TOM Ditto?

EBURY
PRESS

1 3 5 7 9 10 8 6 4 2

First published in 2014 by Ebury Press, an imprint of Ebury Publishing
A Random House Group Company
This edition published in 2015

The Random House Group Limited Reg. No. 954009

Addresses for companies within the Random House Group can be found at:
www.randomhouse.co.uk

A CIP catalogue record for this book is
available from the British Library

The Random House Group Limited supports The Forest Stewardship
Council® (FSC®), the leading international forest-certification organisation.
Our books carrying the FSC label are printed on FSC® -certified paper.
FSC is the only forest-certification scheme supported by the leading
environmental organisations, including Greenpeace.
Our paper procurement policy can be found at:
www.randomhouse.co.uk/environment

Printed and bound by CPI Group (UK) Ltd, Croydon, CR0 4YY

ISBN 9780091919085

To buy books by your favourite authors and register for offers visit:
www.randomhouse.co.uk

To Wag and Will

The boys

DANNY WALLACE

WHO IS TOM Ditto?

'Be well'

Ezra Cockroft, 1982

one

The evening of June the 12th was unusual for many reasons in the end, of course, but it was unusual mostly because the evening of June the 12th was the evening my girlfriend did not leave me.

Tom,
I have not left you. But I am gone.
Please just carry on as normal.
Love always
Hayley

I stared at the words and sat down in my chair.

two

I am not saying I'm not a trusting man.

I'm not saying you can't trust most people. But usually, when you meet someone you can trust, you know. It was as obvious with Hayley as her big blue eyes; as the curl of hair she'd keep tucking behind her ear.

Here, her – Hayley – *this* was a girl you could trust.

The second she gave me her number, I did the thing I always do when someone gives me their number.

I looked at it, then said, 'Wow, no way! That's my *favourite* number!'

It's a pretty good thing to say.

All you have to do after saying something like that is sit back and wait for the laughter to subside. It's a banker. A deal-sealer. If that doesn't get a laugh, you're doing it wrong, and maybe you should start questioning how you do everything else in your life, too, because maybe you can't even make a sandwich properly.

And now I sat in my flat, in the dark, on the chair in the corner, dialling that number again and again and again and again and again.

It was fast becoming not-my-favourite.

A strange thing, being left, while being assured you have not been left.

What are you supposed to do with that? Just switch to solo behaviour? Just think 'fine' and start buying meals-for-one?

Four hours had passed and I was still sitting in that chair. Jangling my keys. Listening to the dogs outside. Dusk had turned to dark. Confusion had turned to anger and settled, lump-thick, deep in my stomach.

Where had Hayley gone?

I guess that was my main question.

But also, and obviously … why? How long would she be gone? Was she *gone* gone? Why didn't I *know* where she'd gone? Why didn't I know she was going? Why was she saying she was going but not gone?

Almost two years we'd been together. We had responsibilities. We had direct debits.

I'd left messages, of course, tonight. I sounded confused on the first one. Furious on the second. Worried on the third and fourth. Desperate as I hit the fifth, and sixth, and then silent seventh.

I'd texted.

Where are you?
Where have you gone?
Hayley, call me.

I'd made calls to other people, too. Lots of calls.

Her best friend, Fran. Her brother, her sister …

'Annie, it's Tom,' I'd said, head down, shoulders hunched, headache starting, standing by the window, one hand against the wall, phone pressed too hard against my cheek, because this feeling, these nerves, they had to go somewhere. It was loud where Annie was. Restaurant? Maybe drinks? 'Is Hayley with you?'

A moment.

'No, Tom …'

She knew. She knew she'd gone. It was right there slotted between the pause and where a 'What do you mean?' should have been. So yes, her sister knew she'd gone, but worse – she'd known she was *going*.

'Why didn't you tell me?'

'Hayley wanted it to be a surprise for everyone.'

'A … *surprise*?'

She sounded distant. What did that mean? Was Annie preparing to say goodbye to me? Backing off? Fading me out of her life? That was bad. The ex you can keep hold of for a while, they owe it to you while you talk things out, they're still in your life, but the friends, the family … they start drifting away the second they see the iceberg from the ship.

'Well, it's definitely a surprise,' I said, loudly, angrily, trying to keep her engaged, stop her from jumping overboard. 'What does it mean, Annie? Where is she?'

'She's not left you, Tom, if that's what you're worried about.'

If that's what I'm worried about?!

But I had to play it carefully here. Annie sounded testy. Like I was overreacting. Like that was *typical* of me to overreact to the disappearance of a loved one. Like it was a *gerbil*, or something.

'No, that's what she says, Annie, and yet she *has* left me, if you look at the basic fucking facts.'

My voice was trembling now.

'Don't swear at me.'

'Where is she?'

'I don't know.'

'Bullshit.'

'Don't swear at me, and I don't *know*, Tom, honestly. Did she not tell you any of this?'

The backs of my eyes sparked with rage.

'Do you think I'd be phoning you up if—'

'Okay, Tom, sorry, yes—'

'Because this is quite a fucking shock to the system, and—'

'Don't *swear* at me, and look—'

'Annie, she's disappeared and you know where she is, don't you?'

'Take care, Tom.'

And there, in those final words, my biggest clue.

Take care, Tom.

Click.

She was gone, wasn't she?

'You know what'd be a good name for a band?' asked Pippy, spinning in her chair. 'REM.'

'I think there's already been a band called REM,' I said, barely looking up, eyes sallow, skin dulled. 'The world-famous band REM.'

It was 4am and I was at my desk.

'I'm just saying, REM would be a good name for a band,' she replied. 'Not asking for you to recite all of musical history. I'm just saying, REM would be a good name if you were starting a band.'

'It would be a terrible name,' I said. 'Because there is already a band called REM, and by that I once more mean the world-famous band REM.'

'Because it makes you think of music, doesn't it, saying REM?' she said, oblivious.

'It makes you think of the music of REM, yes.'

'Bingo,' she said. 'So I say REM, you think music.'

'Yes, I think REM music.'

'Point proved, case closed, many thank yous and happy returns.'

Jesus, I wished Pippy sat somewhere else. Like maybe Belgium. She was nice enough – very short, heavy fringe, jumper with a dog on it – but such an unlikely producer for London's #3 urban R&B station. You'd see her walking along the corridor with Bark and Lyricis like she was their care worker. She's a little older than me, but acts a little younger. Wants to stay 'relevant'.

'You look knackered, mate, are you ill?' she said. 'Just sayin'.'

DANNY WALLACE

Pippy liked saying something insulting and then saying 'just saying' because she felt this meant she could be as insulting as she wanted without other people being able to take offence, because after all, she was 'just saying' it.

'I didn't sleep,' I said, reading and re-reading the first line of my script again …

It's Wednesday June 13th, I'm Tom Adoyo with the stories you're waking up to …

'Oh, you *need* to sleep,' she said, like this was advice straight from the Dalai Lama. 'Hashtag "earlies", mate.'

I was covering for Kate Mann on Talk London's *London Calling with Leslie James* all week. The breakfast show.

Two questions everyone wants to know the second they know you have a job like mine. The first is 'what time do you have to get up?'. The second is 'what time do you have to go to bed?' The answer to both is 'too early', but here you go:

I aim for bed at 9pm. I Sky+ the things I'll miss. I understand and accept this means I'll always be slightly behind the national cultural conversation. I'm up at 3.45, on the bus at 4.10, in by 4.50, apart from days like today when being with Pippy at four in the morning is better than lying in the dark listening to the foxes mate outside.

Then I gather the news (by which I mean look at what the person before me has done), I plan ahead (by which I mean work out how to slightly change each bulletin to make it sound like I'm working), I check Burli for audio, then the wires – PA, Sky, Reuters – and then see if there's anything in from the police.

(And those, by the way, are the releases that need the most rewriting. Why do the police speak in their own weird language? '*The suspect was seen proceeding in a westerly direction.*' No one speaks like that. Not a single functioning human being on God's green

[7]

WHO IS TOM DITTO?

earth. There was that pop star they caught on the A6 recently. '*At oh twenty-two hours a suspect was spotted driving erratically and upon bringing the vehicle to a stop the strong aroma of intoxicants from the forty-six-year-old male driver was immediately detected*.' Dude – you stopped a drunk driver. You're not writing a perfume ad.)

I write my copy, I read my copy, I'm in studio at six and done by twelve.

I'm well aware this is pretend news. Very few people are doing the actual heavy lifting. I just help spread the word. I'm just part of this mass illusion. But at least I write my own stuff. Or at least rewrite other people's stuff myself. Some newsreaders just read news. They have writers, they swan in and swan out. They're 'show and go'. But that's when mistakes happen. If you write it, you know it. You know your own voice, how you say things, just when to pause, just what to stress.

Talking of stress …

'You're never going to up your game if you come in sleepless,' said Pippy. 'Just sayin'.'

Christ, I thought, if you're just saying it, just say it. Don't say it and then say you've just said it. That's not just saying it. Just saying it is just saying it.

'Yeah, well, there's a lot going on right now,' I tried, and immediately I ached for home. I'm not one of those people who hate my job. I like it a lot. Though sometimes I worry I like it because I find it easy. That said, what the hell was I doing here? Four am in a strip-lit office with bright blue chairs and grey, grey walls waiting to start my shift in a city that's still an acquaintance and, despite a woman called Pippy, completely *alone*.

I wanted to talk about it, of course I did. But there'd only been Hayley and Hayley's friends since I moved to London. Everyone in Bristol – my old boss, my dentist, my best mate Calum – told me it was a mistake. It was too soon; I hardly knew this girl.

Only dad remained quiet. I'd phoned him late one night – it was about lunchtime for him, I could hear his wife and her kids in the background, I think they were on their way somewhere – and he'd told me to do what I felt was right. That he was sorry he wasn't there to meet her.

But before I knew it I'd found myself a job, moved my stuff to Stoke Newington, and now here I was. So no: I hadn't slept. And no: I didn't want to raise this with my friends back home, because maybe it was just a blip, maybe couples do stuff like this all the time and maybe I didn't want to look like the total tool they'd all quietly predicted I'd end up looking.

All I'd done last night was make it from the chair to the bed and just lie there. Stunned. Running through the past few weeks, trying to work out what had happened, what had been the catalyst, what had made her go.

'How's Hayley?' asked Pippy, maybe sensing something. She's one of those people who fancies herself mildly psychic and I'd made it my job to disprove this whenever possible.

'Hayley is *wonderful*,' I said, and then stood up to be somewhere else.

'Is she still working at Zara?' she asked, as I was halfway out the door, and I stopped.

Because that was a very good point.

'It's Wednesday June 13th, I'm Tom Adoyo with the stories you're waking up to ... Four arrests after man's body found ... Teacher speaks out about classroom birth ... and in sport, it's all change at Chelsea ...'

London Calling with Leslie James. 6 'til 10 in the capital and beyond. Some people tune in online from the States, or Singapore, or Australia, for a little slice of home and the opinions of Leslie James. Let's just say he's an acquired taste. Cabbies love him – they say he's one of them. Tells it like it is.

Kate – his regular news presenter, or 'desk jockey' as he says, expecting a laugh even on the thousandth time – is on maternity leave, and I'm the guy the news department sticks anywhere that needs it. I'm moveable. A man without a home. If I was a suspicious man, I'd say I'm given the worst gigs. Early mornings, generally. Late nights. It's up to Maureen in HR, a woman who took an immediate dislike to me, based, so I hear, on my 'moods'. Some of this is my fault. The rest I blame on the fact that my natural resting face is one of dark concern. People think I look deep, troubled, like a poet or a serial killer or a judge on some talent show wrongathon. Sometimes I am troubled, of course, but really I'm just as likely to be thinking about a dog, or badminton. So she said I needed to work on them. And in the meantime, she'd do nothing to help. It would be unkind of me – so unkind of me – to say she is a woman who relishes her minuscule powers.

I checked my emails.

....

From: MAUREEN THOMAS
To: ALL

If you are UNABLE to place your pieces of paper in the GREEN RECYCLING BIN we will take these bins away from you as you are NOT FIT to use them. I am SERIOUS.

....

Delete.

So one day I'll be on Talk London, the next evening attempting to subtly change my accent so I fit in with Bark and Lyricis on Vibe.

SoundHaus takes up two-thirds of a strikingly bland building just off High Holborn, the third-biggest commercial radio outfit in

Britain, home to Talk London, Vibe, Jazz Bar, Rocket!, Harmony, and one or two others. And I'll tell you what – not one of those stations I'd listen to voluntarily. No way. Are you mental? They're stations you hear as you drive home in an illegal minicab. And they're all struggling to keep up with the stations of Global or Bauer ... except maybe Talk London and its stand-out star, *Hitachi Commercial Radio Talk Presenter of the Year (1 million TSA plus)* Leslie James.

Leslie James is not a man who will apologise for his opinions.

Here are some opinions Leslie James will not apologise for.

'Fox-hunting. Bad, yes, but I see both sides of the argument. And I make no apology for that, and I say that sincerely.'

'Women should have equal pay, but – and I mean this, and I do not apologise for saying this – the work they do should be equal too. Or greater!'

Just yesterday:

'The Muslim world *has* to take some responsibility for the actions of some Muslims who do *not* represent them all but do do bad things in their name, and I make no apology for that, but I must be clear, I am *not* saying *all* Muslims.'

It's pretty controversial stuff.

On-air he can be a bit of a dick, but off-air, he's actually a bit of a dick.

'*... and in showbusiness, another award last night for Jay Z as Beyoncé took to the stage, and later in your Showbiz Update with Jen Latham, she'll be talking to pop star Aphra Just about her move to France, and the new man in her life ...*'

I'd rather be reporting on Syria.

'*It's 6.32, and now you're up to date ...*'

I gathered my stuff together. I'd be back before seven. I try not to stay in studio during the show.

'I've forgotten your name again,' said Leslie, as the ads played out. He pointed at me, vaguely.

'Oh, it's—'

'But I don't like you saying, "now you're up to date". I think it's pretty self-evident that people are now up to date because you've just updated them.'

'Ah. Thing is, it's from the news team,' I said. 'They want everyone on the station using it. Sense of unity.'

'Sorry, is this the station or is this my show?' he said, which was a tricky one, because the answer was 'both'. 'I'm telling you to lose it. So lose it. And now *you're* up to date ...'

Five past twelve, shift over.

I'd done my handover notes in a hurry, then just googled, clicked, read.

Facebook. No updates.

Twitter. No update since the restaurant the other night.

I'd even checked her MySpace, which is where she would always joke she'd go when she wanted to be alone.

No updates.

Do I tell people? Because I have no idea what to tell people.

I tried Fran, her best friend, again. Fran likes me. We understand each other. But I was getting nothing back and it made me paranoid. Did Fran know? Was Fran in on it?

But Pippy made a good point: Zara, on Long Acre. She's Deputy Store Manager. Her colleagues would know where Hayley was. They'd have to. She'd have told them, because you have to tell your employers these things, don't you, if you're not coming in any more?

But what if you *are* still coming in? What if it's just me she's away from? And if she's in there as usual, then great, I'll confront her.

Cause a scene. Ask her what she means by all this. Ask her where she stayed last night.

Jesus, *where did she stay last night?*

I could walk there in ten minutes, and by the counter: result. I spotted Sonal. We'd only met maybe twice before, but I knew her name. And also, she was wearing a name badge.

'Sonal ...'

'Hi ...' she said, half-smiling.

'It's Tom. Hayley's boyfriend.'

'Tom! How are you? Did she forget something?'

'Oh. So you know?'

'I know what?'

'You know Hayley's gone?'

Busted. Gotcha. You knew, you bitch.

'Yes, I know she's gone,' she said, brightly. 'Of course I know she's gone. What do you mean, I know she's gone?'

'I didn't know she was gone.'

I sounded panicked and crazy. A couple of women holding a black dress – they're all black dresses in Zara – turned to look at me. Sonal lowered her voice and clearly hoped I'd lower mine.

'You didn't know she was gone?'

'Where's she gone?'

'Sorry – you don't know where she's gone or you didn't know she was gone?'

'Either. Both. I got a note last night.'

She blinked at me, once or twice, eyes widening for a second, then back.

'A *note*?'

'Where is she?'

'Hayley? She's gone *travelling*, I think.'

She called over to a colleague.

'Jo? She said she was going travelling, Hayley, yeah?'

Jo nodded. All hooped earrings and scraped-back hair.

'She said she was going travelling,' said Sonal.

'Travelling *where?*'

'She said she didn't know where.'

'Oh, so just general travelling? Just like that? Sudden aimless travelling?'

'Well, not just like that – she gave her month's notice.'

'A *month?*' – fuck! – 'You've known about this for a *month?*'

'It was her leaving do last week,' said Jo.

My knees weakened.

'She had a *leaving do?* Sorry, just to be clear, my girlfriend had a *leaving do* last week and has now gone travelling?'

Sonal tried a smile, then a shrug, both unconvincing.

'What night?'

'What?'

'What night did she have her leaving do?' I said.

'Um, Thursday, I think,' said Jo.

Thursday. She has Pilates on Thursdays.

My head started to spin.

She'd known for a month. A month at the minimum. She'd even celebrated.

'Well, this is very unusual,' said Sonal, shaking her head, and now the world became just noise, just till rings and door beeps, just traffic and wind, and 'Yes,' I said. 'This is very fucking unusual indeed.'

[1]

Kosinski, M/Columbia Journalism School 3/15/84
Michael Berg Award entry

AN INTERVIEW WITH EZRA COCKROFT

It is Christmas 1982 and Professor Ezra Cockroft sits at his table at Keen's on 72 West 36th Street and picks at his salad. Like me, he has ordered for himself the recommended house salad with a twist and left the beets and candied walnuts to the side in one neat little tower.

He is a tall man of eighty with delicate hands and long limbs, still tanned from an autumn spent in Floridian sunshine, though dressed now in New York black.

He sips at his drink – a thin green daiquiri, which I too ordered because I happened to notice the recipe was the very same my great-aunt had at this time of year so often used.

I ask him about this.

'You ordered with confidence,' he says. 'I invested in your confidence. Investments made with confidence tend by their nature to carry lower risk – it implies assumed knowledge, and thereby affords those you carry along with you a greater chance of reward.'

He takes his napkin and cleans a corner of a leaded casement window. A barman prepares another daiquiri behind a robust mahogany and brass bar.

My steamed Finnan Haddie with drawn butter arrives, as a heartbeat later does his.

three

'*Thursday June 14th, I'm Tom Adoyo with the stories you're waking up to... ...*'

I'd managed maybe two or three hours of fitful sleep. Got out of bed, somehow, and made my way to the nightbus. Ah, the nightbus. My people.

It's actually pretty full at just gone four. You'd think it'd be empty. But there are people. Cleaners, mainly, heading into town, keeping a low profile for an invisible job. A couple of the homeless upstairs, bedded down for the night, pale faces pressed heavy against smeared windows. The people you don't treat as real.

'*... Thousands trapped after Mexico storms ...*'

The nightbus is where I write my weather. It's pretty simple. Of course, I check the BBC website. But you have to check the Met Office app, too – you can't just rely on the BBC. I don't know how they get away with it. It's people like me that get the grief for it. All day, you'd get people complaining to the station, texting in, saying 'you said it was going to rain today and it has not rained today'. Well, why are you texting me about it? Just enjoy it. Grow up.

So I tapped it all out, checked the news, and emailed myself the script. I sometimes wonder what people must think if they're reading over my shoulder. 'Wow. This guy writes *very* formal emails about so many topical world events.'

Anyway, highs of nineteen today.

'… *US officials say North Korea could be planning multiple missile launches …*'

My eyes are so heavy in this studio. Pits musty. I haven't showered, just topped up with Lynx. Adewale, the security guard on reception, had made a joke when I floated in. I didn't listen, just pushed through the heavy doors to the corridor, where today each of the six LCD screens had been programmed to read WELCOME TO OUR FRIENDS AT AIG INSURANCE!, a couple of small pink animated balloons juddering from side to side.

'… *Benefits cheats to face ten-year terms …*'

I had to blink hard to focus on the copy on the page. I'd spent last night at the Builder's Arms, on the chair by the door, thinking, not wanting to be in the flat, not wanting to be just listening out for the scratch of a key or waiting for a text. I don't drink, really. I just wanted to be around people who did. That's when you hear the really heavy laughs, the guttural *woofs* of shared joy, building, rising, exploding like fireworks in a dim pub sky.

'*And later, in showbiz, which pop star has drawn criticism from the Vatican after filming the video for new track "Carry On" just metres from the papal residence …?*'

Shoot me now.

'*It's 6.03, currently four degrees in Soho, with highs of nineteen this afternoon – and now you're up to date.*'

Finger point. Sweeper. Ads.

'Hey dickhead,' said Leslie, as I rose, his eyes dead. 'Thought I told you to drop that.'

'Sorry Leslie,' I said.

'Fucking *know your place.*'

I checked my phone. No messages.

Jesus, nothing? *Nothing?*

I sent another: 'Where are you?' and watched it whoosh away to nowhere.

Travelling. She'd never mentioned wanting to go travelling before. We didn't even have a holiday booked. I'd been on at her for months about a holiday. Anywhere, I told her. Egypt. The Algarve. Didcot Parkway. Just anywhere but London. It'd do us the world of good. I guess at least one of us had taken my advice.

There were other people I'd tried, as I'd sat in the pub.

I left word with Fran again.

Hayley's dad in King's Lynn. I had to look that one up, remind him precisely who I was, and have him gruffly deny all knowledge.

I tried other colleagues, friends I had numbers for. I tried our landlord, Mohammed, who seemed mainly concerned that I'd still be paying in full and wasn't trying to negotiate some kind of discount.

No one seemed worried.

'Oh, she'll turn up,' said our neighbour, Edith, ninety-four, and you can imagine how reassuring that was. 'Have you tried calling her?'

Her phone, of course, was constantly turned off. Though it still went to voicemail. She was still paying the bills. She still needed a phone.

So who had she told? Who do you tell when you want to disappear?

'Maybe she found you smothering,' said Pippy, just a thick Kilbride accent like a knife through London around her. She put her hands up defensively. 'I'm only being honest.'

She took a bite of her garlic bread. We were in Eatalian, on the corner. I'd ordered nothing, just water. Pippy hadn't noticed. She'd drawn love hearts and shooting stars on her hand again.

'It's just so frickin' hashtag "mental",' she said, still only being honest.

I knew I needed to run through all this with someone. Pippy would do for now. Though I was slowly working out she wasn't exactly delicate.

'Do you think she's met another man?' she said.

I stared at my drink.

'Or does she have a history of … anything? You know. Mental illness, or whatever?'

'She seemed fine. She even did a Sainsbury's shop. Online. She *knew* that was too much food. Who *does* that?'

'Mad people.'

'She's not mad.'

'Evil, then.'

'Bit strong.'

Pippy is single. She'd tried match.com but had her fingers burnt when she began her profile with the words 'I am a thirty-seven-year-old Scottish girl' and then didn't get any replies. It was three weeks before she realised it was because what she *actually* wrote was 'I am a thirsty seven-year-old Scottish girl'.

'Maybe the shopping …' she said. 'Maybe that's what she meant by "carry on as normal". Maybe she just wants you to just carry on as normal.'

'Really?' I said. 'So she wants me to cook two meals a night? Set two places at the table?'

'You eat at the table? Not in front of the telly like everyone else in the world?'

We never eat at the table. We'd bought that table together in IKEA in Edmonton, imagining we'd have friends round, and make homemade salsa and buy rustic breads, then eat dinners with interesting figures as we talked long into the night about Vladimir Putin and high finance. In reality we put our keys there.

'Sometimes we'd eat at the table, yes, we're not animals.'

'It's just so *weird*,' she said again, sighing, and I was just grateful to have anyone at all agree.

Back at home, that evening, I sat on the floor surrounded by her clothes, my head in my hands.

Above me was her wall calendar. Full of things that would now never happen. 23rd – Janey's wedding. 10th – Fraser & Iona/dinner at ours. 12th – Cinema?

I'd torn the wardrobe apart. I'd lost it. Forty-five seconds of rage – at the lack of information – at the limbo she'd left behind.

There was a suitcase missing – the middle-sized suitcase of a set of three. What did that imply? A week? A month? Maybe it implied she might be back. If you know you're going forever, you take the big suitcase, right?

Unless you realise there's so much you just want to leave behind.

I stared at myself in the mirrored doors of the wardrobe.

What was wrong with me?

I'm not bad looking. Tall, like my dad. His Kenyan genes give me that, though he remains leaner than me. Mum was French, and I'm told I have her doleful eyes. She always said they'd make me a heartbreaker, but so far it's been pretty much an even split. Other than that I strive for neutrality. Neat hair, mainly black clothes. I don't think there's anything there that would immediately make someone run away.

So hopefully it's my personality.

I'm quick to anger but speak up rarely, though when I do I speak clearly and well.

I don't suffer fools gladly, but I do suffer them.

Instead, it brews and boils inside me. Makes me moody and quiet and want to be alone, though not alone like this.

And then the doorbell rang.

It was 8pm. That's an unusual time for visitors.

She's back. It's over.

I scrambled to my feet, clunked my shoulder on the doorframe and fast-limped to the hallway, heart racing, blood pumping to my head, grabbed at the door handle …

'Sainsburys, mate,' said the man, surrounded by blue crates and orange bags.

I'd wondered why she'd ordered so much. She was looking after me. Making sure I ate. That I got my five-a-day.

That scheming bitch.

I ate at the table that night, making myself a little corner amongst the keys and bills and paperwork and takeaway leaflets and magazines.

I'd begun slowly to resent the flat. This one-bed with ideas above its station, five minutes from the chip shop but just around the corner from Clissold Park, and lazy Sundays by the paddling pool in the summer. Mohammed had said we could decorate, but I'd begun to dislike it for how little it now represented me. The bright pink feature wall in an otherwise magnolia lounge. The 'quirky' kitchen cupboard knobs from whatever that shop's called … Apostrophe? Apology?

All this was Hayley's personality. Or, at least, what she'd quite openly *decided* was her personality. She'd spend hours marking the pages of back issues of *Living Etc* when we first moved in, circling Cole & Son wallpaper or Farrow & Ball paints and writing weird words like 'Rockett St George' on brightly coloured Post-its. I tried to remind her this was a one-bed in Stoke Newington, not Babington House, but she kept buying, kept circling. Hayley likes magazines. *Heat*, *Grazia*, *Stylist*, *Elle*, *Cosmo*. A great big pile of them, dog-eared, bruised, rumpled by bath water. The enemy within. Had they given her ideas about me? Were they talking about me behind her back? Suggesting she was unfulfilled, in this rented flat in North London, with an average man in his average clothes and their average life together? I picked the top one off the pile, looked at its cover.

FASHION. STYLE. FOOD. GLAMOUR. TRAVEL.
For the woman who wants it all – and usually gets it!

These magazines did not think I was good enough; that I was a slob; a Neanderthal.

I threw them down, and pushed my plate away. My kebab had gone cold anyway.

And then, in the corner of my eye.

A small red light, blinking on the floor by the sofa, in a pathetic attempt for attention.

The answerphone.

I clicked Play.

'*Hello Ms Anderson, this is Mark, the Sainsbury's driver, just confirming your delivery slot of between 8 and 9pm.*'

My heart sank.

I sank to the floor, with it.

But the answerphone kept going.

'*Wednesday. Eleven … Nineteen … am.*'

An old message. Already listened to.

I went to delete.

'*Hayley …*'

A man's voice.

four

Half past five and I sat, staring at the screen, the cursor blinking back at me.

I hate that wink.

'Go on!' it's saying, full of beans, always bouncing. 'Write something!'

Yeah, cursor? Why don't *you* write something?

'Morning,' said Pippy, as I stared at my blank page. 'You grabbed that audio?'

Some report or other. We'll have one reporter in the field in the morning, another to take over at lunchtime, recording on their phones, sending stuff back to us. They pretty much go and get vox pops. So someone gets stabbed in east London, they'll find someone to say, 'You just don't expect this kind of thing to happen round here.' That's the job. Getting people to say, 'You just don't expect this kind of thing to happen round here.' It's the same every day. You could just use the same person's disembodied voice in every report for every story. Mugging in Kilburn? You just don't expect that kind of thing to happen round there. Lottery winner in Kennington? You just don't expect that kind of thing to happen round there. It's like no one expects anything to happen anywhere at all.

I clicked the audio open and found my headphones.

Someone hadn't expected something to happen to them, and for the first time, I knew exactly how they felt.

Because who the hell was Andy and what was 'the place'?

I'd played and replayed the message.

'*Hayley... it's Andy from the place.*'

One more time.

'*... Andy from the place.*'

Again.

'*... Andy from the place.*'

So I say again: ... who the hell was Andy and what was 'the place'?

It continued.

'*Just wondering if you'd made your arrangements after all. I'll try you on your mobile.*'

The voice – flat, emotionless. No obvious class association. Generic English accent.

'*Just wondering if you'd made your arrangements after all.*'

After all? So whatever these arrangements were, there'd been doubts? Had she been talking to Andy about going? Had she been confiding in him? He didn't sound like a man calling a lover. He sounded like a man checking someone had done a spreadsheet, or forwarded an email.

'*... Andy from the place.*'

No pause as he said 'the place'. No hesitation, no thinking necessary. He always called it that. No emphasis on the words, either – he wasn't making any concessions, wasn't putting imaginary speech marks around them, he didn't have to explain. She would know. Hayley would know exactly what the place was.

And it wasn't a bar or a restaurant or a place called The Place. This was the place – not The Place. Casual, throwaway, familiar, secretive.

Secretive.

You probably think I'm insane, analysing in this way, but look – I know words. I know how they sound. I read for a living. Out loud.

For strangers. I can see those words in the air as I hear them, like subtitles in a film only I'm watching. I can *feel* words.

And these words felt *weird*.

Seven-forty-five am, and Leslie was performing a paid-for read.

These are tricky. Sales & Promotions people love them, but they're not in S&P for their writing skills. You could see Leslie trying to make sense of the words in front of him, correcting their spelling, moving words around, trying not to spit them out with disdain, trying to act like it's completely natural he wants to tell you that …

'*… if you're anywhere near Lakeside in Thurrock today, don't forget to join Tony Ram and the Talk London street team as they hand out vouchers for a whopping 20 per cent off purchases over £15 at The Body Shop!*'

The veins in the side of his head were throbbing … the problem with S&P, he'd tell you, was that they saw him as a mere *vessel* for their words, not as an *artist* trying to *cope* with them … his fists clenched, now …

'*Though remember! Terms and conditions do apply, and all the info is on our website!*'

He plastered on a smile, coming through the worst of it …

'*Find the crazy gang at The Body Shop, shopping level two, just opposite Foot Locker! And tell Tony to buy me some foot scrub for my cracked heels! Happy shopping!*'

Jingle. Ads. Done.

'I hate these bloody things!' he said. 'I'm not a salesman. I'm an ideas man. Why am I talking about 20 per cent off body bollocks at Lakeside? I should be talking about Iran!'

He wouldn't be talking about Iran. He'd be talking about a new survey in the *Daily Mail* that says nine out of ten dog owners wish their dogs could talk.

'Happy shopping? Why did they put that? Why do I have to say "whopping"? Just give me the facts and let me get on with it! I added that bit about the foot scrub and the cracked heels.'

'It was very powerful,' I said.

He scanned my face, coldly, for signs of mockery, then gave me the benefit of the doubt.

'*Exactly*. That's how you bring something to life. That's how you get Mrs Bingo in Stroud Green to sit up and take notice! Not "terms and conditions apply"!'

Janice, the producer, scuttled out of the room. She could sense the darkness coming.

'How much is Tony Ram getting paid for doing that?'

The red 'phone' light lit up.

Someone didn't mind the cracked heels stuff as it was on message but didn't think Leslie should be referring to the street team as the 'crazy gang' in case it made people uneasy in their presence.

Leslie told them where they could shove his heels. It was a startling image which took some working out.

The news travelled upwards.

Ding Ding.

A text message.

Hayley?

I was home, now, the day a wasted blur, waking up on the sofa. I rubbed my eyes, focused on the words.

Tom. It's Fran. I'm sorry I'm late to reply. Can we talk about Hayley?

I hadn't seen Fran in what seemed like forever.

This city can do that to you. Pure intentions fade with time and distance and exhaust fumes until barely there, like a tube map left in the sun.

The last time I'd seen her, we'd had fun, the three of us. We'd been full of 'we should do this more often!' and 'next time come round ours!' and talk of picnics and roasts.

For a while, Hayley and Fran had seemed glued together and with a shorthand impenetrable to others. They'd met one day a few years ago in town – bumped into each other in some shop, went for drinks, got on furiously. They'd found an easy friendship in one another. I liked her, and I sat, waiting, at the Daily Grind on Clerkenwell Road, another one of those places that wasn't there yesterday and probably wouldn't be tomorrow. All wrought iron and stained wood and elaborate eggs Benedict, a 'Director of Coffee' behind a brushed steel counter, ordering beautiful Latvians to bring out more £5 croissants.

I stirred my coffee and stared at the wall, feeling heavy as I did every day at the moment. A black cloud over my head and under my eyes. I knew this feeling.

I decided that maybe I'd got it wrong. Maybe Fran was here to tell me about Andy. That made sense. We get on, me and Fran, perhaps Hayley thought it best to send in a third party; someone to ease the blow and make caring faces and say things like, 'she still loves you, Tom, but she's not *in* love with you,' and 'Andy's a really great guy, I really think the two of you would really get on.'

And now she was here. Vintage dress. Red lipstick. Handbag on the table. Furrowed brow.

'Tom …'

'Hey, Fran …'

'You look …' – struggling to find the right word as she sat down, brush a curl of red hair behind one pale ear – '… well.'

I lift a spoon to check my reflection. I think it actually makes me look better.

'I'm sorry for … what you're going through,' she said. 'It's so …'

She shrugged, shook her head, looked to the waiter and ordered her coffee.

Fran paints small trees on plates and then sells them for a fortune to hipsters at markets. I don't know how she does it. They're just small trees painted on plates.

'I don't actually know what I'm going through,' I said, noticing her brooch. It had a small tree on it. 'Hayley's been a little unclear about things.'

'So that was it? You got that note and nothing else?'

'Did she say anything about it to you?'

Fran raised two thin eyebrows in mock-surprise.

'Tom, I hardly ever saw her.'

I narrowed my eyes.

'You *always* saw her.'

'When was the last time I saw her?'

'I dunno. Couple of weeks back?'

'January.'

I frowned. Her coffee arrived.

'We had a fight,' she said, as the waitress left and we could talk again. 'She didn't tell you?'

'No, nothing,' I said. 'Wait, what? You had a fight about what?'

'I said things that I meant at the time but which probably seemed a bit harsh.'

'What things?'

She took a moment.

'We were out one night,' she said. 'Mayfair. She seemed so distant, like she was more concerned with what was going on at the table next to ours. I couldn't get through to her any more. Seemed like she was always on the lookout for something better, or someone more interesting.'

'She'd been unhappy at work,' I said. 'Maybe she was just distracted.'

'She was always distracted,' she says. 'And I told her as much. I made up some excuse about iffy tapas and said I had to go, but she hardly even took that in, just kept listening to these guys banging on about their Christmas bonuses or something and so I told her how much I hated it that she'd changed so much and ...'

The words were starting to wash over me. None of this made sense. I was drowning. I waved her back.

'Wait – stop. Changed how?'

Now it was Fran's turn to frown.

'You don't think she'd changed?'

'No. She was just ... Hayley. Maybe it was you that changed, not her.'

Fran gave a small smile, and said, gently: 'Who's the one you're sitting having coffee with? Who's the one that's actually *here*?'

I stared at my reflection again.

'I just felt she was trying to be somebody else. Small things at first. The hair.'

The hair. So what? She'd changed her hair. People change their hair. I'd noticed that she'd changed her hair and said 'nice hair'. We'd talked about it. That had been us talking about it.

'The clothes.'

And? People buy new clothes. People buy whole new wardrobes sometimes.

'The make-up.'

Jesus Christ.

'And then there were the other things ...'

Oh, what was she going to say now? She'd started buying Crest instead of Colgate?

'She wanted to go to all these new places all the time.'

Travel. I started to feel a little sick.

'Places that weren't us. And that I just didn't think were all that *her*. It was fine at first, because it just felt like adventures, but it was starting to get really ... pompous.'

Pompous?

'I mean, I love a good restaurant. But she was like, "let's go to Nobu!" Pricey, you know? And it'd be fun so you would, but then the next day she'd be texting saying "let's go to Roka!" Or Hakkasan. Or, like, *nightclubs*. I'm too old for nightclubs! I've got a job, I need to be on site at eight, I don't—'

'Hang on,' I said, relieved I could join in on this one, relieved I wasn't totally in the dark. 'She did mention clubs. She said there was an indie night at the Islington Academy and that we should go sometime. Britpop, old Suede, that kind of stuff.'

'No,' said Fran, leaning in, pointing a finger at me. On the finger was an oversize ring with a small tree on it. Hayley had one of those. 'I mean, like, *Chinawhite*. Boujis. You know?' She laughed. '*Those* places. Places Russian Oligarchs go to get off with Moroccan pop stars. And if I said no, she'd get all funny and say I was acting like a loser – she actually used that word – and I was boring and all this stuff. And that's basically when I told her to fuck off.'

Sitting back in her chair, Fran fiddled with her brooch defensively.

'*Chinawhite?*' I said, startled.

She'd never once mentioned Chinawhite to me. We used to just go to the pub. Maybe pick up a bottle on the way home. What the hell did she want to go to *Chinawhite* for? I didn't even know where it was. I'd read about it in the papers, of course, and Fran was right. It's just people from reality shows and David Hasselhoff and girls in short skirts looking out for Prince Harry.

It was all a bit … tacky.

'When did she have the time to—'

But I stopped. I'm brushing my teeth by 8.30. Often she'd just be getting ready to go out. But not to clubs. To … well … see people like Fran.

'When I first met her, that day in Topshop, she was this ray of sunshine. I turned round and there she was, out of the blue, telling me she loved my necklace, and where did I get it. I didn't want to talk to you about it because I thought the old Hayley would grow out of it and come back,' said Fran, 'and it just felt disloyal going to you. And I thought you'd think I was boring, saying no to Nobu, or whatever, because I'd started to think that I must be.'

'I … I don't know what to do with this information,' I said. 'I thought she was just going to Pilates or seeing you guys, or—'

'But didn't you notice? The changes? Come on, you must've noticed.'

'She changed her hair, yes, I noticed that, I told you,' I said.

'Don't be a cliché. Don't lie to yourself. How could you have lived with her and not seen it?'

'Fran – genuinely. She never once mentioned going to a nightclub or wanting to eat at … wherever. Never once. I would remember. I would have taken the piss *relentlessly*. Because that's just not *us*.'

Fran leaned back in her chair. I let the words hang. And I realised that maybe I was the problem after all.

'Can I ask you something?' I said, and Fran nodded. 'Who's Andy?'

'Andy?'

'Andy.'

She looked blank while she thought about it. I shifted, prepared myself. If Hayley had been seeing someone, she'd have told Fran. And Fran would have told her to put an end to it. Fran's good, she's moral. Maybe that's why they fought. Maybe that's it.

But: 'I don't know who Andy is,' she said.

'What about "the place"?' I said, now feeling a little desperate. 'Did she ever even once mention a place she called "the place"? Or do you know what "the place" might be?'

'I don't know,' said Fran. 'Oh, God, do you think Andy is …'

'I don't know either,' I said. 'Did she ever mention a man?'

'I wish I could help you …'

'I'm so *angry*,' I said.

And she reached across the table and squeezed my hand, and it was then that I realised I was crying.

I felt heavier than ever as I got home. Hayley was a magnet beneath me.

I sank to my knees as I walked through the door.

Reached behind and slammed it shut.

Darkness.

Limbo.

I was powerless. I had no moves.

What can I do, here? I can leave her, but how can I leave her when I can't even tell her? I can do as she asks, and carry on as normal, but there *is* no normal, because she took that with her, along, it turns out, with most of the crazy.

All I can do is just … be here.

What do I have left? A job that I like but which doesn't make me *happy*, a flat I share with someone who's gone, no real friends in the city, no idea where to turn.

I closed my eyes and lay down on the floor, the rough prickles of the sea grass mat scratching at my cheek, the smell of must and dust and mud dancing around me, my energy sucked through my pores, and I thought about things for a minute, maybe an hour, maybe much longer.

And when I was at my lowest, I turned my head and stared at the phone cord, the taut, white phone cord, thick and strong and unbreakable, fastened to the wall with gun-grey staples, and I reached out and touched it, and a thought I'd not had before came to me.

five

'It's 6.01am, Saturday June 16th, I'm Tom Adoyo with the stories you're waking up to ...'

The last text I'd had from Hayley I knew off by heart.

It read: 'Five mins away. Passing wine shop. Cheeky bottle of sauv blanc?'

I'd replied, 'Sure.'

Just that. The last text I knew she'd got.

'... and in showbiz, Jay-Z remembers Glastonbury, and who won the double, with two MTV Europe Awards in Paris ...?'

Saturday today, meaning no Leslie, thank Christ. He'd be at the Yewtree – his vast faux-Tudor Surrey pile – where I imagine he'd be flabbing about by his indoor pool or twatting golf balls with his neighbours, all of whom seemed to be fading radio stars, big in the 80s, bitter now.

Leslie hated it here. He didn't get the respect he deserved, he said. He constantly referred to 'Management' and their 'Ideas' and made liberal use of visual quotation marks. He was on his second warning with the company, after swearing at a vegetarian on air, and for some vague rumour of bullying a suddenly-no-longer-there intern, but that's just idle gossip, and I don't deal in that. The plus side was that he now tended to keep his rants within studio walls.

'There's a reason the canteen only has eggs on a bloody Friday,' he bellowed once, while the ads were on. 'And it's to keep the workers docile. They want us compliant so they starve us of fuel. Feed us fucking porridge like we're Dickensian orphans. Crush our spirit so that the advertisers from Tango know we won't have a bloody meltdown. That's all they fear, "Management" ...' – there go the fingers again – '... freedom of expression! What's the obvious way to quell it? Pretend you can't have fucking eggs delivered in London in the twenty-first century except as a fucking treat on a Friday!'

Still. We were free of him on Saturdays.

'... *with highs of nineteen in the Capital today ...*' I finished, and then, from force of habit ... *'And now you're up to date.'*

Oops.

Mic down. Red light off. Ads.

'Sorry, it's Tom, yeah?' said the girl at the mic. 'I'm Cass?'

She said her name like it was a question, held her hand out and I shook it. She had a limp handshake, like she expected everyone else to do all the work. On the plus side, she'd fit right in.

'I shouldn't have said "now you're up to date" just then. Sorry.'

'You what?'

I knew who Cass was. She'd been here maybe three weeks. I hadn't covered Saturdays before. But Cass used to do drive on Key 103, up north. Won a Sony Rising Star. Interviewed bands. She was a music presenter, really. A jock. Not a *serious* presenter, or a 'broadcaster', as Leslie would have it.

'Leslie doesn't like it when I say "now you're up to date". But I keep doing it, because I feel like I've just updated people and that now they're up to date. And also, it's just something to say.'

Cass laughed. This ... cackle. Her eyes were bright and I noticed her arms. Tanned, lithe. Her laugh went on a little too long, though. Particularly as I hadn't actually made a joke.

'You serious? He cares about that?'

I drained my coffee and quietly put down my mug. I glanced at Janice in the corner. She'd usually be behind the glass, but I guess she was in here for the first month with Cass to make sure all went well. She didn't look up. She'd been Leslie's producer for years. She acted like his PA, too, making sure he had his Starbucks ready and waiting when he got in, making sure he got his eggs on a Friday. There were rumours she made sure he was comfortable in other ways too, but that's just idle gossip, and as you know, I don't deal in that. But the fact was, Leslie expected a lot from those around him. It's a brave move to laugh at Leslie James. Everything gets back to him. *Everything*.

Then Cass said, 'That guy's a dick, man,' and got on with her show.

....

From: MAUREEN THOMAS
To: ALL STAFF

Will newsreaders PLEASE remember to take their mugs back to the kitchenette when their shift is done. I do NOT expect cleaning staff to have to do this. PLEASE REMEMBER we are a COMMUNITY and we DO NOT pick up after one another.

....

I went to get my mug and then picked up my phone.

'Hi, I'm just calling about my girlfriend's phone bill ...'

This had been my idea last night. My big idea. What if she'd phoned Andy back? She'd have used her mobile ...

'And are you the account holder?'

'I just need to get access to it is all.'

'I see, and are you the account holder?'

'No, my girlfriend is the account holder, but I am my girlfriend's boyfriend.'

'Well, I would need to speak to the account holder.'

'She says it's absolutely fine.'

'Well, I would need to speak to the account holder to verify that.'

'I can give you all her details?'

'I would need to speak to the account holder.'

'Ask me anything.'

Hayley Grace Anderson (phone carrier: TelSun, payment plan: PayMonthly, account password: Hayl3y1) gave me her number the night we met (07700 etc, etc) and I made the joke I always make when someone gives me their number which I told you already and which you've probably already decided to use yourself.

And Hayley had laughed and laughed at this, because remember, it's a great thing to say, and I had beamed so widely and felt so good about life that I suppose I must have seemed very attractive at that moment, because then she immediately took the slip of paper back, amended it, and handed me her *real* number.

Hayley's friend had won tickets to a gig on Bristol CitySound 98.8. We were a small team, sharing responsibilities, and gave them out in person instead of posting them because we were spending too much on first class stamps. But we were assured that 'this was a fantastic opportunity for us to engage with the listeners one-on-one'.

I could only imagine Leslie's fury at that kind of thinking.

'They see us as thick bloody sheep!' he once yelled, banging his fist on a filing cabinet, as everyone around him pretended it wasn't happening. 'Just sitting around in this horrible office waiting for their wonderful pronouncements! "Great news, guys! We're halving your wages! This will be a *really exciting opportunity* to get back down there on the floor, to remember our roots, to see how we earn our money. This is a great chance for us to really make our budgets stretch and *get the best out of our money*. Nice one, everybody!" Well they've got one spin and it's absolute bollocks.'

So anyway, we used to ask these competition winners to come to reception, and more often than not they were these confused middle-aged women who couldn't remember what tickets they'd won. There's a whole network of them. Bored housewives who all text each other when they hear there's a competition on and then share the prizes. Doesn't matter what they are or what station it is or whether they've ever heard the show before. Tickets. Trips. Tiaras. Greedily snuffling about for whatever's going. Pete Lawson on Vibe calls them GigPigs. He did it on-air once. No one noticed.

But Hayley and her friend looked different. They looked like they might actually listen to the station.

'Do you listen to the station?' I asked.

'No,' they said.

Then the friend, Laura, who Hayley used to see all the time – and I don't know why she doesn't any more, now I think about it – said, 'How many tickets is it again?'

'Four,' I said, and I handed them over.

'There's only two of us,' said Hayley.

I never went out back then. Well, hardly. A couple of nights a month with Calum, before he got the job offer in Dublin. We'd been mates since school, and he'd helped see me through the things that had happened ... but he'd always been that little bit ahead of me – he had a family, these days. A proper, grown-up marriage with date nights and anniversaries and big family parties. Trampoline in the back garden. A back garden! Corporate car, a home mobile and a work mobile, the trappings of adulthood. But back then, even with someone I knew so well, I felt I should spare the world my company.

That night, though, I had fun. I let go. Went with the flow. Did what my old doctor used to say I should do – 'do what everyone else is doing!' It was at Colston Hall, Abbey Grant, the last gig of her first tour, signed by Universal and on her way, rumour had it, to America ... but here in Bristol first.

And it was Hayley, Laura, me and a stranger from the queue we'd given the spare ticket to. The girls had asked me straight away because they didn't know anyone else in Bristol and I fancied Laura so said yes straight away.

'She's got an aura, hasn't she?' said Hayley, when Laura had gone to the toilet. 'I call it a Laura-aura.'

And then I felt a bit ashamed that I'd been so obviously into her. And like I'd been rude to Hayley. So I started talking to her more, as we found a bar down by the marina. And the more I talked to her, the more I tried to impress her, the more important it became to me that she liked me too.

They were in town from Stockport for a few days for a friend's wedding in a chapel near Frome, but they'd grown restless.

'I thought you two were sisters,' I said, when Laura sat back down, and I thought I saw her bristle slightly, like I'd said they were wearing the same tops or something.

'We've just got very similar tastes,' said Hayley.

Things moved fast.

We'd met up the next day, the three of us, and I'd taken them to see Clifton Suspension Bridge, and I've no idea why, because as impressive as it is, you're still just taking someone to see a bridge, so we found ourselves food and we chatted and hardly noticed when Laura slipped away.

And the next day, when Laura said she had a headache and just needed to get some work done, we hit the countryside on our own, walking the two miles along the canal from Bath to the George in Bathampton, sinking slow pints by the lock in the sun as kids played cricket over the bridge. It was easy, talking to Hayley. It sounds too simple and childish, but it was like everything that was my favourite was her favourite too.

Bands. Albums. Specific *versions* of tracks.

Countries. Cities. Specific *areas* of cities.

TV shows. Characters. Specific *lines* delivered by characters.

And the weirder it became, and the more we pretended to be freaked out by it, the more we loved it, because it meant we didn't have to take responsibility for this – it was like the heavens themselves were willing it.

'Laura? It's Tom … Hayley's Tom …'

My voice was upbeat, friendly, delightful. I'd rehearsed, and I can *do* delightful.

'Tom?'

Her voice wasn't delightful.

'Yeah! Hey, can you speak?'

'Not … not right now, not really, Tom … what's this about?'

She was distant, unfriendly. Maybe because she knew? Was she hiding Hayley? Had I cracked it already and she was struggling to work out how?

'I was just wondering … have you heard from Hayley at all?'

A pause.

'I have not heard from Hayley, no,' she said.

I waited. I'm not sure for what. A question, maybe. Some concern. But nothing.

'Do you know where she might be?' I asked. 'I'm only calling because—'

'I haven't heard from her and I don't expect to,' said Laura, and I thought that would be the end of the sentence, but something crackled and spiked in her voice, like flint against steel, some small spark of fury and impatience, and she said, 'And I thought I made that really, really clear, so if this is some kind of set-up, or some kind of trick, then I'm not interested, Tom.'

I blinked.

'Sorry?'

'She's a bloody psycho. Please don't call again.'

And the line went dead.

[2]

Cockroft takes a sip of his wine. It is a brooding, blood-red wine – a 1975 Chateau Patache d'Aux. He raises his glass, holds it to the light, tings the crystal with a single blackened fingernail.

All the while, a couple at the other table drink their bottle of wine, oblivious.

'It's delicious,' he says, one hand softening his now-silver beard, 'Berries. Black licorice. Full body. Long finish. Try some.'

'You like that one?'

'Never had it before. Never even heard of it, truth be told.'

I smile, I can't help it. I notice the long-stemmed churchwarden pipes behind him, once smoked by Roosevelt, Hoover, Ziegfeld. Once, for $5 a year, patrons could keep their own pipe here. When a member passed away, the stem of their pipe would be cracked. Cockroft would look good with one of those pipes. The bar-room philosopher; the thinker.

'You're resisting,' he says, and I realize he's been staring at me for some time.

'I guess,' I say.

'You avoid the water I order, you don't take of the wine ...'

'I'm not trying to be rude,' I say.

'This happens a lot,' he replies, and I notice his body language mirrors mine. I shift, uncomfortable at the thought he might think me in his awe. 'But you must know, you are already in. A stage hypnotist will tell you that the people who go to his show are already hypnotized; they believe; that's why they are there. Why are you here?'

'Not because I believe,' I say. 'Because I'm a journalist.'

'You report. You see the world from afar. Do you never feel you want to engage? Why choose to report? Why not choose to *involve* yourself?'

six

6.27am. Monday. Second bulletin.

I feel restless, distracted.

Adewale on reception had given me a can of Tango. He'd drunk three himself already today and he couldn't stop moving his knee. He sat, grinning, next to three more, under a giant plasma screaming WELCOME TO OUR FRIENDS AT BRITVIC PLC!

He could not believe his luck.

A bloody psycho, eh?

I sat down, checked the wires.

Oh, great. A story about First Capital Connect. I bloody hate First Capital Connect. Too many *kahs*, too many *chks*.

First. Capital. Connect.

Who named it? Who thought that was a catchy name? Try saying it fast. Now try saying it fast, on air, with half of London listening. First Capital Connect. You have to spread the words. First. Capital. Connect. Slow it down. It just doesn't flow. What were they thinking? Why wasn't there a meeting? I dragged my eyes across them once more. I had to stay focused.

Psycho. Psychopath. Someone thinks my girlfriend is a psychopath.

Is she even my girlfriend?

Christ – Stanislas Wawrinka was playing Murray tonight.

I'm no tennis fan, I know nothing about it, my job is simply to sound like I do, to deliver words and numbers with authority, to learn the most effective way of implying knowledge, to know how to pace 'six-two, six-two, six-four', or 'twenty-two under-par' or 'two hundred and sixty-five for seven', but I genuinely wish Stanislas Wawrinka nothing but ill in his career. I hope he loses, badly, then immediately decides to retire, preferably after changing his name by deed poll to something like Bobby Easyname.

Stanislas Wawrinka.

The arrogance of it.

'Tom,' said Pippy, standing next to a clean-shaven kid of maybe nineteen in a bright lime hoodie, nervously running his hand through messy brown hair. He was still proudly wearing a grubby wristband from Rock Ness. He also looked knackered. Like until this moment he hadn't even known there *was* a 6.28 in the morning. 'This is Work Experience Paul, he's starting with us today, and …'

'Stani*slas*. Vav-*rink*a,' I muttered, barely nodding then pushing through the studio door, and picking up from some subtle clues that Leslie was less than happy.

'Those absolute *pricks* with their fucking gas of words and corporate speak – billows out of their mouths like a fog, a green fog, filling the room, suffocating ideas, any new way of thinking, anything that isn't theirs or been proven by a focus group …'

He looked at me, wild-eyed, then back at Janice.

'Have you ever seen these focus groups? Have you? Slack-jawed simpletons paid in Pizza Hut vouchers. And *they* have a say in what *I* do.'

His eyes flicked to his screen. Forty-two seconds 'til on-air. He relaxed, and pointed at the cupboard.

'You know what they did last month?'

Here we go.

'They said we couldn't keep jam in there. They sent a fucking company-wide memo to say we could not keep jam in that specific cupboard.'

I looked at the cupboard. It was just a cupboard. He shrugged his shoulders, bewildered.

'It's empty, that cupboard, and yet we can't keep a simple pot of jam in there in case a client walks in—'

'It's Britvic today,' I said, trying to interject.

'—and for some unknown *bloody* reason Billy bloody Britvic decides to look in a cupboard, sees some jam, and thinks, "I don't think I'll spend any of my hundreds of thousands of pounds of advertising budget on any of the radio stations in this group because once I opened a cupboard and there was some fucking *jam* in it."'

'Isn't the kitchenette the proper—' began Janice, never expecting to finish.

'The *kitchenette* will see the end of that jam in less than five seconds flat, because the engineers bloody stand around the fridge eating jam with their spoons, Janice. I've seen it. It's disgusting, they're barely a rung up from focus groups. Honestly these people, these bloody people up there ...'

He pointed at the ceiling, jabbed his arm up and down ...

'... they're fucking *ideas jockeys*, they thrive on it, they see us as their pets, just tame and docile, and they leap on our creativity and they ride it to death. Why don't they just build us a fucking exercise yard and be done with it?'

What amazed me about Leslie was that he still didn't get it. Thirty-five years in radio and still the penny hadn't dropped, shrouded and cosseted as he was in his own arrogance. The ads aren't there to support his show. His show is there to bring in ads. He's just a placeholder, someone who can hold a room, keep everyone listening until the next Kwik Fit ad or paid-for read comes round.

'So in the next bulletin—' I said, hopefully, but he was off again.

'Fucking *blotterjotters!* It's a constant battle with these nitpicking sods! I watch them walk in, in their bloody pink bloody shirts, invent a problem, magnify it, and walk out like they've *solved* something. What a way to earn a living!'

I glanced down to concentrate.

'Devoid of talent! Devoid of empathy!'

Fifteen seconds 'til on-air. I tried to point at the screen with my elbow but now Leslie was really going for it.

'They piss about the place in their ill-cut suits, chosen by wives who stopped caring *long* ago, or turning up in new ones from Burton, which means they've got a mistress or an eye on one, and they don't walk, they leer, they prowl. You know what they might as well call themselves? These fucking sods? They're Programme *Prevention* Officers! They're bloody PPOs, the lot of them!'

And then, like the pro he is, it was ads done, mic up, voice low …

'… just coming up to 6.30, so let's get your news, weather, travel, sport and showbiz, with …' – he looked at me, searched my face for a name, relaxed as he realised it didn't matter – *'… Kate Mann.'*

Eyes down. Mic up. News bed.

Usual three stories plus sport from me, plus the inevitable warning about the Blackwall tunnel, finish on the highs.

Stanislas. Waw*rin*ka.

'It's Monday June 18th, I'm Tom Adoyo with the stories you're waking up to …'

I was starting to think that maybe Hayley divided opinion.

I mean – What. The. Hell.

Laura's words whirled thick through my head.

I was also, I think, starting to hate Hayley. Really hate her.

I sat at my desk, my world under a cloud, and I bent a pen until it creaked, until it teetered on the verge of snapping.

'Is there anything I can do for you?' said a voice, and I immediately snapped my pen.

It was Work Experience Paul. He looked so keen to be of service, so happy to help.

Ding.

....

From: MAUREEN THOMAS
To: ALL STAFF

Will newsreaders PLEASE remember to take you're mugs back to the kitchenette and NOT JUST LEAVE THEM BY THE SINK. You're mugs are YOU'RE RESPONSIBILITY and if you cannot use them PROPERLY we will take you're mugs away and you will have to bring you're OWN MUGS IN.

....

Oh, why does she have to send these to ALL? She knows it was me. Everyone knows it was me. Why the need for such passive aggression? Why the need to embarrass?

But this was the least of my worries. Because I started to consider: what if I *needed* Hayley? What if I couldn't live without her? What if I fell ill? What if there was a problem with one of our parents? What if I got hit by a bus? What if our flat burned down? Who would I turn to? Who would the authorities contact? And just how did she think I'd react to this?

This wasn't just selfish. No, this was now cruel.

'Not a coffee or a tea or anything?'

Jesus, Work Experience Paul was still there.

'I'm fine, thank you,' I said. 'Maybe just take a seat and if I think of something I'll let you know.'

He wandered off to find a chair as I considered this nagging doubt, this element of fear, that I was to blame for Hayley's disappearance. I had noticed but not cared that she'd seen Fran less. I didn't question it. Same with Laura, before her. It's just what happens. You're in a couple, you see your friends less. It's relationship maths.

And of *course* it must be difficult for someone like Hayley – flighty, an enthusiast – to be with someone like me. Tied to my hours. Early to bed. Ever-less-inspired. God knows *what* she'd been doing, I now realised. But I'd trusted her. We'd been a couple.

A good couple, too, I'd thought. Not like Calum and Joanne, of course, because they were always on about being soulmates. But people always said to us, 'you've got so much in common!' or 'you're like *peas in a pod*!', and that had seemed enough. She'd stayed with me more and more on Bragg's Lane, and Bristol is where I'd wanted us to have a life, but she wanted to go where the opportunities are. Laura had moved to London the year before, and Hayley had been planning on moving in with her but chose me instead.

It felt like the first time I'd ever been chosen. By anyone. For anything.

I sighed.

Her phone bills were paperless and inaccessible. I'd tried her passwords, all the usual ones, from Hayl3y1 to And3r50n to whatever else, but no, nothing, none of them worked. I suppose that showed the level of trust between us now. Not just her keeping her passwords to herself, but me trying to *guess her passwords*.

I wanted Andy's number. I wanted to speak to Andy. Speaking to Andy was *necessary*.

'Not being funny,' she said, not really having to tell me that. 'But you are asking me to break the law.'

'Only a little. Is that a problem?'

'No, I don't care,' she said. 'I'm just saying. I'm not being funny but that's what you're doing.'

I bristled but tried not to show it. I needed Pippy for this.

'I'm just making you aware that that is what you are doing. You are reaching a certain point in life where you are risking a very steep downwards spiral. I'm only being honest.'

'I can cope with this,' I said.

We were in the corridor, by the stairs, under a giant photo of Bark and Lyricis from Vibe. Lyricis had his hand on Bark's bald head and Bark was finding it funny. We quietened, as an engineer walked past.

'Weather today?' he said, spotting me.

'Highs of nineteen,' I said, and on he strode.

'And what are you going to do if you get his number?' hissed Pippy. 'Are you going to—'

'I'm not going to attack him, don't worry. Look, I just need you to say you've forgotten your password and get them to take you through security. I've written it all down for you. Date of birth, middle names …'

She took the details.

'You owe me,' she said, one finger in the air.

I left her to it.

It was just past 10am. I took my mug back to the kitchenette, washed it to the company's exacting standards and got back to my desk. I had to tee up the next reports, get them ready for Colin Jay at midday.

A footballer bit another footballer.

Blackwall Tunnel's cleared. Traffic stacked back to Clackets.

Lady Gaga has dressed unusually. Aphra Just says she's keen to settle in Paris with rap star Blaze.

Highs of nineteen in the city today.

I think I'm pretty good at my job. It's not as hard as it seems. There's just a few tricks, is all. Like, for a lead story, you're looking at forty-five seconds. But you want audio for at least fifteen of those. You need to mix it up. Now, that's not a problem if someone's grabbed some off Sky News. You'll roll on a press conference, clip it, whack it in the in-queue. You add what we call a 'slug' – BLAIR AUDIO RAW, maybe – and boom, if it's big, you snap it. Get it on the twelve o'clock and you sound like you went round his house yourself.

But you might not have any audio, and that's when you have to get inventive. Let's say there's been a smash and grab at Westfield Stratford. When you're prepping, you'd write, 'There's been a smash and grab at Westfield Stratford ... *my colleague Simon Lamp has more ...*'

Then you'd saunter down to the kitchenette, maybe stopping at the vending machine to see if they've replaced the Topics on the way, and you'd find Simon Lamp making a cup-a-soup in someone else's mug.

'Read this out,' you'd say to Simon Lamp, and then Simon Lamp would put on The Voice (we've all got The Voice we use) and hey presto, suddenly it sounds like Simon Lamp has been chasing down the big story himself, probably with hundreds of other dedicated journalist newshounds, pounding the streets of London for scoops, sources and snitches, flatfooted and grim-faced, press cards poking out of their whiskey-stained trilbies, cocked fivers in hand, all 'maybe *this* will refresh your memory ...'.

In reality, Simon Lamp wouldn't even know what he was reading and now he's halfway back to his desk with his cup-a-soup, probably stopping at the vending machine to see if they've replaced the Topics on the way.

It's necessary smoke and mirrors. It's its own little showbiz.

'And now you're up to date.'

Ten am is always my best hour. *LC with LJ* was over, and the workers with regular hours had started to arrive, still bleary-eyed despite their comparative lie-ins, clutching their Costa lattes or their slicks of greasy croissants pressed up against Pret bags. Constant dings of the lifts.

Top floor: management (with full access to roof garden). Third floor: marketing teams (with full access to café). Second floor: sales (with full access to coffee *and* snack machines, *and* first stop for the sandwich man). Our floor: reception and station teams (with full access to some toilets). I think you see the varying levels of importance here.

It might have been nice to socialise with some of the others, I'd sometimes think. But the hours ... it's always the hours. I'm finished just as they're thinking about what to have for lunch. I could hang around for a bit, but then I'd be the office sad case. I could come back into town later, but that looks desperate too. Permanently out of sync, the best I could hope for was a leaving do, or retirement drinks, and when the retirement drinks of a sixty-five-year-old man you've never really spoken to is the best you can hope for you have to start radically reassessing your life. I wanted to talk to someone about Hayley. But how could I raise it? You work with people you barely know, you can hardly drop something like that into conversation too soon. I suppose I could just say we split up, me and Hayley. Go for the sympathy. But these days people always want to know *how* you split up. It's like the first question, after 'why?' How fast would their concern turn to gossip?

No. Better I internalise this. Better I keep this solely between me and Pippy.

'So I heard your girlfriend fucked off!' said Leslie, towering over me, one hand on my shoulder while I sat at my desk. He was saying it loudly; loudly so the whole office could hear how witty and brave and how wonderfully un-PC he was.

Leslie hated 'the PC brigade'. He hated how political correctness had gone mad. He hated how these 'do-gooders' were always doing good.

'These bloody do-gooders!' he'd say, flicking the pages of the *Telegraph* or the *Mail*, shoulders tense at the thought of meddlers telling him there is real concern about the polar ice caps, or that people should drive slower near schools.

I sometimes thought he hated do-gooders more than do-badders.

But this? What had happened to me? He loved stuff like this.

'She's just gone travelling,' I said, my face flush, knowing every ear in an office of sixty was on me.

'Where to, then?' he said. 'Where's she gone?'

I wanted to say something witty. Now was the time. If only I could say something witty.

And then, like lightning, like *magic* …

'I'm not sure.'

Leslie rocked his head back and hooted. I'd never heard anyone hoot before, I don't think I've ever even used the word, but he hooted and honked and he wanted everyone to know how funny he found this; a river of laughter in full flow.

'But she didn't break up with you? She just went?'

'Yep,' I said, and his shoulders began to shake from the sheer joy of it.

'And you're still with her? You haven't ditched her?'

And all I could do was listen and smile, because 120 ears and 120 eyes needed to know I found this as amusing as Leslie did, otherwise I was just part of the bloody PC Brigade. A bad egg. Someone who couldn't take a joke.

'You poor bastard!' he exploded, and the laughter went on for a day if it went on for a minute, and when the torrent finally slowed to a brook, his hand left my shoulder and off he tramped to Soho, this garrulous, polo-necked, razor-burned man, so he could record a concerned voiceover for a dementia charity 'very close to my heart', for just £400 for the hour and only five grand in usage.

I collected my things, started to shut down my computer, cast a glance around. So now they knew. Amazing how people you don't know that well react to news like mine. They don't know you, so what's happened isn't like something that actually happened. It's not an event. It's like a bad thing you read about, or a disease or something, and they don't want to catch it or jinx themselves. Girls avoid your eye because you're a boy, and a boy who's been left, and they don't want to give you the wrong idea or be seen to be moving in. Boys avoid your eye because boys want an easy entry into friendship – a common bond, an interest, a mutual friend, an opinion – not this heavy stuff, not straight away, not right from the start.

No one wants to be a counsellor except a counsellor.

I should call Calum. Calum would make it all right.

I caught Pippy's eye as I left. She was unwrapping a new mobile. I gave her a hopeful thumbs-up and a raise of the eyebrows.

'Not yet, my love,' she called out, holding up the slip of paper I'd given her. 'Totes on my list!'

I sat on the 73, letting six cups of Nescafé trickle from my pores after a sweaty half-jog to catch it. My head throbbed from the caffeine, the watery coffee with its cheap beige foam. They order catering tubs at SoundHaus. That can't be good for you. I'm sure they cut in some cheaper stuff, too, bought off some spiv in some alley round the back of Chinatown. Leslie doesn't have to worry. He keeps a vacuum-packed bag of Carte Noire in his pigeon-hole. For a while he tried to make interns bring him cafetières. Then the company bought some of those instant hot taps. Now you just hold your cup over a sink and you're done in four seconds. It's how Leslie says he imagines they make coffee in prison.

'They might as well rename the terrace the bloody exercise yard!' he'd fumed.

He made that joke maybe once a week.

A weak rain began to speckle the windows as I wondered whether to call Laura again. It wasn't the sort of conversation I wanted to have on a bus, next to a man who may very well have won awards for his cough before. It was the only thing to do today. My work was over. My chores done.

I'd picked up my prescription. Got my pills. Ended up telling Dr Moon the whole story – missing girlfriend, missing sleep. He was a good man, and he'd smiled, sympathetically, though with one eye on the clock. So I'd left and bought a crayfish wrap.

My afternoons seemed to have so many more hours in them now that Hayley was gone. Calling Laura was a great big highlighted tick on an otherwise empty calendar, whether she wanted to speak to me or not. And why didn't she? Because she thought I was *part* of something. What, though? Some conspiracy? Some plot? Plus, she thought Hayley might have put me up to calling. Why?

I drafted a text as we motored past Sicilian Avenue on Southampton Row. I'd keep it in my phone, I'd wait for the right time.

Laura. It's Tom again. Sorry. I only rang yesterday because Hayley's gone. She upped and left. But need to know what you meant by her being a 'psycho'. I promise I'm not one. Please? T x

I wondered what could have happened between those two. They'd seemed such kindred spirits. There was something familial about them. You know those people who are the best of friends one minute, and enemies the next? Frenemies? And when they're in a frenemy phase they say, 'we're just too *alike*, that's our problem!'?

It was that way with those two. *Peas in a pod*. Which is what made Laura's attitude all the more strange.

I shrugged. Shook my head. How did everything change so fast? Everyone is insane.

I pressed Send on the text.

And, half an hour later, as I walked down Church Street, towards Albion Road, my phone buzzed as I searched for the keys in my pocket.

Laura. It had to be Laura.

Number unknown.

Hi guys! This is my new number! Pip pip! Pippy xxx

Sour, beaten, I pushed open the door of our flat – my flat – and there was that moment again, the one I'd become so familiar with. The listening, the making sure, the sheer silence. No one home. Everything the same.

I stepped in, my shoe sliding on something for a second.

A menu from Wok 'n' Roll. Another from Thaitanic.

I kicked them aside, wiped my shoes on that mat, and then saw, just next to them ... a picture.

I stood above it, not yet ready to pick it up. I took it in.

A mass of small cars, circling an arch. A deep and powerful blue stretching out above it all. Not one cloud in sight.

A word in the middle. Block capitals and underlined.

A name.

seven

Tom,
I'm sorry I've been so distant, I am just elsewhere.
You must be so confused and wonder if I still care.
Hope you're just carrying on as normal.
Love
Hayley

I wasn't angry, as I read, as much as I was fascinated. What could be going through her head?

'Love' was not a fair word to end on. Love equals hope but what if love is intended as friendship or pity? So stick your love where the sun don't shine. Stick it in Ecclefechan.

So, er … WHY DID YOU GO? I mean it, now. I just want to know.

Then: Sorry you've been so distant? Yes, you're pretty fucking distant. You're in Paris.

Next, *WHY ARE YOU IN PARIS?* You have never once mentioned Paris.

So of course I'm confused. At least you know what's going on, and knowing what's going on is the basic requirement for *not* being confused.

But yes, yes I bet you do hope I am 'carrying on as normal'. Because that would relieve you of all guilt and responsibility, wouldn't it? You wouldn't need to worry about me then, would you? This is a selfish sentiment and you are a selfish person.

There. I said it. And I said it all out loud, as I got up, got out of bed, stormed around the flat, fists slamming hard on tables, stairs kicked, a single shoe booted down the corridor against a door where it now lay, confused and sad, like a little leather puppy.

And then I saw all her magazines, lying on our table. And I thought about what Fran had said, about Hayley's changing look, her changing clothes, her changing tastes, her change in location …

FASHION. STYLE. FOOD. GLAMOUR. TRAVEL.

For the woman who wants it all – except her boyfriend!

I swept them off the table and let hard spines and staples and pages clatter against the wall and slide to the floor, where dog-eared pages spilled open and small neon Post-its next to shoes and tops glimpsed out.

I got my phone out, saw Pippy's text still there on the screen.

Number unknown.

Hi guys! This is my new number! Pip pip! Pippy xxx

I pressed CALL BACK. She answered straight away.

'Hiya!'

'Have you done it yet? Can you just do it? I feel like I'm going mad.'

'Cool your jets,' she said. 'First of all, did you tell Work Experience Paul to sit on a chair and await your instructions?'

'What? No. I mean, I told him to take a seat and if I thought of anything—'

'He was there five hours. He skipped lunch.'

'Pippy, did you call Hayley's mobile people?'

'I just talked to them.'

'And?'

'They said they couldn't help. They asked me my "secret question". I had no idea who her favourite teacher was at school so I just said Mrs Barbara Teacher.'

'Bollocks.'

'But then I begged them. And I said it was a matter of life and death. I said I had to be able to change my password because I was afraid my abusive boyfriend had it so he could check who I'd been calling.'

'Abusive?'

'I used that word, yeah, so I imagine the authorities may be in touch. The girl seemed to understand.'

'So you got a new password?'

'No, but she said she understood.'

So I couldn't check her bill. I paced, both of us silent on the phone.

'Can't you trace iPhones?' she said, a beat later.

'Tried it,' I said. 'She's turned that off. But I know where she is. She sent me a postcard.'

'Oh, that's … thoughtful?'

'She's in Paris.'

A pause.

'Paris,' said Pippy. 'Someone mentioned Paris the other day. Who was it?'

'What?'

'Someone mentioned Paris just the other day. I'm certain of it. Because I remember thinking, "Oh, Paris".'

'Lots of people mention Paris. It's pretty famous.'

'Yes, but this was some kind of *special* mention,' she said.

'Who mentioned Paris?'

'I can't remember.'

'*Think.* Who mentioned Paris?'

Another pause.

'I think it was *you*.'

Why would I mention Paris? I would remember mentioning Paris. Perhaps she'd confused me with someone else. Maybe I *was* going mad. I still wasn't sleeping properly. I couldn't remember the last time I'd slept well.

I'd phoned Calum. I needed his take. He didn't answer. I guess it was maybe bath time for the kids, or story time, or bedtime. But he'd texted back.

jesus, man. did i not tell you she was an oddball? did i not call it? are you still up?

I didn't want to talk, now, two hours later. Calum hadn't been a huge fan of Hayley. I reasoned some people just don't gel. But now came the self-pity. I felt ashamed. I felt embarrassed.

I leaned against the wall of the living room, slid down, sat in silence.

I should probably tidy up the magazines. That's what Calum would have done. Calum with his sorted life and his flexible mortgage and his Waitrose home delivery. I flicked a page or two, pages Hayley had highlighted. Outfits she liked, I guess. Retailer numbers. Website addresses. Shoes. A few things I recognised, too – a navy blue top, some bright yellow heels. Stuff she'd bought for her trip, maybe. I flicked to the next marked page.

Another list of numbers. Phone numbers.

Retailers?

But no, hang on, because these were 07 numbers. Mobiles?

These belonged to *people*.

So why were they on a bright pink Post-it on page forty-seven of *Harper's Bazaar*?

'*It's 6.01 on June 19th, I'm Tom Adoyo with the stories you're waking up to ...*'

Autopilot.

Phone numbers. Post-its. Postcards. Paris. Psychos.

Leslie was barely looking at me. He was fuming. There was an email open on his computer.

....

From: MAUREEN THOMAS

To: ALL

ONCE AGAIN: CUPBOARD'S MUST BE KEPT EMPTY AT ALL TIMES. These are not YOU'RE cupboards, they are the COMPANY'S CUPBOARD'S and must be treated AS SUCH.

....

He was shaking his head, his fingers hovering over a keyboard, priming themselves, warming up, ready to respond with a sharp shot of sarcasm and bile.

'*Sir Alex Ferguson wades in to Manchester United referee storm ...*'

I was pleased he wasn't looking at me. Imagine how he'll look at me when he finds out about the postcard. Oh, God, he'll love it.

'*Child protection system "creaking" say MPs ...*'

My phone was off, as is studio etiquette. You just do it automatically, you don't need to be asked; the way a man clambering up a cherry picker doesn't need that sign to tell him to pop his hard hat on.

'*... and police chiefs call for "drunk tanks" in the capital ...*'

Was she depressed? People hide depression from their partners. They can find sneaky ways of distracting from it. They can mask it. They can act in hugely unusual ways. Maybe she was depressed and this was her solution. She'd had a breakdown. That had to be it.

'... *highs of nineteen in the city this morning* ...'

No one had replied last night, when I'd sent the texts out. Why not?

'... *and now you're up to date.*'

I stared at the screen. Blinked.

Was I done?

Sweeper. Ads. Yes, done. All done.

'These fucking cupboard *NAZIS*,' said Leslie, eyes on his laptop, barely moving his head to the left to indicate he was addressing me. 'I'd happily see every one of those *cunts* up against a wall and shot if it meant I could keep my fucking jam in my fucking cupboard.'

I was just pleased he hadn't noticed I'd ended with 'now you're up to date', and as I spilled back in my chair and looked round to murmur some vague notion of support I caught Janice's eye behind the glass.

She looked terrified.

Properly terrified.

She'd just walked back in, coffee in hand. She'd been away from her side of the desk.

I guess that was quite a word for Leslie to use – the worst – but acting offended? This was something else. She was on another level. Eyes wide, her hands clutching papers, now raised to her head, barking something to someone. Urgent.

I frowned.

How had she heard us from behind the glass?

'Absolute fucking *Nazis*,' said Leslie again, oblivious, and as my eyes searched the room, searched for the source of the fear, I saw, just above his head, on the wall, by the clock ... the bright red light.

Lit.

eight

Leslie and I were suspended on full pay before the papers could make the decision themselves. Janice received a formal warning and now couldn't look anyone in the eye or herself in the mirror.

'You cretin,' Leslie had spat, inches from my face, so close I could inhale the Weetabix from his teeth. 'You absolute bloody cretin!'

I wanted to defend myself. The light was on! The fader was up! You could've seen it! But it was my mic. My fader. My responsibility. If Janice had had a chance to slap the Dump button she'd missed it when she hot-tapped a coffee. I could sympathise. The news was on. None of them listened to the news. It was just a break for them. What could happen when the news was on? They'd caught the end of it, of course, but the main meat – the word – that had slipped out of the studio and into half a million little radios, in homes, in cafés, on school runs …

And out of the studio Leslie had stormed, his agent already dialled, and I watched him as he paced back and forth, one arm on his forehead, the veins in his neck strained and blue, angry fingers pointing every now and again at me through the port-hole window, not quite sound-proofed enough to mute his rage.

He apologised straight away on air – profusely, professionally – but Twitter wasn't on his side. Radio Today tweeted a link minutes later. The *Media Guardian* jumped on it with glee. Radiofail preserved it for all eternity and the *Standard* managed to get it on the streets, in black-and-white, irreversible, unchangeable, by the end of the day.

TALK LONDON LESLIE'S MAD NAZI JAM RANT

Leslie was mainly concerned they kept referring to him as a 'local DJ'.

'London's as good as *national*,' he kept saying, over and over. 'We're on DAB! We're online! It's pretty much *inter*national.'

That didn't really help his cause. All it meant was, he'd sworn all over the world.

He'd been summoned to the fifth floor in minutes, and it wasn't to look at the roof garden. Mike Brundell was told to start his show two hours early, and I could hear him now, sitting outside Jenny Gardener's office, talking about immigration through a sleek walnut Revo, just opposite a poster of a grinning Leslie wearing acid-washed jeans and a waistcoat and giving two thumbs-up.

I knew I'd be back on in a week. It was my mistake. I'd do a studio etiquette refreshers course and sign some forms to say I had, but I wasn't the one who'd said the 'C' word on air, and it turned out that was the element a lot of people had chosen to focus on.

I could hear nothing from the office in which Leslie now sat, where no doubt he'd be explaining himself to Jenny Gardener. Janice should've been on hand to stop the offending moment go out, he'd be saying, so why was she making a coffee when the news was on?

But it was still him that had said it.

By the end of the first day, fourteen complaints had been filed with OFCOM.

Two hundred and sixty-six by the time the *Mail* had made its outrage known the next morning.

Leslie's suspension was over.

Leslie had done his last show.

It had distracted me from the wait for replies from people, I'll give it that.

Problem was, waiting for replies had distracted me from my job.

I'd remembered Pippy's text, the night before.

Number Unknown.

Here's my new number.

And it struck me how people trust that kind of text. You accept it. You just do. No one bats an eyelid. *This must be my friend. How could it not? It's come to me!*

So I'd tapped it out, to see how it looked.

**Guys. Lost my phone! This is my new number. Hayley.
Xxx**

Anyone who got that would just think, 'oh, Hayley's lost her phone'. Not 'oh, I appear to be about to engage with the disgruntled partner of a friend or acquaintance of mine adopting the guise of their loved one'. They'd just assume. I mean, I'd believe it, and I'm the one that typed it.

Then they'd reply, and if I played them right, by a process of elimination, I could work out which, if any of them, was Andy-from-the-place. Because one of them was bound to be Andy-from-the-place, right?

But nothing. Nothing at all. From any of them.

Sent home, staring at my phone, I wondered whether to text Leslie to apologise again. He'd left the building that afternoon and headed straight for the Nellie Dean with Janice. Apparently she'd sat wordlessly nursing a flat Pepsi while he hit the Macallan and railed against the industry, saying, 'They'd been *looking* for a fucking excuse. Well, the listeners won't stand for it. They want to see the revolution that'll hit, come Monday morning. They won't know *what* to make of it.'

Even before he'd stormed out of SoundHaus, I could sense his anger turning to glee. For Leslie, his sacking was just proof of the conspiracy against him. He was too old, he was too white, he was too experienced, he was too powerful, he was too expensive. They feared him. How do you contain fear? You crush it. Well, you don't crush Leslie James. He'd be back. Maybe he'd start his own station. You only needed a microphone and some sort of equipment. He could do podcasts, set his own hours, do it from home. This could be the best thing that ever happened to him. And who would replace him? Mike Brundell? Good luck. No, they'd have to bring in a Titchmarsh or an Edmonds. Maybe poach Nick Ferrari, if he'd come back to local. But were any of those going to quell the uprising? Not on your Nellie Dean. Leslie was on fire. Leslie was fury.

So no, I didn't text him in the end.

Instead, I picked up the home phone, and I dialled a number.

'Hello?'

'Don't hang up.'

'Who is this?'

'It's Tom, I'm ringing from home ...'

'I already—'

'I cannot *stress* how much I need to meet with you right now.'

A pause. Uncertainty.

'*Please.*'

nine

I checked my emails as the sun stretched across the table. Flies skimmed the water, lit as they chased through a calming amber.

The canal looked pretty tonight; ducks quietly bothering each other by the houseboats, the dull thunder of another train leaving King's Cross a half-mile or so away. The tall, arched windows of the red-brick factories in the distance lined up, ordered, uniform.

....

FROM: MAUREEN THOMAS
TO: ALL STAFF

ALL STAFF PLEASE NOTE from 2pm tomorrow that ALL STAFF ARE EXPECTED TO ATTEND a STUDIO ETIQUETTE and BASIC DESKWORK WORKSHOP which ALL STAFF MUST ATTEND due to several indescretion's of late which CANNOT be aloud thank you.

....

Did that mean me? I was suspended. Which rule should I respect? I'll respect the suspended rule.

Laura had agreed to meet here after several assurances that we were on the same side. I suggested her place or mine: she chose this pub. It was unsaid, but clear she wanted to meet in public.

I hoped she had the sense that I now had a greater feeling for what she'd been talking about. And I wasn't a wounded boyfriend any more. I wasn't the victim I'd felt previously. It was odd, but I was almost a bystander now. A witness to a crime. And when she finally got there, forty minutes late, already I would guess a glass or two of wine in, I was quick to back that up.

'I know what you mean by bloody psycho now,' I said, swirling the last of the Coke in my glass.

She furrowed her brow. She hadn't changed a bit. How reassuring that is, when someone doesn't change a bit.

'I think she's had some kind of breakdown or something. But I know she's in France now.'

'She's in France?'

'Paris. She sent me a postcard. But I don't know where and I don't have a number for her apart from her mobile and she doesn't reply to emails. And I think I sort of know why she went even though I don't at all understand it, and—'

'The problem is she hasn't changed at all.'

I smiled a false smile, pretended to be distracted as a man threw some bread at the ducks.

'I'd take issue with that statement, I think,' I said, as lightly as I could.

'You serious?' she said. 'You didn't notice? You never spoke about it?'

'Please just say whatever you want to say.'

Laura leaned in, dropped her voice.

'When Hayley met me she fell in love with me. That was how she put it. How long had we known each other by the time we met you in Bristol?'

I shrugged.

'I don't know. Ages.'

'Two months. We'd known each other two months.'

That didn't seem right.

'I thought you'd, like, grown up together, or …'

'Listen, I thought she was fantastic. We had exactly the same tastes. Hit it off brilliantly. It was like, I could say whatever, and we'd find a connection. Any old thing. Favourite film? *You've Got Mail.* Both of us.'

'She hated *You've Got Mail.* She said she hated that film. I remember, it was on last Christmas, she said she hated it.'

Laura laughed, smacked the table, spilled her wine.

'No – *you* hated *You've Got Mail. You* hated it.'

She rocked back in her chair, stared at me, waited for it to sink in.

'What else did she hate?' she said, as I sat there, stumped.

'Tacos? Talent shows? Oh – rosé.'

'And which of those do you hate?'

'So you're saying …'

'She's a pleaser. That's what I think. She tries to please, she tries to fit in, she moulds her tastes around stronger personalities. And then she stays like that, for whatever reasons she has, until something else comes along. Something bigger. With me, it was you. Do you have any idea how much rosé we used to drink? Do you remember what you said when you saw us together in Bristol? You thought we were sisters.'

'Or … or cousins, it's—'

'The hair, yeah? The clothes. The bloody sunglasses. Everyone thought it. Do. You. See. What. I. Am. Saying?'

But I was ignoring her now, because I was thinking of the walk we'd taken, the walk to the George in Bathampton, and the chats we'd had … deep and meaningful and staring straight into each other's eyes and laughing at all the stuff we had in common, all the things we'd liked, all the plans we coyly shared in the hope the other might have the same …

'I hated it when I realised. Because that's not friendship, is it? That's creepy and sociopathic. I told her where to go, and she just kept turning up everywhere she knew I was going to be. You two were going out at that time, thank God, and you have no idea how pleased I was when she found you, so that I could … well …'

'Get rid of her.'

'Yeah.'

'She's always been someone else,' I said, and it hit me hard, and suddenly I wasn't just a bystander any more, I was very directly affected by it. I felt … robbed of something.

'I don't know what to do,' I said.

'Move on,' she said.

'But how do I—'

'Just move on. Don't look back. Told you last time, I'll tell you again. People like that aren't good for you. You're better off out. Especially after … well, the way you were.'

I waved that away, made it seem like nothing.

'A girl who could do this to you after all that,' she said. 'After you credited her with getting you out of it. After you said she *helped* you.'

'Okay.'

'Well, I mean it. You used to say she saved you. And now look at her.'

A thought struck me.

'I've forgotten how you two met?'

'I was in Topshop. She was just suddenly there. She tapped me on the shoulder. Told me she loved my necklace.'

I felt sick. Was that her thing?

'There's something else to all this,' I said. 'I think there's a guy involved.'

'Oh, Tom,' she said, sadly. 'She's capable of anything.'

Somewhere close by, a dog barked. Ducks took flight.

I walked up Caledonian Road and crossed over, towards Barnsbury, past the tall Victorian houses, now updated with slats and fake plants, too green to be convincingly British. Richmond Avenue, with the strange pyramids and coal-black sphinxes standing guard out front, though no one ever seemed to know why, or be curious enough to ask.

I'd left Laura upset. Part of her missed Hayley too. Or, at least, her version of Hayley. She'd texted me straight after, saying it was good to see me, and that we should meet up again sometime, but we both knew that we wouldn't. Our link had been Hayley – at least I'd thought it had been. Now we didn't even have that. We were just two people who'd met, once.

My phone vibrated in my pocket again, but I couldn't face another text from her, knowing it'd be a 'chin up' or a 'sorry' or a sad face or something. I'd wait until I'd found a cab. I didn't want to walk home tonight.

I waved down a black cab near the Regent and climbed in.

'Stoke Newington,' I said, and the cabbie nodded.

'Good night?' he said.

'Can we have the radio on, please?' I said, shooting that down.

He obliged. Some dance track and a DJ with ideas above his station. Quick joke about the weather, time check, song intro. One link, one thought – that's what they tell you is all the public can stand. Maybe they're right. Sometimes you want radio to not listen to.

I pulled my phone out, wondering how to reply to Laura.

But the text wasn't from Laura.

Number unknown.

Hi love. Good luck. A. x

A?

A for Andy?

My heart raced. It had to be him. Come on. 'Hi love', with a kiss? It *had* to be the guy.

What do I write back?

Or do I phone him?

He'll think it's Hayley – he'll answer.

But then what? How do I keep him on the line? How do I get answers?

I stared out the window as we took the back route round Islington, towards the roundabout.

And then …

'Mate …' I shouted. 'Mate!'

The cabbie, startled, turned.

'What?'

'What is this?' I said, panicked. '*This*, what is it?'

'This *what*?' he said.

'This music!' I said, trying to be as quick as I could so I could still hear it, but it was slowing, it was ending, 'What's this *music*?'

It was still in my head as I got home. I kept it there, repeating the words over and over.

I was sure I'd heard what I'd heard.

But what if I hadn't? What if I was going mad?

I'm sorry I've been so distant, I am just elsewhere.
You must be so confused and wonder if I still care …

I grabbed the postcard from the table. Read it. Sank into my sofa.

The words. The words were the lyrics.

I got my phone out again, ready to dial, ready to launch into something at this Andy guy, but then I thought wait, wait … be clever, here. You have his number. Bide your time. There must be a better way.

I flipped open my laptop.

Tapped his number into google.

One result.

CC UK – Wednesdays. 6.30pm. Holiday Inn Express.
Wandsworth.

Then the last few words …

Call Andy, on …

[3]

I sit on the Eames chair in the corner of his apartment on Bleecker.

There is a fresh pot of coffee on the stove, and *Saturday Night Live* plays out on the television set in the corner of the room. Comedian Eddie Murphy is pretending to be the musician Stevie Wonder, at which the audience whoops and hollers.

The old man tends to the plants at the window, kneeling on a patchwork ottoman.

'The aspect many have trouble grasping,' says Cockroft, standing up to turn the television off, 'is that most people are other people.'

'How so?' I say.

'Their thoughts are someone else's opinion, their lives a mimicry, their passions a quotation.'

'Is that true of you?'

'I should say so,' he says, turning to me. 'I just quoted Oscar Wilde.'

'How did you fall into it?' I ask, as he sits down at the table.

'I did not fall into it,' he says. 'I leapt into it. I leapt into it with great vigor, and longing, and passion.'

'But why?'

He lays out two cups, and pushes a bowl of brown sugar toward me.

'Because I had found something.'

I take a sugar cube and drop it in my cup.

'Was finding it enough?' I ask. 'Did you not have enough?'

'I had found something, and no, finding something is not in and of itself enough. To know you have found something worth finding, you must first have lost something worth losing.'

He takes a sugar cube and lets it slide down the curve of his cup.

I say nothing, allowing the silence to drown out what is unsaid. What I would have asked the last time we met is not necessarily what I might ask now. I would rather he tell me than I ask him to.

He takes a breath.

'I lost Mae first to another man, and then to the Gods.'

American Airlines flight 330 out of Chicago.

'She was coming back to New York, maybe to tell me, maybe not.'

It was 1965. They knocked on his door that night. He did not yet know, but he had already lost her to the man she'd booked a seat next to.

'I struggled with it all, of course I did. When she was gone I was struck by what was left. Me. Only me. Our infant daughter, of course, but our memories halved. And I was left not with a bitterness that she may have sought comfort elsewhere, but left instead with the fact that she was gone and I was not.'

He could not cope. He could not look at his life. His past was gone, ruined with his future.

And this was when Ezra Cockroft first realized there must be something else he could do.

ten

The Holiday Inn Express, Wandsworth.

Thirty minutes of free Wi-Fi per night. A new snack menu in the lounge bar including Chicken Tikka Masala (£9.95) and Chilli Con Carne (£8.95). Free hot breakfast with (selected) hot items. Work desk and hairdryer in every room. Just metres from Trinity Road roundabout.

I know this because I'd checked the website on my phone as I sat in a Costa nearby, and now that I was here ... well, was this where they always met? Hayley and Andy? To have an affair? Or do ... whatever it was they were doing? Why the Holiday Inn Express? Why not just treat yourself, and go for the Holiday Inn? What was the rush?

The lounge bar was quiet. Bucket seats. Faint music – prominent clarinet – the odd thwoosh of someone cleaning a milk frother or banging a coffee pot behind a thin wall.

On my left, an unhappy couple sat silently at a too-small table.

She was younger than he was. Pale skin, straight black hair, skinny jeans, maybe mid-twenties. He was a larger, older, black man with a copy of the *Mail* and a plate of eggs, trying to avoid her eye.

He took a sip of his water, and she took a sip of hers.

He put his glass down gently.

They sighed.

Bad news? Fresh argument? Or just misery in sync? A tactic to avoid conversation, based on years of experience? Neither looked up as I crept past, trying not to catch whatever they had. She stared at him. He now stared at the window. No one ate the eggs.

I found a seat near the back, on a low, stiff sofa where I could see the whole room. Just me, skinny jeans and the egg man so far. And then, on a wallpapered pillar, just below an ineffective lampshade, I saw a small and laminated sign.

cc →

I sat a moment more.

Got up.

Followed the arrow.

The thing that Laura mentioned. The times that Hayley got me through.

Let me just clear that up.

Let's say Hayley, for the sake of it, is a mild depressive. Let's just say that, and let's just say it's mild. But strong enough to affect.

Because mild is what Dr Moon calls it, and I suppose compared to the depths to which others slip, it is, but to the person involved at the times you feel it most, it's not mild. It's no more possible to call it mild than it is to call a murder mild, or for someone to suffer mild death. It's not mild. It just is.

Think dank, at first. Foggy. Blurred. Think the moss on an otherwise normal tree, think the oil that coats the water. A growth, a barrier, think of it however's easiest. It's not glass-half-empty, either, before you confuse it with pessimism. It's a total and consuming belief in one's own worthlessness, hopelessness, helplessness, which affects everything the moment you notice what I know some have called that black dog … it's in your peripheral vision, now. You don't have to look at it to know it's there, you hear it panting, you hear it settling, and immediately whatever sense of well-being or self-worth was there rises like a spirit from your body and like in a dream where you can't find your footing there is nothing you can do but watch it go and allow despair and fatigue and emptiness their place at the table. Watch the water rise, watch the fog glide in, watch the dog strain at his leash.

So let's say Hayley, for the sake of it, is a mild depressive.

She isn't.

But if she were, then she'd be just like me.

And now you know why I need clarity about Hayley. Now you know why I need purpose. My days are foggy enough when it hits. Actually, 'hits' is the wrong word. Creeps – that's better. And when it *creeps* – just as it's crept every day since I was sixteen, stretching this gauze across my life – I need to push through it; break the surface for breath. I wanted to know what was going on here. And I needed to stop my spirit rising from my body.

I'd had it under control these days. I could laugh instead of cry. Sometimes I'd do both.

But I had to know.

Because times were changing. And I felt like I was going mad.

You'll find that the meeting room at the Holiday Inn Express, Wandsworth, has access to a coffee machine and benefits from full air conditioning. It also has ten seats around a lacquered pine table, eye-straining carpets and tartan curtains.

When I approached, and hovered by the door, four of the seats were taken.

What was this? Where was Andy? Was this … a support group? Swingers?

'Pia may or may not come,' said a woman, middle-aged, small cheap glasses. The kind of woman who's always happy to have information others don't. 'And Jeremy's not coming, of course.'

I cleared my throat and a huge maroon jumper with a man in it looked up at me. He was mid-forties – salt and pepper hair, huge anticipatory grin, big badge saying 'I'm Tim!'

This, I thought, was not Andy.

'I'm Tim!' he said, apparently delighted to see me, one pale hand reaching for mine.

'Hi Tim,' I said, low-energy. 'I'm …'

'You here for …?'

He stopped short of saying it loud, instead opening one palm for me to deliver the answer …

Clever. What was I supposed to say?

'No,' I said. 'I'm just … I was looking for someone, and …'

'Uh-huh,' said Tim, and I noticed he was still holding my hand. This handshake should have ended by now.

'Yeah, I was looking for my mate, and …'

He wasn't letting go, and now the woman had got up – a slip of a woman, just bones and oats, and she looked at me hopefully, and I noticed her badge.

CC ME.

'CC?' I said, changing tack.

'Oh, *Italian*, are you?' said Tim, now smiling, now finally letting my hand drop. '*Si! Si!*'

He laughed a lot at this, his eyes searching the room for someone to enjoy it with. But he was clearly letting me stay.

'It's £5, then, just to cover coffees and biscuits and the like,' he said, and I scrabbled about in my pocket for change. This really didn't seem like Hayley's scene at all. Not even what I thought had been her new scene. £5 for coffee and biscuits does not equal a Chinawhite crowd.

'You just ignore Tim!' said the lady, sitting back down at the table. 'He's always doing his Italian joke to newbies!'

'Guilty,' said Tim. 'Guilty as charged!'

'I'm Jackie and you're very welcome,' said the woman, who looked like she was probably a knitter and goes to sci-fi conventions for little-watched eighties cartoons held in grim Derbyshire boxing halls. 'What's your name, poppet?'

'… Serge,' I said.

Serge? Where the hell had Serge come from?

A thick-set orange teenager looked round from the coffee machine.

'Where's Andy?' he said. 'Andy should be here by now.'

The hell was that? Fake tan? Jet black hair, too, the kind of pure black nature can't compete with.

The fourth of four stood by the window, fiddling with one tartan curtain, staring out at the road.

'That's Victor,' said Jackie. 'It's his first time too.'

Victor did not turn round.

But Andy was coming. *Andy*.

Because this was *the place*.

And then Andy walked into the place and he was not what I was expecting at all.

'First off,' said Andy, who was a hundred and fifty pounds if he was ten. 'Let's meet the new folks and assess their expectations.'

He was late thirties. Khaki combat trousers. A huge checked shirt. Bifocals under a thinning mop of long, curly hair and red clipboard in hand.

He did not seem a natural nemesis.

'So Victor – you first! What first drew you to us?'

Victor shrugged.

'Okay, that's fine,' said Andy. 'But what do you hope to get out of it?'

Victor shrugged again.

'Dunno, not sure.'

'Uh-huh, uh-huh,' said Andy, nodding. 'And how did you hear about us please? Because as I always say: the first rule of CC is no one talks about CC!'

Tim started to laugh so hard at this that he slapped his thigh. Victor just shrugged.

How the hell did Hayley fit into this? This bunch of … *dweebs.*

'How about you, Serge?' said Andy, and the room turned to me. 'How did you hear about us?'

I hadn't expected this. I didn't know what to say. I could make something up, I suppose. Or I could just play it straight. Get the upper hand early on.

'My girlfriend told me about you,' I said.

'I see,' said Andy. 'Ordinarily people don't … I mean, is she a member of this chapter, or another, or …?'

'When you say "this chapter", you mean …?'

'I mean, does she use this CC? Or does she attend another CC, perhaps—'

'Her name's Hayley,' I said, and the only person who did not react when I said that name was Victor.

'Hayley Anderson?' said Jackie.

'We don't use full names here,' said Andy, eyebrows down, face darker.

He turned to me.

'*The* Hayley?'

I'd expected to be angry. I'd thought I might knock things over. Yell. But instead, I sat, eyes fixed on my shoes.

'Hayley takes it very seriously, Tom,' said Andy, nodding, the room in rapt silence around him.

Jackie had been pretty quiet since realising. Tim wasn't finding much funny any more. The orange kid – whose name I now knew was Felix – just stared at his thumbs. Victor had left when he worked out this wasn't a swingers thing.

'And we were there for her,' he said. 'Always there for her.'

'There for her how?' I said, not looking up, not yet able to.

'She'd only recently joined Wandsworth,' he said. 'She'd been with ... Highgate before that, was it, Jackie?'

'Highgate, yes.'

'And Stockwell before that?'

'Stockwell, yes.'

'But she didn't find them particularly ... inspiring.'

'How long?' I said. 'How long has she been coming here?'

'I don't have that on record.'

'Did she say why she started?'

Andy shook his head.

'Or *why*? No offence to any of you, you all seem perfectly ... but why would she need this in her life? Because I'm sitting in a Holiday Inn Express in Wandsworth and *I don't know why*.'

'We help people,' said Andy, and that stopped me.

'What people?'

'Lost people. People who don't quite know who they are any more.'

I stared at him.

'I don't understand.'

'People can run into trouble,' said Tim, gently. 'It's like a car. Sometimes the battery runs down. And you need another car to help jumpstart it. We sort of provide the leads.'

'You help people who are lost or whose batteries are flat. So far you sound like the RAC. So I'm going to ask you again: what do you do?'

Andy shifted in his chair, leaned in, spoke with care.

'Sometimes someone might be in an unfamiliar city.'

'Hayley *knew* London.'

'They might not know what they're doing with themselves.'

'She had a *job*. She *liked* it.'

'Maybe they moved here and they left their friends behind, or their family, and they look around and they're alone.'

But Hayley had *me*.

'Or something might happen in their life which catches them off guard and throws them off balance and they suddenly think, "Who am I?" You know? "What am I doing?" They might have a history of something. They might feel completely *uninspired*. And we are all about *re*-inspiring them. Recharging their batteries. Showing them who they could be again.'

I looked around the room. Felix with his leather bracelets. Tim eating coleslaw from a tub. Jackie's cheeks, rhubarb red and with faint silver hints of glints of hair.

'So it's self-help? It's a self-help group? You sit around and read mottos out to each other?'

'Not exactly,' said Andy, with patience, and perhaps a little drama. 'That's not exactly how we help.'

'How, then?' I said, embarrassed, because maybe only I knew this, but at some point – around the time we started talking about inspiration, about someone losing sight of themselves – it seemed like we weren't just talking about Hayley any more.

'We copy,' said Jackie, breaking the deadlock.

'You copy,' I said, but the words made no sense.

'We copy others,' she said. 'We follow, we copy. We copy others.'

Andy nodded, gently.

'Why?' I said. 'What?'

'You go to bed,' said Andy. 'You get up, you go to work, you go home, you go to bed. You eat the same dinner every night and shop in the same supermarket. You buy the same things and you eat them in the same place.'

'So?' I said. 'Loads of people do.'

'I don't mean you specifically. I mean people generally. And what we do is help combat that. It's so easy to fall into routine. To think that your way is the only way.'

He smiled, took a Sharpie from his top pocket and pointed it at the window.

'But if you pick someone out there—'

'Someone you think is the way you should be—' said Felix, out of nowhere.

'Then maybe you'll learn to be you,' said Jackie, and I blinked a couple of times, took in the whole scene.

'This is insane,' I said.

'Something you should know is, you will never know our full names. We protect our members' identities.'

'And who's protecting the identities they're nicking?' I said. 'Hang on – is this even legal? You're stealing identities—'

'Yes, Christ yes,' said Andy, flustered, wagging his finger.

'There's no law against it,' said Jackie.

'What I mean is, you'll never know my surname. You'll simply know me as Andy Double. Everyone here does.'

I shook my head. This was insane.

'That's Felix Echo over there.'

Felix raised a hand. I noticed he was wearing an ironic 'N Sync t-shirt.

'They call me Jackie Ape,' said Jackie, smiling. 'I thought that was quite fun.'

'You'll like this,' said Tim. 'I'm Timitate.'

This was the most *uncool* conversation I had ever had. This was *so* uncool.

'So some people start with simply following,' said Andy, still with that gentle tone, still with those kind eyes. 'A new route home, a different park. Some do it jogging, because it's less suspicious that way. Maybe they'll go to a different shop, try a different meal. It's about broadening horizons. Finding the best options. Ones that excite you.'

'Or being someone else entirely,' I said. 'Why would you do that?'

Andy leaned forward, put his hand on mine.

'We like to say, "We're Repli*cans*, not Replican'ts".'

A gentle titter from Timitate.

And I stood.

And I said, 'Well, it was lovely to meet you all.'

Their faces fell. Andy, it seemed, had thought he was getting somewhere.

'And it's great to see that Hayley used to spend her time sitting in a hotel meeting room in Wandsworth with a bunch of weirdos to talk about copying people.'

'Oh dear,' sighed Tim. 'Uh-oh.'

'There's actually no law against it,' said Jackie, again. 'It's honestly not weird. It's just a tool. We just say it's just a different way of subscribing to life.'

'Where's Hayley gone?' I said, now as forthright as I could manage. 'Someone here knows and you need to tell me right now.'

Andy held his hands up.

'I can't.'

'Yes you can. Yes you will, or I'll phone the police right now and have this whole thing shut down.'

'There's actually no *law* against it, actually,' said Jackie again, and it worried me that she'd had to check.

'I can't tell you because I don't know,' said Andy. 'Her story is her story. What she's decided to do is something I personally advised her against but all I could do was advise.'

'You knew she was going. You knew because you left a message on my phone and that's how I found you. You did nothing about it. You knew she'd do this to me and you did nothing!'

And calmly, Andy stood, and looked me dead in the eye.

'Tom, look …' he said. 'The thing you have to understand, the thing that'll help you to know, is that Hayley didn't do this *to you*, Tom.'

He lay two fat pink hands on my shoulders.

'She did this *for her*.'

Out of the Holiday Inn Express, Wandsworth I stormed.

Left at the roundabout, and over the bridge, my head down, my pace fast, never looking up as cars and vans and bikes shot by.

How was I going to explain this to people?

'How's it going with Hayley? Oh, not bad. She decided to meet up with a bunch of oddballs in a hotel to copy strangers and then went to France. But don't worry, she did it *for her*. Have we still got the flat? Oh yes. And me? Yes, I'm fine. I get up in the dead of night every day to read out loud and my name's a footnote in a story about a man complaining about jam on the radio.'

On I blazed, because I just needed to move, to get away, to pound the streets like I had a purpose, because I was now redundant, just a purposeless chimp a girl would rather run away from than be anywhere near. And so I turned right on the King's Road and walked up, past the turning for the World's End estate, and on, up to Green Park, down Pall Mall, the Strand, never looking up, never looking around, and when my feet could take no more I veered onto Waterloo Bridge, leaned against its triplet of white railings, legs aching, and stared with a face full of accusation at the city that had done this.

I'd almost have preferred it if Hayley had gone out of spite. Or left me for another man. But the fact that she left 'for her' made it impossible to get it out of my head. Her life was lacking.

Well, you know what? So was mine.

So what should I do?

Move back to Bristol, that's what.

Sack this whole thing off.

Tell Mohammed he can stick his flat.

Tell Talk London they can stick their job.

Just get home, home to familiar things, familiar people.

God I missed Bristol. The bridge, the cathedral. The butcher's in Southville. The floating harbour, the Tobacco Factory, the gorge. Once it had seemed boring. Now it seemed manageable. Safe. Unsurprising. Perfect.

So that's what I'd do. Forget progress, forget London. Forget my career. Go back to where people don't do as many strange things in as many strange ways. Embrace Bristol, good people, spend my days in the pub by the canal, maybe get a job on a farm, *anything*.

And as I felt for a pill in my pocket, chased it from corner to corner, I could feel the shadows of the city – the phallic Gherkin, the arrogant Shard, the Eye, Big Ben so proud and so full of itself – all of it so big, all of it towering over me, mocking me for having the temerity to stand here, mocking that brief window of genuine optimism I'd somehow allowed myself, and I cast a glance to the right and I caught someone's eye.

I was being followed.

[4]

'Come,' he says, one arm over my shoulder, paternal, nurturing. 'Let's try it.'

'Try what?' I say.

'You want to be immersive,' he says. 'Then immerse. Channel your inner Salinger. Go Gonzo. Choose someone.'

I smile, then laugh.

'I'm serious,' he says. 'Pick a toy.'

'They're toys to you?' I say. 'These are people.'

'You must think of them as toys. You cannot be subservient. Make no mistake: you are the master. They are your subjects. If you bow down to them, you will never rise up; never be anyone but a pale imitation of everyone else. They are the toys, you are the child.'

I look around. We are back in Greenwich Village, on West 3rd Street, next to Golden Swan Park.

'Him?' I say.

A man leaves Café Reggio, and skips across a road, holding a briefcase.

'No,' he says. 'You've chosen someone just like you.'

I look at the man. He's not like me.

'You chose a white man, similar age, similar build, similar clothes, probably a similar mother, probably a similar guy. You chose something you know, you chose familiarity and familiarity is not what discovery is about.'

He knows what I'm thinking.

'Yes, okay, Berlin, you're right. I was drawn to the familiar. But remember – it was also alien to me. Because my choices had taken me down a very different path. That man was living a life that was absolutely not like mine. It was like a shadow of what could have been. Put simply, I knew what I was missing. You on the other hand think you have it all worked out. Ergo, you *don't know* what you're missing.'

He pushes me forward, and we fall in behind a Chinese man furiously barreling through the crowds.

eleven

There was a Tesco Express on the corner.

I could lose her in the crowd.

She'd tailed me right across the bridge, and that was fair enough, because your options are fairly limited on a bridge, but she'd crossed the road when I did, paused when I did, doubled-back when I did. She'd put a jacket on since the first time I'd seen her. Big blue parka. Army boots over black jeans. Grey beanie pulled back over hair. She looked like a little Eskimo.

I kept my head down as I went in, eyes flicking up to the CCTV screen in the corner, circling the newspapers for a second, and picking up *The Times*. I flapped it open and let my eyes rest on the automatic doors.

I shouldn't have come in here. I should've just got a cab home. But I was intrigued. People don't follow you in real life. This was just a series of extraordinary coincidences. Must be. Had to be. All I had to do was break the cycle. Get some distance.

The doors opened and in she came – Christ! – eyes darting around, searching, hungry. I closed the paper, shoved it back and turned.

My neck prickled.

She saw me, followed.

I slowed at the jams to allow her to pass. She didn't want to talk. What, then? I stared at some small packets of jelly until she went by. I turned and went the other way.

I darted down an aisle to the milk, picked up a small red-top of skimmed, checked my sightlines, moved on, grabbed some sausages. I wanted something in my hands, I hated looking suspicious.

She was nowhere to be seen.

Part of me wanted to laugh. This was ludicrous. But I was too certain I wanted to be annoyed to let the absurdity show. I'd been like that with Hayley when we fought – too determined to be angry to smile when she said something funny, when the tension could have been broken. How much time had I spent choosing to be angry rather than letting something go?

I padded on, thought I saw her, then kneeled at the booze aisle, picking up a half-bottle of rum and flipping it round as if I needed to study the label. A young lad in a Tesco tabard swaggered by holding tall green bottles of elderflower cordial, laughing at something a distant colleague was shouting, a vapour trail of hair gel and Lynx in his wake.

Then she rounded the corner, raised her eyebrows at me, half-smiled and continued on.

Black hair, skinny jeans. Small badge on her lapel: 'I LOVE VEGANS'. She hadn't been in the meeting, this little Bjork. But I'd seen her. Sitting in silence with the big fella at the hotel, not eating his eggs, trying to look like he was ignoring her.

She sauntered past, all wide eyes and innocent, freckled face, and as she did I looked down, and in her basket she had a small bottle of red-top milk and some sausages.

I scanned my sausages in the self-service aisle, then scanned my milk. Then the jelly. Peanuts.

Maybe it was my medication. Maybe it was the lack of sleep, the early mornings, the confusion of Hayley and all that she'd done.

Each *be-bloop* of the till was joined by another a half-second later from directly behind me.

The rum.

'*Age restricted item,*' said the voice from the machine.

Then, a second later, from behind me, the other machine: '*Age restricted item.*'

On the screen: '*Please wait for a member of staff.*'

Jesus.

I turned and scowled at the girl.

Her screen: '*Please wait for a member of staff.*'

She avoided my eye now, looking for whichever member of staff was going to get us out of this one.

We stood four feet apart in complete silence.

She knows I know, I thought to myself. *She knows I know and she knows I know she knows I know.*

Her eyes rested on mine.

'What are *you* staring at?' she said, with enough attitude to make me feel *I* was the weirdo.

'Why are you following me?'

'I'm not. I'm shopping.'

'You were.'

'What?'

'Following me.'

'I know.'

'Why?'

'You seem interesting.'

I stared at her. She stared at me.

'SANDRA!' – *wow*, that was loud. '*SANDRA!*'

A Tesco woman under a cloud of thin orange hair was waving at someone I could only assume was Sandra. Let's call her Tesco Sandra.

'*I'll* do it!' she shouted, waving at Tesco Sandra to remain where she was, then looked at the rum, looked at me. 'Sorry, I need my fob.'

She strode off. We were stuck.

'Where's your mate?' I said.

'What mate?' said the girl.

'The big black guy with the eggs.'

'What big black guy with the … oh, the big black guy with the eggs at the hotel?'

'Yes, that's the big black guy with the eggs I meant. Where's that big black guy with the eggs?'

'Where I left him, I s'pose. He's a senior manager at Foxtons.'

I shrugged.

'I just thought that was an interesting detail. No, I don't know where he is. I don't know him. I read the Foxtons thing on one of his bits of paper he kept putting up to his face.'

She was pretty. In a sort of damaged goods way. Pale, with that constellation of light brown freckles and two green eyes.

I'm not sure why I said 'two' there.

But what did she *want*?

'We never talked, me and that guy,' she said.

'You were eating with him.'

'No I wasn't. I was sitting opposite him. We never talked.'

'The place was empty.'

'And?'

'Did you sit with him or did he sit with you?'

'I sat with him.'

'You just sat down, in an otherwise empty room, at someone else's table?'

'He seemed interesting.'

A micro-shrug, a tilt of the head, the implication being: *what's your problem?*

'Look, I know you're one of them. One of those … from that thing.'

'I know. It's pretty obvious. And I also knew you'd know that.'

'Right!' said the woman with the orange hair, and we fell silent as she took the bottle from my basket. 'Rum, is it? Ooh, very nice.'

She swiped or tapped or did whatever it was this great gatekeeper of goods had to do, using her vast power to allow me to buy a half-bottle of something I'd never drink, while I struggled with how to be. This girl, was she friend? Was she foe? Did she know Hayley? Had she encouraged her?

'And now, you, m'love ...' said Tesco woman, turning to the girl, and then, noticing her stuff: 'Oh, you're *shopping* twins!'

She pointed at the items, her excitement growing.

'Milk, skimmed – sausages, same brand – the exact same bottle of rum!'

We both just stared at her.

'Peanuts – jelly ...!'

She made a huge open-mouthed 'surprised' face.

'Sandra!' she shouted. 'You're *never* going to believe this!'

Outside, I hovered by the doors. Mad Girl stepped outside and magicked out a roll-up from a deep blue pocket, limp plastic bag hooked over one thin wrist.

The orange-haired woman had tried to get us to agree to get married one day. All the guests at the wedding would have to eat sausages, jelly and peanuts, she said. And drink milk and rum. The Mad Girl said that sounded like the worst wedding ever and accused me of copying her shopping. That was when the orange-haired woman had started glancing around, looking for security.

I moved off, glowering.

She lit her fag and started after me.

'You're *still* following me,' I said.

'I live this way,' she said. 'Deal with it.'

'Your whole life?'

'What?'

'You *live* your *whole life* this way?'

'No,' she said, scrunching up her nose, and pointing down the road. 'I *live, this* way.'

I stopped in my tracks, frowned at her.

'Well, I'm walking this way.'

'So?'

'So follow someone else.'

'Nutter,' she said, overtaking me, slipping an earphone into one ear and hitting Play on an unseen iPod, and turning round once – and only once – to quickly flick me the V, then smile.

twelve

I'd been called in for a meeting at work. I knew what it meant. I was being shelved. Taken off London Calling to make way for Mike Brundell and his sidekick, Sharon News. She'd been called Travel Sharon for ages, but it was felt that made her sound like something you'd buy from Halfords, after you'd popped into the supermarket to get yourself a Tesco Sandra.

Radio does that. Compartmentalises. Pigeon-holes. It's understandable. You need simple, identifiable figures, with simple, identifiable jobs. I'd escaped it so far. I think Adoyo as a name helped make the station sound more multicultural. I think it made it sound like they'd bussed me in from Kenya, rather than asked me to get the 17:30 from Bristol Temple Meads.

Halfway down Great Portland Street a jogger buzzed past me and padded on. Moments later, so did another.

Since CC and the girl on the bridge, I'd been keeping an eye out. I saw followings and followers everywhere. Who's to say it wasn't going on all around me? Or that it hadn't been happening for years? What if everyone was at it?

The girl, there, leaving the newsagents, now walking behind the old lady weighed down by bags. What if that was something? Why couldn't it be?

Or the man running to catch the bus. What if it wasn't the *bus* he was after? I mean – these people meet up, for God's sake. They hire rooms at the Holiday Inn. Where had Andy mentioned? Stockwell? Highgate? Where else were Tims and Jackies and Felixes meeting up? They said it was like a support group. Who else had left, the day Hayley left? Who else had jacked it all in and for what?

And why would you give it all up? Who in their right mind would want to live *someone else's life?*

Ding.

....

FROM: MAUREEN THOMAS
TO: ALL STAFF

Please do NOT bring your OWN WASHING UP LIQUID TO WORK.

....

Delete.

I'd had to hand my ID over to Maureen the week before, like a renegade cop rather than a disgraced local newsreader, but I still got her emails.

Adewale kept his eye on me as I sat in reception, waiting to be picked up and led upstairs by some work experience or other. I looked around.

'WELCOME TO OUR FRIENDS AT BONJELA.'

And next to that screen, in huge letters painted right across the wall, the SoundHaus mission statement:

WE ARE THE VOICE THEY HEAR!
One voice, unified, passionate! One voice for London,
one voice for the United Kingdom!
We are here to serve, to entertain, to inform – this is
SoundHaus Plc.
And you're <u>welcome</u> to it!

It had been an internal competition. Jonathan in Online had won. He called it 'One Voice'. That was on all the stationery now – '*SoundHaus – One Voice*'. Jonathan got a night in Barnsley House for his trouble, and even with a prime Cotswolds dinner it was maybe 3,000 per cent cheaper than paying an actual marketing company to do it instead. The only stipulation was that it had to use the word 'passion' because they'd done some audience testing and 'passion' was ranked top by almost two in every three ABC1s in the coveted 18–34 demographic when asked to identify most-looked-for attributes in modern music or speech-centric commercial radio endeavours.

I found my way to the newsroom. Generally, I avoid this place, because this place is not a fun place to be. Eight desks, six computers, two tellies, strip-lit, windows facing a stained brick wall. Sky News running constantly at just above a whisper. Head of news in a small office to one side. It's the travel people you really avoid. Eight hours a day looking at cameras, studying tailbacks. It's not conducive to very good anecdotes.

'It's stacked back to Clackets,' they'll say, most days, shaking their heads very slowly. It's always stacked back to Clackets.

Bron poked her head out of her office door and beckoned me in.

'I hear your personal life is suffering some strife presently,' she said, one eye on the screen. Was she reading this? Did she get an email from HR with a script? 'Please know we wish you to feel supported and hope this does not affect your work.'

My work. That implies …

'So here it is and brace yourself,' said Bron, her voice suddenly changing as she clicked the email away, the buttons at the bottom of her shirt straining as she leaned back in her chair, her Telford accent as thick as she was. 'You're back on breakfast from Monday.'

I mustered up a smile.

'Okay,' I said. 'Thank you for your understanding.'

'OFCOM are going to rule against us. Of course they are. We broadcast the very worst word you can. Have you seen the list?'

She pushed a file across the desk towards me.

There they all were, the words, neatly divided into sections.

Slang words for sex.
Insults with sexual connotations.
Everyday words.
Ethnic words.
People with disabilities.
Terms of racial/religious faith abuse.
Religious words.
Body parts and/or bodily functions, eg 'tits'.

And there – right there, right at the top, in bold, so you couldn't really miss it.

The word Leslie said.

'There's no way round it,' said Bron, shrugging, reading an email off the screen. '"*Radio broadcasters must have particular regard to times when children are particularly likely to be listening.*"'

She made a face that implied this could arguably include breakfast time.

'"*The transition to more adult material must not be unduly abrupt.*"'

I made a face that implied I accepted it could be said Leslie's outburst could be described as unduly abrupt.

'I suspect we're looking at a fine that could well be record-breaking. You're lucky to be here at all, but it wasn't your fault.'

It kind of was.

'It was Leslie's responsibility,' she said, swatting a fat fly away and watching it go. 'It was Leslie that had to take the fall.'

Her gaze found me again and she half-smiled. That said it all. Leslie was right. They'd been looking for an excuse.

'Of course … Leslie has a different opinion. He might be coming after you, press-wise. If he does, please just alert HR, I'll make sure they're across it.'

A full-smile now, with sly eyes.

'Have you seen the videos?'

Oh, I'd seen the videos. Leslie had gone viral. JAM NAZI was massive. Six hundred thousand views in five days. The show had been removed from Listen Again almost immediately, but not before the website crashed under the weight of traffic, and the audio stuck up on SoundCloud. There were dozens, now. Some set to music. Some animated. Some just with a sombre black-and-white publicity photo of Leslie someone had found of him holding a kettle while presenting the 2004 *Which?* Awards. There were the usual parodies and remixes – a screaming Hitler, a dubstep version, something with kittens. It had even made a few in-roads into America, but it was over, done, yesterday's viral, replaced almost immediately by someone else's mortification. A fat woman stuck in a McDonald's high chair, maybe, or a naked drunk man running into a wall.

'It's actually had a few upsides,' said Bron. 'Station awareness is … well, statistically word-of-mouth has increased. Chris Evans was talking about it on Radio 2.'

Radio 2? Oh, Leslie would be delighted. He'd taken it hard, truth be told. He was yet to understand how quickly it spread. He still thought the internet was probably just one big 'forum', and that live radio was gone the second you'd finished.

Well, he knew all about it now. The engineer who'd been told to take Leslie's stuff and drop it round at his house said he found him in his conservatory, hunched over his PC in a short navy dressing gown, railing against 'the trolls', demanding to know what PMSL meant, a bottle of Glenfiddich broken in the corner, one more in the wastepaper basket.

'So I'm working with Mike Brundell, I guess?'

God, Mike Brundell was boring. His career had peaked in 1988 with an ITV version of *That's Life!* called *What's Your Story?* He'd been a newsreader on BBC Northwest up until then, had a column in the *Reader's Digest*, still pops up on 'Dictionary Corner', and wastes no time in telling you about the time Noel Edmonds performed an elaborate Gotcha! on him, and how if it hadn't been 'cut from the show due to time constraints' it would have changed *everything*.

'No, not Mike Brundell actually.'

Who, then? Tony Ram, with his jumpers? Passive-aggressive Ray Singer?

'We're switching things up. Reflecting the changing tastes of the key demographic. We haven't announced it yet, but you'll be working with Cassandra Tailor. Though we're just calling her "Cassandra". That'll be her name. Or maybe "Cass". We're testing both.'

They test names.

'Cass?' I said. 'But isn't she … I mean, she's a *jock*, isn't she, not a *broadcaster*, and—'

'This has always been the plan. That's why we gave her weekend breakfast. It was supposed to be another year or so.'

Just in time for Leslie's contract renewal.

'She's … less experienced,' said Bron, by which she meant cheap and malleable. 'We've done three off-air pilots already. She's good. *Fit*, too …'

She flashed me a dinosaur smile, face hard as steel when her teeth were bared.

' … and I've specified she's not to talk about her cracked heels. Leslie talked about his cracked heels a *lot*. Said it made him one of the people. I said it made him one of the people with cracked heels.'

I shrugged my agreement.

'So we want you there for stability. Familiar voice for the listeners. Just until Cass has settled in. So welcome back.'

Cass was in today. She'd been dotting the i's and crossing the t's with her agent. Apparently she wanted to see me before I left, so I hung around the kitchenette and kept an eye out.

'Tom!'

I span round. Pippy, dragging Work Experience Paul behind her.

'I just got some good news,' I said.

'*You* think you've got good news?' she said, beaming, sidling up to me, pleased as punch.

'Oh yeah?' I said.

She tapped the side of her glasses. She doesn't normally wear glasses, Pippy, much less glasses like these, because these were *statement* glasses.

'The man who made these glasses …' she said, 'was nominated for an Oscar!'

I blinked.

'Wow,' I said, a little confused. It wasn't Oscars season. Was I missing something? 'Who is he?'

She leaned forward, conspiratorially.

'Tom Ford,' she said.

She leaned back, tapped them again.

'Tom Ford … the designer?' I said.

'Exactly,' she said.

I was struggling to work out how this was good news.

'And … do you know him?'

'No,' she said. 'But he directed a film, and it was on telly last night, and the bloke announcing it said that Tom Ford had been nominated for an Oscar for it, and then I remembered that I had a pair of Tom Ford glasses.'

'Oh,' I said. 'And are they … bespoke?'

'No no,' she said. 'Bought them in a shop.'

'Well,' I said, doing my best for her. 'That is good news.'

'I couldn't believe it,' she said, shaking her head, like she was telling me she'd milked a cat and pumped out liquid gold. 'I was like, Tom Ford? Oscar?! He designed my glasses!'

She glanced at Work Experience Paul, who did not look as enthusiastic, and she held his gaze until he did. Poor kid still had nothing to do, except scratch.

'Have you told Bron?' I asked.

'Do you think Bron would be interested?'

'I think Bron would *love* to hear this piece of good news.'

'I'll away and tell Bron.'

'I'm *stoked*, man,' said Cass, coming in for the hug. 'So stoked.'

'Yeah, it's great news, Cass,' I said, not knowing where to put my arms. I was sure there must be a rule. Maureen was probably hovering around her keyboard just waiting to fire something off. 'Congratulations.'

'No, I'm stoked to be working with *you*. I *asked* for you.'

She smiled, flashing a row of perfect teeth made for billboards.

'They're going to keep an eye on us for a while. Plenty of snoops, apparently.'

Snoops. Great. An hour after the show to listen to random segments and be told why they're awful. Jen Latham once had a snoop in which they told her she was saying her own name wrong.

'I obviously feel bad for Leslie, though, man,' said Cass. 'That was really … unfortunate.'

'That's one word for it. I guess you'll be in charge of the mics.'

She started to laugh. She found that funny. It wasn't even a joke.

'This is why I wanted you, man. The bants.'

Eek. She used the term 'bants'. This could be a warning sign.

I'm not sure I can work with someone who uses the word 'bants'. Mind you, I just used 'eek'.

'Though Christ, I hate that word, "bants",' she said. 'If I ever say it again, slap me down. It's my sister. I live with her. She overuses it. We need a bants ban.'

'You just said it again.'

'You're funny,' she said. 'Literally.'

I was literally being literal, but I let that one go.

'I'm heading out with my agent for a drink, I was going to get Janice to come along and maybe Pippy – she's had some good news of her own today, have you heard?'

She winked at me.

This was the first time I'd been invited anywhere in forever.

'Sure,' I said, warming to her already.

Janice couldn't make it. I think she still felt bad about Leslie. She'd worked with him for years – since his Radio Trent days. And she'd followed him faithfully through the regions, to Rock Radio for the Love Hour, his late-night call-in show on West Country Gold, and all the way to London Calling. London – the big time. And there'd always been rumours about those two. And she'd been getting more and more mysterious calls that meant she had to leave the room of late. But that's just idle gossip, and as you know, I don't deal in that.

Serena from Ketsu Talent put her card behind the bar of the Punch & Judy and drifted off to smoke and run her Blackberry down. She'd started the company, dragged a bunch of clients away from Allied Agents when she left, and only recently discovered that accidentally leaving the 'i' off 'Ketsui' meant it was no longer the Japanese word for 'determination' but instead a Japanese slang word for 'bottom'. She was currently coming up with new names.

'So come on,' said Cass, touching my arm. 'We're going to be working much more closely together. Tell me everything.'

'What? About the job? About what to expect?'

'Well, I meant about you, but yeah, if you want to tell me about the job – go on.'

I thought about it.

'Well, you'll sort of know this from working on the weekends, but when you're out so early during the week ... well, you're out before London even wakes up. Before the sun rises. And London is all orange and dark and sort of abandoned ...'

She leaned in. Gestured me on.

'Well, I mean ... you get to know the sound of a milk cart, the sound that the bottles make, which you've probably forgotten from you were a kid. And you notice little things as you stop at the traffic lights or whatever.'

'What things?'

'I dunno. White vans with their ceilings all nicotined. Men flipping back doors open to get newspapers out or whatever, and they've got their radios up far too loud for that time of the morning. And ... you know ...'

It felt like it was just me and her, now, despite a man three tables away who just kept finding excuses to stare at her.

'Battered estate cars. The last illegal minicabs of the night, taking drunk single girls back to wherever they slurred they needed to go. And the girls have got their sticky windows down for air, and you just know they've got damp fivers clutched in one hand and their purse is all spattered with Sambuca.'

'Sounds magical.'

'It sort of is, in some dirty way. You're seeing the tail end of something. The hangers-on, who nearly made it into your day, and they're finishing the story of their night. Like clubbers. Or a couple of Rorys in tuxedos sitting with a bottle of red by a statue, fresh from some corporate marketing awards where they lost out on – I dunno – International Outsource Team of the Year to the guys from

Capita but still toasting their own good fortune. And they don't know how lucky they really are because just metres away—'

'"Rorys". Remind me of that one day.'

'—because just metres away you see piles of newspapers left outside shops by overturned bins and flaps of kebab skin, all dead and grey because no one's cleaned them up yet, and men with hoods and backpacks circling stacks of milk by the Tesco. Everywhere's just nervous eyes and faked bravado. You're in the night bus and you see this shadow, papering up the inside of the phone box with bits of old Metro so he can smoke his crack in peace. Or the woman in the alley off Theobalds Road looking out for stragglers before …'

'What?'

'Before *we* get there.'

'You make it sound horrible. And sort of beautiful.'

'It sort of is. I mean, it's much, much more horrible than beautiful, but it can be beautiful because it's real. It's not manufactured or controlled. No one's cleaning it up. It just is. People always talk about the listeners waking up to a show, the ones in bed, or listening in the shower. I like to think of the people who aren't listening. Who are oblivious. Untouched by … radio chatter. Pop. Who wouldn't know what to do with a traffic update.'

'I thought when you said you were going to tell me about the job you meant "the coffee machine's usually broken" and "Maureen in HR likes an email".'

'And then it's dawn,' I said, registering what she'd said, acknowledging her smile, but on a roll now, with more somehow to tell her, 'and it's the Poles and the Nigerians and the Afghans that pour out of the buses, all in black, heads down, so they can clean our offices or man our casinos or get us ready, and then they slink back to their estates or bedsits and they turn on the radio … and they hear Leslie James telling them how unneeded or unwanted they are.'

'Well,' she said, picking up her glass for a toast. 'Here's to change. Let's lead London to a brighter dawn.'

She laughed. That was pretty clever and she knew it. But it also made her sound a bit like Hitler.

'I'm not a leader,' I said, clinking glasses.

'Fine by me,' she said, and that man, probably Italian, found another excuse to look at her. 'Here's to followers.'

A pause, as she built up to something.

'Now tell me about *you*,' she said. 'And what happened with that girlfriend of yours ...'

'You know about that?'

My neck prickled.

'Dude,' she said, putting one hand on mine. '*Everybody* knows about that.'

They didn't know the half of it.

I felt hopeful after that. She'd asked for me. And as I walked down Parker Street, trying to find my way to Kingsway and the tube, night falling all around me, one easy eye out for a lazy cab home, belly full of Ketsu Talent pinot, it was the other half of it I was thinking about when I turned my head, slight right, and began to feel uneasy.

There was a man and he was close, so I started to cross the street and as I did so I realised in that gut-wrenching, heart-sinking way that you do, that once again I was being followed.

For a second I considered stopping, and laughing, and introducing myself, because how often do you get followed twice in quick succession, but he was big, and he was closer now, so close his foot clipped at my heel and as I stumbled the side of my thigh was barged and I found myself walking backwards in an alleyway off the main drag as this man now inches away, hand on my chest, pushed me, pushed me back, neck craning to see if we'd been spotted, and I realised this wasn't what I thought it could be, and I pushed back against him out of instinct, tried to turn, but now he had a grip on my neck, and the grip tightened and my head was forced round and forwards, pushing hard towards the wall, my hands rising to protect my face but my body clashing hard against the wall, my hip bone striking and scraping and the first splinters and shots of pain firing down through my legs like a nail through bone.

thirteen

The grip tightened, then released.

'Money.'

'What?' I said. 'Oh, fu—'

The first punch was to my kidneys, the second, straight after, a little higher. Back of the ribs.

'Gizzit,' he said again, as my knees began to buckle and I could open my eyes again.

'I haven't got—'

The next strike was harder. Kidneys again. I felt something give, and God, you imagine something like this happening, and you imagine fighting, but really, I wanted to cry.

The hand was back on my neck, now, and pushed me round, my head clipping the wall, but my legs were going and I didn't want to see who this was, because if I couldn't see, maybe they'd just stop or cut their losses or something.

'I haven't—'

And then my eyes sparked and the stars came out as he slapped me, hard, fast, loud, open-handed and round the cheek.

I cowered now; my hands up.

'I've got a phone,' I said, quickly. 'Here, I can give you my wallet ...'

I searched around in my jacket for it, looking up at him now and for the first time. Blood-red eyes, veins as one. Broad. Thousand-mile stare. *On* something?

That was the worst bit. You can't reason when they're on something. I'd meet them sometimes, outside the building, waiting for security to let me in. They were friendly, generally, but there were some who'd let the madness take them over. And these were the ones who could turn. Fast. Aggressive. They'd approach, maybe asking for money, maybe asking if I had a light, circling like a shark. If there was one of them you were usually okay. Two and you could have a problem, but you were *never sure*. If they engaged you in conversation, all you could do was listen. You had to smile. Placate. Give them nothing to be paranoid about. Say nothing smart. Act like everything they say impresses you and everything they say is news to you. Make them feel you believe them, whatever it is, whether it's about the government or the dole office or the man that gave them those cuts, that broken nose. You calm them, you never contradict or patronise, and while you keep your hands out of your pockets and ready, of course, you give them no reason to dislike you. They'd dislike you if they thought you reckoned you were above them. They'd dislike you if they thought you found them in any way amusing. Funny; funny's usually a trait people covet.

'I've also got an iPod,' I said. See? Show willing. Offer them something they didn't know was there. At best they'd think it was just weakness, congratulating themselves on their cleverness for finding the right target. At worst, pity and maybe just a slap for fun.

Over his shoulder, London carried on. People shot past the alley, eyes down, headphones on.

But 'What else?' he said, and 'That's it,' I replied, and with a flash of anger he brought another mighty fist down on my cheek, the contact not registering for a second, and then my skin screaming as the shock turned to pain and the taste of hot metal crept over my tongue as blood crawled around my gums and between my teeth.

'Mate, wait,' I tried, and *boom* – another open-handed slap to the face and now this wasn't just for effect, this wasn't to punctuate his points, this was an *attack*.

I just wanted him to go, he felt like a giant and I wanted to be safe, and I reached into my pocket to grab anything, anything else at all to offer him, and I clutched at a fiver and some mints and pathetically held them out in front of me as I stood, bent, no longer a man, no longer someone with a name, just six foot of useless in an alley off the main drag.

Then: 'Yoohoo!'

A girl's voice.

Yoohoo?

The whole world stopped. Silence. No car moved, no bird sang.

I stole a glance, my hands still up … the man turned, shocked, ready for another fight …

Big blue parka. I LOVE VEGANS. Phone out in front of her. The unlikeliest of angels.

'Big smiles.'

The world burst into action again. She was recording. I didn't know how to feel. Relief, that help had arrived? Humiliation that it had arrived like this? The man hid his face. Turned away. Realised it was too late. Turned back to intimidate. Shoulders up, chest out.

'Oh yeah, that's good, that's a better shot,' said the girl, backing away, backing into the street, where now there were more people, not many but more, and they could be witnesses, they could have cameras too. A woman had to stop in her tracks then go round her, sighing, oblivious, like she was the most important woman in the world and her hurried walk home the only thing that mattered.

'Yeah, come into the light,' said the girl, backing off, but no fear in her voice. 'Nice one.'

He had my iPod. He'd grabbed it from my pocket the second he'd seen it. The wallet and balled fiver he'd leave. He wasn't taking them on camera. He wasn't doing anything else on camera, either. He tried to shrug his head into his shoulders, and swaggered off, hood now flipped down, past McDonald's and on, people curving around him, sensing his mood, avoiding his eye.

I staggered to my feet, one hand on the wall behind me, stabs of pain from my back as I shifted my weight.

'Are you okay?' said the girl.

Bruised cheek was the worst of it. Red on the other side where he'd slapped me. Slapped! Who gets *slapped*? Mind you, who says *yoohoo*? Rib-ache, too, but otherwise I think his moves had been designed to intimidate, not hurt or show.

I looked at the girl in the seat next to me as the taxi hit a sharp left on Amwell. Great. Speed bumps for the next three miles. *Slow, slow, quick quick slow*. The cab driver's foxtrot.

'You were following me again,' I said.

'Complaining?'

'It's a bit weird.'

'You *are* complaining!'

'No. No, not this time, no.'

We'd grabbed the first cab we could. I just wanted out of here. I just wanted to go home. The girl had climbed in with me. It seemed fair enough. My ribs ached, but I was grateful to feel anything. Shock would come soon, I suppose. Weirdly, right now, I felt pretty good. Adrenalised.

'I'd only been following you since you left the pub,' said the girl.

'Well, how did you know I was in the pub?' I said.

'I followed you there.'

'Yeah, so you'd been following me for longer. How long had you been following me?'

'Only since work.'

I sighed.

'And how did you know where I work?'

'There was the fact that you've named your crotch.'

This girl was mental. Well, why not? Why not share a cab with a mentalist, who claims to be able to tell your name by looking at your crotch?

And then she pointed at the ID dangling from my belt.

My name in big blue letters.

'Couldn't help but notice last time we – you know – met.'

'The last time you *followed* me,' I said.

A thought struck her and she turned to me, very seriously.

'Hey, I googled you. I'm so sorry to hear about the whole Jam Nazi thing.'

Jesus.

'Yeah, that was unfortunate.'

'There are some great videos. Have you seen the one where they—'

'I've seen them all, yeah.'

'We should call the police.'

'Yes,' I said, realising, remembering. 'God, of course. Christ, it's so crazy …'

'What?' she said.

'You just don't expect that kind of thing to happen round here.'

I hadn't thought about the police. My head wasn't yet clear. But of course we should phone the police.

'We'll do it from your place,' she said. 'I'm your witness.'

'And you've got the video.'

'Oh, I wasn't videoing,' she said. 'I was just *implying* I was videoing.'

'What the hell is your name, anyway?'

She smiled.

'Lincoln Racksmackle,' she said.

'What?'

'I'm Pia,' she said. 'My name is Pia.'

I made for the bathroom while Pia – who I found a very unsettling presence – made herself a cup of tea.

I kept an ear out, in case I heard drawers being opened. I don't know what she'd find in there to steal. A few takeaway menus. A quid or two.

I stared at myself in the mirror. When had I stopped trusting people?

Oh yeah, that's right …

Man, I was going to be bruised. I'd always wondered how I'd react if I was mugged. I suppose at least now I knew. I'd put my hands up and collapse.

I found an extremely old bottle of TCP and some cotton wool.

'Why are you doing it, Pia?' I called out, dabbing at the one area the man had broken skin. 'Why follow? Why me?'

'You should know,' she said. 'You went to a meeting yourself.'

'Yeah, but I didn't go for that reason. I didn't go because I was *missing* something.'

'That's exactly why you went.'

'I went because of my girlfriend.'

'Who was exactly what you were missing.'

In the living room, she now sat with her feet up and an open tin of Christmas biscuits I didn't even know we had.

'You smell nice,' she said, and then pretended to vomit.

She was very confident, I'll give her that.

'I like your place, though,' she said, looking around. 'Oh, and there's the woman herself …'

She pointed at the mantelpiece. A picture of Hayley, the day we moved in. Hair in a scrunchie, collapsed on the sofa, surrounded by boxes.

'Do you know her?' I said. 'From those meetings?'

'I know her a bit. As much as you can know anything at those things. I'm not sure she knows me.'

'Did you know she was going to do what she did?'

'Yes.'

I stared at her for a second or two.

'Yes?'

'Yes, I knew from day one. She walked in, and I knew. She was so into it all. Full of ideas. She'd been to other meetings. She wasn't doing it to help herself.'

'Why, then?'

'I'm not sure if there was something wrong with her,' she shrugged. 'Something compulsive. Because she kept pushing it.'

'But did you know she was going to run off?'

'I think she wanted to ... win. She wanted to show her commitment to it. That she'd drop everything and become someone else. I think she was doing that for Andy.'

Andy?

'For him? What, you mean – she found him *beguiling*, or something?'

'Andy is not beguiling. I've been round Andy's house. He lives near that big Lucozade sign in Brentford. He's got an extension cord on the floor with eight Ambi Purs plugged into it. It's like walking into a field of toxic lavender.'

She made the vomit face again.

'You should chill,' she said. 'I mean, she didn't drop you, technically, did she?'

'Did you ever talk to her about it?'

'I never actually spoke to her. I listened at those things. That's what I thought it was all about. Listening. Not pushing your own agenda.'

'How often do you do it?'

'What?' she said.

'Follow. Copy.'

'It's only if I find someone interesting. I find you interesting.'

'Why?'

'Because of what happened to you. I wanted to know what it would do to you.'

I shook my head at her, still standing, looking down on her.

'I think it's *you* something's happened to. Because you're a proper fucking oddball.'

'You should try it.'

'Try what?'

'Following.'

I laughed, bitterly. Yeah. Sure. Definitely.

She reached into her giant parka pocket and brought out the half-bottle of rum she'd bought the other day. She twisted it open, took a swig. How do I get rid of her?

'Has she been in touch, at all?' she said. 'I mean, considering what she's done to you, it'd be cruel not to.'

'Once. Yes. A postcard.'

'Can I see?'

I thought about it. I hadn't shown this to anyone. I'd stared at it a lot, though. Stared at it at night. I'd emailed Calum about it. He called me, sounded concerned for me, suggested a trip over to Dublin to clear my mind, but I told him I needed to stay in London. I had to be here just in case. But just in case what? She called the landline? She suddenly reappeared? Calum told me to take care, that he was thinking of me, to call him straight away if anything happened. Said he had a presentation to prepare for a conference in Utrecht next week, otherwise he'd have been on the first flight over. I could hear his kids in the background, *Peppa Pig* finishing up, his life calling him back. I felt silly. This was humiliating, and it was childish, and I felt small.

But why not show this girl? That didn't matter. She was all but a stranger.

She read it to herself.

'The weird thing is,' I said. 'I think it's lyrics from a song.'

'What?'

'I was in a cab and I heard this song and I googled the words but she must have changed them a bit.'

'She's sent you *song lyrics*?' she said. 'Instead of an explanation? Oh, you should totally start doing it yourself.'

I put my hand over my eyes and smiled.

'You *should*,' she said, and I sank down onto the sofa, another laugh coming from nowhere.

'Who do you want to be, Tom?'

I crossed my legs then crossed my arms.

'Stupid question.'

'Who would you like to be *like*?' she said, passing me the bottle.

'Honestly?'

'Honestly.'

'A *million* people. Axl Rose. Bradley Cooper.'

'Why?'

'Stop it. I'm not a child,' I said, a quick swig of rum and then the cap back on, twisted shut, tight. 'I can't just be like those people. I'm not even sure why I said Axl Rose.'

'Okay, someone from real life, then,' she said. 'Who do you know that you'd like to be like?'

I was humouring her. I don't know why. To make sense of it all? To talk to someone? To think of something else? To *have a conversation*?

'From real life?'

'Yeah.'

'I wouldn't say any of the people I know in real life are particularly … inspiring.'

'Because of how they are or because of how you engage with them?' she said, taking the bottle, immediately untwisting the cap, flicking it across the room.

She offered it to me. I put my hand up to decline.

'Medicinal,' she said.

I relented.

'Come out with me,' she said. 'Right now.'

'No.'

'We'll follow someone. I'll show you. It's fun.'

'You're out of your fucking mind.'

'There's a whole world out there. Billions of people doing billions of things. Do you honestly think that not one of those billions of things is better than what you're doing right now?'

'What I'm doing … what I—'

'You're saying "this is it?", are you? "This is all I want? Keep your billions of interesting activities and pastimes, not one of them can interest me?"'

'That's not what I'm saying at all—'

'What do you think Bradley Cooper's doing right now? Do you think it's better or worse than sitting in your flat after a botched mugging without a girlfriend you're not sure is your girlfriend, probably already thinking you've got to get up at quarter past three or whatever mental time you're supposed to get up?'

'That's a good point,' I said. 'I should probably rest. How about Axl Rose? I wonder what Axl Rose is—'

'What does Hayley think you're doing right now? And what would show Hayley?'

She pointed at the photo on the mantelpiece. Held up the postcard.

'What would piss her *right* off?'

Ah, my weak point. Well played. Because yes, maybe it was time to hit back. Hit back even if she couldn't see it. Pia saw she was onto something.

'You. Out there. *That* would piss her off. You, showing her how to do it. Then getting on with your life.'

Bottle to my lips.

But no.

'Much as I'd love to see how you follow people about,' I said, handing it back, 'the resting thing sways it for me, and—'

'Why rest when you don't *do* anything? What are you recovering from? At least do something to rest from!'

'Pia, I've just been beaten up.'

She smiled.

'That's a very *passive* activity. You even let someone else do *that* for you.'

She stole a laugh from me.

'One hour,' she said.

'I shouldn't leave the flat! I should be calling the police and—'

'Come on. Come with me! Give me one hour. I know it sounds crazy, but you have to *see*.'

I thought about it.

No.

Maybe?

'You *owe* me.'

'Well … I need milk.'

'We'll get milk. We'll go out to get milk. If anyone tries to attack you again I'll duff them up. Come on. I saved your arse tonight.'

I couldn't argue with that.

'And then,' she said, taking another long, sweet swig from the bottle, 'we'll see what happens next.'

I sort of wanted to see what happened next.

[5]

'Why do this?' I ask, as we take cover from the rain in the entrance of Delmonico's on South William.

The Chinese man is long gone, swapped for a mustachioed homosexual in a leatherette sailor's cap on his way to a party downtown. We followed him until the rain ran slick through our hair.

'Come,' he says. 'Inside.'

We take a table in the center of the room. He wipes the rain from his brow, and takes a menu.

'You know this place?' he says. 'First printed menus in the US. First tablecloths, too. This place has a lot of firsts. First place to use the term Baked Alaska. Claims to have been the first to make eggs Benedict. Manhattan clam chowder – started right here, in those kitchens just three feet through that door. And you know the best one?'

I remove my jacket and shake my head.

'The Hamburg Steak.'

I have never heard of it. Cockroft looks startled.

'The first hamburger!' he says. 'Here. Right here. In 1834. So you see, it pays to be original, it does, you need that moment of inspiration, for you will forever hold your place in history!'

I look around, because I sense that's what he wants me to do.

'And yet,' he says, leaning toward me now. 'What if you don't do anything with it?'

He holds my eye and takes his time.

'You know how many McDonald's we passed on the way here today? You know how many there are in the country? Nearly 6,000. They made $7 billion last year. This place? Sells maybe twenty burgers a day, I don't know. You can buy a 39-cent burger in *London* now. Tokyo – can you imagine! But did McDonald's invent the idea? Did they diddely. They followed. They took inspiration. You could argue the hamburger belongs to them now. And therein one sees the power of an idea.'

'But you're not in this for money,' I say, and I am reminded of the question he so elegantly avoided out in the rain. 'Why do you copy?'

'Hmm?' he says.

'Why copy?' I say.

'Why copy?' he says.

'Yes,' I say.

'Yes,' he says.

'Yes?' I say.

'Yes?' he says.

I sit back, unwilling to play.

He shoots back in his chair, too, an exaggerated look of confusion across his face.

'I'm sorry, I'm joking,' he says, his wild blue eyes softening. 'Copy? I just told you. We all copy. It is in us. It forms the greatest part of our own personalities. You think we are all born original? We are not. Every book you've read, every movie you've seen, every idea you've ever thought was yours ... all of them were somewhere else first. If we see further, it is because we stand on the shoulders of giants.'

'That's a nice way of putting it.'

'I didn't put it that way. Isaac Newton did. But the fact remains ... I mean, "Books serve to show a man that those original thoughts of his aren't very new after all." Abraham Lincoln.'

'I see,' I say.

'Pretty original thought. Although Marie Antoinette said it before him. On it goes. Shakespeare, all of them. Everything that can be put has already been put. Everything that can be done, be felt, be heard, has already been done, felt and heard.'

'I'm not certain I understand what you're saying.'

'What I am saying is what others have said and it is simple: why not take a short cut and get to the good stuff? Why go through all the legwork, the tedious invention of the thousand and one things that have to happen before you discover a thought, a moment, an intention – why not just find someone who's already there, or on the cusp, and *piggyback their joy?*'

fourteen

We stood on Stoke Newington Church Street, outside 5 Star Cleaners, underneath the lamppost by the bus stop.

Another bus went straight past.

'Well, this is fun. I can certainly see what all the fuss is about.'

'You just have to be patient,' said Pia. 'What about him?'

She pointed with one elbow – her hands deep in her parka.

'That guy? You want to follow that guy?'

Fifty feet away, a man in his mid-thirties crossed the road from the town hall, looking both ways as he did so.

'Why not? Look at his shoes. Converse. That shows he's grounded.'

'Or cheap.'

'Laptop bag, worn leather. So he's professional, but probably creative. Bag from the wine shop.'

'So he's going home.'

'He might be going to a party. He might be going to a wine-tasting. You don't know.'

'He looks very … normal.'

'Don't you want to be normal?' she said. 'Get a mortgage? Order the same curry every Friday night from the same place you always use? Get an office job, answer the phones, "*Good morning, Kitchen and Home Supplies, Tom speaking* …?" That's what most people want.'

'So you just want to follow normal people as they order their favourite curries?' I said.

'Sometimes I see the value in that. Sometimes I see the value in *"Good morning, how can I help you please thank you?"'*

'What's your codename, anyway?'

'My what?'

'Andy Double. Felix Follow-everyone-about. What's yours?'

'Mine's double-barrelled,' she said. 'Pia Likewise-Xerox.'

'You just made that up.'

'I did. I find all that *so* uncool,' she said, scanning the street, looking down towards the library. 'What about her, then?'

A teenage girl in a pink velour tracksuit barked loudly into a cheap handset, a box from Luigi's in the other hand. Her words floated over us.

'*Lemme ahks you a question, right? ... Nah, lemme ahks you this ...*'

She walked past John's Garden Centre, then stopped to shout into her phone.

'No thank you,' I said.

'I'm just saying. All these people are going somewhere. They've each got a story. A destination. Isn't that interesting?'

'Nope.'

'Come with me into town. Let's go to Trafalgar Square. Do you know how many stories start there? At this time of night it's a story a second!'

'We'll end up following a tourist to Heathrow. That will be our story. Standing in WH Smith as they buy a travel pillow and some mints. And how do we know when to stop? When we hit Osaka?'

'Hey – look ...' she said, ignoring me, and I followed her eye.

Now this – this *was* interesting. A gentleman. Not a man. A *gentle*man. Older. Maybe mid-sixties. Hat. Classic Burberry trench in almond. He'd been in The Fox Reformed – the wine bar with the red frontage I'd always fancied going to but never felt I'd fit. He stood for a moment under the bust of Edgar Allen Poe and fixed his hat by the orange blush of the streetlight, leaves fluttering around him.

'He's brilliant,' said Pia. 'Check out his briefcase.'

It was old, cared-for. Brass locks over dulled maroon leather. He wore brogues, and tan leather gloves. A beard and small round glasses, face rich and flush as the bottles of red on the Fox's wine list.

I took it all in. I think it was the longest I'd ever really looked at a stranger. I saw them all the time, strangers … just never *looked*.

The man checked his watch as he approached and smoothed down his jacket as he passed.

'Let's follow,' she said, and she tugged at my sleeve.

'I don't feel comfortable with this,' I said, staying where I was.

'Just for a bit,' she said. 'He's going …'

She stared at me, like a little girl on an adventure who can't believe her boring uncle won't join in with the make-believe.

And so I humoured her. We kept our distance. We walked down Church Street, a hundred steps behind.

He turned right on Green Lanes and then upped his pace.

'He's late for something,' she said, upping hers. 'He's got to *be* somewhere. That's exciting.'

'He could be going anywhere,' I said, annoyed. 'Slow down …'

'The *whole point*,' she said, 'is that he could be going anywhere!'

On Green Lanes, he broke into a pained jog as the 141 approached, raising one hand to catch the driver's attention, but the bus didn't even slow, didn't even raise a 'sorry' hand as a basic courtesy. Everyone's busy. Everyone's got some place to be.

'Okay,' I said, surprised to find I'd been jogging too. 'He's missed his bus. That's that. We'd have followed him to a bus stop and then watched him go. Can't believe we missed out on that.'

'Your sarcasm bores me,' said Pia. 'Look – he's got a plan.'

He checked his watch again and continued to stride down Green Lanes, past the Brownswood and on, past the Pirate's Playhouse.

'He's heading for the tube,' she said. 'Manor House. That's the Piccadilly Line. Where's he going? Kensington?'

'That's the glamorous way of looking at it. He might be going to Uxbridge. Or Heathrow.'

'You up for it?'

'Uxbridge? No! Pia, we've followed a man to a bus stop and now we're walking to a tube station. It's ten to eight, I sort of feel I've had enough for one night.'

'Come on,' she said. 'You've got an Oyster Card. You've got an Oyster Card because I stopped someone *nicking* your Oyster Card! And what's the difference? Let's give it an hour. You can be tucked up in bed by half nine, I promise.'

Something in her eyes had changed. They were shining now. And only now did I see how dulled they must have been before. This was what she wanted to do. I could stop it all in a heartbeat. Or I could go with it. It was only a tube ride, after all.

'Tucked up in bed by half nine,' I said.

Into Manor House we ducked, swiping our Oyster Cards behind the man, who was moving quickly now, skipping down the steps, hand trailing lightly on the banister. She was right. He had to be somewhere. I suppose it was interesting. I suppose part of me now wanted a hint of where he could be going. Some minor resolution.

'First test,' said Pia. 'Northbound to Cockfosters, or Southbound to *excitement*?'

We watched the man study the signs. He chose Southbound. She gave me a nudge in the ribs. A look that said, 'See?' … and we followed him down to the platform, deep down below the streets and flats and parks of London, and when the train arrived a minute later we jumped on board, five or six steps behind him.

'Fiver says it's King's Cross,' I whispered. 'And that'll be that. I'm not just going to spend my evening doing someone else's commute.'

'We have to keep our distance,' she said, pulling me to the other end of the carriage. 'What's he doing now?'

I cast a glance to the other end.

'He's sitting down. He's got a newspaper out.'

'Which newspaper?'

'*Telegraph.*'

'So he's a traditionalist,' she said, and I rolled my eyes.

'Are we supposed to make up a story for him now?' I said. 'Like we're young lovers in a Simon & Garfunkel song? Are we supposed to say he looks like a spy?'

'He *does* look like a spy!' said Pia. 'We should get a copy of the *Telegraph* later, though. See what he's reading. It might give us some ideas.'

'Later?' I said.

On we rode, past Finsbury Park, Arsenal, Holloway Road ... at King's Cross we prepared ourselves, knowing he'd probably alight here, minding the gap and heading for the Metropolitan Line, or the Circle, or maybe heading up into the vast Georgian arches of the station above to find his train back to the provinces.

But he remained in his seat, ruffled his paper.

'He's going into town,' said Pia, squeezing my arm. 'We're off!'

And past Russell Square we bounced, then Holborn, then Leicester Square, Covent Garden ...

'He's getting up,' she said, hushed, in my ear, pretending to be looking somewhere else. 'He's getting his things together ...'

'Okay, so, Piccadilly Circus ...'

'He might be going on a date! Maybe there's some cool, out-of-the-way restaurant only people like him ever know about! Or a sex club!'

'You would follow this man into a sex club, would you?'

The train slowed, tracks screeching, and we tensed ourselves to deal with the moment of hard stop.

The man was already at the door.

'You've got another thirty minutes,' I said, and she made a miniature triple-handclap like I'd just told her that, actually, we were going to Disneyland.

Up the escalator he climbed, and we climbed after him, moving quickly past still passengers, gently squeezing the odd tourist to the right, and through the barriers we pushed, up the stairs and out, beneath the huge neon signs of the Circus.

He moved with speed now, checking his watch again, adjusting his hat and moving head down, gently using his briefcase to guide slower pedestrians out of his way and nipping gracefully between them. It was a busy night in Soho, all crowds and buses and cabs, and we moved with him down Shaftesbury Avenue, past Rupert Street – Chinatown and stag parties to our right – until we found Soho fire station. He raised his briefcase in thanks to the bus that let him cross and dashed over the road.

'He's doubling back on himself,' I said. 'This looks weird.'

'He's no idea we're following him,' she said, as we pounded across. 'He's heading into Soho. Maybe Ronnie Scott's. He looks like a jazz musician.'

But we passed Frith Street.

'Maybe he's a theatre director. Maybe he's late for the opening night of his own musical.'

He turned right on Dean Street.

'Maybe he's going to Pizza Express,' I said. 'Maybe he's going to eat a pizza.'

'I think you're wandering into the realms of fantasy now,' she said, then: 'Look.'

The man was sidestepping a group of paparazzi outside a grey building with giant red flags outside. He was trying to get through, politely raising one hand but not afraid also to *accidentally* bash one in the small of the back with his briefcase.

'That's the Randolph,' I said. 'Private members bar. Well, I guess that's that.'

'Why is that that?'

'That's that because we can't go in. You have to be a member.'

The man was through the door. And the door – vast and black and solid – was closed.

'No, you don't have to be a member,' she said. 'I mean, you *do* have to be a member. But you can also just *act* like a member. Which is good for you, because you've been acting like a member all night.'

She rabbit-punched me in the ribs. It really bloody hurt.

'Sorry!' she said. 'No, you just walk in.'

We stood outside, away from the photographers.

'I'm not just walking in. All they'll do is ask us to leave. Don't you have to have ID or something?'

'Not in a place like that. They daren't ask for ID in case you *are* someone. And you just don't let them ask if you're a member. They've got a guestbook. You just say, "Hey everyone!" and act like you're always in there, or you say, "Is upstairs open tonight?" and before you know it you've signed in and they just assume you're someone who belongs there. You think these places recognise all their members?'

'You seem remarkably comfortable in situations like this.'

'Come on. You take the lead. Just say, "Hey everyone!", sign in, and keep walking.'

'Absolutely not.'

She pushed me, along the pavement, towards the doors.

'No. Fun's over.'

She kept pushing. I tried to play it off, tried to make it look normal, but now one of the paps had turned round, sensing something. He raised his camera, just in case.

'Stop it,' I said to her. 'People are looking.'

I did not want to be the centre of attention. I had to act normal. I got to the door and pushed it open while Pia giggled behind me.

Inside a small anteroom, smart girls in black looked up from behind a tall oak desk. Three sets of bright red lips, three friendly smiles.

I raised a pathetic hand.

'Hey, everyone!' I said, so they wouldn't ask me if I was a member.

'Hi,' said the first girl, her smile fading now, and then: 'Are you a member?'

Shit.

I looked at Pia, who was already at the guestbook, pen held in one clenched fist like a child, already trying to move things on.

'No,' I said, shrugging. 'Nor's she.'

'We're actually *meeting* someone here,' said Pia, shooting me a look. 'And *they're* a member.'

'And what's the member's name please?'

'Matthew Channing,' she said, without missing a beat.

Who? I looked again at Pia, confused, then saw she had a finger on the guestbook. A random name. Someone who'd already signed in. Matthew Channing.

'Is Matthew expecting you?' said the girl. 'He didn't say he was expecting guests.'

'We've been texting,' said Pia. 'It only just came up. He said to swing by. Said he was sitting his usual spot and to ask you where that was.'

'Okay,' said the girl, walking round her table and opening the door. 'He's in the upstairs bar ...'

Through the doors, laughter. A mahogany bar, art on the walls – a Damien Hirst? – fat leather club chairs, espresso martinis, piano music.

Only she stood in our way.

'I'll just take you to him,' said the girl.

'Oh, you don't have to do that,' I said, suddenly panicking, because we could really do without being presented to a blank-eyed stranger. 'It's fine. Honestly. We'll find him. I mean, it's not that big up there. Or is it?'

'We *usually* take people to him,' said the girl, and I could see an out here. 'If they're not members.'

'Well, that would be *very kind* of you,' said Pia.

What?

'Please do lead the way.'

Inside the main bar, on our right, was the man we'd followed all the way from Stokey. His hat was off now, and his trench, too, revealing a jaunty yellow jacket and polka-dot tie. He'd opened his briefcase and pulled out sheet music … then moved to the piano, in the shadow of a Peter Blake original. Old Man Stokey was the resident pianist. And he was *good*. Pia shot me a look as we walked through and up the stairs, brushing past a rock star hand-in-hand with that-girl-from-that-thing.

'This is better than Pizza Express,' whispered Pia.

'Pizza Express is highly underrated,' I said.

'Matthew always takes the upstairs bar,' said the girl, smiling, and as Old Man Stokey hit his stride with 'Paint It Black', immediately I realised we were about to meet a man named Matthew who was not expecting us at all.

'Hi Matthew!' she said, brightly, flirtatiously, and a handsome man in a well-cut midnight blue suit put down his cocktail menu and looked up. 'Your guests are here.'

'Hi!' said Pia, brightly.

'Hi,' I said, quite quietly.

I thought about how we looked. A small girl in a big blue parka. A tall man with a now very swollen cheek who now realised he'd used far too much TCP.

'Hello …?' said Matthew, slender eyebrows arched over dark green eyes. He had a confident moustache; the type of moustache only the truly handsome or murderers of the nineteenth century could really pull off.

'Hi!' said Pia again, while the girl in black looked on, and then she sort of stooped, awkwardly, to kiss him on the cheek. 'How are you, honey?'

'I'm fine, I'm fine,' said the man, playing it off. 'How have you been?'

He was pretending he knew us.

'Is everything okay, Matthew?' said the girl in black, pretending she was asking about the drinks or the seat, but really saying, 'Just checking these clowns are with you?'

'Everything is fine, Berenice, thank you …'

'I apologise for that smell,' she said, sniffing around. 'Someone must have been cleaning the tables.'

She left, and Pia leaned towards Matthew and said, 'Can I come clean?'

God. This was quick.

'We're not your guests.'

'Sorry?' said the man, and I began to inch away.

'We're friends of Lucy,' said Pia.

'Oh! Ha!' said Matthew. 'Thank God, because I was struggling to recognise you. Which Lucy? Lucy Parker?'

No!

'Yes. Lucy Parker.'

What was she doing?

'How *is* Lucy?' he said, reaching for a memory. 'Is she still working at the Tate?'

'You know Lucy,' said Pia, who I was fairly certain didn't. 'Work work work. Tate Tate Tate.'

'I haven't seen her since Berlin. God, sorry, were you there too? Is that where we …'

'In Berlin? No, we didn't meet in Berlin. What was Berlin?'

'Edgar's thirtieth. Oh, I hope I haven't put my foot in it …'

Pia made a that'll-explain-it face.

'Ah, well, I don't actually know Edgar all that well, so no, you haven't!' Then: '*Sorry*, I'm being so rude. This is Tom.'

'Hello Tom.'

'Hello Mister Channing.'

Mister Channing?

'Haha. It's Matthew. So is Lucy here tonight?'

He seemed familiar, suddenly, this Mister Channing.

'She wanted to be. But no. So we're just—'

'Can I get you any drinks?' said a girl in a tight skirt, smiling. She was holding a small tumbler of Twiglets, which I remember thinking was odd.

'Yes, sit, sit,' said Matthew. 'Now it's *me* being rude, not that *you* were being rude, please, join me for a drink, and then I'm off to dinner …'

And suddenly I knew who this was. It was the way he made us sit. The flustered Brit, full of self-deprecation and generosity. Where had I seen it? Jonathan Ross? Graham Norton?

'You're an actor!' I said, sitting, finding myself too-low in a surprisingly small chair. 'You're Matthew Channing the actor!'

The waitress cast him an awkward glance which he smiled away, a nod to say 'it's okay'.

Matthew Channing wasn't just an actor. Matthew Channing was one of the hottest young actors in the country. He'd been tipped to play Dr Who, he was a name that came up when they mentioned a future James Bond, he'd made his name leading *The Valley of Fear* at the National, been nominated for an Olivier but lost out to Colin Firth, made it onto the cover of *Vanity Fair* (inside flap). Now, Scarlett Johansson was said to have chosen him to be Mister Darcy in a more rock 'n' roll adaption of *Pride & Prejudice*. He was on the cusp. He was *that* Matthew Channing.

He looked mock-surprised, like I'd caught him. A weary smile, implying can't-I-just-be-*me*?

I kicked myself for playing his game. But Christ – why had Pia chosen *his* name? Why not someone innocuous? Someone with a normal name, like Bill Fletcher? Sally Pipe? If it had to be media in a place like this, why not just someone who worked at ITV2, or writes the back covers on DVDs?

'I'm an actor, yes,' he said. 'But I'm also a drinker. I'll have a negroni, please ... God, I'm so sorry, I've forgotten your name?'

The waitress blushed, and broke into a huge smile, perhaps imagining this man below her, all but on his knees, was moments from proposing.

'It's Alice.'

'A negroni please – Alice.'

He shut his eyes as he said her name – showing he was committing it to the vast vault of women's names in his mind, giving it a special shelf all of its own, giving her an I Know Who You Are. Her pen tapped her order pad, excitement finding a way out, the way bubbles of air find their way to the surface.

'Well, I think I'll follow suit,' said Pia, raising her eyebrows at me, making sure I knew she was showing me how it was done. '*I'll have a negroni too*. Tom?'

'What's a negroni?'

'Three negronis then,' she said.

'Actually, it's *negroni*,' said Matthew, and though this was the kind of thing that I'm sure would normally have made her thump someone, Pia laughed and laughed ... and it struck me how she'd changed since she'd walked in here. She was more confident, louder – maybe even posher. The *voice*. She was blending in. Aping. Following. Suddenly that parka didn't look scruffy. It looked … creative.

'What *is* a negroni, actually?' I said. 'Only I'm a bit allergic to gin.'

I'm not allergic to gin. I was only trying to join in. Pia was a master at this. It was effortless. I couldn't do it. I tried, and immediately started assigning myself fictional allergies.

'Well, there *is* gin in it, I'm afraid,' said Matthew, kindly, as if he was telling me that although it had put up a fight, it was time to put my puppy down. 'In fact, it's pretty much gin-based. Shall I cancel it?'

'Nah,' I said, waving his concern away. 'I'm sure it'll be fine.'

'So what are you working on?' said Pia, leaning in, fascinated, and I looked around the room. I'd heard about the Randolph. It was always in the papers. I never thought it would look so much like a British Airways business class lounge, though. Carpeted floors, sleek bar, brass fittings. A splash of colour here and there, low lighting, with dark slats keeping Soho at bay. Around me, people sat – the dominant or more powerful of each group sitting with his back to the wall, facing the room, to see and be seen, eyes flicking up and over shoulders every time someone new walked in. Strange pauses in conversation whenever a story was interrupted by a new arrival, as the teller considered for a half-second whether it was worth ditching the thought to welcome the newcomer instead. Vast canvases on the walls. A spot of neon. Denise Van Outen with a face on. Bloody hell! Brandon Flowers at the back, sitting back as a coked-up man in a suit (but no tie, so he's cool, he's basically one of The Killers) talked passionately and with constantly bobbing leg about something Brandon couldn't seem to care less about.

'Wow!' said Matthew, and my head snapped back to the conversation. I had no idea what he was wowing about. 'That must be so much fun. And what about you, Tom, what do you do?'

I looked at Pia for clues. What had she said? Had she lied about what she did? Actually – what *does* she do?

'I work in radio,' I said, nodding my head to help his reaction along. 'Yeah, I work in radio.'

'Oh, what station?'

'Talk London? I read the news on Talk London Breakfast. London Calling. Or it was. Now it's not. Or, soon. Anyway.'

'Talk London. What did I read about that recently?'

My heart sank.

'What was it?' he said, his arms now crossed, his brow furrowed, one finger tapping his lip. 'It was something about …'

'The Jam Nazis?' asked Pia, helpfully.

'YES!' shouted Matthew. 'The Jam Nazis! Oh, that was brilliant. The Jam Nazis. "No jam in the cupboards! But I want jam in the cupboards!" Oh, man.'

'That was him!' said Pia, pointing at me.

'Well, it wasn't me—'

'That was you?!' he said, lurching forward, his hand on my knee, a look of unfeigned excitement across that face.

'No, it was … it was me who left the fader up, and—'

'HA!' said Matthew. 'A. MAZING. The guy sounded like a twat, was he a twat?'

Pia looked delighted. Matthew was all over me.

'Well, he's … a little twat-like.'

'Are you all pleased to see the back of him?'

'Um …'

'Genius. Genius. Wow. Have you seen the videos? The videos are brilliant. I forwarded one on to a guy I know in the States. A director, actually. Oliver Stone, as it happens. His reply was, "Fuck yeah!" He's a man of few words, Oliver, but he's able to convey the correct emotions through them.'

Oliver Stone knew about Jam Nazis. He knew about the *cupboard in our studio*.

'So, wow, here you are. Internet celebrity. I want a picture with you. We can't take one in here, they won't allow it, but outside, okay? I want a picture with you and I want to send it to Oliver Stone.'

This was not a sentence I'd ever heard before.

Outside, three *negroni* later, a flushed Matthew Channing burst through the doors of the Randolph with me in a headlock under his arm, manicured fingers ruffling my hair before I was free.

'Why take a shitty photo on a phone when we can just do this?' he said, and the paps went mad.

He grabbed me again as they did their thing, lighting us up with a thousand flashes from a dozen cameras. On the other side of the street, by the Thai place, people stopped and stared and pointed. Now he span me round, pretended to dance with me, then held my arm aloft as photographers jostled and elbowed for space.

'Just go online later and google my name,' said Matthew. 'You'll find the pics, they'll have 'em up in five minutes, I bet. And I've got your number, I'll text you mine, right?'

We watched him walk away, as Alice in the black skirt guided him to his Addison Lee, the paps following, still wanting one last shot, still not quite convinced that any of the previous million might suffice.

I turned to Pia.

'Well, that was—'

'*Fucking Jam Nazis!*' was the last thing we heard as he roared past, one clenched fist held from a straight arm salute from the open window of the car as it disappeared down Dean Street.

'Who are you, mate?' said a man, suddenly next to me, camera round his neck, piece of paper in hand.

'Tom,' I said, confused.

'Tom *Adoyo* from Talk London,' said Pia, and he scribbled it down and wandered off.

'That was awesome,' she said, digging in her pocket for a roll-up. 'Where now?'

'Ha!' I said, booze in my veins. 'I think I'm finally over my gin intolerance!'

'You don't drink much, do you?'

'I don't really drink,' I said. 'But I am currently experiencing an *enormous* sense of well-being.'

'Ditto,' she said. 'Hey – I know who you are! I've got your name!'

'Eh?'

'Tom *Ditto*!' she laughed.

'I do not want a nickname,' I said.

'Tom Ditto!'

'I genuinely find it a bit sad,' I said.

And then, as a group of drunk Irish lads in rugby tops started playing up to the paps, 'Who now? Where now?' she said. It was kicking out time at the pubs. The lads were looking for a bar.

'It's … Christ, it's 11.30,' I said. 'It's so late, Pia, I need to—'

'Wait,' she said. 'One more thing. Let's do one more thing.'

She was hailing a rickshaw.

'No, no,' I said. 'Look, we've …'

'Where to?' said the rider, all legs and backwards cap.

She grabbed me, pulled me on board. Just ahead, a tall black guy I vaguely recognised – boyband? DJ? – was stepping into a cab, its yellow light flicking off as two girls in short skirts carrying bottles of something tailed behind him.

'Follow that cab!' yelled Pia.

'Who *are* you?' I said, as the rickshaw lurched forward.

fifteen

' ... and the traffic on that route, as usual – stacked back to Clackets ... highs of nineteen in the city today, which means, at 6.31 on Monday morning – now you're up to date.'

First show with Cass. I felt energised by it. There was something in the air. A new start. The clouds were clearing.

Dad had emailed. A round-robin. Pictures of the family on a trip to Dunedin, the kids dancing round an extinct volcano. I replied and he wrote straight back, asked me how I was, how Hayley was doing.

I said fine.

'Thanks, Tom!' said Cass, hitting the music bed.

I silently wondered if Leslie would be listening.

'So good morning London, such a pleasure to be with you, you're with the all-new London Calling with me, Cass Tailor ... coming up ...'

Big, dramatic music. The show sounded *important*.

'Mayor Anthony Jackson joins us by phone ...'

I gathered my papers together and got ready to go. It had been quite a weekend, in all sorts of unusual ways, but now I had the next bulletin to prep, and also I fancied a—

'Tom, before you go ...'

—coffee. Hang on.

'What's happened to you?'

The dramatic music had stopped, cut short.

I stood, confused by the silence. What was happening here? My eyes shot to the On Air light. Yes. We were On Air.

'No. What? Nothing,' I said. I was startled to be spoken to. 'Sorry, what did you—'

'Your face, mate. What's going on with your face?'

Silence. Dead air. Awkward.

What was I supposed to say? Fell down the stairs? Walked into a cupboard? I had to speak. Six seconds of silence and the emergency tape would get ready to kick in. London would inexplicably start listening to Elton John instead of topical debate.

'I … my face. Yes. It's …'

'Have you been *beaten up*?'

I looked at Janice, through the glass. Was this okay to talk about? Or should I laugh it off?

'Yeah,' I said. 'I, um … I got mugged.'

I expected the music to come back up. Maybe she'd hit a sting, or a stab, all of which now sounded a little too violent. Maybe just a glib remark and a let's-move-on.

'Where?' she asked, leaning back in her chair, no urgency to move the show on, sounding genuinely concerned, the only thing that didn't make her prying a little offensive. 'Did they take anything?'

Suddenly I could feel the weight of my words. London was listening. Focus on me. Normally I'm a voice but right now I'm a person.

Through the glass I could sense Work Experience Paul, sitting down with nothing to do except stare at me.

'My … iPod,' I said, nodding, the unwilling centre of attention, still trying to keep things a little bright, a little breezy, a little breakfast. 'Though of course other MP3 players are available.'

'Scumbags,' she said. 'Proper scumbags. Maybe they're listening. And if you're listening …'

Dramatic music back, now.

'You're a *scumbag*. What is going in London that this can happen? Have *you* been the victim of crime in the capital? Or have you been a witness? This is something we should raise with Mayor Jackson when he's on the show after eight this morning. That's what we'll do. That this can happen in a—'

And suddenly, she wasn't talking to me any more.

I moved to leave, but she put her hand up to stop me and smiled.

'And we're going to talk more with Tom about what happened, too … morning London, this is Talk London Breakfast with me, Cass Tailor – and scumbags ain't welcome …'

Swoosh. Ads. Done.

She turned to me, concerned.

'I'm amazed you're in today,' she said, concern on her face.

'Couldn't miss the first show,' I said. 'Anyway, it was Friday.'

'Friday after you saw me? God, you poor thing. Did you report it? What did you do after?'

'After the mugging?'

'Yeah,' she said, her face now maternal, now comforting. 'Did you call someone? You could've called me. What did you do?'

I thought about how to phrase it.

'I got on a rickshaw and went to Chinawhite.'

Pippy grabbed me as I left the studio for the newsroom.

'You're in the paper,' she said.

'What?'

'You're in the newspaper! How the hell do you know *Matthew Channing*?'

She held out a copy of *The Londoner*. There we were, look. The lads. In the Wild Weekend section.

The caption: '*On triumphant form after his win at the Oliviers last week, actor Matthew Channing celebrates with friend Tim Adoyo in central London.*'

'Oh … he's just … I met him and we got on.'

'He's the new Mister Darcy!'

'Yeah, well. He doesn't like to be labelled. He was just very flattered that Scarlett asked him. He's worried that might be an albatross round his neck.'

'On his back.'

'Anywhere near him, really.'

'Why's he got you in a headlock?'

'Oh, you know,' I said, shrugging. 'Bants.'

'Amazeballs?' she said, like a question. Fact: there is no answer to a question like 'Amazeballs'.

'Hashtag: think-you-know-someone …'

I smiled, as I sat in the tiny box near the kitchenette, sourcing audio for the next bulletin. That was pretty cool. Matthew Channing. Imagine if Hayley saw that. Maybe she'd see it on some celebrity site. That'd teach her. She'd be desperate to know why I suddenly kept such glamorous company. *Desperate*. I checked what else had come through to the news team. Oh, look, Blackwall Tunnel's clear. Updated statement from the Vatican about those cardinals. Another Manchester City player in a fight in some try-hard champagne bar. And—

'*Tom! Get in! Quick!*'

The door was open. Pippy again. Wild-eyed. Manic.

'Get in what?'

'*Studio*! Cass needs you!'

'What?'

I panicked, dropped my papers, started to pad towards 4K. I slapped my ID on the lock, opened the first heavy doors, heard the muffle of her voice, saw the sober red On Air light, peered through the glass wall. Cass saw me, beckoned me in, eyes wide.

I pushed through the next door, as quietly as I could, found my chair, heard Cass saying, 'But surely, Mister Mayor, the problem is not what you *are* doing, it's what you *haven't* done?'

Jesus. The Mayor? Why was I here? Leslie wanted a clear studio for his cosy chats with the Mayor.

I grabbed my cans, pulled them over my head, heard the tail end of his reply.

'Mister Mayor,' said Cass. 'The next voice you'll hear will be that of Tom Adoyo ...'

She nodded at me.

'Hello?' I said, and immediately wished I hadn't said it as a question. I sounded like someone trying the first telephone.

'Hello Tom,' came the response, and you could tell he was wary, because he was using my name, and why was he suddenly speaking to me, what trap was this, what might this be? A muffled moment, a question to an aide, a hand over the receiver, then clarity again.

'... and just this weekend, Tom was pushed into an alleyway and robbed – at knifepoint – by a criminal who is still very much at large on the streets of this city ...'

Well, yeah. I hadn't reported him. And hang on – *knifepoint*?

I did the best mime I could to show there'd been no knife, pointed or not. She frowned and waved it away.

'Well, obviously, Tom,' said the voice I knew so well, from TV, from radio, from press conference after press conference, 'let me first say this – I'm obviously appalled by what happened to you and in any—'

'What are you going to do about crimes like this, Mister Mayor?' said Cass, interrupting.

'Well, the question is not what we—'

'That's precisely the question, with respect sir, which is precisely why I asked it.'

'Let me be absolutely clear—'

'I *want* you to be absolutely clear, Mister Mayor – what are you going to do about crimes like those suffered by Tom?'

'In any—'

'And what's more – as our elected representative – the Mayor of the greatest city on Earth – are you going to *apologise* to Tom, because I'm looking at his poor broken face right now, sir, and breathing in the very faint whiff of TCP, and whatever you're doing … it ain't working.'

She had him on the run. I knew this would be on all over the building.

She gave me a little thumbs-up, like I'd done anything to make this happen at all.

'Absolutely brilliant, guys,' said Bron, straight after the show. 'Top-notch. Honestly. We've clipped that Mayor interview and sent it out already. We're running promos throughout the day. I mean – an *apology*—'

'It wasn't really an apology, it was—'

'An *admission*, though – from the Mayor! That something isn't working! On your first show! Well done. *Both* of you, well done.'

Cass put her arm in mine, and squeezed.

My phone buzzed as I stood in Frank's where a fat man was arguing with another fat man. I answered.

'Yo, Tom Ditto,' she yelled. 'Wanna go out later?'

'Yeah,' I said, automatically. 'Yeah, okay.'

'Great, because I'm right behind you. I've been following you for the last forty minutes.'

I span around.

Nothing but fat men in a café.

'Only joking,' she said.

We were starting to get a shorthand, me and her. She'd crashed on the sofa at mine after we got back from Chinawhite, sometime around 5am Saturday morning … the guy we'd followed turned out to be a low-level TV star from that Welsh dance studio reality show. *Last Tango in Powys*, or something. Late Saturday morning turned into a moment-by-moment deconstruction of what had happened over Co-op cheese and onion sandwiches. How the man had led us where he'd led us, the whole Matthew Channing incident, the clinging to the tail-end of the *Powys* group to sneak into the club ... then microwave beans on toast, a snooze in front of *E!*, and then miraculously it had been Saturday night and we'd headed out for food.

I took her to the vegan place on the corner of Albion Road.

She took one look at the menu and scrunched her nose up.

'Is this not good?' I asked.

'*Avocado quinoa and kale?*'

'I thought you were vegan,' I said, pointing at the badge on her lapel.

'What? No, I just took one because someone else did. Followed him to a conference of some kind. He had some pace on him. A remarkable energy. Made me rethink my whole diet.'

So we got up and headed down the road, and wandered aimlessly, and mock-bickered about what to do, until she spotted a couple who looked like they knew *exactly* where they were going.

We sat at the next table. He looked to be a banker, and from what she was saying, she was taking a year off to redecorate the house. She couldn't decide whether to paint the hallway in London Clay or Cornforth White and it was really getting her down.

We all ordered the fish.

'Did something happen?' I said, gently. 'To make you do things like this?'

'I felt sort of born into it,' she replied. 'And look! It worked out! Fish instead of kale nuts and asparagus balls or whatever.'

'Yeah, but ... come on. You can't have just got up one day and thought this seemed like a good idea.'

'No, that's true.'

'So …?'

She shrugged. Moved her knife and fork around.

'You only ever wear black, don't you?' she said.

'What?'

'You only ever wear black. It's like your whole life is a funeral.'

'Don't change the subject. And I find black flattering. How did you start? Who did you follow first?'

'Some girl,' she said. 'She looked … sorted. Happy.'

'Where did you go?'

'Walthamstow. She was going to a house party. I stood outside for half an hour and then went home.'

If I'd been expecting inspiration, I was sorely let down.

'Okay,' I said. 'But you continued.'

'It was better than being at home.'

She looked fragile, now. Small.

'Meaning?'

'What do you mean, meaning?'

'Why was it better than being at home?'

'Look, there was a guy,' she said. 'It was serious. It didn't work out.'

'It was serious?' I said. 'You look about *nine.*'

What I meant was, this girl didn't seem the commitment type. She didn't seem the type to commit to anything – a restaurant, veganism, anything, let alone something serious.

'And you split up?'

'Mm-hmm.'

'Whose fault?' I asked, sensing I was pushing it.

She shrugged, bit her lip.

'It's not as simple as that.'

'Do you still see him?'

Again, *Are you over him?* is what I wanted to say. Is that why you do it? Is that why you follow people?

'Yeah, sort of. We talk. It didn't end badly. Well, it did end badly, but you know what I mean.'

'What does he do?'

'Do you mind if we *don't*, actually?' she said. 'I'm tired. And I'm not very hungry. And I'd prefer to just keep things ...'

'*You* ask *me* questions,' I said. 'Questions about my life.'

'You need me to, is the difference. I need you not to.'

I wanted to know more, of course. What do you do? Where do you work? How old are you? Where do you live? What's your favourite colour? Despite myself, I liked her. I found her fascinating. She didn't make sense to me. I didn't get her. All my life I thought I'd been able to work people out. Get the gist of them the second I saw them. So much for that. Hayley proved me wrong. So now maybe I shouldn't try and do that. I should just go with the flow, and discover people as they develop in front of me, like film in a dark room, the way Pia let a story unfurl in front of her. But there was something about the way we'd met – the strangest way I'd ever met anybody – that made her like my secret. Something in my life, maybe the only thing, that Hayley didn't know about, and therefore a victory in some way. I wasn't going to pretend to be anyone else for Pia. I've never seen the sense in reinventing yourself for the sake of a new friendship. Seems to me if you do that, the only thing you're inventing is the friendship. And it seemed weird thinking all this about someone I'd just met. Because as far as I could tell, as we nibbled at our fish, I would never, ever see her again.

'I heard the show this morning,' she said, and I snapped back to the phone call, still standing outside Frank's. I guess I might see her again, then. 'I thought it was very nice of the Mayor to apologise to you personally for the mugging.'

One of the fat men next to me had called the other a wanker and walked off. I caught sight of my reflection in the window. I was wearing all black again. It just seems to happen without thinking these days.

'Yes,' I said. 'Though it wasn't really an apology, so much as—'

'You forgot to mention you'd been saved by a girl much shorter than you.'

'It didn't seem the right time.'

'So where are you right now?' she said. 'What do you want to do?'

'Great Titchfield Street,' I said. 'We could get a coffee?'

A pause. This had not filled her with excitement.

'Yeah, maybe,' she said.

'Or ... cinema?' I tried, but I knew what she wanted to do, I knew she wanted me to do it too, and as I waited for her response, my eyes came to rest on a guy on the other side of the window – fifties, jaunty, German phrasebook, *excellent* pipe. He opened his jacket – Harris tweed, waistcoat underneath – and brought out a silver pocketwatch.

'Actually,' I said, 'I've just spotted an interesting man ...'

'Yeah?' she said, her voice rising, a trill of thrill now there. 'Shall I come to you?'

How had this happened?

'No,' I said, now out of the café and halfway down the street, getting ready to cross when he did, a flash of pink lining exposed as he tucked his pocketwatch away. 'I'll let you know where to meet us ...'

sixteen

As often happens to a Monday, two days later it was Wednesday.

I arrived at SoundHaus to be greeted by three six-foot pandas and a woman called Eileen.

'Hi, do you work at SoundHaus?' she said, flanked by the giant bears. 'Only they wouldn't let us into reception.'

She made a pleading face.

'Well, three of you are dressed as pandas,' I said.

This was always happening. PRs and marketers trying to create a buzz around completely invented 'national conversations' like National Bread Week (in association with Warburtons bread) or British Pie Day (in association with Jus Rol pastry) or maybe Egg Week (The Egg Council) or Shed of the Year (Cuprinol wood stain) or British Sausage Week's Global National Day of the Sausage Month (when Simon Rimmer might turn up outside the studio with a small plate of Plockwurst and a smile).

'Yes, but it's just that it's International Week of the Red Panda,' she said.

'In association with?'

'Why does it have to be associated with anyone?'

'Who's it associated with?'

'Epping Forest Safari Adventure Park and Zoo,' she said. 'Just off the M11 near Chigwell. I've got your Panda Packs to drop off.'

I knew the deal. There'd be a stuffed red panda. Maybe a red panda baseball cap. A press release talking about the plight of the red panda and the latest two-for-one family-friendly deals at Epping Forest Safari Adventure Park and Zoo, just off the M11 near Chigwell, complete with suggested hashtags and interesting on-air talking points. Leslie used to rail against this stuff. 'We're here to report! Not to *help!* You can shove your bloody hashtag!'

'Do you think it's something you might talk about on-air?' she said. 'Do you work with Bark and Lyricis on Vibe?'

'No,' I said, and her face fell.

'Well, you can take one anyway,' she said, holding out a bag, sulking.

One of the panda men took his head off.

I sat down at my desk and turned my computer on.

Ding.

....

FROM: MAUREEN THOMAS
TO: ALL STAFF

Oweing to recent events, PLEASE DO NOT ALLOW UNAFFILIATED STAFF onto the BUILDING PREMISES even if they USED TO WORK HERE.

An incident yesterday evening in which a FORMER member of staff attempted to gain entry to the STUDIO'S means ALL STAFF must now attend a SECURITY AWARENESS briefing run by Adawale on the third floor THIS AFTERNOON. NO EXCUSE'S.

....

'It was Leslie,' said Pippy, eyes alight with the joy of it. 'He was after you!'

DANNY WALLACE

'What?' I said, closing the fridge door when I realised absolutely everything inside it had someone else's name on. Who puts their name on a cling-filmed *carrot*?

'Gary the engineer let him in,' she said. 'He said he'd forgotten about the whole Jam Nazi thing.'

'Oh, yeah, that little thing,' I said.

Leslie had been in town, recording a voiceover for Denbigh's Rally Kart and Paintball Centre. He'd usually use the ISDN line in his house for such small jobs, but fancied a trip to the city, and while he was round the corner, rage brewing over a balti in Shikara's, his ears being filled with the injustice of it all by Len Barker who now covered overnights on Radio 2 of all places ('He used to make me tea!' Leslie used to rage, pointing at his tiny name in the ever-smaller radio section of *Time Out*. 'I bloody taught that little oik!'), he decided to pay SoundHaus a little visit. Gary had let him in just after five, and he'd come looking for me on the news floor, gold pack of fags bent and wet in one tense fist.

'What hours does he think I work?' I said. 'Does he just think I'm here all day and night?'

But that's exactly what he thought. He had no idea because he just associated me with the place. He didn't know what time I got in, he'd never asked about my home life, either, save for that one day he took such pleasure in ridiculing me.

He couldn't find me, of course. He'd hovered by my desk for a while and then made his way up to the studios, rattling the doors of 4K until Jess 'Drivetime in My' Carr alerted security and had him removed.

'You wanna watch out,' said Pippy, importantly. 'You wanna watch he doesn't start following you ...'

'He's about sixty!' I said.

'That's the problem,' said Pippy. 'Who's hiring guys like him?'

*

[157]

Later, I resisted the urge to text Pia. But here's the thing.

The forty-eight hours I'd spent with her were all it had taken to make London look brighter, make life look a little better.

The interesting man I'd seen in Frank's had led us first to a meeting with an interesting woman in an interesting hat in an interesting building which turned out to be an open council planning application meeting, and that had been less interesting, so we'd left.

Outside, and almost at once – a group of jolly older men dragged us in their wake with the pull of a planet as they headed towards Wardour Street wearing t-shirts that said 'Ale Trail' …

'What's an ale trail?' I said, and Pia laughed, and said, 'Does it matter?'

And so we'd spent an hour in the midst of these real ale freaks – Roger, Michael, Roger and Stan – moving from the Dog & Duck to the Three Greyhounds to the Pontefract Castle, laughing with these sixty-five-year-old men, friends from university on their annual pub crawl, making up names for unusual beers and brews and Indian Pale Ales with them.

'The Beast!' I tried.

'The Rat Bastard!' yelled Pia, a little too loudly.

'Oh – Pia is an anagram of IPA!' said a Roger, at one point, spitting as he talked but pretending he wasn't. 'That's interesting!'

That was when we decided to leave them.

We tramped through Soho until Pia nudged me and we matched an eccentric couple step for step as they headed to Old Compton Street, all silver PVC ponchos and silver hair and gold sunglasses and black cigarette holders, and we held our breath as they led us into an erotic bookshop, which turned out to have a man standing at the top of some stairs with a clipboard, taking reservations for whatever hidden bar lay deep within. We skipped down the stairs, lit red by neon, and sat by a mirrored bar and ordered whatever the people next to us ordered, then skipped out again as a gaunt, interesting, slick-haired gent in a waistcoat unwittingly led us to Frith Street, and Garlic & Shots, where he ordered a Bloodshot, an All Black and a Sweet Death all within the space of ten minutes.

'He's a vampire,' said Pia. 'He's totally a vampire.'

Making up stories about the people we followed didn't seem necessary. They were showing us their stories. Little slices of their lives, small moments, bite-sized chunks.

And at five to one in the morning, a smile now aching across my face, we followed a couple into Chinatown, and we winced as they chose Mr Fu's, we eavesdropped as they talked about the show they'd just seen.

She was Jane. He was Steve. They were down from Middlesbrough for the night, these two, and it had been disappointing, because one of the actors that was supposed to be in it wasn't in it. Some guy they'd voted for on X Factor. Never mind, said the man, all Burton slacks and top. In a few months they could probably see him for free in Nando's.

Pia and I burst out laughing at that, and he'd turned and looked at us, three tables away, in this otherwise silent restaurant.

We moved tables when someone more interesting walked in.

'Half a crispy duck to start,' he said, this man, with his copy of a theatre programme and his wife in her sparkly dress. 'Then one kung-po chicken, one beef chow mein, one sweet and sour pork, two special fried rice, and … the *special* tea, please.'

He winked. The waiter noted it all down.

'We'll have half a crispy duck to start,' Pia called out, not missing a beat. 'Then one kung-po chicken, one beef chow mein, one sweet and sour pork, two special fried rice, and the *special* tea, please. Whatever *that* is.'

The man looked at his wife. They sat there in silence.

Pia winked.

'I can't do this forever,' I told her, later that night. 'But it's fun for now.'

She cocked her head, and poured me another covert shot of post-licence beer from the teapot.

'Why can't you do it forever?'

'Because eventually you have to live your own life.'

And she put her fork down.

Minutes later it occurred to me how much we'd laughed that night. More than I could remember laughing since I was a kid. I forgot.

All this made me *forget*.

seventeen

Two days later, Pia texted me after the show to say she would meet me outside the newsagents on the corner.

I mooched towards it, and saw a girl standing by the lamppost.

'Yo,' she said, as I got nearer.

She was blondish. Black-framed glasses. Bright red lips. Well-cut black dress.

But Pia's face.

'Oh ... you've ... did you ...?'

'Yeah,' she said. 'New look.'

'Based on ...'

'Remember Alice from the Randolph?'

'I *do* remember Alice from the Randolph,' I said, cautiously. 'Do *you* remember the film *Single White Female*?'

'I just thought she looked interesting,' she said.

'If I were a brain doctor, I'd say *you* looked interesting.'

'I'm gonna dye it back tonight.'

I stared at her for a second.

'Actually, genuinely: do you ever wonder whether this might be a sign of some kind of illness?'

She slapped my arm, not taking me as seriously as I'd hoped, which I took to be almost certainly a sign.

'I got you this,' I said, and handed over my gift.

She stared at it.

'International Week of the Red Panda,' she said. 'I was just wondering when that was.'

'I think a baseball cap with panda eyes is what your look has been missing,' I said.

'Did you know there are less than 10,000 of these in the world and often they are acutely affected by inbreeding depression?'

I blinked.

'I did not,' I said.

Where the hell did she pull that from? Or was she messing with me?

'So – any good?'

She indicated the guy I'd left behind. He was nose deep in the *Daily Express*, a *pain au chocolat* sitting uneaten on his plate, just as on the table to his left my *pain au chocolat* sat still uneaten next to my copy of the *Daily Express*.

'Nah,' I said. 'We just sat by that café not eating.'

She smiled.

'I was early,' I said.

'You're getting into this,' she said, putting her cap on. 'I knew you would.'

'I'm stopping soon,' I said.

Pia thought I was just escaping. Trying something new. But the reality was – she was that rare thing for me. A new friend. Someone I could talk to like I'd talked to Calum. Yes, she was damaged, and God knows she could be annoying, but I'm not arrogant enough to say I wasn't damaged, too. For now, this felt good, because it had lifted me, and it had lifted me because, I think, it made me think of other people. It meant I could talk about Hayley with someone who might understand. Who might help me understand.

'So what do you want to do?' I said, happy to welcome distraction. 'The world's our oyster.'

She span around.

'I was thinking … that guy,' she said, choosing randomly, and we fell in behind a guy in his twenties wearing scuffed brogues and brown corduroys and carrying a cycling helmet.

It was half past twelve on a beautiful day – the kind you see in adverts. The kind that sell the place to tourists.

'What's new?'

'I've pretty much just been working,' she said, and we slowed as the guy fiddled around in his pocket by the Barclays bikes on Clerkenwell Green.

People were already outside the Crown Tavern, under Union Jack bunting left over from something or other, twin red telephone boxes standing guard with the trees.

'Yeah, it's a busy time,' she said, and I found my credit card, put it into the reader on the corner of the street.

'I never asked you where you worked,' I said. 'I wasn't sure if you'd let me. I wasn't sure if you did.'

'Did what?'

'Did work.'

'What is it about me that seems unprofessional?' she said, digging me in the ribs.

'You like hitting me, don't you?'

At the bikes, the man was having trouble releasing one from its rail.

'For Christ's *sake*,' he muttered.

'Jesus H *Christ*!' bellowed Pia, and by the time he looked round she had her hands on her hips and was shaking her head. 'Man *alive!*'

I got my code, found a bike at the end of the stand.

'I've not ridden in forever,' said Pia, smiling, clunkily bumping out a bike. 'You see? This is fun!'

The brogues guy had his helmet on now, bony fingers finding the strap. He looked like he could probably play guitar, this guy.

Probably spends his Sunday mornings looking for old vinyl at car boot sales and then listening to them all afternoon on some vintage record player he bought at a Dalston junkyard sale, as he reads the papers and noodles around on his mandolin and makes hand-pressed espressos. He looked like all his girlfriends had probably been French.

He kept glancing at Pia. I think he liked her.

'You've managed not to tell me again,' I said, testing my saddle. 'You're unemployed, aren't you? That would make sense in this scenario.'

'Yes,' she said. 'The unemployed are always out and about on rental bikes. We're just absolutely carefree.'

She clambered onto her bike and we started off down Clerkenwell Road. Brogues guy put his hand out to signal left, and we followed suit.

'So do you avoid questions because you don't like the answers?' I asked. 'Do you hate your job?'

'I like my job,' she said, quickly. 'Sometimes I think it's the only thing that keeps me going. That, and this.'

'This?' I said.

This? Us?

'*This*,' she said, clarifying, pointing in all directions.

Oh. *This.*

Down Farringdon Road we rode, down the wide street with proud buildings, banks, bankers and bluster.

'Do you think he's hungry?' I said, after another minute or so, a bus tearing up the lane alongside us. 'Because I'm hungry.'

'Who?'

'The guy we're following.'

'Oh, we're not following him any more,' she said.

'What? Who are we following then?'

'*That* guy,' she said, nodding at an older man, also on a bike, now slowing by a florist's. We hung back as he leaned his bike against a lamppost, gave it a second, followed him in and found him at the counter, bright red and purple flowers in his hand.

Pia picked up a bunch of white lilacs – stroked their heads almost tenderly – then said, 'We'll take these, please,' as the man stepped around us, smiled at us, made sure the tissue paper was just so.

Five minutes later, we crossed Blackfriars Bridge, the three of us – a train rumbling past the bridge on our left – Pia holding the flowers in one hand, just like the man in front.

But then an arm slung to the right and we bumped onto River View.

We slowed, ditched the bikes, followed him and his flowers a little further, up Milroy Walk and beyond, to a sweeping reception area at the base of a tall building.

'Good call,' I said. 'Lunch.'

Eight floors up, at the top of the Oxo Tower – London on its back before us – the older man had taken off his cycling helmet and found his companion.

'Follow me, please,' said the *maître d'*.

'We would be happy to follow you,' said Pia. 'Do you like my hat?'

Another glance told us the woman the older man was with was delighted to see him. Kiss on the cheek and a long hug, hands on shoulders and meaningful stares as it ended. Not colleagues, then, nor in the first throes of something romantic. They were married, and it seemed they were married to each other. Anniversary?

We took advantage of a late cancellation and were led to the balcony, Pia's lilacs between us on the table. Nearby, tourists with cameras stood on the viewing platform gazing out over London. The view was too good only to allow paying customers – anyone could walk in and ask to see it, a fact the restaurant perhaps understandably prefers is discovered, not advertised.

Inside, the couple had started with a bellini.

Ours arrived.

'So a man at work might be trying to kill me,' I said.

'Cool,' she said. 'Who?'

'The Jam Nazi man,' and she nodded her understanding.

'Yes, I can see that.'

'Talking of which' – man, I'd been clever here – 'let me try again. What is your job? What do you do?'

I figured asking straight out left little room to wriggle.

'We're here to talk about *you*,' she said. 'And by the way you appear to be the talk of London. I heard it this morning – that new thing you do ...'

Cass had insisted. A new feature called *What Did Tom Get Up To Last Night?* She'd ask me, and then I'd be honest. It started after the mugging, but since all this following, it had been easy to find things to say. Tomorrow, for example ...

I rented a bike!

I bought some flowers!

I ate up the Oxo Tower!

I had a bellini with a girl in a panda hat!

But this was Pia's trick ... to guide the conversation away from her ...

'*Please*, Pia, give me something. Where do you work?'

'I work at London Zoo.'

I sighed.

'Yeah, okay ...'

'I do.'

'No you don't. You own a panda baseball cap from a safari adventure park near Chigwell and you're now pretending you're an expert.'

'I refer you to my panda fact of earlier on,' she said. 'Anyway, I work with the marmosets.'

'Sure you do. You work with the marmosets.'

'Have worked with marmosets.'

'You have nothing to do with marmosets. You work in an office or something. What are marmosets?'

'Primates.'

'Monkeys?'

She was taking the mick. I made a face that showed I wasn't going to be taken for a ride. I waved her on. Indulged her. She sighed, then smiled.

'Marmosets are primates from Brazil.'

Sure. That sounded convincing.

'We should go there one night,' she said, sipping at her bellini, the glass peach-orange and lit and glowing in the golden hour – that hour of sunshine where the world looks the way it looks in your dreams.

'I'm not going there at night. You can't go there at night. Look at you, pretending to be all kooky. I bet you think you're kooky. There's a difference between being kooky and being weird. Being kooky is charming. You're just weird.'

'Piss off.'

'You see? No one kooky uses words like that. But weirdos do. All the time. They leap out of bushes and shout things like that. I gave you a panda hat and you've made it kooky. I'm just your enabler.'

I tried again.

'Tell me something about yourself. What's your favourite colour? How old are you? Twenty-six? Twenty-seven?'

'Let me ask *you* something,' she said, leaning forwards, and I prepared myself. I decided I'd be happy to tell her anything. 'And this might sound a bit weird, but you've reminded me ...'

'Go on.'

'What do you think happens when you die?'

I frowned.

'Wow. I reminded you to think about what happens when you die? That's what you're saying? How am I supposed to take that?'

'Because I read this article in, like, the *Reader's Digest* or something,' she said. 'Because this quite stylish woman was ahead of me in the queue at WH Smith, and she bought—'

'I'm way ahead of you.'

'Anyway, it said you go to this place and you meet everyone you're related to – everyone – but here's the thing: they're all in their prime.'

'In their prime?'

'They're all in their *prime*, yeah. Like you and me are now. Well, like I am. And it doesn't matter how old they were when they bit the bullet or bought the farm or joined the choir invisible. You *meet them in their prime*.'

Her eyes were huge, now, like this was the greatest thing she'd ever heard. I considered it.

'It sounds disastrous,' I said, and she looked at me, quizzically. 'So you meet your grandma and she looks about thirty. Then you meet your uncle and he looks about thirty too. Where's the hierarchy? Who's in charge? The whole of Heaven will just look like an episode of *Friends*.'

She smiled, looked away.

'But … you know, if you believe it …'

'I didn't say I believe it,' she said. 'I just wondered if it was believable.'

'I'm not sure I'm in my prime,' I said. 'How are you supposed to know?'

Inside, the older man ordered a bottle of champagne. His wife had given him a card and whatever she'd written in it had made him stop in his tracks.

'Well, are you happy?' asked Pia, staring at him.

'What do you mean?' I said. 'At this moment?'

Her eyes moved to me, now.

'I mean, are you a happy person?'

'I'd … like to be.'

'We'd *all* like to be. There's no one walking around thinking, what I'd *really* like is to be *not quite* happy. But do you think happy people are born or made?'

'I think you can make yourself happier.'

'I don't mean, like, buying a cheeseburger. I mean, do you *find* happiness? If you look hard enough? If you follow enough people? Because sometimes it feels like I see it, and it's in reach, but if I try for it, it pushes against me.'

'I don't think it's a "thing". I don't think … I don't know what I think.'

'Your problem is you think about being unhappy. You don't think about how to be happier. Remember when you were at school and you learned about magnets—'

'I'll be interested to see where this is going …'

'—and you knew magnets stuck together because you had some on your fridge or whatever, but then you saw how the wrong sides push against each other? Like they don't get on? That's what my life feels like sometimes. Like, happiness doesn't want me. And no matter how hard I push for it, it pushes back at me with just the same effort. Enough so I can still see it. Enough so I keep trying. But just enough to stop me. Whatever I give, it gives back.'

We sat in silence for a moment or two.

I looked at the older couple.

'Are *we* supposed to order champagne now?' I said.

'Can I dye my hair back at your place?'

On the bus, a tubby lad in sneakers was on the phone doing his weekly shop.

'Yeah mate, one medium Meat Mayhem,' he said, staring at the legs of a woman outside. 'One bucket of chicken … bottle of Fanta.'

Pia nudged me, pulled her cap back.

'Sorry about getting a bit weird back there,' she said.

'I'd prefer it if you saved that kind of talk for your monkeys,' I said. 'Look, I don't pretend to understand your whole … thing. But if I can help …'

'Thing is, you want to know all these facts. Favourite colour. How many A Levels I got. Mother's maiden name. Who cares about that stuff? Identity thieves and the people who write those security questions for online banking. Knowing those things is just knowing facts. I'm right here. Why isn't that enough?'

'It's just … what people do. I'm thirty-four and my favourite colour is blue,' I said. 'And now you know more about me than I do about you.'

'You're still so hung up on Hayley,' she said.

'Would it kill her to call me? To pick up the phone? How hard is that? Where are you from? I'm guessing Yorkshire.'

'Are you listening to me? You're hung up on Hayley and you've got to let that go. She detached from you.'

She what?

'It's a thing. People who follow detach. They either detach from the people they were with or they detach from the people they follow. Detachment. That's the technical term for what Hayley did to you.'

'There's a technical term?'

'For those who follow, yes, and look, she said it herself – carry on as normal.'

'How? Everything's changed. I can't carry on as normal because nothing is normal, and I can't move on, because I don't have closure.'

She smiled. Dug me in the ribs.

'Which is why you need this,' she said. 'You need some not-normal for a while. You can't live in limbo. You have to puncture the clouds.'

I looked at this small, pretty girl next to me.

What clouds did she live under?

At home, I ordered our food while she found the bathroom and started the shower. She managed to knock over every bottle in there.

God, she was noisy.

I could hear a car slowing to a halt outside. The rough grumble of an idling black cab. Edith from upstairs, maybe. Two doors slammed shut.

Woah. Maybe Edith had company.

'Have you got any towels?' Pia called out. 'Can I ruin one with the extremely potent hair dye which I bought for a quid from a Happy Shopper?'

'Yeah, I'll ...'

Thump-thump-thump at the door.

I looked at my watch, heard the cab's engine lift as it drove away.

8.15. Who comes round at 8.15? Sainsbury's again?

Thump-thump-thump again.

Christ. Hayley?

I walked to the window, slowly.

Parted a blind, peered out.

It was a man.

I recognised him.

[6]

'I am loath to tell you, but this feels unnatural,' I say, on our fifth afternoon together, as we follow a man walking east on 72nd toward Central Park.

The gentleman's collar is up, and we have followed suit.

He carries with him a balloon, and so we, two other men, carry one balloon apiece.

'This does not come easily to me,' I say.

My balloon is blue.

'And yet it is as natural to us both as breathing,' says Cockroft.

His balloon is pink.

'I'd argue not,' I say, stopping as I notice the man ahead stops to tie his shoelace.

For a moment we are simply two men, generations apart, standing on a street corner holding balloons. We stand and watch as they catch a slim wind, and I cross my arms to secure my string.

'Your arms are crossed,' he says. 'You crossed them mere moments after I crossed mine. I crossed mine to see if you would cross yours.'

I straighten my arms, quickly, flushing as I do so, embarrassed.

'Don't worry,' he says, placing a hand on my arm. 'Think of the way a parent imitates the facial expressions of their newborn. The way they smile, or poke their tongues from their mouths in mimicry. It is connection. It is the Chameleon Effect, and it is automatic imitation as social glue. On the most base level, we somehow adapt our behavior to every single person we meet. Including strangers.'

'I do not mimic everyone I meet,' I say. 'I know that I don't.'

'Yeah, you do. We all do. Mirror neuron system. We do it without thought. We alter the way we speak, the way we stand, the lilts and turns of our accents, our gestures, our speech patterns, all of it to *fit in* because all we are is animals and all we want is to be part of the herd.'

We turn to see the man is back on his feet. He stares up at the sky, his hands on his hips, his face darkened, staring as his balloon gets smaller and smaller and smaller, ready to puncture the clouds.

We look at each other, then release our balloons too.

'Isn't this whole endeavor merely wasting your life?'

'How so?' he says, surprised, taking his eyes off our balloons – blue and pink, now dancing with the green one the man had lost.

'If you're always walking in other people's footsteps, you will never make any tracks of your own.'

'You been practicing that?' he says, smiling, and I avoid his eye, because once again, this old man caught me. 'There have been people in my life who have said that to me. People who felt they had to … *detach* from me as a consequence. But they miss the point.'

The man with no balloon is staring at us. He wants to talk about why all our balloons are now in the sky.

'How so?' I ask, beginning to move away.

'This is the opposite of wasting your life. A life wasted is a life spent doing the same-old same-old. You follow, you learn. You can live a thousand lives, a minute at a time, and learn a thousand new things. Or you can do the same shit the same way you always do.'

I smile.

The man is closer now.

We turn and break into a jog.

'Of course,' says Cockroft, 'the really tricky thing is what happens when you get caught …'

eighteen

I did not know what to do.

Literally no idea.

I hovered by the curtain, one foot almost going to the door, the other remaining firmly where it was.

'Are you going to get that?' shouted Pia.

I stole another look out of the window, panicking, wondering whether I should open up, or whether it'd be better just to run and hide.

'What is it?' said Pia, a face like thunder now over my shoulder as I began to hunch. 'Who's that?'

The man looked over, spotted me, gave me a wave. He pointed at the sky. It was starting to rain. His look said, 'Just in time!'

And then he moved, slightly, to reveal a woman – his wife? – and then I felt complete confusion. I knew them. But what were *they* doing here?

A memory. *Wednesday 10th. 8pm.*

Was that still on?!

'You okay?' asked Pia, and I tried to find the time to explain.

'Dinner party,' I said, eyes wide, 'There's a dinner party ...'

'What? Out there?'

'No,' I said. 'In here ...'

'No there isn't,' she said, scrunching up her nose.

I opened the door.

'Tom!' said the man, extending his hand, gripping mine warmly. 'Did we catch you in the middle of something?'

He laughed a gregarious laugh. I tried to join in.

Had it been down to me to cancel? Why hadn't Hayley cancelled her own plans?

'Hi Tom,' said his wife, going for the kiss on one cheek, then the other, barging her way in. 'Sorry if we're a few minutes early!'

'We texted Hayley to warn her but didn't hear back,' said the man. 'Hope she's not too busy in the kitchen!'

Ha.

Ha ha.

'This is for you,' he said, handing me a bottle of red then sniffing the air theatrically. 'What's cooking?'

I don't know what he was sniffing because there was literally nothing cooking.

I tried to think of something to say.

'Come in!'

I wish I'd thought of something else.

And also – what the hell were their names? These were Hayley's friends, I knew that. Or *he* was. From where, though? I'd forgotten. Was it university? No! He runs a cheese shop somewhere! A posh one, in a villagey part of London! Chiswick? Dulwich? And he's always been *so* nice to me – but who's she? Artist? Accountant? Something with A?

'Hello!' said Pia, suddenly by my side, her elbow brushing my waist, just a little bit too close in the narrow hallway. In a dressing gown.

In. A. Dressing. Gown.

But wait – this would be okay if we ignore that. Because she was going to introduce herself. She'd sensed my discomfort and would now say her name, allowing them to say their names in return, and no one would think about the fact that she was in a dressing gown.

But she didn't.

'Hi!' said the man, nodding at Pia, waiting to be introduced, eyebrows raised …

'*ThisisPia*,' I gabbled, hoping that would suffice for introductions, and moving things swiftly on. 'Did you come far?'

'Still in Crouch End,' said the woman, smiling, and I had a vague memory of her saying something snippy about me to Hayley once, but there ended her sentence. She looked at Pia. Dressing gown. Oh, great. Panda cap too.

'Crouch End!' I said loudly, then, with a French accent: '*Crou-chen.*'

They both laughed like they'd never heard it before, followed by a silence that was longer than the Nile.

Right. Just explain. Just say 'your friend Hayley ditched me and didn't even think highly enough of you to properly cancel a dinner'.

Yes. That's the grown-up thing to do.

'Look,' I said. 'There's some news …'

The man's face a picture of concern now, the woman's not so much.

Pia put her hand on my shoulder.

'Yes, and it's bad,' she said. 'It's really bad news.'

'Oh God, what?' said the man.

What was his name?

'I feel terrible that you've wasted your time coming here,' I said, and then a gentle hand on my arm from Pia.

'Because the oven's broken and we've had to improvise,' she said.

What?

'Can I take your jackets?' she said, assuming the role of half-dressed panda-capped co-host.

'What did you say your name was again?' asked the man.

'Pia.'

'Pia!' he said. 'I'm Fraser.'

'God!' I said, grabbing the opportunity. 'God, I'm so rude, forgive me, I thought you'd met. Yes, this is Pia, sorry, and this is *Fraser*, and ...'

I looked at the woman.

' ... his wife—'

'Iona,' said Iona, and now I remembered their names perfectly.

'IONA,' I said. 'And Fraser.'

'You seem interesting,' said Pia, pointing at Iona.

'Oh ... thank you,' said Iona, and I shot Pia a *stop it*.

She could be kooky if she wanted. But this was not a time to be weird.

'There's other news as well,' I said. 'And—'

'Where do you work, Iona?' asked Pia, taking her jacket.

'At UCL, in Bloomsbury?'

'Oh, cool,' said Pia. 'And what sort of time do you have to leave your house to get there in the mornings?'

'*Anyway*, come in, come in!' I said, very loudly indeed, and it was then that I saw the flat through their eyes.

Broken vase. Magazines all over the floor. Meal-for-one packets on the dusty IKEA table. Half-bottle of rum by the telly.

We all stood and looked, disappointment running thick in the room.

'I, um ...'

'We were *burgled* this evening,' said Pia. 'That was the other news.'

Well, why not.

'Oh God, how *terrible*,' said Iona. '*Burgled?*'

'Bloody hell,' said Fraser, and he looked at the room for all the confirmation he needed. 'I'm so sorry.'

'Yeah, it's pretty bad,' said Pia.

'Well, not burgled, exactly,' I said.

'Cats,' said Pia. 'We think a load of cats got in.'

'Cat burglars!' said Fraser, and we all laughed a little too hard.

'Well, no, it wasn't cats,' I said, because that was fucking ludicrous. 'We think someone got in and … maybe a cat came in as well afterwards.'

Why were we saying this? And what was I going to say about Hayley?

'What did the police say?' said Iona.

'They said it was probably burglars and thieves,' said Pia, nodding. 'Where did you get your necklace, I *love* it?'

'This?' said Iona, confused. 'I, er …'

'Listen,' said Fraser. 'We can come back another time, when everything's …'

'No!' said Pia. 'Stay!'

'Really,' said Iona. 'You've got so much to sort out, and—'

'Iona, I will not have it,' said Pia, taking her by the hand and leading her to the sofa. 'But I'm afraid we haven't been able to cook anything.'

I wished she'd stop saying 'we'.

'And … where's Hayley?' said Fraser, finally.

'Hayley, yes,' I said.

Quietly, his hand found my arm.

'Is she all right?'

'She's, well … she's—'

'She's in bed,' said Pia. 'She's pretty down about it all.'

Jesus Christ, Pia. Enough. I had to tell them.

But: 'The burglars took her tiaras,' said Pia, very grim-faced. 'And all her cufflinks that she got on eBay. And one of the cats pissed on her bonnets.'

The words hung in the air.

'Okay,' I said. 'This all sounds very weird, and—'

'Oh, God,' said Fraser, shaking his head, brow furrowed.

'So that's why Tom asked *me* to come round,' said Pia. 'To cheer things up a bit.'

'Sorry, are you Hayley's ...?' asked Iona, hoping Pia might fill in the blanks.

'Comet?' asked Pia.

Stop!

'Wine!' I said, remembering the bottle in my hand. 'Let's open this wine!'

Thump-thump-thump.

Pia looked at the door.

'Dinner's here.'

We sat around the table, all paper napkins and mismatched cutlery. No mood lighting. No candles. No wine glasses for the wine, because they'd been in the dishwasher for over a fortnight now. No fancy food to hum and haw over.

'We only ordered one pizza,' I said. 'But we did get some chicken wings. I hope that's okay.'

'Burglars took his cards,' explained Pia, who'd done me the great favour of putting her clothes back on and taking her panda cap off. 'We also got a two-litre bottle of Fanta. And the pizza is a Meat Mayhem, so hopefully there's something for everyone.'

'It's lovely,' said Fraser, picking up a bright red drumstick. 'What a treat. We *never* eat like this at home.'

Iona smiled weakly. I caught her eye.

'Are you ...'

'I'm a vegetarian, yes.'

'We've got some white bread!' yelled Pia, bolting for the fridge, and by now they were onto us. Something was up. They knew it. They couldn't call us on it, but they knew it. It was horribly obvious. The whole thing was horrible. But I was past caring, resigned to the evening and wherever it took us. Maybe it was my own little rebellion.

God, how different the night would have been if Hayley had been here. We'd have started getting ready mid-afternoon. I'd have tidied up, she'd have started cooking a dessert from a Jamie book she could later unveil with great triumph and then claim had taken no time whatsoever. About fourish, I'd have popped to the wine shop and picked up two bottles of mid-range white, two bottles of decent red, and some Kettle Chips we'd have placed in a bowl to look like amazing people who only eat hand-cut crisps from bowls. Someone would've Hoovered. And right now we'd be talking about property prices, or whether we could be bothered going to Glastonbury these days, or how *The X Factor*'s had its day, or whatever else we could raise a quick opinion on to get us through 'til midnight. And we'd have done a vegetarian option.

Instead, what did we have? A man with a bruised face, a no-show from his girlfriend, a stranger making roll-ups at the dinner table, one medium Meat Mayhem, some chicken wings the colour of nothing else in the known world and a story about cat burglars pissing on bonnets.

My eyes flickered to the clock.

We were only forty-five minutes in.

I suppose it definitely looked like I'd killed Hayley.

'There's no more wine,' said Pia, coming back in from the kitchen. 'They must've taken that last night. *Bloody* wine thieves.'

She put her hands on her hips and shook her head.

I noticed Fraser and Iona swap a glance and something of a smile. Iona put her jam sandwich down. I frowned slightly at Pia to get her to take it easy.

'So we've got a half-bottle of a half-bottle of rum, a can of Beck's Vier or that Fanta.'

'Oh, um … I'll have some Fanta, please,' said Iona, who'd definitely dressed up for tonight.

Anthropologist. At UCL. *A for Anthropologist!* Of course.

'Listen,' she said, as Pia went to fetch the Fanta. 'Tom, are you sure everything's okay?'

Isn't anthropology the study of human behaviour? I wondered whether in her head she was already planning a paper.

'Yeah, all good!' I said, and she glanced at Fraser, who nodded her on.

'Hayley's not here, is she, Tom?' she said. 'She's not really in bed.'

'Can I be honest with you?' I said. 'Hayley's not here, no.'

A momentary silence. They *knew* it.

'She's in hospital,' said Pia, putting her hand on mine as she sat.

'For Christ's sake, Pia,' I said, then, more quietly: 'She's not in hospital.'

'No, she's not in hospital,' said Pia. 'But she's not here.'

The table fell silent as Pia poured the Fanta and unscrewed the remaining rum, placing it in front of me with a little straw. We all listened to the fizz settle down.

'Okay …' said Iona. 'So where is Hayley?'

'She's in France,' I said. 'She left me.'

Pia squeezed my hand, tightly.

They looked at me, at the flat, at the girl next to me.

At the half-bottle of rum with the little straw.

It all made perfect sense.

Fraser and Iona left the minute we ran out of Fanta.

I wrapped a spare chicken wing in cling film and pressed it into Fraser's hand at the door as he left by way of apology.

'Cats pissing on her *bonnets*?' I said, while Pia folded up the pizza box and crushed it into the bin.

'They were Hayley's friends, not yours. Why should you feel awkward? Hayley should feel awkward. They should feel awkward. Not you. Look, think about tonight. Think about how down it would have made you feel. To go over the truth of it all again. To get their sympathy. They'd still be here now. Sitting on that sofa, making you cups of sugary tea, saying things like "you poor thing" and "maybe it's for the best".'

'Maybe that's the kind of thing I want to hear.'

'You know it's not. You need to be active. And let's say you did just buckle like that. Then they'd have left you – all of you knowing you'd never see each other again – and then they'd have sat there laughing in their cab at you and about how boring you must have been to push Hayley away like that.'

'Christ,' I said. 'How hard is it to pick up the phone? Would it kill her? If you love someone, if there's even a *moment* of love left in you, that should be reason enough just to *pick up the phone.*'

She avoided my eye, walked past me.

'They're probably laughing in their cab about it right now,' I said, as she slid onto the sofa, grabbing one of Hayley's magazines from the table.

'Yes, but on your terms,' she said, starting to flick through. 'You didn't tell them because you had to. You told them because you decided to. Now when they tell this story at their next Crouch End dinner party – because yours is a story they'll tell a lot – it'll be about a girl in a dressing gown offering them chicken wings and talking about cats and tiaras as much as it'll be about your girlfriend running off and OH MY GOD LOOK AT *THIS.*'

I span round.

nineteen

Great.

So Hayley was insane.

She was an obsessive. Fantastic. I'd been living with an obsessive. This was all such wonderful news.

Ding.

....

FROM: MAUREEN THOMAS
TO: ALL STAFF

I am DISAPPOINTED TO SAY that only THREE PEOPLE turned up to Adewale's SECURITY FAMILIARITY BRIEFING. This is NOT ACCEPTABLE and NAME'S HAVE BEEN SENT TO MANAGEMENT. We are RESCHEDULING FOR TOMORROW at 5PM. And NO EXCUSE'S!!!!

....

Delete.

And look – I don't pretend we don't all have our obsessions. We all did as kids. I liked *Knight Rider*. But here was a woman in her *thirties* displaying all the signs of an adolescent.

Magazine after magazine.

Page after page.

Picture after picture.

Post-it after Post-it after Post-it.

I'd seen some of these Post-its before but thought nothing of it. Because I hadn't seen the pattern or noticed the volume. I'd assumed she'd just been marking out small details of interest – a brand here, a place there – but now I really looked ... I recognised these clothes; I recognised these places.

Bubbledogs. The weird champagne and hotdog place in Fitzrovia. Had she mentioned it? Had I?

'*Pop star Aphra pictured outside London restaurant Bubbledogs.*'

Maybe. Possibly.

A navy top – one I thought I recognised – one I was sure she'd ordered from ASOS in some fevered rush. I mean, it was just a navy top. Maybe she'd bought one like it. But look ...

'*Pop star Aphra shines at the MOBOs in classic blue.*'

Yellow heels.

'*Aphra hits the yellow brick road to Chinawhite.*'

Hayley had yellow heels. Not the same ones – these were about two grand – but she had *yellow heels*. Well, yellowish. Burnt orange. But the same direction. The same basic direction.

And more, and more, and more.

This was weird. It was sad. It felt creepy.

The feelings I had for her quickly turned to a weird sort of ... disgust.

'The song,' I said. 'Do you think it's ...'

Pia was way ahead of me. She flipped the laptop round, and hit play.

> *Sorry I've been so distant, I am just elsewhere.*
> *You must be so confused and wonder if I care ...*

And as it built to the chorus, this latest hit from Aphra, my knees buckled and the blood drained from my face ...

Carry on, baby, carry on … just carry on without me …

Of course.

Why not.

The lift doors opened to reveal Pippy.

'The hell?'

'Hayley thinks she's Aphra,' I said, laughing, smiling, shaking my head in disbelief, just as I'd done all the way in.

Work Experience Paul span round in a bright blue office chair, grinning, expecting some big joke to equal the laughs.

'*Man* you get in early,' I said, and he nodded, sadly. 'Anyway, Hayley thinks she's a pop star! Or she's obsessed with her. Or she's just been copying her. Or I don't know what. But at least I know it's not me. It's not me! She didn't go because of me.'

The words sounded great. I didn't care any more. I didn't care who knew. I felt light, I felt trippy, I felt for a pot plant to steady myself.

'She went because she's a nutcase.'

Hallelujah! HALLELUJAH!

I'm not sure why this felt like such great relief. I don't know why it stirred such joy in me. To have an answer? Even an answer like this?

It was the first relationship ever to jump the shark.

'Look!' I said, at my desk now, delighted, and digging through the computer. 'I *did* mention Paris!'

I'd done a search – found the news story.

I put on my newsman's voice.

'"*Aphra says she's keen to settle in Paris with rap star Blaze.*" Haha! Wow. So I guess Hayley has gone to Paris to find a rap star to settle down with. Yes.'

'Tom, are you okay?'

Concerned face. Half-frown. Work Experience Paul's face had frozen in some kind of semi-fear.

'I'm brilliant! I'm just so happy for Hayley.'

'You are …?'

'Oh God, yes. She's finally found herself. She's finally found herself and she's Aphra.'

'I'm not sure you should go on air.'

'No, I'm okay, Pippy, I've started following people around London with a girl called Pia who once started following *me*.'

She was moving towards me, uncertainly. Sniffing the air for booze. Instinctively I patted my pocket. I had what I needed in there. I'd taken one already this morning.

'I'm absolutely fine. I'm absolutely delighted, is all,' I said, beaming. 'I hope there are more rap stars in Paris. It would be a terrible shame to move to Paris and not find any other rap stars.'

'Tom, I'm going to call someone.'

'Pippy, I'm fine.'

'You don't look fine. You look like you're about to cry.'

'I'm not! I'm not! It's joy! I'm fine!'

I rapped the table three times, hard, with my knuckles, the way people do when they're absolutely sure they're fine.

The phone rang. We stared at each other. The phone never rang at this time.

One word on the screen: SECURITY.

'Oh, look – it's Golden Boy. The Golden Boy of broadcasting,' he said, choking out a bitter laugh. If he could have spat it at me, he would. 'And here sits thine past.'

My eyes shot past him, over his shoulder, to the brightly lit security desk behind the glass doors. I used to hate it when he'd say things like 'thy' or 'thine'. Adewale stared out from the office beyond, iPlayer on his laptop as usual. He raised his eyebrows to assure me he'd seen Leslie, then slowly shook his head to assure me he'd already denied him entry.

I'd come outside because they didn't know who else to tell, and sending a stranger seemed a cruel way to treat one of our own. Leslie did not look well. Jacket on lap, crumpled white shirt, a trail of red wine from pocket down to once-cream linen trousers. Fag end stuck to his shoe. Small plastic badge clipped to his belt, his name above a Comet logo in faded cyan. Someone somewhere needed to replace a cartridge.

I guessed he'd been hosting a corporate for them, handing out awards for Best Regional Comet or Best Comet Store Manager or whatever. Probably the Hilton, or in the Great Room at the Dorchester. Either way, Mayfair. I guessed he must have taken advantage of the free booze afterwards. Pressed the flesh with the great and the good of the washing machine and white goods industry. Probably exchanged business cards with a chief exec. Maybe followed some of them on. Ended up alone in an inappropriate club, or shared a cab with a hanger-on to some clip joint in Soho. I guessed he'd have looked at his watch, forgotten himself and headed here for work. Tried to get in to do his show. Found out the hard way from Adewale.

'Hi Leslie,' I said. 'Nice to see you again.'

Because what else do you say?

'Nice to see me again? Is it?'

Cold blue eyes, widening as he wondered what level of contempt my platitude deserved.

'How's my replacement?' he said, faking a smile.

'She's fine,' I said.

'Making a name for herself,' he said. 'Not bad for a fraudcaster.'

He was pleased with that. I held my tongue. This wasn't the time. Leslie looked different. Rattled and dishevelled.

'You know where I'm off to?' he said, shaking his head. 'You know the only people even to get back in touch with me?'

'You mean …'

'Work-wise, yes. Not Radio 2. Oh, no. No, my friend there – or I thought he was my friend – no, he put paid to that. You might think LBC would be a good fit. But no, it's a closed shop, one in, one out, thank you very much.'

'Something will come up, Leslie. It's been hardly any time.'

'My agent does not share your optimism, Tom. So come next month I'll be doing an afternoon slot on Sunrise.'

'That's … the online thing, yeah?'

Station. I should have said 'station'.

'People say good things about Sunrise,' I said.

'It's one up from prison radio, Tom.'

'At least they might have an exercise yard,' I said.

'What are you *talking* about?' he said, not getting his own joke. He stood.

'*You* should have gone,' he said. 'Mistake like that. What have you got on them? Or are you there to make up the numbers? Someone's done a survey and found out, "Ooh, we need more of *them*."'

I had to be careful here.

'You mean because …'

'I don't mean anything.'

'Sounds like you do.'

'Don't you try and put words in my mouth. That's your trick. That's how we ended up here.'

'I didn't put those words in your mouth, Leslie.'

'No, but *you let them out*!'

He staggered, steadied himself on the bench. He stank of booze and Embassies.

'You people, you think—'

'What people am I, Leslie?' I said. 'Why do you keep saying "you people"?'

'No, not like that. Stop trying to make it look like I'm ...' – he reset – 'You *young* people, you think the world has only ever been the way you see it now. You don't know how it was. I've been in broadcasting *thirty-five* years, I've seen people like you come and go, young people, people who haven't got the gift, and *one review* in *The Times* means nothing. *Nothing.*'

One finger in my face now.

'You should have gone, not me. I didn't even know your name.'

'Come on, Leslie, go home, mate.'

'I *am* home. This is my ... it's what I'm best at. You know why? Because I know who I am, "mate". I know who I am and that's what you have to know to be a success at this. I've *always* known. What do *you* know?'

He started to walk, brushing past me, though not, I think, entirely on purpose. And as he got to the edge of the pavement, he turned once more.

'Do *you* even know who *you* are, Tom?' he smiled. 'I should come after you with all guns blazing but the truth is, you survived because you're a nobody. You slip through. Low impact. No one cares enough. You don't matter. Nobody cares enough about you to bother doing anything about you because really, what's the difference?'

And he laughed, and shook his head, and walked over, jacket now tossed across one shoulder, out into the street, where he was hit by a cab.

Boom. Screech. Horn.

And 'Hang on,' I remember thinking, straight after, as the howl of the ambulance grew closer and someone – some tourist – took a picture on their phone. '*What* review in *The Times*?'

twenty

I was sent home again. Compassionate leave (one day). Pippy said it was because of the whole Leslie thing, but I suspect it was actually because she'd witnessed what she was pretty sure was the start of some kind of episode.

I think she may have been right. The dog was sniffing around. Trying to find a place to settle. The dog was finding its spot.

I sat in the corner of the room, no longer comfortable on my side of the sofa we'd bought, the chairs we'd bought.

The Times was on my lap. Media section. It was only a small review, but in radio, that's like the cover of *Vanity Fair*. The words, though, were what mattered, and they were enough to distract me for now.

MAYOR'S ON-AIR 'MARE
Talk London's new breakfast show has a snap, crackle and pop at Mayor Jackson. Another serving, please, says TIM EDMUNDS ...

I read and re-read the words.

After the morning snoozefest that was London Calling with Leslie James (the five-year run's only notable highlight being the 'Jam Nazi' rant most recently played out on US network NBC's

late-night talk show, Late Night With Jimmy Fallon, and which
ultimately led to James leaving the station in disgrace), the
capital has a new pretender gunning for morning glory …

We'd been recognised. Cass was the focus, of course. It was her
harrying and prodding on her first show – when the Mayor had
thought it was going to be an easy little press opp with a few new
ears on it – that had secured the story. But I was name-checked too.
Singled out for praise, even.

Talking bravely about his recent and horrific experiences at the
hands of a knife-wielding maniac on London's streets, Adoyo
spoke candidly …

The press like finding something they can say they found. We'd be
ignored from now on, of course, but this is what put Leslie over the
edge today. An early morning copy. A casual glance. A realisation
that he had never once been plucked out of the blue for praise. The
world was moving on without him.

I put the paper down and looked at the TV, so desperate for my
attention, impotent and mute. Took another swig of beer. Then
looked at the picture of Hayley on the mantelpiece.

It had been four weeks. Four *weeks*.

Maybe there's a more innocent explanation to all this, I thought.
Maybe she won a competition and was too embarrassed to tell me
about it. We all have weird things we're into. Some people are into
some really weird stuff. There's nothing too weird about liking a
pop star. Nothing weird about liking their style, what they stand
for, what they represent. Perhaps Hayley won something from a
chocolate bar or a radio station and couldn't turn it down and …

The morning grew hazy and warm, thanks to my pill, the
light blanding out before me, the world a little floatier … the box a
little emptier.

Time to see Dr Moon.

I whistled as I picked through Hayley's magazines. *Grazia*. *Cosmo*. All of them. And I learned more about pop star Aphra than I ever thought I would.

First, it seemed impossible to write anything about pop star Aphra without calling her 'pop star Aphra'. It's like that was on her birth certificate, and if it was, I suppose music seemed an inevitable choice of career.

Born in Trinidad, moved to Miami, spotted in a Walmart, modelled for a year in Paris and Milan, courted Kanye, signed with Sony, toured the world, settled in LA with a pad in Paris, rapper boyfriend, perfume called Raindance.

I guessed I'd probably recognise the smell. I guessed it'd probably remind me of Hayley.

Aphra even had a reality show.

My eyes flicked to the telly.

I switched it on. Found the Sky Remote. Checked the Planner.

Oh, look. *Aphra: Pop Warrior*. Surprised it wasn't series linked.

I started the first episode and went back to the magazines, the twaddle and screeches of a pop star and her entourage now in the background.

Aphra was furious because a puppy she'd ordered in black had arrived in dark brown. Her personal assistant, a camp man with a rictus grin, fanned himself as he called it 'literally the worst day ever'.

How much further could she make my heart sink? In how many more ways? At least try and emulate someone you've got something in common with. Someone you can respect yourself for liking.

I switched the telly off and I wanted to howl.

I'd been seeing Dr Moon since I arrived in London.

He has a nice little practice on a tree-lined street round the back of Green Lanes. Brass plaque outside, parquet flooring, very nice, thank you.

He's maybe two or three years older than me. He tries to stay professional, but I know he listens to the show, because the little digital radio he has in the corner of his office betrays him: 'Talk London' scrolling quickly along its small screen, ready to be turned up between patients.

He usually gives me six minutes. It's the London average. Though today I got more as he popped to the loo at the start of the appointment. He left his Facebook page open when he did, so I know his favourite films are *Shutter Island* and *Gangster Squad*, he enjoys the work of Leonard Cohen, Nick Drake and Kanye West, and he 'likes' the official pages of *Only Fools and Horses*, Olivia Wilde and – weirdly – Smints.

'How are you feeling?' he said, kindly, sitting back down at his desk, quickly clicking Facebook away, hiding the profile pic of him and his rugby mates, pretending he was just a doctor again, not a man with a life and interests.

'Same,' I said, bluffing, just trying to make this normal. 'That sort of … blah.'

'Things not looking up?'

Not really, doctor, no.

'Everything at home okay?'

Not really, doctor, no.

At least this time there was a cause, a root. How to describe it, normally? It's just a complete lack of will. The will to get better, even the will to look for *how* to. Not caring enough.

But it's a feeling that is crawling along so subtly and becoming so insidious that soon five, ten, fifteen years may pass, where you're chained to this feeling of ennui, without ever really realising that you weren't, in fact, crawling along – you were going downhill. That's the fear. The slow and the steady decline just starting to feel perfectly normal. The grey gauze, the black dog, the slowly falling cloak over your head.

'You know, I'm not a psychiatrist,' he said. 'But there are things you can do. Things that may help. Exercise is …'

He smiled, hoping maybe I'd let him in.

'I just came for a new prescription really,' I said.

This guy. Yeah, this one. The one with the stride. He's the one I'll go for. He's the one I'll follow.

I was on Oxford Street, weaving through the crowds, my mood sedated and cosseted by my amitriptyline – my serotonin and noradrenaline protected for now – my mood light, my walk bouncier than I could otherwise hope for.

Anything you can do, Hayley …

The world was just that little bit louder, the scene around me ever-so-slightly blurred round the edges – they say it takes the edge off, amitriptyline, and maybe that's what they mean. I'd get the dry mouth sometimes with this stuff. I'd get the floats, too. Seemed a small price to pay for the rendering it put over the bricks.

Dr Moon was right. There were things I could do. Things that may help.

The guy I'd chosen was a slender white guy with a walk I could only covet. Elegant, confident, not so much a walk as a stride. Look at him go, I thought to myself. Well, let's do it.

He had good hair, this guy – expensive shoes. Flat platinum wedding ring, chunky watch, light tan.

He ducked into Selfridges and I ducked in after him.

First floor. *Men's Designer. Men's Contemporary. Men's men's men's …*

I watched as he glided past the names – names I'd never stop to look at. This isn't my world. *Dolce & Gabbana. McQueen. Westwood.* I had no business here. But this guy did, the way he'd trail his hands down the lining of a jacket, inspect a cuff, check the break of a sleeve.

He was here for a fitting. I sat nearby and pretended to be waiting for an imaginary girlfriend – because I suppose in many ways *you* were just an imaginary girlfriend all along weren't you, Hayley? – as a girl brought his suit out and laid it before him like it was her masterpiece. He slipped the jacket over his shirt, stretched his arms out, buttoned the second button, left the top one just like you're supposed to, smoothed the whole piece down, checked the silhouette. The girl stood behind him, peeking over his shoulder, admiring in the mirror her tailor's handiwork, perhaps imagining for a moment a life with this man in this jacket. I smiled to myself. That man was in control. He tried some shoes – nodded his admiration. She brought out a tie she thought he might like, that she thought might be perfect for him. He shrugged a why-not, then flipped open his wallet and threw a black card onto the counter. I made a note on my phone. *Duchamp three-piece dash check suit. Paul Smith London Stamford shoes, red laces. Canali Jacquard-stripe single-cuff shirt. Tie: Boss, wool, grey with single black stripe.*

I would never buy this stuff, of course. That would be too far. Buying it would mean that I missed this too much. That following *had* me; meant more to me than I wanted to admit. But I enjoyed the moment. Liked thinking I might. Enjoyed the technicolour I'd been missing.

He was off, now, and I was too, keeping my distance, observing, maybe thirty steps behind him as he left the shop and turned left towards Manchester Square, turning round, searching for a cab, arm in the air as one stopped.

In a cab myself, now, my driver excited by the whole thing, chuckling to himself about how he never thought he'd be in a spy film, and how he'd longed to have a whole follow-that-cab! moment. I didn't mention it was my second, though the first was by rickshaw, and as I looked up once more I saw we were slowing.

Park Lane.

I waited in the lobby of the hotel while the man dropped off his suit in his room. I knew that's what he was doing as he'd said as much to the doorman, who'd put his hand to his hat and said, 'Welcome back to the Dorchester, Mister Davis.'

I can't even get Adewale on reception to smile at me.

Ten minutes later, he was back, and he was striding again. Quick stop for a takeaway coffee at Piccolo, then I stood three people behind him in a queue for Yazu Sushi on Curzon Street – followed his example and got the Sashimi Deluxe to go.

I followed him round the corner, feeling like I was stomping but body somehow gliding, on past the Fox Club, and over the road into Green Park, sushi bags in hand, mine rustling behind my back, held there so he wouldn't notice if he glanced over his shoulder, which he had, now, once or twice.

I could just follow this guy forever, I thought. Escape my life. Live his. Pop my pills and eat sushi and stride. I don't know what he did. Banker?

Who cares. I liked *how* he did things. I liked the *feel* of his life.

And there she was: waiting on a bench. The inevitable girl, this vision, this beautiful flame-haired woman, model-pretty, her face lighting up the second she saw him, her arms out for the hug, the kiss on the cheek, the kiss on the mouth, the hug now an embrace and lasting an age.

Now they began to talk excitedly, and I noticed she wasn't wearing a ring, and I studied his hand again and saw that now no longer was he, and 'that's strange' I thought, and I followed them as they walked arm-in-arm, tight like a team or a unit, and he showed her the sushi and said he hoped it was okay, and she took in the trees and the grass and the big grey sky above her, and I thought about the last time Hayley had seemed excited to see me, the last time we'd held each other like that, the last time we'd surprised each other.

Well, except for the time she surprised me by fucking off. But you know what I mean. And that was when I realised I was standing far too close to this couple and he turned to me. Took me in.

Remembered me.

'You were in Selfridges,' he said. 'And my hotel.'

He glanced at my sushi bag – then the coffee from Piccolo. His eyes widened.

'What the hell are you up to?'

I smiled. The girl looked uncertain at first, frightened now.

'So …' I began, not quite knowing how I would finish.

Stoke Newington Church Street. Bottle shop. It was coming up for six. Head home. Sleep. Sleep all this off. The day, the cans, the pills. The wine would help.

But *thump-thump-thump* on the door, just as I was running a bath.

'Hi,' said Pia, when I opened it. 'Jesus, you look rough.'

'You've changed your hair,' I said.

'Bob,' she said.

'And your name, apparently.'

'No, *it's* a bob.'

'I know. What are you doing here?'

'I was passing.'

'You mean someone else was.'

'Yeah.'

I let her in.

'You've been drinking,' she said, opening the blinds. 'I thought you didn't drink much.'

'I don't.'

'That doesn't look like your first can.'

'Well, I wouldn't say I'm particularly happy today.'

She brushed the words away, quickly.

'You should be. You've got focus now, and clarity, and—'

'I followed someone today,' I said.

Her jaw dropped.

'You followed someone? Without me?' she said. 'That's fantastic! Who were they? What did you do? You know what this means? You're free!'

'Am I?'

'Yes. You're in control again.'

'I'm not, Pia …'

'You are! And you have your reason, for why Hayley went. Having that reason means you can move on. You know how?'

'How?'

'It's *Wednesday*.'

The Holiday Inn Express, Wandsworth.

We sat around the table. Me. Pia. Jackie. Tim. Felix. And Andy.

Sometimes it felt like the Holiday Inn was the closest I'd ever get to an actual holiday. We'd planned for it, me and Hayley. I'd saved for it. Just never done it. It felt like London *had* me.

'Guys! Let's start by sharing some of our experiences from the week,' said Andy, clipboard in hand.

I sipped at my coffee, let the caffeine do its work.

Everyone kept stealing little glances at me. They seemed thrilled I was here, though no one asked why. At one point Jackie gave Pia a little pat on the hand. A 'well done', maybe.

'Tim, let's start with you,' he said, full of beans. 'Share your story.'

'Well, it was quite a week for me,' said Tim, smiling. 'The man downstairs, the man who owns the betting shop, well ordinarily on a Monday I'd follow him, wouldn't I? Quick walk through the park, spot of lunch, then he disappears off to see his mistress at Glenmore Villas and I'd hang around by the benches.'

As always, he said all this as if it was completely normal.

'Well, he's off on holiday this week. I can't go, obviously, because I've got my mother to take care of, so I did something completely different.'

He made a big you'll-like-this face.

'So I followed his mistress instead!'

'Ooh!' said Jackie.

'Turns out she's *also* seeing a fella in *Turnham Green*!'

'Ooh!' said Jackie.

'I thought to myself, "if there's one thing that'd turn *him* green, it's that!" Green with *envy*!'

He treated us to a moment of jazz hands after this well-rehearsed joke, and Jackie chuckled in a way that implied she knew she shouldn't.

'I'd not been to Turnham Green in years,' said Tim. 'They've got a Starbucks there now.'

I noticed Pia had moved to the side of the room, now. She'd told me about all of them. Tim was a good man, I knew that, no side to him, an optimist, but he was shackled to his home. The two hours a day his mother was cared for by the woman who also came to clean were his only chance to get out there, to live. This was his way of doing it.

Jackie suffered from crippling shyness. Her first year at CC she hadn't spoken a word. In this room, she was Someone. She was accepted. Now she even brought the biscuits. Although I was concerned to hear that one night, struggling to find anyone worth following, Jackie had spent two hours following a dustman.

Felix had been bullied all his life. His mum's new boyfriend, an army man, hadn't taken to him. It affected him at school. Made him an outcast. He struggled with his identity. He'd been a goth, then a metaller, a boy-bander, all before he was fourteen. Now he was experimenting with spray tan and hairspray. For Felix, it was the purest form of finding himself. He knew he was out there. He just didn't know who.

And again, I thought, the only person Pia hadn't told me about was Pia.

And now she sat, head against the wall, just listening.

'And what about you … Tom?' said Andy, kindly, and this is what everyone had been waiting for. 'You're back, I see …'

I nodded.

'And … is there a reason for that? Last time you were here …'

'Tom went on the follow this afternoon,' said Pia, interrupting her own self-imposed silence, and this changed the whole atmosphere.

'What?' said Jackie. 'Did you?'

'I'm having an … unusual time of late,' I explained, struggling to find the right words. 'The more I find out about Hayley, I … yeah. I gave it a go. No big deal. I did a little follow.'

'No big deal?' laughed Andy. 'You're on the road now, Tom. The road to—'

'He was caught,' said Pia, and Jackie's face fell. Tim put his hand to his head.

'What did you say?' said Felix.

'He said he was a private detective,' said Pia, giggling, and I shot her a look. 'He said the guy's wife had sent him!'

'Is *everyone* just having *affairs* these days?' said Tim, shocked at the world.

'I suppose really before anything else happens, Andy,' I said, trying to move things on, away from my own humiliation, 'I just want to know a bit more about the club.'

He smiled and put his clipboard down.

CC – which I'd thought must mean Copy Club, or perhaps even Copy Cat – stood for Carbon Copy. It stood, also, for inclusion.

'CC me in,' they'd say. Or 'CC all'.

It had started in Berlin in the late 1960s, thanks to a New York academic by the name of Ezra Cockroft on an exchange programme with the Freie Universität. He'd seen the light one night walking down the Kurfürstendamm – papers in hand, another night of nothing but work in front of him – as a man he described as his unbelievable doppelgänger bounded up the steps of the U-Bahn and into the arms of a waiting family.

'In that moment,' he wrote, in a paper he presented some years later at a conference in Connecticut on the changing face of social mobility, 'I wondered what had happened in our lives to take us in such different directions, this other me and me. We shared a city, a time, a look, even – though he was younger than me, far younger than me – and what he had seemed so removed from my own life that it became incredibly attractive to me.'

Fascinated, he'd followed the man, gently at first, from a distance, before the urge to talk to him grew so great that he had to approach. The man – a financial adviser for a large chain of German real estate brokers – was charmed to meet someone who seemed so like him. A father figure, maybe.

They became great friends.

The idea then spread thanks to a student writing a piece on him. Small chapters opened up in New York, San Francisco, Boston, and while they'd fizzled out, that same student had brought it to London some years later. Chapters opened up here and there, usually of no more than six or seven people in size, meeting in pubs or church halls. Most dropped out when life took over, as they had in New York, or San Francisco, or Boston.

But some kept going.

'There's a group in Rome,' said Felix. 'One in Doha, for some reason. And a few scattered around some of the bigger cities in Spain. Everyone does it differently, but the fundamental idea remains the same.'

'Observe, learn, leave,' said Jackie.

'And what about you, Andy?' I asked. 'How did you get started?'

'I was introduced to it,' he said.

'By who?' I asked.

He looked uncomfortable. His eyes flit around the room, landed on Pia.

'Guy called Jeremy.'

I cast a glance at Pia, looking daggers at Andy.

'But anyway,' he said. 'Long time ago.'

'Who's Jeremy?' I asked.

'Nobody,' said Pia, breaking her silence. 'A great big nobody.'

'It might be good to talk about Jeremy,' tried Jackie, with all the courage she could muster.

'No,' said Pia, fixing her with a stare I'd never seen her use before, full of hurt and caution. 'It would not be good to talk about Jeremy.'

And in that moment, with the way she said *that* name, I was pretty sure I knew what Pia's story was.

'So what are everyone's plans for the night?' asked Andy, clearing the biscuits away. By which I mean eating them.

'Nothing,' said Felix, flatly. 'Maybe I'll follow Tom.'

'Haha,' I said, uncomfortably.

'Would you mind if I followed you?' he said. 'I'd do it quietly.'

'Why would you follow me?' I said, confused

'You probably go to cool parties.'

Pia laughed very hard at this.

'You probably meet loads of celebrities. You probably know Will.i.am.'

She slapped the table at that.

Andy kindly changed the subject.

'Pia? What about you?'

'I'm taking Tom to the zoo,' said Pia, calming down.

The others turned to stare.

'You're taking me where?' I said.

'The zoo,' said Pia.

'That is fantastic,' said Jackie, hands on hips, impressed. 'That is great, P.'

Everyone was acting like this was a huge deal.

'So we're going to the zoo?' I said. 'What – on our own?'

'Yes, on our own. You've earned it.'

'No, I mean – without following anyone there?'

'Yes,' she said. 'We will be using our own free will.'

'The zoo,' said Andy, smiling. 'Well *done*, Pia.'

[7]

And so, at last, I broached 1968.

'The university had a deal with the Freie Universität. Especially when it came to economists. We'd send someone over for a year or two, they'd send someone our way for a year or two. Well, I put my hand up for that one pretty quick. I wanted to see Berlin again, wanted to see Germany again, but on better terms this time. I was at Aachen in '44. Crossing the Siegfried Line. Well, you become fascinated, you know? You want to go back.'

He becomes more animated now.

'And so I move there, and I work, and I work, and I work. And soon I realize that all I'm doing is working. I'm not seeing the old place, I haven't been back to Aachen, I'm just preparing classes, delivering classes, marking the papers I ask them to do in the classes … well, I could have been doing that back at NYU, where my counterpart – my *intellectual* doppelgänger – was probably now going to my guy on 5th and probably ordering my favorite sandwich.'

He laughs, and slaps the table with one huge hand.

'And then I saw the guy.'

He flips his hands open as if to say 'and there you have it'.

'So what did you do?'

'Well, I would follow him.'

He stands and walks to the mantelpiece.

I notice a photograph – a beautiful girl, his daughter. A photograph from his wedding, Ezra and Mae before an old white church up in Amenia Union. And there is one final photograph – of Ezra and another man.

'I'd follow from a distance at first, observing, enjoying. He'd spend weekends at the Wannsee with his family, sitting by the beach, enjoying a Weissbier or what have you. I'd always carry a *Berliner Zeitung* for cover. People were less suspicious in those days, more open to coincidence.'

He studies my face for a moment.

'Make no mistake, I realize all this sounds relatively untoward, I realize that, but stay with me. We had a connection, this man and I. Granted, not one he knew about, but that doesn't mean a connection isn't there. One cat doesn't have to know it's related to another cat to drink from the same bowl. So I would watch him, and I would see in him what I had. Except here was a guy who kept his head up, who kept his eyes on the eyes of others, who was *present*. He was living in the moment, and in those moments I would see what I hadn't done. I wanted to know him, because of course I wanted to *be* him. Him, with his beautiful wife. Him, still talking to his beautiful daughter, the kind of daughter whose eyes could light up the sky.'

My eyes found the pictures once more for just a second. He notices but moves on.

'So one day I engineered a meeting. I made sure I was wearing a suit just like the suit he always wore on the days he was going to the meetings that had to go well. I remember it, it was an Anthony Sinclair, a Conduit Cut I bought one frisky afternoon I was feeling flush in Mayfair. And I stood next to him on the Kurfürstendamm, and I said, "My God, we could be *family*!"'

He slaps the table, delighted, and there is a moment of true joy in his eyes. He has spilled a slick of coffee and he wipes it with one hand, sweeping across the plastic tablecloth with its fields and flowers and kittens so its presence might not distract us any further.

'And he laughed, this guy who would actually *become* like a young brother to me, and we talked about where we got our suits and I remember I took an umbrella just like his too, and the next day we met up again at the same place and now we were talking.'

His eyes soften.

'And so it was, for a few years,' he says. 'Just wonderful.'

'And then?' I say, curious.

'Well, and then …' he says, his smile fading to nothing. 'I'm afraid to say that was when I *royally* fucked it up.'

twenty-one

'That was pretty bloody weird,' I said, staring straight ahead as we rode the bus over Westminster Bridge.

'Well, you're the one walking around calling yourself Tom Ditto.'

'I have literally never called myself that,' I said, briefly checking behind me. 'But the philosophy of this whole thing ... the history ...'

She breathed on the window, rubbed out the breath with her hand.

'History doesn't matter. That's just stuff that happened. It's all about the present. And it's not like CC is this huge thing – though they said it could have been, once. The important thing is to find a different way of subscribing to life.'

I fell silent. I was building up to something and she knew it.

'So can I ask you a question?'

'No.'

'Why?'

'Because you're going to ask who Jeremy is. And I don't want to talk to you about Jeremy.'

'Why don't you want to talk about Jeremy?'

'I just don't.'

'It seems important to you, you and Jeremy,' I said, quickly turning again.

'There *is* no me and Jeremy. Why do you keep turning around?'

'In case Felix is suddenly sitting right behind me. He freaks me out a bit.'

She turned to me.

'Can I ask *you* something?'

'Yes?'

'Right now, Felix and Andy and Tim and Jackie are probably talking about what a cute couple we make. Just because we've been spending time with each other. Just because I'm helping you.'

'Helping me? That's how you see it?'

'People always say that men and women can't be friends, like it's a fact.'

'Isn't it a fact?'

'No. Men and women can be friends, it just depends on how important friendship is to you.'

'That specific friendship?'

'Friendship in general. Why can't they be a friend, if having a friend is the most important thing? If having a friend is what you need?'

'Who are your friends?' I asked, because I hadn't really thought about it before.

'Stay on topic,' she said. 'Of course men and women can be friends. Why does no one say to gay guys, oh, well, you like men so you can no longer have any male friends? It's ludicrous.'

She turned to me.

'Are *we* friends?'

'Of course we're friends,' I said, more out of instinct than anything.

'What makes us friends?'

'I dunno,' I said. 'We like each other?'

She smiled, nodded to herself.

'And we don't have to be anything but friends,' she said.

'Well … that's good to know.'

'Do you know what I mean, though? There'll be people who think we want to be together, or who think we should be together, or who think that one day we'll get together, but we won't, will we?'

I shook my head.

'I've got no plans to,' I said.

She hugged me, tight.

'*Thank* you,' she said.

I didn't know how to feel. I'd been rebuffed. I hadn't even been trying to buff.

The bus slowed.

'Who's Jeremy?' I asked.

London Zoo needs to survive like any other institution. Gift shops and cafés and ice creams just don't cut it. Now you can rent suites there to celebrate your twenty-first. You can get married there, swapping rings while an alpaca slathers by. And now it had extended its 'Zoo Lates'. The zoo closes, the kids go, it quietly opens up again for the city's singles, marrieds and others to mix, drink and point at animals. You know immediately who to avoid – anyone dressed up as an animal. Girls with tiger ears, that sort of thing. But the rest of it ... pop-up bars, street food, animal talks ... I mean, why didn't I go out more?

'Why did everyone think it was such a big deal for you to bring me here?' I said.

'You're full of questions, aren't you? Can I remind you of our deal?'

'What deal?'

'I can ask you anything. You can ask me nothing.'

I didn't remember specifically agreeing to this deal. She whipped out what looked like an ID card.

'So you do work here?'

'You're still asking questions,' she said. 'I used to volunteer here. This is just a membership card. I know about animals, it's like a thing. I once followed a cat.'

Something in my pocket vibrated. I could only hope it was my phone.

'Sorry, you once followed a cat?' I said, bringing the phone out and glancing at the screen.

Pippy.

'It was a lean night. No one around. I saw this cat and it just seemed so calm and in control, you know? Serene. Spellbinding. So I followed it for a few minutes and we ended up on this bench and we just sat there – *being*.'

Jesus.

'Hey, Pippy,' I said, answering my phone, moving off to one side, still glancing at the woman who'd followed a cat. Maybe my shift had been cancelled. Please say my shift had been cancelled.

'Just FYI,' she said. 'Leslie is out of hospital.'

'Oh,' I said.

'He broke both his arms.'

'Right …'

'Now they're in plaster, which means he can't operate his own faders.'

I put my hand to my mouth in horror.

'He is absolutely furious. He says you're to blame. He called you his curse.'

'I'm not to blame!'

'He's supposed to get his official pictures taken tomorrow for Sunrise and wanted to do his thumbs-up pose. He says he's done his thumbs-up pose at every radio station he's worked at for twenty years and now he won't be able to.'

'Are his thumbs still visible?' I said, and Pia scrunched up her nose in confusion.

'Well, he's got *permanent* thumbs-up now, hasn't he?' said Pippy. 'They're the only things you can see! Anyway, he says you've ruined his life and you'll rue the day. Where are you, by the way?'

'I'm just at the shops,' I lied.

Somewhere, an elephant trumpeted.

A pause.

''Kay then, bye.'

Poor Leslie.

'Come on – this way,' said Pia, making her decision. 'We need to go round here …'

She led me away from the crowds, and round a corner. A man with his face painted like a walrus zipped up his flies and walked away from the bushes sheepishly. We ignored this.

'We need to find Ash,' she said. 'He should be working tonight …'

'Absolutely not,' he said. 'Absolutely not.'

'You owe me,' said Pia, with a quiet aggression I found unnerving, like she was a tiny Mafioso thuggishly demanding protection money.

'Who's this guy?' said Ash.

'Tom. He's a newsreader.'

He shrugged, not understanding the relevance.

Ash was tall and gaunt with a thin mouth and sideburns that didn't quite know what they were there for. He was carrying a bucket and stank of God knows what, his green overalls patchy and dark round the ankles. He'd been a volunteer around the same time as Pia – which I guessed from their conversation was maybe three years ago – but now he was full-time at the zoo.

'I never asked you for anything,' she said. 'I'm just asking for this. Just five minutes.'

Ash thought about it.

'I will be sacked.'

'You won't be sacked. No one will know. Please. You know why I haven't been back.'

Ash's eyes softened.

'What the hell are we doing?' I said, with what I thought was quite a light delivery.

'Shush your lips up!' she said, suddenly very northern.

We crept in, the door creaking behind me, Pia leaving the keys and electronic fob at the entrance as promised.

This was insane. This was illegal. Surely it was illegal.

'Careful it doesn't lock behind us,' she said, low voice, and I nodded my understanding, feeling around in my pocket for a coin or something to stop the lock clicking shut. 'This is where I used to come ...'

'Won't Ash say anything?' trying to find a way out of this.

'Ash owes me. Ash knows what I saw.'

She said it with quite some conviction.

She unlocked another door, a high one, and we stepped up and onto the platform behind it – the keepers' entrance.

'Tom ... meet the gang.'

Inside, a dozen tiny marmosets slept. The sound of small breaths, squeaks of air through nostrils like pin pricks.

It was ... amazing.

'So these are ...'

'Geoffroy's marmosets,' she said. 'We used to call them our babies.'

'That doesn't seem healthy to me,' I said, and she dug me in the ribs.

She looked different, now. Like she was at peace.

'So was this where you met ... you and ...?' I tried, hoping she'd finish the sentence, break down a wall, let me in, but she didn't.

But I knew this was why coming here was such a big deal. She hadn't been back. She couldn't. She'd met Jeremy here. Worked with him, perhaps. Or maybe split up with him here. Whatever it was, it was hard for her. But she'd brought me anyway.

'Pia – thank you for this,' I said, and as I kneeled down, two small, wet black eyes blinked open as a marmoset registered me for the first time. 'It feels like a privilege.'

Pia grabbed my arm.

'Things have been ... unusual lately. I've had no one to—'

'Ssh,' she said. '*Ssssh!*'

'Sorry,' I whispered. 'They're sleeping, and—'

'*Sssssh!* for Christ's sake!'

The grip tightened. Was someone coming? Someone must be coming.

But total silence.

What *was* this girl's problem?

And then, behind us, I heard the noise of a wastepaper basket suddenly rocking on its base.

'Pia!' I whispered.

'What was that?'

I turned around. I couldn't see anything to worry about.

'The wind?' I tried.

'FUCK!' she hush-shouted, now crouching, eyes darting.

Marmosets began to stir.

'SHIT!'

'WHAT?' I replied, eyes widening in the dark, still adjusting, panic rising though I couldn't work out why yet. '*What?*'

She punched my arm, hard.

'BINKY!' she shouted.

'What? What does *that* mean?'

'Binky's out! Binky's out!'

'What's a Binky?'

She slapped the walls – brick walls painted green to look nothing like the jungle – until she found the switch ... the *blink-blink-blink*

of fluorescent lights above … then the slam of the enclosure door as
she panicked and moved.

'Shit!' she said, pointing at the door we'd come through. I'd
propped it open with the fire extinguisher. She'd said it could lock
behind us. I was trying to be helpful!

She leaned down, counted the marmosets she could see.

'NO!'

'What?'

She punched my arm again as she stood.

'Gone!'

'What is?' I said, playing dumb, hoping if I just kept asking
questions like this I'd never get an answer I didn't want to hear.

'A *marmoset*!' hissed Pia.

'What – because of *us*?'

'Oh, no,' she said. 'He's probably been planning it for years.
He'd probably made himself a tiny ladder out of toothpicks. *Yes*,
because of us.'

'When we opened the door?'

'Are you the thickest man in Britain? Yes – *when we opened the
door*! More specifically, when you *propped it open* instead of *sticking
it on the latch*!'

Better solution, right there. Wow. You read about these things
happening. But usually they happen for good reason … animal
activists, anti-vivisectionists. Not just a girl wanting to show a boy
some marmosets she used to know. Her eyes shot up to the security
camera. The slow, judgmental blink of a green light underneath.

'Right, what do we do?' I said.

'We call Ash,' she said. 'Then we look for him.'

'Binky's a boy?'

'Yes?'

'Binky's a weird name for a boy.'

'Oh God, Binky's out.'

'Well – at least Binky's in a zoo.'

'Yes, he's in a zoo, where they keep *wild hunting dogs* and *lions*. They all get on so well, it's like *Madagascar 3* in here.'

Maybe we should call someone. Security. Or the police. We need to lock down the zoo. You can't have marmosets running about. What if it attacked someone? Who would they sue? Us, or the zoo? Hopefully the zoo.

Oh good God, we're going to be sued.

'Call Ash!' I said. 'Call Ash!'

'Ash is on his final warning. Oh, God, Ash'll get sacked for this!'

'Maybe it's not so bad!'

'We've released an animal into London. That's what has happened here. It's 9.55pm on a Wednesday night and we've released an animal into London.'

'Should we—'

'We should go, yes.'

We looked for Binky as we skulked through the shadows. We kept our heads down to avoid the cameras, though it was a bit late now. We'd just have to hope they wouldn't notice. Or that Binky would make his own way back out of some kind of loyalty to London Zoo's corporate brand. Or that he'd get hungry and faint somewhere safe.

'Ash,' Pia whispered into her phone. 'Binky's out!'

I could hear Ash screaming, all distant, tinny rage.

Pia shrugged and hung up.

We headed south, two green London Zoo caps we'd found in the enclosure pulled low over our heads, and we padded on, away from the Rainforest Life area, past the reindeers and otters, under the bridge, the lovebirds to our left, and through a weak point in the gates where a late 274 to Baker Street sped over Prince Albert Road.

'This is the worst night ever,' I said, as she sank onto a bench. 'Thanks a lot. You said it was going to be magical.'

'You left a door open in a feeding enclosure. Any loss in magic is your doing. I'm not sure I can take all the blame here.'

'Oh, no. Of course not. I'd probably have just done this anyway tonight.'

She smiled. I'd punctured the clouds.

'Are marmosets dangerous?' I said, genuinely curious.

'They're about six inches tall,' she said. 'So yes, to you, they probably are.'

A pause.

'It's just a marmoset,' I said, bewildered. 'At least he's harmless.'

And she started to laugh.

'Like Leslie,' she said.

'What?'

'Armless.'

And now I was laughing.

'That is honestly the worst joke I have ever heard,' I said.

'I'm sorry,' she said. 'I've been looking for a way to work that in for ages …'

And we kept laughing, as the relief of escaping hit us, and the remaining and terrible ramifications started to come at us.

'Could we get *arrested*?!' I tried to say, a moment of horror suddenly upon me.

'We could get *arrested*!' she spluttered back, realising along with me but finding it funnier somehow.

'We must be on about sixty cameras!' I said. 'Me, you and a marmoset called Binky.'

And that's when she really lost it, right there on that pavement, under the moonlight, and as I looked at her laughing, she looked so pretty, like something had lifted from her, some great weight, and I knew that I had helped her somehow, and something made me want to hold her close, and made me want to kiss her.

I suppose the best way of putting it is that the night felt like ours. It felt like we owned it, like more and more these days the night didn't own me, like the darkness had lifted, and the laughter continued as we grabbed some wine from the wine shop and bickered over what flavour crisps to buy and headed back to mine, but the laughter soon stopped as I opened the door and stared, slack-jawed, at the suitcase sitting right in the centre of the hallway.

twenty-two

I'd never have bought a suitcase like that. I'd never thought about it before – suppose I just accepted that it existed and it was in our flat – but bright pink, glossy, hard shell … that didn't feel like it could ever have been in my place.

It was a mid-size, though, so I'd been right – she'd kept her options open. And now here she was.

Back.

'Where is she?' Pia whispered, eyes wide. 'I should go, right?'

I was a few steps ahead of her. I could hear the TV burbling away – some repeat, *A Question of Sport*, I think – and see the low light of the table lamp framing the doorway like a halo.

I pushed it open, inch by inch, and my knees weakened and my heart hurt as I saw her, lying there, asleep on the sofa, Grandma's blanket over her, remote in one hand, cold cup of tea on the floor by her phone. I stared at her, this girl I thought I'd known, and then I felt a hand on my elbow and I let it pull me back, away, outside.

'Are you okay?' said Pia, quietly, out front.

I didn't think I was. I felt shaky. Weak. Relieved. Angry. Grateful. Everything.

'I don't think this is fair of her,' she said, crossing her arms, and now I wanted to laugh. 'Sod this. Sod her.'

And then: 'You can stay at mine tonight.'

She held her hand out to me, awkwardly. Lip half-bit, risking something of herself, vulnerable. Up until now, I'd tried to respect this deal I didn't know we had, and I'd done it out of instinct, to protect what we had, whatever that was. I didn't ask her questions. She didn't give me answers.

Also, of course, that was the path of least resistance. Now? Well, now I had to make a call.

'I don't know what to do,' I shrugged.

'Tell her to get lost,' she said.

'P, I want to talk to her,' I said. 'I want to find out what happened.'

She shook her head.

'Don't. Don't look back. Just look forwards. It won't do you any good to look back. That's not what all this has been about.'

'"All this?" All this what?'

'Us. The stuff we've done. It's been about progress. "Subscribing to life in a different way".'

'Look,' I said, as gently as I could. 'Obviously I have to do this. *Obviously* I have to find out.'

'But how will it help?' she said, now a little desperately, hand on my elbow again. 'What do you think you'll find out? Something that'll make it all better? You won't. Whatever you find out will hurt you. It's always the way. It's better not to know. It's better to do your own thing. Why dwell on it all?'

'Because it's human nature to want answers.'

'You're going to get hurt.'

'I've been hurt this whole time. Maybe this is how I can get un-hurt.'

And then, the creak of the door, the sound of a hand sliding up its frame as she stood there, leaning against it, lit by the glow of the streetlamp just beyond us.

'Tom,' she said, cautiously, then: 'Pia.'

A pause, now, as she folded her arms, any moment of warmth dissipating into the night air, rising above us, escaping.

'Well doesn't *this* look cosy.'

twenty-three

She was like an attack dog that wouldn't give up.

She'd changed her hair slightly. It seemed shorter, the curl she used to tuck behind her ear now behind it permanently. What was that on her wrist? Pink and green thread intertwined ... a friendship bracelet, like something you'd pick up on a gap year? Her white t-shirt made a light tan pop – what was the weather like in Paris right now?

All this floated through my head as she stood before me, angry.

For a while I just let her go at me, amazed by it, fascinated.

'So don't you for a second think I don't know exactly what you've done,' she said, quick as lightning, face like thunder. 'Don't you for a second think I don't know how you met her.'

I really didn't think this is how it would go.

Her bravado was incredible. I smirked, and sank down onto the sofa.

'That girl, that Pia, she is odd,' she said. 'She's always been odd. You don't know the half of it – she's a weirdo, Tom, and I know where you met her. I know what you must have done.'

'Then tell me,' I said, staying calm, remaining cool, keeping my cards close.

'You went to the place, didn't you?'

'You don't have to call it the place any more. You can call it what it is.'

'How did you know about it?'

I just watched her, thoughts pinging through her mind, frustration all around her. I'd found her little secret.

'You went and you met the others, didn't you? How? What did they tell you about me?'

I stayed silent. My power was in my silence and it was my first taste of power in a while.

'Because whatever they told you about me, it's bollocks, Tom. I mean – *Jesus*! – how could you? How could you go there?'

'Why do you think I went there?'

I kept my voice flat, like an amateur psychotherapist, putting it all back on her, letting her dig her own hole, letting her throw the rope over the gallows and test its strength, get it ready …

'You went because …' – she faltered, reset – 'I mean, where is the *trust*, Tom? That's what shocks me most. Where is the trust?'

That was bait. She was trying to reel me in. She was always good at that, the baiting, the reeling, and yes, I wanted to bite. But more than that, I wanted to see what she was fishing for; what she'd say next; how her mind worked; how this could somehow be my fault. I was looking at her clearly now, trying to remain emotionless, acting like a fight technician.

'I told you I hadn't gone,' she said, near wailing, but with top notes of anger. 'I *told* you – I was very clear about it – that you should just carry on. You should have trusted that I was doing something I needed to do. That maybe it was something I needed to do for *us*.'

Oh, but that was it. She did this *for us*?

'What, you just disappearing one day?' I snapped, and she took a step back, allowed me the floor, almost relieved it was someone else's turn to speak. 'Leaving me some cryptic bullshit note? What did you think that would do to me?'

'It wasn't about you, Tom. Not everything is about you.'

The selfish card. That was quick.

'This *was* about me. This was about me being left on my own for no apparent reason and me being the only person not to know. It could have *destroyed* me, Hayley.'

She stood fast. No backing down. I pulled out one of my big guns.

'You had a *leaving do*.'

'You're annoyed you weren't invited?'

'Annoyed?' I said, and was she *kidding*? 'No, I'm not "annoyed" I wasn't invited. You think the worst thing about all this was not being invited to a leaving do? Annoyed is not a word that figures in this. You get annoyed a bus is late, you get annoyed a colleague speaks in hashtags.'

I stood up.

'And how dare you talk about "trust"?'

'You went snooping around behind my back.'

'You disappeared!'

'I told you to just carry on!'

'You left me.'

'You should have trusted me.'

'You shouldn't have gone. But it was worse than that, because you wouldn't even admit to me that you had.'

'I didn't leave you!'

'No, you did worse. You threw me in limbo to go God knows where with God knows who. Except I do know. And believe me, you can slate Pia all you want, but you left me to go and do one of the strangest, most pathetic things I've ever heard about. I feel sorry for you. That's my overwhelming feeling right now. And I know that's something people usually say in soap operas or films when they want to take the moral high ground and hide that they've been hurt, but with me it is absolutely true. I, Tom, feel sorry for you, Hayley.'

She steadied herself on a chair, then sat.

Silence.

'Why do you do it?' I said. 'Why do you follow?'

She said nothing, just looked up at me, all doe-eyed, a real Princess Di of a look, and without warning the words began to tumble out of her like she'd had them ready for years.

Hayley Grace Anderson was not who I thought she was, but more than that, she was never who I thought she'd been.

She'd sat me down, when we'd first met, and taken me through her photographs. Happy summer days, life outdoors, green green fields and bunting. Some big manor house of a school, a life ruled by hockey and lacrosse, and as far away from the grey custard and cold chips of my Fishponds state school as she could get.

They'd shown me, I thought, a girl well brought-up, well adjusted, happy. I knew now these showed the best days of her life.

She'd been sent off to boarding school aged twelve, away from her parents five days a week, and just floating, longing to belong. Soon, she found herself hanging out with the most popular girl in her year. They became inseparable, the friendship bright and vital. Except that girl had a family to go to. Except that girl had friends outside, friends from back home. Hayley demanded more and more from her – her commitment, her time, and her love – until her friend turned on her. Cut her off. Her whole identity depended on that girl, who broke her heart and left her with nothing.

'I think on some levels I've always done it,' she said, her eyes filling and pleading with me. 'I've always adapted who I am based on what I thought people wanted me to be. Or what they wanted to hear, so I could be closer to what I wanted ... I was never myself until I could be someone else ... maybe my personality isn't strong enough, or maybe that is my personality, but it's who I've always been ... it made me efficient. At making friends. Contacts. And it makes me scared, Tom, because do I want what I want, or do I just want what other people seem to want? Have I lost who I am? Is it too late for me?'

I began to understand, I think.

To protect herself, that first time, Hayley had needed another Someone Special. And that had become the story of her life. Change, adapt, please, all to satisfy this need to be liked. And then, at a university she personally wasn't drawn to, while doing a course someone else's heart was in, she met an American student in a low-down dive bar who drank red wine and smoked Spanish tobacco and acted like the wisest twenty-three-year-old the world had ever seen. He told her about Ezra Cockroft's theories. They so chimed with her own that she fell in love with them. She studied them, became if at first not a convert then at least an enthusiastic amateur.

'And it worked!' she said, now, here, in our flat. 'I made some of my best friends that way ... Fran ... Laura ...'

I nodded. I didn't have the heart.

'I found *you* through it,' she said, and she grasped for my hand. 'I get it,' I said, moving it away. 'I get all that.'

She looked up, hopeful.

'But why do you take it to such extremes?'

'What do you mean?' she said, tears in her eyes, mopping one away with the end of her jumper, this girl I'd loved, so vulnerable now, so fragile in my hands.

'Come on,' I said. 'A pop star.'

'You mean—'

'A *pop star*, Hayley,' I said, gently. 'That's the really sad thing.'

She sniffed, wiped another eye. I felt the urge to do it for her, but some part of me that felt stronger now resisted. Maybe just to *show* her.

But 'I don't understand?' she said, and though I should have been angry with her for continuing to play this game, I couldn't be too harsh, I couldn't destroy her.

'Aphra,' I said, just to show I knew. 'You followed Aphra to Paris.'

She sniffed again, and looked up at me with those great big eyes, ready for redemption.

'Tom,' she said quietly, that Princess Diana look making its comeback now: 'What the hell are you talking about?'

She denied it. Denied, denied, denied. Did admit one thing, though.

'Cockroft ...' – an apologetic smile; the first sign of any remorse – 'well, he taught that when we have to deal with something painful, it's okay not to know what to say,' she said. 'He said there are techniques you can use until you're strong enough to handle it yourself.'

'Like?'

'Like "externalising your feelings using pre-established thoughts".'

I shook my head. No idea.

'If someone else has said it better, say it the way they said it.'

'Copy them?'

'A line from a film, a poem, whatever.'

'Plagiarism.'

'Using what's around you.'

'So your postcard—'

'Used song lyrics. It was at number one. The words just fit. I could say what I wanted to say without having to worry about how to say it. It was on the radio all the time, like a sign.'

'But what about Paris?' I said.

'I wasn't in Paris,' she said, dismissively. 'I just *went* to Paris.'

'You just went to Paris. That's the same as being in Paris.'

'I went to Paris for a *little while*, cleared my head, then I came home and stayed at, you know, with people.'

'What people? You've been here the whole time? *What* people?'

Say Laura. Say Fran. Then I'd catch you out.

'Annie,' she said. Her sister. I *knew* she knew. 'You need to give me some space. You need to trust me again.'

I wanted to scream, but our negotiations had become delicate. If I pushed the jealous boyfriend angle that's all we'd talk about. And besides, another thought had come to me.

'Did you listen to the show?' I said.

I don't know why it was important. Maybe if I knew she'd listened, I'd know she wanted to hear my voice, to hear how I was, and maybe it'd be like we were still connected somehow.

'No,' she said. 'That would have defeated the object. My plan was to detach for a while. That's what they call it when you see it through – detachment. You detach from your old life to find how to make it new. You work out what's important.'

'And did you find it?'

She welled up as she looked at me, reached out for my hand, and said, 'Yes, Tom, I think so.'

I thought about what else to ask her, but her eyes flitted up to the clock in the corner of the room, and she said 'Do you mind if we knock it off for tonight? I'm just so, so tired …'

I had a thousand more questions.

'I love you, Tom,' she said, and my eyes pricked with tears, because despite it all that's what I'd wanted to hear, but to avoid her eye I looked around the room, then up at the clock myself for the first time.

Uh oh.

[8]

Cockroft nurses his drink back at Keen's.

For the first time, he has ordered his own drink, an Old Crow, ignoring my Bud.

'The man I saw,' he says, bourbon swirling, catching the light. 'He was at a wonderful point in his life. He was making decisions that I hadn't made. Being the husband and father I hadn't been.'

'And you wanted to – what did you say? – "piggyback his joy"?'

'That makes it sound childish, but yes,' he says. 'And then, when I became strong enough, it became important to me that our friendship was real. I was, I like to think, like an older brother to him. A father, maybe. A mentor? I don't know. But I wanted it to be built on something real.'

'So you told him?'

'So I told him. I told him our meeting was not chance,' he said. 'That I had spent six months studying him from a distance. That I had engineered our friendship based on his choices.'

'You don't mention his name in your book.'

'His name does not matter. His name is not who he is. It was not his choice. It was someone else's.'

'I'd like to know.'

'His name was Andreas,' he says.

He takes a hit of his drink and then shifts in his chair as a new thought comes to him. It is like he is a surfer who has seen a new wave which will take him far away from this

'To meet your follower can cause distress. But the *world* it opens up is *too great to ignore*. To be effective, it must be quiet, covert, hidden.'

He is passionate now; almost preaching.

'You defend it despite everything.'

'It has the potential to radically improve—'

'What happened?' I say, interrupting. 'With Andreas?'

'What is there to say?' he says, and he seems almost physically to deflate. 'I came clean, in 1971, in a bar on Friedrichstraße.'

'And what *happened*?'

'He detached.'

twenty-four

'*It's 8.01 on July 19th, I'm Tom Adoyo with the stories you're waking up to ...*'

I had a feeling this was going to be difficult. Not because I'd barely slept an hour. But because of what had made the news.

I dreaded getting there. Slowed my stories right down. Threw to Cathy James reporting live on a pile-up on the M25 and just let her talk, and when she finished, asked her about it some more. I told myself I was just making the most of a rare outside broadcast. You had to do that with OBs. Even ones just on the phone. *Faux*-B's.

'*... and finally ...*'

Well, I'd put it off as long as I could. The release had only come in on the wires in the last forty minutes. I'd kept it out of the 7.30, because that's when our audience is at its peak. I kept it for the 8, because that's when people are brushing their teeth. They've done research.

'*... some breaking news this morning ...*'

Brace yourself, Tom. Keep brushing, everyone. Drown this out ...

'*... a spokesman for London Zoo revealed in an early-morning statement ... that one of their marmosets is missing.*'

Just. Act. Normal.

I looked up. Behind the glass, eight complete strangers were staring at me.

'*The ... six-inch primate was last seen yesterday evening ...*'

Who the hell were they?

'*... and is now presumed to be on the loose in the capital ...*'

Please say there's no such thing as the Monkey Police.

'*The marmoset is not considered dangerous, but experts say ...*'

'There's a *monkey* on the loose in *London*?' said Cass, interrupting me, eyes mock-surprised, and my heart sank, because now we were going to talk about this. 'Why isn't this a bigger story?! Why's *this* an "and finally"?'

It was a good point. I suppose I'd tried to make it 'fun'. But no, there was essentially a wild animal on the run in one of the world's highest-populated cities. Best not draw attention to it.

'A monkey!' said Cass, again, and the eight people – now joined by Mick from Sales – all started laughing, silently, behind the double-walled glass.

'A marmoset has escaped, yes,' I said, giving in. 'It's not actually a monkey, it's a primate, but yeah, that general area. They're from the Atlantic rainforests of Southeast Brazil. Average lifespan of ten years.'

'So it could be out there for the next *ten years*?'

I now wished I hadn't said that.

'And this is news just in?' she said.

'New news, yes,' I said, keen to move on. 'That being the nature of news.'

'Well, we have to ask: have *you* seen the missing monkey?' she said, switching to presenter mode.

'*Primate*,' I said.

'Text us if you have ... maybe you saw him in Budgens, eyeing up a leg of lamb. Wherever you saw ... er ...'

'Binky.'

Binky! The indignity of that name. I could sense the eight people staring at us, mouthing the name 'Binky'.

And for something so throwaway, the texts came thick and fast.

'Graham in Swanley says – *I saw Binky dressed up as former French president François Mitterrand, trying to start an anti-sausage rally outside a butchers.*'

Cass laughed that laugh, charming London, provoking a smile even from me.

'Penny in Notting Hill – *I saw Binky the marmoset teaching a cat how to drive a van.*'

'More stuff like that,' said Cass, during the ads. 'That's what we should be doing in the eight. Warm-up in the six, proper news in the seven, bit of fun in the eight. Nice one Tom.'

'Weather today?' asked that engineer, shovelling a bacon sandwich into his mouth.

'Highs of nineteen,' I said.

'That was great, that monkey stuff,' said Bron, as we walked out of the studio. 'Well done Tom.'

'Who were those people staring at us?' I said.

'The Pringles people. Thinking of sponsoring the show.'

'Oh, God, really?' said Cass. 'So it'd say, "London Calling with Cass Tailor and Pringles"? I'm not sure I want my name constantly followed by Pringles.'

'It would actually be, "*London Calling with Cass Tailor and Brand New Pringles Cheese, Chilli & Chives – For When Your Mouth Wants a Party!*"' said Bron, nodding.

'Oh, great,' said Cass. 'So it'll just sort of blend in.'

I checked my phone quickly while they bickered. I'd texted Pia when I'd arrived at work. I didn't even know if she'd got home safely. But no reply. Just an email from Maureen telling us someone had spilled coffee in the kitchenette again.

'So Brand New Pringles Cheese, Chilli & Chives aside, we're using the monkey texts for promos throughout the day,' said Bron. 'Also, I think we need to go bigger on it.'

Cass agreed.

'Definitely. We need to own this story.'

'Yeah?' I said. 'Really, I mean?'

'God yeah,' said Bron. 'For sure.'

We actually owned it more than they knew. I checked my phone again, as if in the last few microseconds Pia might have texted. Maybe she'd been listening.

'So you should get down to the zoo this morning,' said Bron, and that snapped me out of it.

'Sorry?'

'Phone the PR, get an interview, try and find out how this happened.'

'You want me to actually go to the zoo?' I said. 'Where they lost the marmoset? You want me to physically go there?'

'You understand English, that's great.'

I can't go back! It's been less than twelve hours!

'But it's an *animal* story,' I tried, and then: 'I have a bold and brave idea.'

'Yes?'

'We send Work Experience Paul. I've been studying him. He's raw, sure, but he's hungry and I think he's ready.'

Work Experience Paul stood up, puffed out his chest, then quickly let it deflate.

'I'm actually not sure I *am* ready,' he said. 'I've done, like, literally zero since I got here.'

'Look,' I said, hands open, shoulders up. 'Is this all really that big a deal?'

I tried to make it sound like absolutely nothing at all.

'There is a monkey on the loose in London and *someone is to blame*,' said Bron. 'So yes. Yes, it is.'

I grabbed my Marantz from a drawer full of pads and checked its batteries. I was sluggish, finding it hard to push through thoughts of Hayley. I searched my desk for headphones.

She'd denied the whole Aphra thing flat out. It was laughable. And she said she didn't remember putting all the Post-it notes in the magazines, that it had to be coincidence or something, but I saw through it all. This was embarrassment. Pure and simple. I'd caught her out, this star-struck girl, acting like the least mature teenager of all time, and now she wanted to prove she was an adult. But at least she was back. At least there was that. Now I could question her. I could be in control. Let there just be some calm after the storm, some moment to gather our thoughts before we decide what to do.

Because whatever happened next would be my choice.

And yes, I know I should have just said 'you're dumped, get out'. But how do you do that, practically? They can't just pack a bag and go. They need to find the next place, you need to work out the bills, you need to see if you untangle your emotions, understand, forgive them or forget them.

No matter what my fantasies had been – a dignified goodbye, perhaps, a stirring and articulate speech, her standing in the doorway with one packed bag and two eyes full of tears as I apologised like a gentleman then slowly closed the door in her face, standing philosophically by the window as I watched her trudge down the path, her shoulders shaking as she cursed herself through the tears for letting the best thing that ever happened to her slip away – the reality changes when they're a real person again. She was there, in our flat, like nothing had happened.

I looked at my phone. Silence from Pia. I should call her.

'You look cream-crackered, mate,' said Pippy, placing what she would always call a 'posh coffee' on my desk. Posh because it wasn't made with a hot tap, I suppose.

'Is that for me?' I said, sort of touched. Maybe the world was okay.

'What, that?' she said. 'No, it's mine. So what's up? Not "heading up the wooden hill to Bedfordshire" early enough?'

'Hayley's back,' I said.

'What?' she said, sensing gossip, sinking to ear level to keep this between us. 'She's back?'

'Last night. Out of the blue.'

'What did she say?'

'That she never left me and that now she's back.'

'That's it? No sorry?'

'No sorry.'

'*So* messed up dot com! What are you going to do?'

I shook my head, slowly. I had no idea dot org.

She sensed the well had run dry and let her grin fade.

'Your best mate's in the building,' she said, standing back up.

My best mate?

'Hello, sir!' he said, striding down the corridor, fresh out of the studios of Harmony, flanked by a stern-looking pair. He stopped, a wave of aftershave joining us a moment later.

'Oh,' I said, looking around, just in case it wasn't me he remembered or recognised.

'Publicity trail,' he said. 'Got that BBC One thing starting tonight. Modern day Spartacus, set in the banking world. Off to LA later. You?'

'I'm off down London Zoo.'

'Ha ha!' he ha-ha'd, flashing a classic Channing smile. 'You serious? I think I know why. The monkey thing, right? *Classic*. Newsreader on the station I was just on was on about it. Guys – this is Tom – *Tom*, right? – I had a very entertaining night with him at the Randolph. You remember the Jam Nazi thing I showed you, yeah?'

'OhmyGodI*loved*that,' said the woman, all sleek PR hair and Mulberry Alexa, while the man – brogues with no socks, pastel shirt under dark McQueen jacket, a manager maybe – showed just a notch above no interest, checking his phone instead.

'Well, behold the genius behind it.'

'Not exactly,' I said, as now the girl broke off to take a call. 'It was more of a mistake, really.'

'A happy accident.'

'*No, there's no statement on that at this stage,*' said the girl, moving away, and Matthew raised his eyebrows at me to register trouble he could doubtless charm his way out of. '*No, we'll be making no comment on that at all.*'

'I sent it to Oliver Stone, did I tell you I was going to do that? He sent it to Matt Damon. Apparently he plays it to people at parties.'

'Oh,' I said. 'Good …'

'Apparently Mila Kunis does the most wonderful Leslie impression.'

'I'll tell him,' I said. 'And then I'll explain who Mila Kunis is.'

'I've got your number, yeah? Take care.'

He slapped me on the shoulder and walked away, *Team Matthew* on the march, out onto the streets of London, a Mexican wave of clammy hands reaching for cameraphones in its wake.

I texted Pia again.

'*Bloody hell. You'll never guess where I am.*'

Send.

I sat with a Styrofoam cup of weak mahogany-brown coffee in a soulless room to one side of the zoo. I was not expecting this to be fun. My neck prickled, I felt flushed, like I was on enemy territory – a spy about to be found out and dealt with.

Opposite, a PR called Tabitha had done her best to welcome me politely, but insisted on staying 'just to make sure you get everything you need'.

It seemed sinister. I tapped the table with a pen shaped like a giraffe.

'He'll be here any second,' she said, not looking up from double-thumbing her Blackberry.

'And this guy, he's …?'

'An expert,' she said, still not looking up. 'One of our keepers. But if you can remember to keep the focus on "let's find Binky!" as opposed to "Binky escaped!", I think that would really—'

She was interrupted by the door swinging open.

A tall, gaunt man stood in the doorway.

We clocked each other.

Tabitha finally put her phone down and looked up.

'This is Ash,' she said. 'Ashley Bilton.'

'Oh,' I said, standing, as the man's eyes registered me properly. *Ash!*

Not knowing what else to do, we shook hands.

'Ash was actually here last night, helping out on Zoo Lates,' explained Tabitha, and Ash shot me a guilty glance. Was I here to drop him in it? Was he going to drop me in it?

'I see,' I said. 'Well, this will just be very quick …'

'Take your time, honestly,' said Tabitha. 'Ask whatever you want. Ash is pleased to help, aren't you, Ash?'

'Oh yes,' said Ash, back stiff as he found his seat, and I smiled at him as we sat for a moment in silence.

How were we going to do this? How were we going to get our stories straight?

'So,' said Tabitha. 'This is for syndicated news, Ash, Tom's here from SoundHaus, and this will go out on …'

'Lots of stations,' I said, nodding, and Ash looked terrified. Why was I suddenly back? Why was I about to probe him on this? Why did I want to *broadcast* it?

'And,' said Tabitha, 'it'll be on Cass Tailor's show …'

'In the morning, yes,' I said. 'In fact we'll be doing a whole phone-in about it. Really getting London involved.'

It is hard to describe Ash's face at this point.

'Let's get started,' said Tabitha.

I turned on my Marantz and held it under Ash's nose. He looked at it, then me, with panic in his eyes. Why was I doing this to him?

'So if you could just introduce yourself …' I said, lightly, like this was all just completely normal. 'Just your name and what you do.'

'My … my name is Ashley Bilton? And I work with marmosets. At the London … at London Zoo.'

His eyes flicked back to me.

'And Mr Bilton … you were in charge the night the marmoset – Binky – escaped.'

'I wasn't in charge,' he said, quite firmly. 'But yes, I was here, yes.'

'And how on earth did that happen?' I said, trying to show Tabitha I meant business and was a professional.

'Well … I work here,' he said.

'No, I mean, how on earth did it happen that a marmoset could escape?'

His eyes were wide. He was scared to put a foot wrong. I smiled, helpfully. *Just take your time, Ash. We'll get through this together.*

'That's a tricky one,' said Ash, not knowing what I wanted him to say, and I realised that maybe I'd come in too hard. I was offending him. I had to soften up.

'But talk me through how that could possibly happen?' I said, making a friendly face and nodding at the microphone. 'That a marmoset could escape a presumably safe environment?'

'Well,' he replied, looking annoyed. 'I suppose someone must have *let him out.*'

My eyes widened. I tried to shake my head without Tabitha noticing.

But: 'Actually, Ash,' she said, 'let's just stick to what we know. Don't want to start flinging accusations about, like a monkey flinging you-know-what about! We'll end up getting someone in trouble!'

She mocked-laughed, so I mock-laughed too. Ash didn't.

'Good point,' I said. 'So Ash … can you describe Binky?'

'Lovely little lad,' he said. 'Real charmer.'

'I meant more physically, in case people spot him.'

'Well, they'll spot a bloody *marmoset*, won't they?'

Tabitha coughed.

'Okay, and just so we know – how did he get out?'

'We are unable to say how he got out at this time,' said Ash, as if he was reading it off a piece of paper, and Tabitha nodded, looking calmer.

'Was there any … CCTV footage at all?' I asked, and I really wanted a specific answer to this one. 'Was anything … *suspicious* spotted?'

Ash sighed, and put on quite a performance to say: 'Somehow the cameras failed in that quadrant of the zoo.'

'Did they?' I said.

'They did,' he said.

'*Did* they?' I said.

'Yes,' he said.

'How *convenient*,' I said.

'I can have another *look*,' he said.

Tabitha dropped her pen, stooped down to pick it up.

Ash mouthed: 'What are you doing?!'

I mouthed: 'I don't know, I'm sorry!'

I reset.

'So we actually don't *know* who if anyone is responsible for this, is what we are both together definitely agreeing here today?'

'Yes,' he said. 'It is a mystery.'

'It could just be something that just happened!'

'That's one of the possibilities I have been keen to promote,' he said.

'And there's no back-up system involving hard-drives that …'

'I'm afraid we suffered significant power outages last night,' said Ash. 'Which could be—'

'How the doors unlocked themselves!' I said, finishing his sentence for him, watching him nod at me, eyes closed. 'Great!'

I caught a glance from Tabitha.

'By which I mean, *great*, well done "technology", God ...!'

I rolled my eyes.

'We are all hoping Binky makes it back to the zoo safely and in one piece,' he said, and from the look on his face, he was saying, *quit while you're ahead*.

'Well thank you, Ash. Thank you very much indeed. For taking care of everything so well.'

Another glance from Tabitha.

'Like the marmosets, I mean.'

Ash sighed.

'I'm not being sarcastic.'

We stared at each other, meaningfully, as Tabitha tried and failed to put her finger on something.

'Can I ask you one thing?' she said, putting her hand on my arm as she walked us out of the room.

'Of course,' I said.

'I heard you this morning on Talk London,' she said. 'And one thing really struck me.'

She stopped, studied my face.

'How did you know the marmoset is called Binky?'

She'd grown colder, now. Her voice less PR, more MI5.

'How do you mean?'

'We didn't name the marmoset in the release. Yet you knew.'

'I think you told me.'

'I've only just met you.'

'You the *zoo*, I mean. I made a phone call.'

'Jesus,' she said. 'Everything's supposed to go through me. I'll look into it. Someone's going to get into trouble over this. Thanks, Tom.'

I grabbed Ash on the way out.

'So we're in the clear?' I said, voice hushed, eyes darting nervously around.

'For now,' he said. 'I took care of what I could. You just better hope Binky shows up, though. The PR department are loving this. They train for it. Usually they go worst-case scenario – a lion or a rhino. Everyone's delighted it's just a bloody marmoset. *Also*, Binky's a complete tool.'

'It seemed a big deal, Pia coming here,' I said.

'Well, yes,' he said. 'It's a special place for her.'

'Why?'

'Didn't you know?' he said. 'It's where she got married.'

'Hey Pia, it's Tom ... listen, sorry it all went a bit weird last night,' I said, waiting for the bus. 'I, um ... well, I wasn't expecting that. Clearly. She ... well, look, we've got a lot to sort through, obviously. But I just wanted to check in with you. Could you call me back?'

I didn't know what to say next. I settled for 'bye'.

I thought about what Ash had told me again.

Married?

Pia was married?

Or she'd *been* married?

It all made more sense now. Her reluctance to talk about her life, about Jeremy, the frostiness in that Wandsworth hotel meeting room at the first mention of his name ...

Do I talk to her about this? She seemed to be ignoring me. Unless this was just her way of giving me space. If it was, it made me uncomfortable. I'd grown used to her. I liked having someone to talk to. Maybe the only person who understood.

My phone vibrated.

'Okay, I'm just going to come straight out with it,' said Pia, as secretly I tried to picture her as a bride. She'd met me off the bus and we walked down the high street as she started to gabble. 'I know you might soften because as hurt as you are you just want something to take away the hurt and the easiest thing would be to take her back. But you shouldn't be with Hayley. You should ditch her and move on because if you're in a bad relationship, you get out, believe me on this.'

I understood now. But to mention I did might seem indelicate. And logically, she was right. But the truth was – and I hated myself for this – I was relieved Hayley was back. It gave me back some control. I could decide what to do, not be decided for – I just needed time. Energy.

'I know that part of you doesn't want to end it properly but that's because she weakened you. She tore down your resolve. She beat you up and now you just want to be wanted again.'

'That's not true.'

'It's classic battered wife syndrome,' she said, nodding, pleading with her eyes. 'Happens all the time. Think of what she put you through, Tom.'

'She went away. And she left me in the lurch and she didn't contact me and I'm angry about all that. I also think maybe it was a kind of breakdown, Pia. Maybe it wasn't technically "cruel". Not compared to what *some* people go through.'

'It was cruel, Tom. She knew what she was doing.'

Maybe she was saying this out of friendship, I reasoned. Or maybe because her own marriage hadn't worked out, because of whatever this guy had done. I studied her face for clues but all I saw was hope.

'Look, maybe I need to be sympathetic for a while and then take a view.'

'Don't put it off, Tom – this is your life.'

'I know,' I said, nodding. 'You're right. I know.'

'Come out with me tonight.'

'Where?'

'Wherever. We don't have to follow anyone. We can just … be.'

I was so tired. I'd barely slept, gone to work and then had to talk about marmosets for ages. I smiled, weakly, shook my head.

She punched my arm.

'Come on. We don't have to go mad. We can be ourselves.'

Ach.

'I'd have to go home first.'

'I understand.'

'I'll call you.'

'I'll wait. But you'll call?'

'I'll call.'

I went home, I slept. All I wanted to do was sleep, lately.

When I woke, Hayley made me some soup. She leaned closer to me, tried to nestle in as I stared blankly at an *All Star Family Fortunes* repeat. I wanted to pull away, but I didn't. I was too tired, too exhausted to not let her.

And I didn't call Pia.

[9]

'You see,' says Cockroft, nudging my ribs. 'This kind of thing happens all too often for my liking.'

He shakes his head, pulls his hat a little further down his forehead. He had been keen to get out there again, to show me the light once more.

We ride the subway from Wall Street to Bleecker.

We had followed a man there and now we were following him back. We decided he may have forgotten his wallet at home.

Cockroft sighs a heavy sigh. I can hear his breathing.

Opposite us, a girl in a t-shirt applies her eye make-up and fiddles with her curls. Her t-shirt says 'Holiday'. There is a picture of another girl on there, with eyeliner and curls of her own.

'You see it more and more these days – that it is easier to live through someone else than to complete yourself,' he whispers, conspiratorially, cheekily, a grin playing around his face, though here, in the light of the subway, he looks older than I've seen him look before.

'That's a quote, right?' I say.

'Betty Friedan,' he says. 'You're catching on, Mister Kosinski.'

He coughs. A long, slow, languorous cough. The winter has been hard for him.

Twenty minutes later and a few steps down from Christopher Street, we sit by the window of the Lion's Head. He's been coming here for years, he tells me, he's seen them all here: Norman Mailer, Frank McCourt, all of them.

'Way I see it, Friedan's right. Living is freedom. An empty highway. There are other cars, sure, and they're all headed in the same direction as you. But where do you turn off? Most of us just keep going, just keep following the herd, sticking to the highway, foot on the pedal, until one day you just get where you were just going.'

I find myself confused.

'Question is,' he says, 'is it better to just go where the road leads, or find your own way there?'

'Surely it's better to find your own way there? Not just follow?'

He shrugs.

'That's what you say in your book. In *Carbon Copy*, you say—'

'You know there are groups now?' he says, and his eyes are a little distant. 'They meet up all over the State. I'd love to go to one of those.'

'In *Carbon Copy*—'

'I know what I said in my book but truth is I'm still finding out, kid,' he says, another cough brewing within. 'Shakespeare said, "We know what we are, but not what we may be."'

'Isn't it strange that you talk of originality, yet you always quote the words of others?' I say, and immediately I wonder if I have said too much.

'No, kid,' he says, shaking his head, putting his hand on mine. 'It is exactly the point.'

We arrive at his apartment and Cockroft struggled with the stairs.

'What was your mistake?' I ask, now that we've spent more time together, and now that I feel I'm able. 'The mistake with your first follow?'

He considers his response, and I see in him the academic.

'My mistake,' he says, pushing his door open, 'was that I should have moved on. I stayed on the one guy. I should have taken what I could and gone.'

He moves to the kitchen in the corner and finds his battered coffee pot.

'You know there are these clubs now all over the world? These "CC Clubs"? Where people get together and they talk about my paper and my book on all this?'

'I do,' I say, and I frown. 'That's why I'm here.'

'That's right,' he says. 'Of course, that's right. Well, I think that's funny. Whole groups dedicated to it. They say it could become a movement. How wonderful that would be.'

He smiles his huge broad smile, and I smile back, but this I do simply to mask my worries.

twenty-five

At home, something was different. There was music.

Editors. *An End Has a Start*.

That's what had been missing from this place. Not just Hayley. Music.

The windows were open, the place was fresh, tidy, brighter somehow.

Hayley was in the kitchen making Bolognese and singing along.

Since she'd been back, she'd been acting like she'd never been away. She was acting like she was auditioning for the part of Girlfriend of the Year in some kind of lighthearted romcom. We didn't talk about it as much as I'd assumed we would; both of us getting used to each other again, circling each other, walking on eggshells. We were polite to one another. Isn't that weird? Like some breakdown in etiquette might lead to all of it pouring out, like lava from a volcano, hot and angry and eating through the earth. For now, we both needed peace, calm. To get used to each other again.

Every now and again a fury would rise in me. But I'd quell it. Dispel it. I needed to think straight. I needed calm. But I knew that every day of calm put me further away from Pia's advice.

There was a small pile of letters on the table, ready to go.

'What are these?' I said, and she popped her head round the corner.

'CVs. I just woke up this morning and realised I need to get started. Can't hang around. There's nothing going at Zara but that feels like an opportunity to me. Why go back to the old life?'

'Some of these are in Bristol,' I said, confused.

She came to me.

'I know you've wanted to go back for ages,' she said. 'And maybe we can.'

I half-smiled. This was too soon, too weird. But part of me wanted it. Her making changes for me.

'I have a job here.'

'That you don't enjoy.'

'That's not true. Things have been changing.'

'But just think how much more they could change. What if we did go to Bristol? I could start fresh there, you could go back to City Sound. Change shift. Get off breakfast.'

I stared at her. She was saying all the right things; all the things I wished she'd said before she went.

'It could be amazing,' she said. 'Going away gave me this fresh perspective. I feel lucky to have you again.'

Again.

'I just needed the space to appreciate what I have. What I hope we can still have.'

I'd been sleeping on the sofa these past few nights. I'd insisted, though she offered me the bed. She'd begged me to tell her if I'd met someone else, if it was Pia, that Iona had told her of their strange night at ours, that Pia had been half naked, freshly showered, acting like she owned the place.

I noticed she'd folded up my duvet, put my pillow away. There were flowers in a bright new vase. She'd put my DVDs back in their cases.

'And this Bristol idea ...'

'We could just see what happens. It's what you used to want.'

I didn't have the words. I should be so angry, still. But what if I repressed it? Let it go? Just went with this? What if it had all been some messed up blip? What if she was right and it needed to happen? To make us stronger?

'I'd follow you there, Tom. I'd follow *you*.'

Pia had texted once or twice after I blew her out.

She'd said it was fine, initially, but there was a tension there now. I knew why she wanted to talk to me. She wanted to make sure I'd ended things. But I was tired. So tired. For right now, I just wanted to be. No more high emotion. No more drama. No more upset or anger. Let me have the calm.

I didn't know if I loved Hayley any more, I thought. Maybe? Not in the same way. But so many couples go through bad times. And this Bristol thing ... I mean, that could sort a lot out, couldn't it? I'd be back on my old turf, my old friends ... I'd have that control I wanted.

'We can find our way out of this,' Hayley said, over avocado, quinoa and kale at that vegan place on the corner, and she kissed my cheek, took my hand.

I still couldn't quite take that.

I pulled away, she bit her lip.

If Pia hadn't followed me that night, then maybe this would be easier. But to have confided in someone, to have had their ear for so long and to have them care about your next move ... because if I hadn't met Pia, I was sure that Hayley coming back would have been the greatest night of my life, so weak, so pathetically grateful would I have been.

Pia had made me stronger.

'Oh!' said Hayley, putting her fork down, remembering something. 'Look.'

She brought a magazine out of her bag.

FASHION. STYLE. FOOD. GLAMOUR. TRAVEL.

For the woman who wants it all – and usually gets it!

'This page here …'

She flicked through, found a mass of Post-it notes, found the one she was looking for.

'What?' I said.

This was brave. She'd avoided the issue of the Post-its, generally. Said she must have done it absent-mindedly, or blamed me. Maybe she'd remembered, or found an excuse. She pointed, still, looked at me, eyebrows raised.

'Well … look at them.'

Shoes.

'Yeah?' she said. 'Come on.'

'What?' I said, again, and she looked surprised.

'Do you really think I'd do that?'

I looked again. Closer.

They were the worst shoes I'd ever seen.

'You would if you were copying …' – I studied the caption – '"*Lindsay Lohan enjoying a rare night off at Spago of Beverly Hills.*"'

She smiled, took a bite of her food.

'What?' I said.

'Nothing,' she said.

'Come on.'

This whole time she'd been building up to something.

'I was just thinking,' she said, clapping the magazine shut and tossing it down on the table. 'Unless Lindsay Lohan's been round … if you had to guess, who else could have done this? Put these Post-it notes in there?'

'You,' I said. 'You, you, you.'

'But who else?' she said.

I shook my head, unsure of what she was trying to say.

twenty-six

So is this just how the world is? You can't trust anyone, is that it?

She'd been all too happy to agree to meet up. I'd texted her. She'd been waiting, she said. She was pleased things didn't have to change just because Hayley was back. I knew if I called her, actually spoke to her, it would all just come spilling out. I wanted to look into her eyes to try and understand why she'd done this to me.

She said she'd meet me in Trafalgar Square at 6pm.

I got there early, standing by the great lions, when I got her text.

Should be there in five minutes. We're just walking up from Downing Street.

I turned to look down Whitehall. All I could see was maybe forty South Korean students in matching tabards and bright white backpacks with little flags on them, all getting ready to cross the road.

And there, in amongst them, right in the middle of the throng – Pia.

She waved, beaming.

'You forget what an amazing city this is until you see it through someone else's eyes,' she said, when she got to me. 'Did you know the Victoria Line was originally going to be called the Viking Line?'

'I didn't.'

'Also on the subject of the tube network, did you know that in 2001 the London Underground introduced its own scent called Madeleine into stations, and that they stopped doing it the very next day because a lot of people said they wanted to vomit?'

'No.'

'Did you know that London's smallest house is three-and-a-half-feet wide and a bunch of nuns live next door?'

'I know what you did, Pia.'

She blinked, confused, took a step back, and I held her gaze.

'I *know*.'

'You know about the murders in the eighties?'

'It's not funny. I know that you put the Post-its in the magazine. It was so mental, so *ridiculous*, but I couldn't see because I'd been blinded by how mental everything else was too.'

'I don't know what you mean,' she said, and she looked little, now, like I'd blindsided her, or tricked her somehow.

'You recognised the song lyrics. And you were just sitting there in that chair and you worked out how to take it further. You made it look like Hayley was some obsessed fan of crappy pop culture because that's all you had time to do. You drew my attention to it and you led me to believe that she'd done something insane.'

'But she *did* do something insane. She left you. I wouldn't leave you.'

'You played games with me.'

'I was protecting you!'

'See, the problem is, I don't think you know what you want, Pia,' I said, trying to be as gentle as possible now, to use these hard words carefully. 'I think you're just as messed up as Hayley in some ways.'

That came out wrong. What I meant was – why can't we all just be cool? Why does everyone have to be *involved* in everything?

'Piss off,' she said, searching around in those pockets for her tobacco.

But I was angry with her – a kind of flat, dulled anger, my pills a wet towel over my rage. And I was tired. I wanted an easy life again. I wanted things to be straightforward. I wanted everyone to be straightforward. Pia was always trying to help me with home truths. Maybe I could help her.

'I think you think if you just keep looking for whatever it is you'll find it. But how can you find it if you don't know what it is?'

She furrowed her brow, narrowed her eyes.

'That's not how life works,' she said. 'That's a life without surprise. You're saying you can only be happy if you *identify* happiness. That's saying you know it all already. You're thinking about things you know. Money or a house or normality or whatever.'

'Isn't that what you want? Isn't that really what you're looking for? You said it yourself once – "don't you want to be normal?"'

'You're talking like that's all there is. What about all the experiences you'd never dreamed of having?'

'What – some new restaurant? Some new coffee you've never tried?'

'No,' she said, forcefully. 'Not just things you can see. Things you can feel.'

'You keep talking about protecting me,' I said, and she shrugged.

'I felt like you needed it.'

'You think I'm a failure that needs cosseting. Well, maybe I just lost control and I needed it back.'

'Why do you think Hayley went?' she said.

'No,' I said. 'Why do you think she came back? It's because she realised she made a mistake.'

She scowled, looked at her feet.

'Truth is,' I said, 'she went, thought about things, regretted it, and came back. That's all. Now, if she'd left me for another man, fair enough, it would hurt but it would be done. At least it's a level playing field. There's no disgrace in that. But I just want to move on. I don't want my life to be a fight. And I don't want people laughing behind my back any more. I won.'

'I never laughed.'

'No, but you get what was in her head. You get this whole failing-at-life-so-I'll-copy-someone-else's thing.'

She blinked at me.

'Failing at life?'

'You know what I mean.'

'You think I'm failing at life.'

It was hard to find the right words. I'd messed up. Around her, the Korean tourists were back, talking loudly and pointing up at Nelson's Column. I noticed Pia was wearing a little flag badge. It made her look child-like, in need of protection, but I had to be strong.

'Look – I just think you and Hayley and for a while me found solace and comfort in relinquishing control.'

'How many times have you rehearsed that sentence? And I have not failed at life.'

'Your marriage broke up. You took it hard.'

She stopped in her tracks, the shock clear in her eyes.

'Who told you?' she said. 'Who told you about—'

'Doesn't matter who told me. And I'm sorry, for the record. But you need to pick yourself up. Stop fucking about.'

'I'm *not* doing that,' she said, a tear forming in the corner of one eye. 'What do you mean? I'm *embracing* life. That's what I've been telling you. CC is a vehicle. And yes, people will think it's weird, of course they will, but "failing at life" is a bit fucking harsh, Tom.'

I went to interject but she hadn't finished.

'You want to talk about failing at life? Failing at life is where you come in. It's hiding away. Quiet as a mouse. Dead inside. Path of least resistance. What's the point of living like that? That's wasting your life. Because some people would give anything to have what you've got, Tom.'

'I've got nothing.'

'You've got *everything*. You can do whatever you like. But what do you do instead? What do you do with your life?'

'Pia, you need to—'

And then I saw.

Her hand was shaking and she leaned against a lamppost to steady herself. She was going to cry now.

'You're so fucking *lucky*, Tom, and you can't even see it. That's all I was trying to do.'

'Pia—'

'But apparently that's failing.'

She started to walk away.

'So let me go and fail somewhere else.'

She turned, one last time, tears streaming down her face.

'But you should leave her, Tom. You should turn around and you should run. You will be very sorry if you don't because it will happen again. It always does.'

She pushed through the cloud of South Koreans and disappeared.

twenty-seven

'God, London is exciting,' she said, holding my hand down by the South Bank. 'You forget, don't you? You need to be away from it to fall in love with it again.'

She looked up at me. Those big eyes, the river behind her.

'I guess so,' I said.

'What shall we do tonight?'

It had been a week. I hadn't heard from Pia. I hadn't tried to contact her. What was the point? She'd taken things too far. It couldn't have lasted. We'd been friends, intense friends, but only because I'd needed someone. It was time to grow up. Crack on. Deal with things.

'There's this amazing Thai place on Percy Street,' she said. 'We could grab a drink, a bite to eat, then, I dunno ...'

'Chinawhite?'

She laughed this off. I hadn't meant to say it bitterly, it had been supposed to sound like a joke, but something in me couldn't stop saying stuff like this. She was constantly unsure of my mood, unable to find the right angle with me.

'Rupert got back in touch with me, by the way,' she said, changing the subject.

'Rupert?'

'Rupert Bryant. My old boss? Says there's something coming up at Zara. Says I should go for it.'

'Zara in …'

'Well, Sloane Square. Flagship branch. Deputy manager again, with a view to managing the launch of a smaller one the following year. Be quite a step up. Be like I've landed on my feet. Like all this was *for* something.'

I'd noticed she'd stopped talking about Bristol around the time I'd started letting her hold my hand.

We shared a bed now, too. Nothing had happened. Nothing needed to. But she had me back where she wanted me.

A jogger whizzed past.

A few seconds later, so did another.

I watched them go, wondered where they were headed. Felt a strange pang of jealousy.

'So do you fancy it, then?' she said. 'Thai food?'

'How did you hear about it?' I said.

She rolled her eyes.

'Not this again.'

'I'm just interested.'

'I went there for Katya's birthday, okay? Is that acceptable? I told you – that was a phase. A stupid phase where I didn't know what the hell I was doing but now I do. So tell you what – to prove it – *you* choose.'

The Oxo Tower. The terrace.

Evening was giving way to night. The sky finding its way to black through purple. St Paul's all lit up, the boats on the Thames chugging by, the odd tiny flash of a cameraphone in the distance.

'Wow,' she said. 'The view.'

'You've never been up here?' I said.

How sad it was I couldn't be sure of things like this any more.

'Once,' she said. 'Yeah, once. You? Have *you* been here?'

I made a face.

'Oh,' she said. 'With her?'

She looked out over the city. This was like a first date, like we were doing everything for the first time again.

'I never liked her, you know,' she said, almost wistfully.

'I know,' I said. 'You say that quite a lot.'

'She's so … outside. Do you know what I mean by that? Like she's judging.'

Hayley had brought up Pia a couple of times already this week. It was uncomfortable. Like she wanted me to do her down; join in. As if that would be a victory for her – she'd got me back.

'Maybe she just observes and people mistake it for judging,' I said. 'Maybe she's just interested.'

'She's weird, though.'

'She's different. But that's not a bad thing. People want to be different. You wanted to be different. I think she's different but that maybe she doesn't want to be.'

My hackles were up. I tried to stay calm, took a sip of my water. There was a pill in my pocket, I knew that. The last of another pack. There was a fresh box at home. I'd thought of little else tonight.

'She tried to break us up, Tom,' she said. 'But you like defending her.'

'That implies you were attacking her.'

'No, I'm … look, Tom, sooner or later you have to let this go. This anger.'

'You've been back about a week, Pia.'

She stared at me.

'What?' I said. 'What now?'

A pause.

'My name is Hayley.'

My phone vibrated on the table. Thank Christ.

A text.

I didn't recognise the number.

Seven words.

I really need to talk to you.

'Hi, this is Tom Adoyo – who's this?'

I stood in the hallway, near the toilets. I could hear my echo from the sleek white floors, and the squeal of the doors as men pushed through them.

'Tom – hello,' said a man. 'Thank you for phoning back, I very much appreciate it.'

Familiar voice. Cultured. Mannered.

'It's Matthew Channing.'

'Oh,' I said, moving away, signalling through the window to Hayley I'd be just one minute. She sipped at her drink, pissed off with me.

'Look, can we meet?'

In the upstairs bar of the Randolph – lights low, eyes everywhere – Matthew was already three negroni in, tie loose, slight slur.

'There's trouble brewing,' he said, after I'd ordered and we were alone again. 'I've been a naughty boy.'

'I see,' I said, lying.

He swirled his drink, took the stirrer out, tapped it.

'A momentary lapse in judgment. Maybe a negroni too far.'

The flash of an insincere smile.

Downstairs, Old Man Stokey was on the piano again. A whoop from an eager drinker as he segued into 'Let It Be'.

'So … what did you do?'

'You remember the last time we were here?' he said, eyes on his drink. 'I was going to dinner?'

'Yes?'

'I didn't go to dinner.'

'Oh.'

Eyes on me, now.

'You remember also that there was a girl here?'

'Pia?'

'Who?'

'The girl I was with.'

'Oh,' – he laughed – 'yes, no, not her. How is she? She was very unusual.'

'Fine,' I said, not wanting to go down that path.

'Well, it was another girl.'

I strained to remember.

'Alice,' he said.

Black skirt. Tumbler of Twiglets. The penny dropped.

'Oh,' I said. 'So …'

'People are sniffing around. Looking for evidence. *The Sun* have it.'

This sounded pretty bad for him. Question was, why was he telling me?

'Well, just make sure there aren't any photos of you together, I guess.'

'But there are. She was standing right next to us when I had you in a headlock that night. She was laughing, she put her hand on my shoulder. Guided me to my car. And that wasn't the first time.'

'So where is she?' I said, looking around. 'Aren't you worried about bumping into her?'

'She's in Ibiza for a bit,' he said. 'I've got a place. It's just … I'm also in a relationship.'

'I see.'

'You've probably read about it,'

'Uh huh,' I lied, again.

'And that relationship, as you may know, is soon to welcome its first child.'

His face fell. Hands up, *mea culpa*. I couldn't tell if he was acting, but he looked sheepish, ashamed. I still didn't know why I was here.

'Look, I need a friendly face,' he said. 'My PRs are panicking, my management think this could distract from and perhaps impact certain projects in the States. No one wants a troublemaker. They only want likeable in the States. Likeable, likeable, likeable. Apparently this isn't particularly likeable.'

'And what do you want *me* to do?'

'Well, I'm told I need to take control. Admit my mistakes. They've drawn up a list of names, before the tabs run with it. But I look at these names, and I know what they'll do with it. It'll become emotive. They'll want pictures of me holding my head and crying and making remorseful faces and it's just so bloody undignified. Tom, I want you to interview me in a straight and matter-of-fact way and put it out on your show and that will be my statement. Keep things British. After that the work can speak for itself. I don't want a big song and dance. Just an interview, get the facts out there, say sorry, and carry on as normal.'

Carry on as normal.

'Why me?'

'Because you seem … straight. Down-the-line. I think I can trust you.'

He paused.

'We're going to try and suppress it. We're pulling out all the stops. But if it happens, if it's next week, or next month … will you do this?'

Of course I bloody would. This was a world exclusive. He was making waves in the States. He was on the verge of household name here. And my name would be all over this story. Cass would be thrilled, Bron would go crazy.

'Yeah,' I said.

'But maybe,' he said, eyes shifty now, 'things are a little unequal.'

'How do you mean?'

'I mean, I trust you, okay? But tell me something. Something no one knows about you. It sounds silly, okay, but I just need something here. I'm putting all my faith in you. Give me a token gesture of solidarity.'

I thought about what to tell him. Did I have to tell him anything? But this was good – gaining each other's trust. So what dark secret to convey? What would be a decent swap? How to convince him of my gratitude while saving my place on the ship?

My girlfriend disappeared one night and even though she has proved herself the worst girlfriend possible I still don't feel that I'm in control now she's back.

I think that's too much.

The one person who's been looking out for me I have lost because I'm not a strong enough man to make the right decision.

Nah.

Oh, hang on.

'You know that monkey that escaped from London Zoo?' I said, and he leaned forwards, a smile now playing on his face.

In the downstairs bar, Hayley was in the middle of a small group of strangers, talking to a guy.

Flirting?

Her hand on his shoulder for a second longer than it should have been. Where did she get that drink?

'Tom!' she said, beckoning me over. 'This is Trevor.'

Trevor was wearing a stupid little hat.

'And Jay – and Rob? – and Anna.'

I smiled at them all, said hi. It was loud here. Fuzzy. The light played with your eyes. The mahogany, the brass. It was like drinking on a galleon.

'Shall we go?' I said.

'Trevor is a musician, isn't that cool? His band's called ... what's it called?'

'Disused Disco,' said Trevor.

'Great,' I said, and the girl, Anna – all biker jacket and jeans – whooped as Old Man Stokey finished another tune.

'I *love* your jacket,' said Hayley, feeling the collar as Anna pulled away. 'Is it Stella McCartney? It's Stella McCartney, isn't it?'

Waiters in black brought drinks to tables while wide-irised men eyed up girls who pretended they didn't notice.

'So hey, look – I need to be up early, so ...'

'Let's have a cocktail. One more. Can't hurt you. What *is* this?'

She held her drink up to the light. She seemed drunk, now. Like she'd come to life in here.

'We're off to Gerry's Bar,' said Trevor, but to Hayley, not to me. 'You're welcome to follow.'

She looked at me, hopefully.

'Shall we follow?'

'I really need to go,' I said.

'So what did the great Matthew Channing want?' she said, looping her arm in mine. 'You read so much about him. How long have you known him? He's married to that actress, the one from that show. Is she nice?'

I've literally no idea.

'I can't really say too much about it all,' I said. 'You know. It's work stuff.'

She nudged me.

'You used to tell me everything.'

'Yeah, well, it's not really mine to tell.'

'God, his life must be exciting. Can I meet him?'

'No.'

'I wish I'd been an actress. Maybe it's not too late. Maybe I could train. Maybe that's what's next for me.'

'Yes,' I said, barely listening, trying to find a cab.

'Acting. Being someone else.'

'Mm-hmm.'

'Hey, how funny would it be if we got a rickshaw home?' she said, eyes bright, as some glamorous-looking people, bottle of wine in hand, and Trevor in his stupid little hat, pushed their way onto one.

twenty-eight

One week bled into the next. May even have bled into the one after that.

Talk London was fine. The routine was back on. Early to bed, early to rise.

At home, Hayley and I allowed ourselves to get used to each other some more. It was amazing how quickly you can reach a level of comfort again, just by being near each other.

I'd stopped asking her questions. She'd stopped having to think of answers. I'd stopped the digs. I'd stopped digging. I'd even made her laugh once – properly laugh – and the shock of it, seeing her face light up like that, a glimpse of the old Hayley sitting with the old me, was enough momentarily to make me forget, for the clouds to be punctured, for some joy to escape the barriers and rise on through …

But the dog.

Ah, the dog.

The dog had been at the door, but now he'd set himself a place at the table.

Monday. Or Tuesday.

Standard show so far. The Blackwall Tunnel was closed. Delays at the Ted Danson Interchange. Did you know there was a Ted Danson Interchange? There's a Ted Danson Interchange. Well, it's the Danson Interchange. Sometimes the traffic guys call it the Ted Danson Interchange. You have to find the fun where you can.

Work Experience Paul plonked a tray of hot-tap coffees on the table. The colour had slowly been draining from his face these last few weeks.

I stared out the window. I'd have to give the weather soon. How did it look out there?

Cloudy.

I'll just say cloudy. I'll just say highs of nineteen.

Cass had raced through the show this morning. It was a good one. Had it all: politics, entertainment, the 'quirky, sideways glance' at the news Bron was always on about. She got that comedian with the glasses, Matty Collins, in for Paper View, he'd made some off-colour jokes about women's thighs, and she'd segued beautifully out of it. Things were going well for Cass. She had a shoot with *ES Magazine* straight after the show. BBC3 were interested in her hosting *Young Voters' Question Time* this year. Bron seemed very keen on her too, though perhaps for less professional reasons.

But that's just idle gossip, and as you know, I don't deal in that.

Maybe I need to get myself sorted out. Start again. Commit to Talk London properly. Commit to this life of getting up at God knows when to read out loud to strangers. Accept my lot.

But now Cass was signalling me and I shook myself out of it.

'And of course,' she said, 'regular feature time here on London Calling … so let's find out …'

She hit a button.

'*What Did Tom Get Up To – Last Night?*'

She looked delighted. They'd done a jingle. They were surprising me with it. We waited quietly for it to finish while my mind raced – what did I get up to last night?

'So – Tom?' said Cass.

'Oh … well … not much, actually,' I said.

A pause.

Dead air.

She willed me on.

I shrugged an apology.

She hit the button again.

'*That's What Tom Got Up To – Last Night!*'

'Are you okay?' said Cass, by the kitchenette. I was making a hot tap coffee and was terrified because I'd spilled some granules. 'You seem … a bit different, lately.'

'You mean crap on air.'

'No, no …' she said. 'But yes.'

'I'm fine,' I said, as brightly as I could. 'Yeah, you know. Maybe I'm coming down with something. I don't know. Just taking it easy. Having some downtime. How are you, anyway?'

She paused, wondering how to put something.

'What's changed?' she said.

'I'm honestly fine.'

'Do you want to talk?' and without warning, that engineer was there again.

'Weather today?' he said.

'Highs of nineteen,' I said. 'Oh – and cloudy.'

He walked off, happy.

'Talking of getting on,' I said, moving away.

'Tom – listen, do you want to hang out later?' she said. 'I've got this ticket to the *M* Style Awards thing and my sister's dropped out. Which surprised me because Michael Fassbender's going to be there and she's been testing Fassbender out as a surname for about six months now. And anyway, I thought maybe we could hang?'

Hang? Was this, like, a work thing? Or something … else? Could it be?

I thought about what else I had going on. Another evening of awkwardness with Hayley, pretending nothing had happened, commenting on the haircuts on *EastEnders*, sloping off to bed, her sliding in an hour or so later, checking to see if I was awake. Me faking sleep.

'Sure,' I said, and I felt this surge of relief to be offered a momentary escape.

'I mean – you'd need to wear a suit. Smarten up a bit.'

'Yup,' I said.

'What are you doing now, anyway?' she said. 'You lunching?'

I checked I had my wallet, my phone.

'I'd love to,' I said. 'But I've got to be somewhere.'

My appointment was for 12.30. It was 12.29. That's an on-air man for you.

I had a copy of the *Standard* in my lap. Something had caught my eye. Not for me, but for Pia. She might like this. She might smile.

Should I tear it out? Keep it in my wallet? Just in case? Because what if I run into her? It might make a good ice-breaker, or …

But who was I fooling? That was over. I was pretending. Holding onto something. I just had to accept that life was back to normal.

Ding.

....

FROM: MAUREEN THOMAS
TO: ALL STAFF

Will all staff PLEASE REMEMBER the kitchenette is for the use of EVERYONE and SPILLING COFFEE EVERYWHERE is totally UNACCEPTABLE. The bins are there FOR A REASONS and if you don't USE THEM you will LOSE THEM.

....

Delete.

'So it's been a while, Tom – how are you keeping?'

'Up and down.'

'And the—'

'Comes and goes.'

His eyes scanned his notes. I studied his badge.

Dr J Moon. The one good thing about having a job with a name badge: you're never in any doubt about who you are.

'You stopped taking the amitriptyline for a while, didn't you?'

He looked up at me, studied my face for signs of happiness, tried to see if some weight was off my shoulders.

'I did. I didn't mean to. I just … some stuff came up.'

'And at that stage you found you didn't need them?'

'I did,' I said.

'No incidents?'

Well, we freed a marmoset.

'No incidents,' I said.

'That's good,' he said, writing something down. 'Has something happened recently to make you feel you need them again?'

'No. Yeah. I mean, things are just … back to normal. Back to how they were.'

He held my gaze.

'The last time I saw you was when your girlfriend left you.'

'She didn't leave me. Technically. She was just … missing.'

'And now she's back?'

'Yes.'

The words hung in the air.

'Look, remember: GP,' he said, finally, pointing at himself. 'Not psychiatrist. But you shouldn't necessarily be afraid of change.'

I crossed my legs, folded my arms, closed up.

'I'm not really comfortable talking about my relationship,' I said.

'Well, on a smaller scale, then, I just mean – are you getting exercise?'

This again. Exercise. The idea that depression – even mild – can be solved by star jumps.

'Or enough sunlight? Levels of light exposure can be very important.'

I get up when it's dark. I sit in a striplit room then move to an airless box. In the winter, I go home and have a nap and when I wake up it's dark again.

'Or finding new ways to release your frustration? Are there people you can speak to? Often things get worse if there's no one to share things with.'

There's Pippy.

'And if you don't feel comfortable talking to one of your friends, you can release the frustration in other safe and responsible ways. Walking. Running. Dancing.'

'Dancing?'

'Dancing, yes.'

'You want me to *dance* my troubles away?'

'Well no, not dance them away exactly, but you need to acknowledge them.'

'Through *dance*?'

'Look, sometimes when people go through this …'

He thought about how to put it.

'… it can be because they're angry. At themselves. Sometimes with reason, often with none. You may be turning your anger in on yourself, Tom. Ask yourself why.'

I unfolded my arms, and considered his words.

The dog had found me after Mum died.

I was sixteen. She was only forty-two. One of those vivid people, filmed in glorious technicolour, the ones who see music in everything. I was her world. She told me that all the time, all the way through school, kissing the top of my forehead, breathing her baby in, stretching up to do that even when my own height far overtook hers. I was her world, yes, and I was at that point we all reach where I was denying she was mine. I'd never quite forgive myself for that. Blame youth, blame hormones, blame me trying to work out who I was, but would it have killed me to take a moment, take a breath, just hug her and hold her just a few more times, instead of pulling away or watching the clock to see how long it'd be before I could run off to the park to drink cider with Calum and not talk to girls? As history would prove, I had many, many years not to talk to girls.

No one had seen it coming, when it came. The doctors said it had spread too far, too fast. She had an illness – *the* illness – she couldn't fight.

All over in a matter of weeks.

Shock, anger, rejection, acceptance, help. The five stages you're supposed to face. I'd got as far as anger before she'd gone, and then I'd had to start all over again.

But rather than face the pain, I'd tried to find a drawer for it, somewhere to keep it until I was stronger. I postponed it all. Gave the dog a spare room rather than have it put down. Hoped if I just dampened it, kept it just below the surface, I'd be okay.

But I'd never be truly okay, because somehow, now, I felt I'd always be alone. Dad dealt with it better. He moved on quickly. They say that's quite common. Three years later I was heading for university and he was heading for New Zealand. Invercargill, just down there at the bottom of the South Island, just 11,902 short miles away from his old life, his memories, from me. He'd met a Kiwi nurse at the Grain Barge one night, and grabbed the opportunity at something. I remember him holding me, saying how sorry he was, but that I was a man now, and I didn't need him, at least not as much, and this could be his last chance at a new start, and that

Mum would be happy for him. I think he was mainly telling himself. I assured him I'd be okay, but I knew I wouldn't. I assured him I didn't blame him, but I knew I did. Nowadays, I'm pleased for him. I love him. But right then and there I felt like I had lost two parents, I felt like I had lost so much love, I felt like I had lost any importance, and I felt …

Well.

Lost.

I'd always felt lost.

'Can I tell you how I feel these days?' I said, when the story had been told, and the doctor had fallen silent. 'I feel robbed. I feel like I had a lot of my choices taken away from me. Like everyone else has a say, just not me. I feel like it's been that way since my mum died. Like one day I had a world around me and then bit by bit that world fell away and I woke up briefly at thirty-four and found I had *no control*.'

I'd never told him about this; never opened up to him or anyone else apart from Hayley. I'd always tried to just keep things moving along until he got his pad out and dashed out another prescription.

'So take back control,' he said. 'Find a way to exercise your choice. Show yourself who's in charge. This is very unprofessional of me to say, but why be a victim in all this? Find a way, no matter how small it is.'

'How?'

'You could join a club,' he said, and when I started to laugh, *really* laugh, he stuck with it, dug deeper. 'I just mean find some likeminded people. You don't have to be alone, Tom. You can lighten your load.'

'I'm not laughing at the idea of a club,' I said. 'I'm laughing at the club I have an idea of.'

He smiled.

'I know you think it's simplistic,' he said.

'I think star jumps can cure anything,' I smiled.

'You have an illness,' he said. 'But you can *fight*.'

I sighed, and glanced up at the clock. Twenty-three minutes. A new record.

'Thank you, doctor,' I said, after a moment. 'But if it's all the same to you, I think I'm just going to take the pills.'

He sat back in his chair, conceded, and opened up his pad.

The *M* Style Awards were at the Troxy in Stepney, this art deco theatre in a part of London where the risk of mugging is just low enough to guarantee A List guests, but just high enough to make it seem edgy and cool. At least for the night. Something like this would be the only reason half the people inside would ever even have heard of Stepney. It's not like on any other day of the week you'd be jostling for elbow space at the Rajboy Tandoori or Michael's Chinese Food with Harry Styles or Cara Delevingne.

You had to walk past thirty models in little black dresses to get inside. It was a horrible gauntlet to run. One of those nights where someone might realistically ask 'who dressed you?' and you'd end up panicking and saying, 'Well, I dressed myself.'

I like to blend. Not stand out.

Cass looped her arm in mine and we walked through them all, these women just standing there, silent, hands on hips like plastic mannequins, smiling at you as you walked out of the lift, perfectly reflecting your inadequacy in their disinterested steel eyes.

'You look great,' said Cass, smoothing down my tie, brushing something off my collar. 'I suppose I should say, "Who dressed you?"'

Duchamp three-piece dash check suit. Paul Smith London Stamford shoes, red laces. Canali Jacquard-stripe single-cuff shirt. Tie: Boss, wool, grey with single black stripe. To be honest, I don't know *who* the guy that dressed me was.

'I feel a little out of place,' I said.

'Just be yourself,' she said. 'Best advice ever. Anyway, it's something we can talk about on the radio tomorrow ... What Did Tom Get Up To Last Night? "Well, Cass, I was stared at by thirty Sexbots from the future."'

Cass fitted in here. She could be any of these people, with her hair up, and a tight gold dress accentuating the things she wanted to accentuate. A small child from a boyband nodded at Cass and smirked. She smiled back, a beacon of early-thirties confidence, and he flushed and walked away.

'That dealt with that,' she said, and she passed me a drink as we made it to the other side of this warfield of glamour.

I was allowed the occasional drink, the doctor told me, and thank God I was.

'Check it out,' she said. 'Ronnie Wood.'

There he was, skinny tie and wild hair, mixing with the guys you'd see in a magazine like *M* – the M for Men, but Men like this.

David Gandy smiled enigmatically at no one in particular. Jake Bugg nodded at Miles Kane. Russell Brand floated past, and I took another deep slug of champagne, Cass passing me another glass the second a waitress was near.

Bloody hell.

Bradley Cooper.

I thought back to Pia, what she'd said that day.

'*Who do you want to be like?*'

Well, look at me now! I'm doing the exact same as Bradley Cooper! Maybe I should follow him tonight. For old times' sake. See if I can make it all the way to the bar at the Savoy. God help me if Axl Rose is here too.

Another buzz in the crowd now, as people tried to pretend they weren't pointing Justin Timberlake out as he arrived, the flutter of photographers' flashes like a tropical storm in the corner of your eye. I took another slug of champagne.

'I'm just popping to the loo,' said Cass, and my knees nearly buckled.

'Do not leave me.'

'I'll only leave you for a second.'

'Do. Not. Leave. Me.' But she just laughed, turned on her heel, and swayed away.

Christ.

My eyes darted around. Black ties. Velvet. Diamonds. Huge, manly Breitlings. I wanted to get my phone out and pretend to text. But that would send out the signals that I was alone and uncomfortable. People would notice me trying not to be noticed. I had to just not be noticed, and the best way not to be noticed was to not try not to be noticed.

A girl was next to me, now, and she too was on her own. A saviour. Model-pretty, expensively dressed, she stared out at the crowd in front of her, blank, cool, totally in control of her own solitude, totally unfazed. Maybe we could team up. Save each other.

She held the smallest canapé I had ever seen.

'What a small canapé,' I said, eyebrows raised, pointing at it.

'I'm married,' she said, moving immediately away.

I took another huge hit of champagne.

I realised now I was standing by a giant *M* cover, blown-up, huge, and on it, the tanned and smooth face of an absolutely massive Matthew Channing.

'NEXT BRIT THING,' said the coverline, next to other, smaller lines, like 'Lose that Belly!' and 'How to Make Her Yours!' and 'Ten Ways to Drive Her Wild!'

I suddenly felt just a little inadequate. Walking back, Cass could tell what I was thinking.

'Amazing that we're always trying to be something we're not,' she said, holding two fresh glasses of Moët, and there, just over her shoulder, I saw the man himself: Matthew Channing.

I tried to shrink into the background.

'Christ, this is embarrassing,' I said.

'How so?' she said.

'Matthew Channing. I saw him just the other night for a drink. And I saw him at the station too. And once before that.'

'I'm sorry – what?'

And then there he was, turning away from another photograph, on his way past us, hand clasped tightly to the hand of a woman behind him, dragging her through, and …

'Oh!' he said, stopping.

Cass raised her eyebrows, seemed impressed.

'Tom, hi …' he said, a little flustered, then, smiling, 'are you following me?'

'Hello Matthew,' I said, going for casual, but all I could think was, there's another really *huge* you right behind me. Tom looked to Cass.

'This is Cass,' I said. 'Cass, this is Matthew Channing, the next Brit thing.'

That was a ridiculous thing to say.

'I feel a little narcissistic standing here,' said Matthew, smiling, pointing at the cover.

'I hate narcissists,' said Cass. 'I only really want to talk about me.'

Matthew smiled, charmed, was about to say something clearly very clever back, and then the woman he'd been dragging behind him stepped forward.

'I'm Olivia,' she said, open, friendly, full of warmth, but very definitely cutting in. 'How do you do?'

She was beautiful – stunning, really – and heavily pregnant. She put one elegant hand on Matthew's arm.

'Darling, we said we'd catch up with Piers …'

Matthew shot me an apologetic look, but a millimetre deeper than that I could tell he was embarrassed. I knew his story. I knew what might be coming. And now I'd seen exactly what he had to lose; now I understood the depths of his stupidity; now I saw exactly why he needed me.

'I'll catch up with you later ...?' he said. 'Nice to meet you, Cassandra.'

They wafted past, heads turning, eyes scanning them for flaws.

'He's *very* charming,' said Cass, watching them go. 'And she's *very* pregnant.'

I took another deep sip and nodded.

The awards rumbled on. Confident, loud men took to the stage and thanked each other for voting them Most Stylish, or Best British Breakthrough Use of a Cummerbund, or whatever. Spotlights, strobes and speakers on a stage dominated by one giant, multi-bulbed 'M'. I spent much of the evening staring at Jeremy Piven.

Matthew Channing was awarded the perspex *New Man Award in Association with Bvlgari Man* and made a self-effacing speech in which he pretended to be overawed and wowed by the company in which he suddenly found himself.

'We should go to the pub,' whispered Cass, mock-yawning, but moments later a barrel-chested Eastern European stooped by our table and whispered something in her ear. She smiled, then nodded.

'You know that lad out of that band we saw on the way in?' she said.

'The fifteen-year-old?' I said.

'He's just invited me to the after-party ...'

The plan had been to go to these awards and then head home. That's what I'd told Hayley. But I didn't want to go home. I didn't want the cup of tea, the how-was-your-day, the awkward peck on the cheek, the lying in the dark in the silence. Plus, I couldn't let Cass go on her own. What if that fifteen-year-old tried to kiss her?

And at the heart of it all, the honest and true heart of it all – I was sick of always knowing what happens next. I wanted some of that not knowing back. I wanted to ditch the running order.

Behind two oak gates on an otherwise normal Camden street, the great and the good relaxed, laughed, snorted and quaffed, safe in the knowledge that the public was two gates and twenty guards away.

'This is Damien Laskin's house,' said Cass.

'The PR?'

It was huge, sprawling, modern. A central courtyard surrounded by folding glass, the whole house more a gallery than a home. I counted four Banksys, a couple of Damien Hirsts, and a truly awful painting of a cigarette carton with legs that probably cost close to a million.

Jesus Christ – there's Axl Rose.

'This place is amazing,' I said, turning to Cass, but …

'Cass!' – a shrill voice and a middle-aged blonde woman thundering towards her, over the moon to have seen her. I was about to be left again. Cass shot me an apologetic glance and whispered, 'I have literally no idea who this is,' and then squealed and held out her arms to receive the approaching hug from whoever this was.

And then …

'Bloody hell, you're everywhere,' said a voice. It was Matthew. Slightly dishevelled, but somehow the cooler for it. 'Look, Tom, don't take this the wrong way, but we probably shouldn't be seen together …'

'I'm not following you,' I said.

'What?'

'Just in case you genuinely thought I was following you.'

'Oh. No, I did not think that,' he said. 'Why would I think that?'

I made a 'no idea!' face.

'No, I just mean – look, it's looking more and more likely that we'll have to do this … "interview" …'

'Ah. And you think if we look too chummy …'

'Exactly. I mean, we *are* chums. We are. But my PRs are saying we should be doing this with a name journalist. You know – a Gordon Smart, a Clemmie Moodie, someone like that – but I'm trying to tell them that this way it'll look better. It'll look proper. Me and Tom, I keep saying. I tell them, look, this guy's not a name, he's a nobody, and that works for us …'

He stopped himself, put an embarrassed fist to his forehead. I smiled, shook away the insult.

'I don't mean a nobody. That's not what I meant. You're not a nobody. You're just not part of …'

'No, I get it.'

In fact, I'd been hearing this a lot lately.

'I don't mean you're a nobody. I just mean we can *control* you more.'

We both knew that sounded worse.

'By which I mean, you're part of the team. Because we're chums, like I said. Oh Christ, have I ballsed this up? Have I insulted you?'

But the truth was, he hadn't. I knew what he meant. He meant he'd be the only focus. I wouldn't have to prove anything. I didn't have my own agenda. I had no editor to please, no readership who expected tougher questioning from me.

'This will be good for both of us, is what I mean.'

He looked pained now, but it was acting, the same acting I'd seen as he accepted his award tonight. He was a charming actor, but he was an actor.

I didn't think we were chums. I didn't think that once we'd done this he'd ever call me again. I was cool with it. I'd have my name on something. A story. For once, I wouldn't be taking stuff off the wires. I'd be at the heart of it. And besides – part of me just wanted to help him. He'd messed up. Badly, of course, but he'd still just messed up.

'I didn't mean you were a nobody,' he said, again, much more sincerely this time. 'I just mean … it's very important to me to do this right. You met Olivia tonight, poor thing hates this stuff, had to go home, but you saw how …'

'Pregnant she is?'

'Yes.'

'And you have to stay likeable …'

'Yes! Exactly! You remembered. You get it.'

His eyes landed on Cass, in the corner, now approached by the kid from the boyband.

'You've done *very* well there, by the way,' he said, and I felt uncomfortable as he took a long moment to take in every inch of her, then playfully punch me on the arm.

Cass beckoned me back over once she'd rid herself of the kid, and we both watched as a security guard gently persuaded a TV comedian it might be time he went home.

'I might have a story coming up soon,' I said, leaning against the wall. 'A big one.'

'About you?'

I laughed.

'No, not about me.'

'I only want to hear stories about you tonight,' she said, and to anyone else that might have seemed flirtatious, but it was a sisterly look I saw, I think. 'I wanted to say … I heard your girlfriend came back.'

I sighed, said, 'Yep.' Bedded in. This had clearly been coming.

'That must be weird.'

'Yep.'

'So did she say why she left in the first place?'

I laughed, the vodka burning an empty stomach, now.

'You would never, ever believe me if I told you.'

'I'm supposed to say "try me" now, aren't I?'

I smiled, stared into my drink.

'Come on. We're not just colleagues. We're mates.'

And so I told her.

I told her about the note. About the confusion, and the anger, and I tried not to scare her when I mentioned the dog. And then before I knew it, and after swearing her to secrecy, I told her something I hadn't told anyone, because it had been too weird, too embarrassing, too difficult to explain:

I told her about turning up at CC, about making a scene, and about how I'd been followed by a girl.

At this, she cocked her head, sipped her drink, nodded me on.

So I told her about this absolute weirdo, this girl I found an annoyance until the night she saved me, this girl called Pia who made me angry and happy and curious and sad. How no one had ever brought out so many conflicting emotions in me. About how she said she was trying to protect me and despite all the evidence to the contrary I sort of believed her.

'Tell me about her,' said Cass, turning to catch a waiter's eye, ordering more drinks. 'What's her story?'

I laughed, and shrugged.

'I was never allowed to know,' I said.

'Well, where's she from?'

'Yorkshire maybe?' I said.

That kid came back, leaned on one arm on the wall, smiled.

'Definitely not now,' said Cass, and he scowled and turned on his heel.

'That's what I'm saying,' I said. 'I have her name and I have her number. But that's all she'd let me have.'

Cass thought about it.

'Married? In a relationship?'

It had never once crossed my mind.

'She'd been married. I think to some guy called Jeremy. Didn't work out.'

'Was she lying?' she said. 'What if she's just not happy? What if she's hiding all this from somebody? A lot of people aren't happy in their relationships.'

The words hung in the air.

'I don't think she was lying.'

'Why wouldn't she tell you anything about herself?'

'I tried. But she had rules. She asked me to respect them. She said this wasn't about her, it was about me.'

Cass smiled.

'Maybe she's an angel.'

'An angel in a parka who smokes roll-ups.'

'A fallen angel, then.'

The drinks arrived. I took a long pull, and waited for the waiter to leave.

'Sounds like she was looking out for you, anyway,' said Cass.

'She was, I think,' I said, and then Cass tapped the table and looked me deep in the eye.

'So who's looking out for her?'

The words stayed with me.

I didn't know. I had no idea who was looking out for her.

I texted Pia several times that night. I got no replies. I took another pill. I wanted the world to be more bland, more manageable.

I missed her, now. The vodka had helped with that, but I knew I'd missed her since the second I'd last seen her.

I'd been blind. I'd been mean.

I texted her again, standing at the edge of the party.

Pia. Please - text me back. I'd call you but I want you to want to speak with me. Text me back and I'll call you straight away.

I stared at the phone, willing a reply, then it all got too much – the noise, the laughter, the music, the party, and I found myself leaving, walking, waving to Cass, her nodding her permission with kind and hopeful eyes.

And as I made it to the exit, a security guard eyeing my jacket to make sure I'd not nicked anything – I caught someone's eye …

Felix.

'Felix Echo!' I thought, panicked. 'Felix Echo is here!'

He was in full black tie. His jet black hair spiked straight up. His bright orange skin suddenly completely normal in an environment like this.

He looked *great*. He was holding a *goodie bag*.

'What the—?' I mouthed, eyes wide, and he smiled back.

He was talking to four men, one of whom was Justin Timberlake.

He made a little 'walking' gesture with his fingers.

He followed me in.

'Yeah!' he mouthed, seeing me realise.

'Just here?' I mouthed, confused, but impressed.

'Yeah!' he mouthed back, nodding furiously, and he did the little gesture again. He must've heard Cass talking about it on the radio. Been waiting in full black tie outside the awards. Snuck in straight after us. I smiled.

'Are you having fun?' I mouthed, doing a little mime for 'fun' at the same time, which appeared to be the twist.

He just pointed at Justin Timberlake. I remembered his 'N Sync t-shirt. Not so ironic after all.

I laughed as I walked out onto the street, but the night air hit me, and I wasn't so much walking as staggering.

I could find a taxi on the high street, I thought, and a second later heard the putter and growl of a black cab, but as I turned I saw it was taken, no bright yellow light, just two figures in the back, close together, comforting …

And as they passed, I recognised them.

It was Matthew.

And next to him – it was Alice.

A text. *Ding-ding.*

Hayley.

Where are you?

I put the phone away.

Why hadn't she just been straight with me?

Pia, I mean.

I stumbled. I wasn't steady on my feet right now. Maybe I shouldn't have taken that pill. I definitely shouldn't have had those drinks.

But would she have told me her story if I'd just insisted she did? Again, Pia, I mean. She'd always resisted, but I'd never pushed it. I convinced myself it was out of respect for her. But actually, wasn't it just because I was self-obsessed? Didn't I just want this to be about me? I'd needed someone to talk to and someone to distract me and there she'd been, this fallen angel, this oddball, and I'd taken advantage and selfishly dominated and what if *she'd* needed *me*?

Hang on – what was *Alice* doing in the car with *Matthew*?

But if Pia had needed me, wouldn't that explain why she'd followed me that day?

I'm not texting Hayley – where were *you*, love, never mind where I am?

I steadied myself against a tree.

So was Matthew still seeing Alice?

And was he right – was I a *nobody?*

Pia was always there for me. She didn't think that about me. She was just a phone call away from me.

I found a cab, I was woozy, immediately pulling one window down, a fresh bag of chips in my hand from God knows where, and fifteen minutes later I was approaching Stoke Newington.

I wouldn't be able to do this inside.

Sod it.

I dialled the number.

Come on, Pia.

A memory. '*Wow – that's my favourite number!*'

The thing is, for the first time ever – I think it actually *was.*

I waited.

A flat tone.

This number is no longer in service.

[10]

'The problem with having what others have,' says Cockroft, 'is that you no longer covet what was already yours.'

We had begun to talk of Cockroft's daughter. What he had left behind.

'It wasn't for want of love,' he says. 'I changed after her mother … after I discovered the choices her mother had made. She didn't approve of my ideas, the way I lived. I had never lived that way with her mother. I suppose you could call my behavior at that stage – after I moved to Berlin, after I taught there a while – I suppose you could call it a breakdown of sorts. She was just a child. My sister took her in. I continued to develop my theories.'

'Do you ever see her?'

'I do not,' he says, softly. 'But I tell you this: she is a beautiful girl with beautiful hair and a beautiful smile and eyes that could light up the sky.'

'There must have been others,' I say. 'That doubted you?'

'There were many that doubted me,' he says. 'Who saw my ideas as a freak show. And of course that is to be respected. I had to detach and I think they accept that.'

'You mention detaching a lot.'

'Detachment is a necessary part of the human experience.'

'You detached from your daughter.'

'And she detached from me.'

'You detached from Andreas.'

'Not by choice.'

I say nothing.

'What,' he says. 'You think that every person you meet you must be tied to forever? That every person you went to school with, or happened to be born near, or happened to be related to, you have to stick with for life?'

He seems angry now, and there is a darkness that cloaks his face, as he delivers an argument that seems forced and rehearsed.

'Connection is random. You live next door to whomever you live next door to. You sit on the bus with whomever you sit on the bus with. You think you have to like them? Of course not. You must choose to detach. You must choose to make choices.'

'But you advocate making other *people's* choices. You advocate obeying the choices of *others*.'

'Yes, but only when it hurts, son,' he says, his head shaking, and his voice softer now. 'But only when it hurts.'

twenty-nine

I woke up on the sofa.

Christ, my head.

It was bright, and I squinted, held my hand up to shield myself from the light.

Wait.

The light? I don't get up in the light. I live in the dark.

What time was it? Am I late? Shit, I must be late. It's light. Usually it's a good thing, isn't it, to see the light? But in my profession it's a very, very bad thing indeed.

Jesus. Oh, no. The sweat started. I felt flushed. Sick. It's 9.03.

My phone. 1 per cent battery. On all night. Three texts. Six missed calls. Two voicemails. All unknown numbers. The studio.

I scrabbled to my feet, bundled over to the kitchen, flipped the radio on.

'... and the world of theatre is mourning the passing of West End actor Stephen Langbridge this morning ... 'He was a one-off. There will never be another Stephen Langbridge,' said the late actor's son, Stephen.'

Who was this?

'... highs of nineteen in our capitals today – and now you are, you're, updated.'

Bron! Bron was doing the news herself. She sounded terrible, and oh, God, if she sounded terrible I could imagine the texts flying in, appearing in real-time right in front of her nose on the screen:

'Who's this? SACK HER! Why can't she read properly? Where's Tom?', as people so used to one thing inexplicably get another.

This was all bad news. She can't have been able to find cover. My boss had had to do it *herself*. What time had she been woken?

'Morning!' said Hayley, brightly, spilling out of the shower with a towel round her head. 'You didn't say you had the morning off.'

I hardly heard her. I read my texts. A rising tide of fear in Cass's writing.

Just checking you're on your way.

Tried your phone, it's on - where are you?

Are you close?

Shit, are you still asleep?

Have you got Kate Mann's number?

Christ, Bron's come in early to do it herself! I'll cover for you! If they call you say you had a dodgy curry!

A heartbeat later the phone rang.

I answered.

'Well, good morning, sunshine,' said a voice, but one without the warmth you might expect of such a sentence.

'Bron, I had a bad curry,' I said, before the battery went dead, making it sound for all the world like I'd simply decided to tell her what I had for my tea last night and then hang up.

I lay back on the sofa. She'd be ringing me again now. Getting my voicemail. I wondered how many swearwords she'd be using. Whether she'd get out her OFCOM file and just read aloud from that.

'I thought you were coming straight back after the awards?' said Hayley, in that innocent but frosty way people do when they're actually pretty angry. 'I was worried when you didn't come back. I texted you and you ignored it. And to be honest I'd really appreciate it if you didn't do that to me again.'

I slowly turned to stare at her until she listened to her own words back and walked away.

I closed my eyes.

Pia.

Nothing from Pia.

But I knew what this was, now.

Pia had talked about it that evening on the bus. Hayley had mentioned it the night she got back.

Detachment.

Cockroft's Way. I'd realised some nights earlier there'd been a copy of his book on the bookshelf – *Carbon Copy* – nestled between a Lonely Planet guide to Crete I'd bought while optimistically hoping we might eventually plan a holiday, and a Taschen book about chairs I'd never once looked at.

I stood and found the chapter on detachment.

To disengage.
To be easily removable.

She considered herself easily removable. Something isolated, unneeded, unmissed.

Pia had detached from me and now I knew for sure I wanted her back.

thirty

Wednesday. 7.45pm.

I'd been milling about in the BP garage outside for the last fifteen minutes, pretending I was having a difficult time choosing between M&Ms or a Bounty.

I could see the entrance to the Holiday Inn from here. I wanted to catch Andy on his own. I reasoned he'd be more open with me then. No one else around to chip in, or caution him, or distract from the story. No one to stop me finding out what I needed to know.

First, I saw Tim, bleep-bleeping his small red Polo open, climbing in, Classic FM rising for a second until he could quell the strings, then roaring off.

A moment later, and there was Andy, shoving his clipboard into a small red Eastpak that now looked ludicrous across the acres of his back. He was with Felix and Jackie. They walked to the bus stop together.

I choose the M&Ms and paid.

'Quite a decision,' said the cashier. 'Sure you don't want to think about it some more?'

I tailed the three of them – such an odd group. Jackie, the oldest, her silver hair lapping her shoulders, her limp more pronounced now, in the real world. Felix in his black skinny jeans and Slayer t-shirt, prepping his iPod, presumably with death metal or hardcore for some kind of furious march home. Andy and his tiny rucksack, taking his glasses off and cleaning them with his tie. A strange family unit, but tight; they way people are when they share a secret.

Their bus approached, and as it did, Jackie and Felix peeled off, each with a hand in the air, leaving Andy to hop on – if hop is the right word. I sprinted across the road, dodged the cars, whipped out my Oyster card and squeezed through the doors, the back of my coat nipped for a second as the driver – blue jumper, nicotine fingers – rolled his eyes at me and gently pressed his foot down.

Andy must have gone upstairs. I can't talk to him here. Not on the bus. Too many people, too public, so I sat down by the window near the stairs, my prey trapped in the box above me.

I'd catch him outside, or wherever he lived. Where was that, I wondered? What bus was this? The 22? But barely a half dozen stops had passed when I saw him again, white knuckles tight round the handrail, another on the wall to steady himself, noises of effort and concentration as he balanced himself onto each new step.

Old Church Street. Chelsea.

He thundered past me, and I rose to my feet, jumped through the doors after him, ready to shout his name and suggest a coffee when I saw what he was doing.

He was on the follow.

Andy was not the best follower I had seen. He was pretty bad at it. Lumbering, unsubtle. No elegance. His size, of course, made it harder for him to blend in. But there were his clothes, too. The blue trousers. The baseball cap. The bright red rucksack. This guy was an amateur.

He'd followed two black guys in their early twenties off the bus and tailed them to a café where one of them seemed to work. He'd walked closely behind them, almost bumped into them at the door, then sat down and perused the menu, while I found shelter from a thin rain in the launderette opposite, the hot air thick with Persil.

Then he'd simply pointed at the jacket potato an elderly man was enjoying by the window.

I didn't think he was getting the best out of this system. It's not like he could claim he'd never had a jacket potato before.

Over his shoulder, one of the guys he'd followed appeared from the kitchen wearing an apron. Andy clocked him, and I watched as he took in the details. His eyes went from the guy's hair to his clothes to his watch to his shoes. He took out his clipboard and made some notes.

Behind me, on a TV screwed to the wall, *University Challenge* blathered away.

'Your bonuses are now on quotations about shellfish,' said Jeremy Paxman. I glanced at the man on a plastic chair opposite, half-asleep, a well of drool forming in the corner of his mouth. I'm not sure how either of us would do on that show.

Five minutes later Andy was finishing his jacket potato and can of Fanta. He noted something down on his clipboard, then held the can up, read what I had to assume was its ingredients, and noted that down too. He asked for the bill, and laid down a fiver on a plate with great care, a finger and a thumb at each end.

He stood, left the café, and started to trudge back to the bus stop, his head down, his great jacket potato adventure over.

I couldn't work out why he'd followed that guy. I couldn't work out what he'd seen in him, or what Andy wanted to be. What did he get out of that? At least when Pia did it, there was a sense of fun, a sense of adventure. It was about bettering yourself, making the best use of your time, losing yourself in a vast crowd of Koreans. Not just filling your day.

I considered approaching, as I left the launderette, leaving nothing but a roomful of scowls behind me, but Andy was on the move, and where Andy went, I went.

*

Turns out where Andy went was the Trocadero Centre to watch the new Jason Statham film. That was what Andy did when Andy was being himself.

I couldn't let him suffer like that.

'Hey Andy,' I said, sitting down, his popcorn spilling over the brim of its cup and bouncing from taut trouser legs from the shock of it.

Andy didn't have anything. Anyone. All he had was this. Well, this and his job.

'Database administrator,' he said, almost apologetically.

'That's cool,' I said. 'We all need databases.'

He helps people with CC. But it doesn't work for him, he said, at least not as well as it can for others. He doesn't know what to look for. He doesn't know what he wants to be. But he enjoys helping; he likes the company.

'Maybe you're just you,' I said, nursing my coffee. We were in the Costa on Regent Street, surrounded by Italian students on MacBooks, Skyping home with cheap rubber earbuds.

'Being just me, yeah … that's what I'm afraid of,' he said. 'When I read Cockroft's book, I just thought, this is incredible. It's a million windows into other decisions. It's like a bus you can hop on and hop off. You're *life*-jacking, that's what I call it. You're piggybacking on the fun stuff that other people do. You're—'

'Having a jacket potato and a can of Fanta.'

'Yeah, okay, look – there are degrees. It doesn't always work. The Japanese chapters took it further, before they were shut down. One guy in Kyoto lived in someone else's apartment for a year. Hid above her boiler cupboard at night. Used to wait until she'd left the apartment then slide out and eat her leftovers before heading out to work. There was nothing weird about it, though.'

'Nothing *weird* about it?'

'*Sexual*, I mean. But we'd never do that over here. I've done things, though. Some pretty great things.'

'Like?'

'Like seen art I would never have seen. Did you know Leonardo da Vinci spent twelve years painting the Mona Lisa's lips?'

'You saw the "Mona Lisa"?'

'Well, no, but I followed a bloke into an art lecture on the Strand and he had it up on a PowerPoint. But if I'd stayed home and watched *Rip Off Britain* I wouldn't have. Or I've been up Big Ben. That was on the follow, too. Tour group. Pretended to be a German. Did you know Big Ben, which is the bell, by the way, weighs the same as a small elephant and he's wider than he is tall?'

I shook my head.

'I was the only one in the group to understand that, to be fair,' he said. 'But those are the moments I live for. The *unexpected*. And I'm getting better.'

'Pia told me why Tim does it …'

'Tim's trapped. He's been trapped for years, in that semi with his mum. He doesn't have time for his own life because he's got to look after someone else's. So when he does what he does, it's because someone else has done all the work to build up to it. They can go to restaurants, they can form relationships, they can go and see Kenny G at the O2, they can do whatever they want. Tim can't. That's what I mean about life-jacking! He gets a glimpse into what his life could have been.'

I sipped at my drink as Andy leaned forward.

'Look, *you've* followed,' he said. 'I know you've done it. You did it tonight! I know you get it.'

He was right. I did get it. Despite it all, I'd seen the point. No, that wasn't fair. I *saw* the point. But I was done. I'd moved on. I was getting my life back together. And then I thought of Hayley, of the tension that hung thick round the flat.

'It's different for Felix,' he said. 'He's younger. He hasn't tasted true failure yet. He does it because he's impatient. He's in a hurry to find out who he is. I keep telling him, "Just wait! You'll figure it out!" He doesn't realise he has his whole life ahead of him. He wants it now.'

'And Jackie?'

'Well to be honest with you, Jackie's just a bit odd.'

'I see.'

'But that doesn't take away from the whole. Someone like Pia – someone who needed this once – enjoys it now. Pia's got the right idea.'

I grabbed my chance.

'That's kind of why I'm here. It's about Pia.'

'What about her? Is she okay?' he said, his face now concerned. 'She hasn't been to the place in a while.'

'I don't know if she's okay. We had a fight. Hayley came back.'

His jaw dropped.

'She's back? Did she say why?'

'She said she needed to go away to work out why she needed to come back.'

He nodded, hid his mouth behind his cup.

'Pia said I needed to move on. Said Hayley would only ever hurt me. I said some things. Now she won't take my calls. I keep looking over my shoulder in case she's there. But she never is.'

Andy put his cup down, wondering how to phrase something.

'Maybe she had a point. About Hayley.'

I blinked.

'I thought you were all for people doing this? You encouraged Hayley.'

'I didn't encourage her. I told her to follow her heart.'

'That sounds like pretty much the same thing.'

'But I also told her I didn't agree with what she was doing.'

It wasn't Hayley I wanted to talk about, to be honest. It was Pia. Pia was the important thing.

'Look, here's the thing: I think that after she broke up with Jeremy, she spiralled into some kind of depression. Some dark place. I get that.'

Andy raised his eyebrows.

'So she broke up with him.'

'Yes,' I said. 'I mean, didn't she?'

'Well, good. That guy was not a good guy. I'm pleased you know about him, to be frank. He was a user. Powerful personality, quite magnetic, but *over*powering. That was always her problem: personalities are her magnet. We used to talk about that so much. Her whole life has been like that. I suppose it makes sense she was attracted to him.'

'Do you think she's over him?'

'I don't know,' said Andy. 'Did she tell you she was?'

'She'd always change the subject. I mean, a break-up's tough, of course. But especially if you're married.'

Andy stopped now, no movement, nothing, just frozen as I continued.

'And then there's the zoo thing,' I said.

'Hang on,' he said, the spell now broken. 'Wait.'

'And if I ever asked her about it, about her marriage, she'd tell me those weren't the rules. That she was here to talk to me about my stuff, to protect me, not to help her. She was acting like she was my guardian angel or something.'

'*Stop*,' said Andy. 'Can you go back a bit, because I'm really confused?'

'Pia,' I said.

'You're talking about Pia?'

'Of course I'm talking about Pia. Pia and this Jeremy guy.'

He sighed, looked around, didn't know how to tell me.

'Tom, Pia wasn't with Jeremy,' he said, as gently as he could. 'Pia had nothing to *do* with Jeremy.'

'Well, who the hell is Jeremy, then?' I said, and Andy put his hand over his mouth.

[11]

Ezra Cockroft disappeared from my life soon after the night we had talked of the hurt from which he'd run, and the hurt that he still felt.

He detached.

I called him, of course, and I visited his apartment, but all to no avail. Perhaps, I thought, he has escaped for the sun once more — perhaps he needed the warmth in his life.

I still returned to Keen's when I could, where I would sit by the bar and scan the room, just in case.

Six weeks passed before I found a note, pinned to my door, folded once, a tear of Royal Blue ink running down one side where the weather had found it.

I had returned from following a tall Jewish man from the azaleas in the Botanical Garden — to which I am ashamed to say I had never before been — via a bookstore on W 155th Street to a small diner on Broadway where quietly we ate latkes with Smetana and read our new books (*The Running Man* by Richard Bachman).

For the Attention of Michael Kosinski
Cc: The World

Michael, I was passing, and I was thinking.
    Maybe one day there'll be born a man who's got it all worked out.

Maybe statistically, that has to happen one day. And I wish that had been me.

Truth is, I messed up. When I was young I worked too much because I was trying to be who I thought everyone wanted me to be. I didn't feel like I was enough. But maybe I always was, and if I hadn't tried so hard to be someone else, I'd have realized that everyone was happy with me being me. But I was desperate to be someone else, Michael, and to hide away in someone else's world.

So I found someone like me who'd made the right choices. I decided to step into his shadow, because being in his shadow was better than always being at the foot of my own. Only when I was being someone else could I be myself. And soon I lived a life that was anyone's but my own.

Maybe, Michael – despite it all … the fun, the fights, the girls … maybe I should have just lived my own life. Seen it through. Maybe following is something to be shared. Because following by its very nature means that despite the presence of the person you could be, you are alone.

But these are the ramblings of an old and stupid man.

Our old friend Oscar Wilde would say: be yourself; everyone else is already taken.

Me? I take a different road. Be whomever you want to be, Michael. Be you, be me, be the kid you pass on the stairs. But be well.

– Ezra

thirty-one

So there it was: the banality of truth.

No pop star, no great adventure, no 'detachment', no 'finding herself' cod-psychology 1960s New York bullshit – just an investments analyst named Jeremy who'd wowed her with the force of his incredible investments-analyst personality.

She'd left me. But she didn't have the balls to leave me.

The mundanity of how it happened shocked me. That a relationship could be put in jeopardy in such a pedestrian way.

She'd been out, one night, with Fran. Picked her up from Spitalfields, headed to Mayfair. Sat at a table next to a group of men celebrating some kind of win. Listened to them bellow and brag. Fran had found it boring, the way Hayley was never quite there, ears cocked to the table next to hers, taking nothing in, not being present. She'd made her excuses – 'iffy tapas' – and left, stormed out, had *that* argument, leaving Hayley to settle up and make her own way home. Home to me. But she knew I'd be asleep. Home promised no fun. And anyway: she'd found her next follow.

So Hayley had stayed, listened, made sure she was leaving at the same time, caught the eye of Jeremy at the cloakroom, laughed at his jokes, said she'd been stood up, accepted the invite to follow on with the group.

Soon, it was just those two.

I walked to the tube, shoulders hunched, my fists in a ball, not knowing if I'd ever be able to unclench them.

She hadn't gone to Paris on a whim. She hadn't seen it on some travel show and thought it seemed nice. She hadn't come straight back to Britain, either, staying at her dad's in King's Lynn, or her sister's in Brighton, or whatever else she'd told me that seemed a good enough dead end.

She'd been with Jeremy.

I felt around for the pills in my pocket. Found the packet. Brought them out.

Stared at them.

When I got home, I found a note.

Just popped out. Back in a bit.

Where now? Where this time?

There was a bag by the door, cream with brown cotton handles, tissue paper billowing out. I peered in. She'd bought herself a new biker jacket.

Stella McCartney.

I walked to the bedroom. Found what I was looking for in the drawer by the window.

I took it out, and stared at the picture in the back of her passport. Those big eyes. That curl. I'd been there when she'd taken this picture. We'd found a booth in a tube station, had one taken together afterwards. I still had it in my wallet. We still had one on our fridge.

I took a breath. Flicked through.

They don't always stamp them, of course, I told myself.

But there – look – *there*.

SOUTH AFRICA. A visa. Stamped.

She'd had to apply for *visas*. That put the leaving do in perspective.

I sat down.

Soul aching. Stomach sinking.

I turned the page.

DUBAI. Stamped. Same month.

Disgusted, heart punched, I sat in the dark until I heard the key in the lock.

thirty-two

I was still holding it when she got in, Sainsbury's bags under her arm, milk in hand.

She saw me, saw the passport, put the bags down, slowly.

'Baby, I can explain.'

'So you were in King's Lynn with your dad, yeah?' I said. 'And you were in Brighton with Annie?'

'Tom ...'

'But actually you were all over the place,' I said, holding back my killer blow until now. 'With Jeremy.'

I spat that name out, and she looked weak now, pale. Like her knees might buckle. Her hands were raised, maybe to placate, maybe to defend. I'd said the name she never wanted me to know.

'How?' I said. 'How did you even afford this?'

And then I realised.

'It was a business trip, wasn't it?' I said. 'Good hotels, nice wine, expenses, insurance broker bonuses ...'

She swallowed. Defeated. Busted.

'It was a business trip,' she said.

'Too good to pass up? Better than another night in Stoke Newington?'

'I ... it sounded ...'

'You went off with some guy, Hayley.'

My voice was flat, emotionless, drained.

'I don't know what to say, Tom,' she said, and she sat now, her head in her hands, all the signs pointing to tears, but none appearing. 'I'm so, so sorry.'

'Sure.'

'It just happened.'

'Yes, no worries, I often join strangers on business trips, it's such an easy trap to fall into.'

'I should have told you.'

'Yes, but also, you shouldn't have gone.'

'I know. I know. I hate myself. I do. Please believe me, this wasn't supposed to … I just got carried away, I …'

'So why did you do it? Because this wasn't just an impulse decision, this affair, Hayley. *This* kind of spontaneity takes planning.'

She shrugged. I sounded more bitter now, more lively, gunning for a fight. Because come on, Hayley, why don't you tell me why you did this? Hurt me, be brutal, I don't care, just tell me.

'He was different.'

Wow. That should have sent me scuttling, made me think of my pills, but I was finding a different way through it now, I was doing what the doctor ordered …

'Different from me?' I said.

'From anyone. From me, as it happens. He was different from me. Confident. It all seemed to make sense. I wanted to see what would happen.'

'So you quit your job and left me a note.'

'I hated my job, Tom. I hated it. It's so boring. It was killing me. I was trapped.'

'Yet you want to do it again in Chelsea?'

'I want to be normal again. Normal with you.'

The words made me shudder. I didn't want to be normal any more. I didn't want to be anybody's 'normal'.

'I didn't want to leave you, Tom. I knew I was making a mistake, which is why the note I wrote you—'

'Left your options open.'

'I needed to make sure that there wasn't ... I don't know ...'

'A *better* option?'

'No!' she said. 'I love you. I do. I ended that other ... thing. But our life, I mean, is this it? Is this flat the best flat we'll ever have? Are our jobs what we're meant to be doing? You're asleep when I go to bed, you're gone when I wake up, we never saw each other ...'

'All that crap about how you were when you were growing up, how you never knew yourself ...'

'That was true! I just ...'

'You just used the jigsaw pieces to let me come to my own conclusion. You were just doing it again – telling me what you thought I wanted to hear. But the truth was so much more mundane. So much more *disappointing*.'

She sat, cowed, dumb, caught.

'So you should have talked to me,' I said.

'You were always so tired. You had a routine you had to stick to.'

'I moved here for you,' I said. 'This was *our* routine.'

'But routine's not what I want ...'

Turns out we both wanted the same thing in the end. Something else.

'And what about Jeremy?'

'Jeremy is not what I want,' she said. 'Please believe me. I never thought he was, I just wondered if that *life* was. But it isn't, Tom.'

'So it didn't work out.'

'It's not like that.'

'It didn't work out with this guy so you've returned to your fallback.'

'It's not *like* that.'

'You slept with him, Hayley.'

She said nothing, now. There was no comeback to this. No justification. I realised, in that moment, that this girl had something right. She'd gone looking for herself. But she'd never find herself. Because as sad as it was, she was absolutely nothing.

'I'm surprised it took you this long,' she said, leaning against the frame of the bedroom door, wine glass in hand, wounded pride across her face, as I packed a bag. 'Considering your little girlfriend knew about it all along.'

'She's not my little girlfriend,' I said. 'She's my friend.'

And then I stood. Stopped. Turned.

Took the bait.

'What do you mean?' I said.

'She knew,' she said. 'They all did. Andy. That little weakling Felix. Your *friend*, Pia. Surprised she didn't drop me in it. She can be a judgmental little bitch.'

'They knew?'

'It started with a follow. I talked about it every week. They tracked it. It was like their own little soap opera for a while. But they never thought I'd go through with it. Well, I did. Sad – they just wanted to live vicariously through me.'

She looked defiant; proud, almost.

'Imagine that,' I said. 'Imagine only living through other people.'

Her eyes fell a little. The words were a dent in her armour, a scratch on her new car.

I was done here.

'Goodbye Hayley,' I said. 'Just try and carry on as normal.'

'Wait,' she said. 'Are you coming back?'

I walked out.

'Tom, *are you coming back?*'

*

The cabbie asked me where to.

I didn't know what to say, so I said, 'The Holiday Inn Express, Wandsworth.'

The ride through London was fast at this time of night. The lights bouncing off the river, the blue neon of lit bridges, the orange of the streetlamps, the white of St Paul's, each a floating moment in an ink-black sky that seemed to stretch on and on forever.

thirty-three

'It's 6 o'clock, I'm Tom Adoyo with the stories you're waking up to …'

I had several missed calls on my phone.

Hayley, Hayley, Home, Home, Blocked.

The Blocked, I reasoned, was her again, hiding her number this time, trying to fool me into picking up. She'd fooled me enough.

There was that, of course, to keep my mind occupied. But there was also the fact that Pia had known about this guy, this Jeremy, yet she'd chosen not to tell me. She'd made stuff up to hide it from me. Whose side was she on?

'Arsène Wenger insists he made the right choice with the starting line-up on Saturday …'

There was a picture of Leslie James on Digital Spy this morning.

He'd arrived for his first show on Sunrise. A couple of photographers had turned up to document his fall from grace. He'd made a statement saying how proud he was to be starting his brand new afternoon show for Kent, especially on such an exciting online platform.

Then, with both his arms still in plaster, he'd become trapped in the revolving doors of the building.

He batted back and forth in there like a moth against a window.

The photographers must have taken a thousand pictures before anyone thought to get help.

A passer-by made a video and it was starting to get some real traction on YouTube.

'And in showbiz, multi-award-winning pop star Aphra Just says her next album could well be her last ...'

Yeah? Good.

I paused.

'And now you're up to date.'

Straight after the show, I took my phone off silent and sat at my desk.

It was empty, as always. It wasn't even my desk, really.

A desk as metaphor for life.

Ding.

....

FROM: MAUREEN THOMAS
TO: ALL STAFF

Will you PLEASE REMEMBER our CLEAN DESK POLICY. Personal items are FORBIDDEN. We are a PAPERLESS ENVIRONMENT. Any personal items found on desks AFTER OFFICE HOURS will be DESTROYED.

....

I was starting to feel these emails in my soul. I read it again. Clean desk policy?

Let's start by deleting your email.

Leslie had always said there was something else going on with that.

'It's nothing to do with the environment,' he'd spit. 'It's so they can disappear you in the night, like a Mexican bloody cartel.'

I sort of missed Leslie now.

'"Oh, keep their desks empty so no one notices when they've gone." That's what happens! That's what happened to Jenny Stevens!'

Jenny Stevens, of Harmony. She was just coming up to her

eleventh year on the job. Taken to one side on the Friday before her contract was up. Told she'd done her last show. They don't let you say goodbye to the listeners; there is no time for cloying sentimentality, they say, not in a commercial operation. Doesn't matter that these people have had you in their lives for so long. They say the listeners will find it distressing. Best just to go. Disappear. They tell you afterwards, so you don't say anything on-air, and people leave early on Fridays – less chance of a scene. You have the weekend to calm down, think about your options, work on your statement, say you'd like to thank the station for eleven great years but the time has come to 'explore new opportunities'. They thank you for your time and talk about how exciting the new-look Harmony is going to be. Seems a good approach to life. Send out releases to friends and family. 'I'd like to thank Hayley for two really interesting years. I'm proud of all we achieved during our time together – including replacing an old kitchen pedal bin with a stainless steel Brabantia one with a removable plastic inner bucket which is certainly a decision I will be replicating moving forward – but the moment has come to explore some exciting new opportunities on the horizon.'

My phone rang.

Blocked.

I nearly pressed Decline. Hayley again. She'd listened to the show, maybe, or just checked her watch – she knew I'd be out of studio.

But what if it wasn't?

What if it was Pia?

'Hello,' I said, fumbling for it, answering it.

'Tom?'

Not Hayley. Nor Pia. Who?

'This is Jo Ward, I work with Matthew Channing?'

'Oh,' I said, sitting up straight. 'Yes?'

'Matthew's filming in LA right now, but asked me to pass something on?'

'Okay.'

'He says he's going to call you tomorrow evening and that you need to be ready.'

'I see.'

'Do you know what that means?'

'I do,' I said. 'It means something's about to happen.'

'That's right,' she said. 'It means something's about to happen.'

'I need to book a studio,' I said. 'Tomorrow evening.'

'Why?' said Pippy. 'Why tomorrow evening?'

'A story.'

'Ooh, I love stories.'

'Good.'

'What story?'

'A big story.'

'A secret story?'

'A big secret story.'

'I'll book 6A.'

The Matthew Channing story would be a good distraction. That's what I should concentrate on. Get my name out there.

Pia would love it if she knew. She'd laugh about how it had happened. An older man with a pipe. A tube journey. A bar. A lie. Now this.

And maybe Hayley had been useful. Maybe her instincts had been right when she'd mentioned going back to City Sound. She was only saying what she thought I wanted to hear, but there was a reason I wanted to hear it. And this could totally help me get my old job back. But it'd be different this time. No early wake-ups. A nice cushy drivetime show. Rock up about midday. Some basic office noodling. In studio at four. Bit more noodling from seven. Dinner by the quay at eight. Maybe meet a completely normal girl who's never followed a stranger in her life before.

Yeah, man. *Drivetime*.

Could get a flat in the centre. One of those new developments. Just a studio, or maybe a one-bed. See my friends again. Hang out with that completely normal girl who'd never followed a stranger in her life before.

I knew what I'd do. The second the Channing story went out, I'd clip it. Send the audio to my old boss. See what was going on.

Positive. Thinking. Can't let this beat me. *Can't*. Must be proactive. Move my own narrative forward.

So I had my questions – straightforward, to-the-point, designed to allow Matthew simply to present the facts. That's what he wanted from me – his nobody. But there'd be fallout as the media picked up on it. I'd probably be asked to do interviews myself. I'd be known as his confidant, and I had to be careful there. I needed to position myself as a serious journalist who landed the story. But if I wanted the follow-ups, I had to play by Matthew's rules. Not make him look like a bad guy or the kind of man who takes his wife to an awards do and leaves the after-party with the girl he's been seeing on the side. That disappointed me. But no. I was doing the right thing by helping him on this. The right thing for me. It was important. It wasn't just dealing in idle gossip.

So …

Can you tell me in your own words what happened?
How do you feel about this?
Is this something you feel you've learned from?
How are you moving forward?

I stared at the questions. I shook my head. What was I doing?

My phone rang again.

Home.

I thought of Hayley. Of Jeremy, whoever he was and whatever he looked like. This man, so much better than me. So much more interesting. So *different*.

Investment analyst.

Dubai. Cape Town. Paris.

Decline.

I had to be the bigger man.

I could not obsess.

He worked in Covent Garden.

His picture was on the board in reception, under 'Partners'.

Jeremy Minshall. Senior Investment Analyst. Jellico/Slade.

He was looking off camera, smiling as if someone had just told him a joke, one finger to his brow and pointing a pen.

Twat.

He'd been easy enough to find. Basic googling, an hour at most. Andy's description had been thorough, the company one of only three in the area.

I followed him from this wide silver shark of a building where he worked – a glass lift running down the outside, an alleyway packed with smokers.

He had an easy gait, he moved quickly, past the chuggers and homeless, this captain of industry, this master of his universe. I don't know why but I assumed he'd be stocky. He was tall, lean, in a grey suit, shiny. Burnt orange brogues with thin brown laces. Short silver hair, tan, good skin. Big watch. Samsung Galaxy in one hand, matt black wallet in the other.

He was heading for The Bear and Staff.

I followed.

'Ladies!' he shouted, clapping his hands on the shoulders of the biggest of his friends. They looked like a rugby team that never played rugby.

I found a chair, turned away, listened – a copy of *The Times* turned to the TV pages in my lap, letting me blend.

He was seeing a girl, he said, and now my interest was really piqued. Colombian. Completely mad, apparently. Met her at Spearmint Rhino on Tottenham Court Road. Not his favourite, he prefers the gateway pubs, they're less cynical there, more easily impressed. Anyway, took her to Paris, made her drink 'til she sicked-up cut-price shots of Grand Marnier from the hotel bar. Check out the pics on his Facebook page. No, not his *actual* Facebook page. His *other* Facebook page. She went spare when she found out but whatever. At least she didn't call him up constantly, like that Joanna or whatever her name was. Marketing. Face like a slapped arse. How had Alec put it again? 'Body off of *Baywatch*, face off of *Crimewatch*', something like that.

They all laughed like they'd never heard that before. He kept a cocked twenty between two fingers, used it as a pointer, continued: anyway, Alec was a prick who couldn't hold his drink, Jamie didn't have two farthings to rub together, Welshie could never get laid, Graham went to the polytechnic of the West of bloody England … and they all laughed and lapped it up, this alpha male with his opinions and his put-downs and his cocked twenty and his fat wallet and his fat head.

And then someone asked him about that bird he was showing about the place for a while.

'Nah, mate, moved on from that one. Fucking nightmare.'

His eyes never left the girl at the next table. He sucked at his pint, his eyes on her, predatory, looking for a wound, a weak point.

'Sad eyes, my weakness. Not getting what she wanted at home.'

My hands tightened around my pint.

'All I did was give her a smile, she wanted to commit!' he said. 'I told her, look, it's not me – it's you.'

They thumped the table with joy. This guy was their king.

'Food!' he said. 'Come on, you pricks.'

They wouldn't notice a guy like me, and I was now pretty good at following, but men like this don't see the quiet. It's like they can only register their own kind. The suits, the shoes, the watches, the only things that matter.

I wondered what Pia would think of me doing this. Gathering information; setting my mind at rest. It was cathartic. I was freeing myself.

Since I discovered the world of Jeremy, my vision was clearer, the universe in sharper focus.

I sat in the corner of the restaurant, made slow work of my poppadoms.

They mainly ordered beer. Half an hour in, one of them tried to light a fag. The waiters were good about it, polite, they talked him out of it, but the second they walked away the impressions started. The laughter soared.

They went to the Casino after, the one in Leicester Square, now down to just four of them, ties undone, faces flush, a gas of booze trailing in the air behind them.

I sat, facing the Empire, for an hour and a quarter until he came out, on his own, the fresh air now hitting him, a bouncer trying to steady his gait but being shaken off in a flurry of obscenities.

These people. These people who just know who they are. Who think they live their life as the only important person in the world when they share it with so many others. Who don't realise what they're like. Where do they get the confidence? They're the ones who need to change. They're the ones who need to find themselves, not us.

We made eye contact for just a second and I saw him judge me. Or perhaps try and place me. He gave up and moved off. I let him. Why confront him? I was nothing to him. He wouldn't give me the time of day.

I'd done what I'd wanted to do. Seen the man who won. The *better* man.

And then, there, huddled by the Burger King, just metres away, I saw someone else.

I stood. Moved closer.

My heart stopped for a second when I saw him. It beat faster now, my left hand shaking slightly from adrenaline, the hairs on the back of my neck rising with the fight or flight of it all.

Blood red eyes.

The same hoodie.

It was him.

I froze for a second, the memory of it all washing over me.

And then I snapped out of it.

'Hey,' I said, and this man looked up, confused, already agitated. He looked smaller, hungry, less angry, not like the same guy who'd trapped me, slapped me, stolen from me in an alleyway off the main drag. But I didn't care about any of that now.

He didn't recognise me.

I lost confidence; faltered again.

Fuck it.

'You'll never guess what,' I said, trying to make my voice more blokey, more man-on-the-street. 'That guy just won *massive* on the roulette wheel.'

I pointed at Jeremy, stumbling away, telling some guy with chips to F-off home.

Maybe this, too, is what the doctor meant about taking control.

I watched this other man heave himself up to his feet, nod me his gratitude and slowly follow Jeremy into the night.

thirty-four

'*And finally,*' I said, using The Voice, '*not to end on a disappointing note ... but despite our best efforts here at Talk London, Mayor Jackson was once again forced to express his disappointment at the latest crime figures which show yet again that muggings are* up *in the capital ...*'

Cass shook her head, disgusted.

'*Highs of nineteen today – it's 6.33, and now you're up to date.*'

'Okay, before he goes,' said Cass, 'let's just get this out of the way ...'

She pressed a button.

Jingle.

'*What Did Tom Get Up To – Last Night?*'

I found a man I'm fairly sure was a convicted criminal and I think I got him to beat up a love rival.

'Curry in town and a stroll through Leicester Square!' I said.

Then I took my prescription amitriptyline and squeezed it through the plughole of my filthy sink using the base of my kettle.

'Followed by an early night with a cup of tea!'

We may meet again. But bye for now, *mon ami.*

'That's lovely!' said Cass, hitting the button.

'*That's What Tom Got Up To – Last Night!*'

'Pippy said you'd booked 6A tonight,' said Cass, nudging me. 'What's this for? Doing your showreel?'

'Can I help?' said Work Experience Paul. 'Like … please?'

'Leslie James headhunting you, is he?' said Cass.

I laughed.

'The story,' I said. 'Talking to someone sometime after five. Between five and eight.'

'Oh, the story?' she said. 'The big mysterious story that only you know about.'

'Can I know about it?' said Work Experience Paul.

'I got the nod,' I went on, simultaneously shaking my head at Paul. 'I think you'll be pleased. It'll be for tomorrow's show.'

'So we should leave some space in the running order, should we? You sure about this?'

'Yes I am,' I said. 'You leave some space …'

I could have told her. But this was mine. I couldn't risk it getting out. Didn't want Steve Penny or Lydia Barnes swooping in on this one.

'Talking of stories, how's yours? What's happened with …'

We both stared at Work Experience Paul until he got the hint and wandered off.

'Pia?' I said.

'Pia.'

I sighed and shook my head.

'She's gone off-grid,' I said. 'I went to a guy I thought could help. He did help, but in a different way.'

'Facebook? Twitter?'

'She's on neither. Which is weird, because you'd think Twitter would be natural for someone so keen on following.'

'Is there anyone else you know that knows her?'

Andy didn't know her address. She'd been round to his, once, after her first meeting. She'd just followed him home straight after, surprised him outside his house, asked if he had any squash. Andy invited her in. He told me he'd never found someone so lost. He told me a lot of things.

Then there was Ash. I'd rung him at the zoo. He told me never to phone back. I asked if there was any news on Binky. He told me never to mention his name. I asked if he'd heard from Pia. He told me to go jump off a fucking bridge.

She'd disappeared.

Pia could have been a million things, I now realised.

Maybe she'd been a military kid, always moving, always adapting, always having to fit in. Always making new friends but never friends that lasted.

Or maybe she was on the run. Or she was an orphan. What if she'd stolen money from her parents and fled?

Cass said I should wait for her in reception. We'd go to lunch, we'd brainstorm, we'd come up with something.

I sat under a screen that said WELCOME TO OUR FRIENDS AT TOYOTA! The receptionist whose name I could never remember was fielding calls.

'*Hello, SoundHaus, what department please?*'

Click of a button.

She never fitted in, she said that once, so maybe to cope, she'd fit in with whomever and whatever she could. Or what if maybe she'd been too popular? Maybe she didn't like it and changed her life to suit?

Maybe she'd been all of those things, maybe she'd been heavily into drugs, maybe she'd suffered amnesia, maybe she'd been none of these.

Everything about her was a little off.

Which is why when something seemed just right, it stood out.

Of course she wore that parka. It looked right.

Of course she knew obscure facts about pandas. That seemed right.
'*Hello, SoundHaus, what department please?*'

Jesus, I wished this woman would give it a rest. How did she do that? The relentlessness, the repetition. She needed to shake things up. She should start following.

I stared at her. Listened to her. These words, this rhythm, the beats of the sentence must be drilled deep into her dreams, chiselled into her subconscious. One of those jobs. Pick up the phone, say the sentence, next call, say the sentence, next call, say the sentence …

Escaping this sort of thing – that's exactly what CC was for.

And as I heard '*Hello, SoundHaus, what department please?*' one more time, I felt a shadow at the door. A thought. An idea.

And the shadow grew stronger, and the shadow grew richer, until I realised the shadow could be real. I stood.

'Where's Work Experience Paul?' I said, a little too loudly, barrelling towards the lift as Cass was stepping out. 'I need Work Experience Paul!'

And the woman on the phone paused and stared up at me, no one in this building ever once having heard those words before.

thirty-five

'And this is for the story, yeah?' said Work Experience Paul, picking up one of the landlines, his face a picture of eagerness, willingness, gratitude. No one else in the newsroom knew about this. I'd waited for Bron to leave for lunch.

'It's for a story, yes,' I said. 'That's right.'

'Your story, I mean?' he said. 'The one you were talking about?'

I considered it.

'Yeah, let's go with that,' I said, and excitedly, he began to dial.

There'd been something that had struck me as odd, that first night with Pia – the night we stood on Church Street, moments away from spotting Old Man Stokey, moments away from my first follow.

I couldn't work out why it seemed odd, at the time, because everything seemed odd that night ... but now, here, it hit me: it's precisely because amongst all that, it seemed so *normal*.

I found a number – made sure Paul had his – and dialled.

I know words, I'm sure I do; I know how they sound. I know what they look like as they leave a person's mouth. I know when someone's reading, I know when someone's ad-libbing, and I know when someone's said something a million times before.

'Hello, I wonder if you can help me, I'm calling from SoundHaus Radio,' said Paul, when someone on the other end picked up, and as someone picked up my own call I said the same ...

Pia had said what she'd said a million times before, I now realised.

It was too casual, too quick to trip off the tongue, too *easy*.

Paul hung up, shook his head, found the next number on an incredibly long list of kitchen and home supply stores in north, east and north-east London, and started to dial.

[12]

Ezra James Cockroft passed away on 17 September 1983. He was eighty-one.

I attended his funeral. I brought white lilacs, the same white lilacs he'd laid at the grave of Mae, his adored but imperfect wife, every Sunday since 1973 and his return to New York.

There were mourners at his funeral. The small white church in Amenia Union rang its bells loud that morning. I read on a plaque that it was considered one of the finest imitations of an English country parish church in the country. I guess he would've liked that.

I stood at the back, with the guys Ezra would see every day in Greenwich Village. Ray from Ray's Pizza and the girl from the Chinese takeout on Franklin mixed with the guys with whom he'd seen the tail end of the war, and the few academics from the university who still spoke to him.

The reverend spoke tenderly, and I noticed in front of him a beautiful woman with beautiful hair and a beautiful smile and eyes that could light up the sky.

She was crying.

I knew I would go home, but when the service was complete, and the mourners began to move, and the cars started up, I followed instead.

Found myself by her side.

The truth of this piece is, I'm not sure Cockroft had the answer.

To be or not to be. To live or to live like some other guy.

He fell into following because his life was suddenly out of his control.

He saw a man who looked like he had what Ezra no longer did.

He wanted it back, because it had belonged to him, once.

And the only way he could take it was by pretending. He was a mimic.

He'd admit that. He'd be the first.

Or the second, of course – being a mimic.

He may have spent much of his life being someone else. But whomever he was, and whenever that was – he was the greatest man I knew.

I shared a bus back to the city with the girl with the smile.

We sat adjacent to a man who'd travelled to the funeral with his family. I noticed they had more luggage than most.

I extended my hand and introduced myself.

'Andreas,' he said, with a hint of an accent.

thirty-six

Grey office, strip lighting, and I'd say probably plenty of Pippies and Maureens.

Cars shot by, buses in both directions.

It was quarter past five. I stood across the road, wind flicking polystyrene takeaway boxes down the street, cellophane wrappers and crisp packets rising and dancing round bins.

Work Experience Paul had struck gold. The one thing in our favour had been her name. Pia. Just rare enough. We'd tried kitchen supplies, kitchen and home supplies, kitchen and home suppliers, kitchen fitters, kitchen installers, kitchen and home advisers, kitchen makers, cabinet makers, commercial kitchen supplies, commercial kitchen suppliers, the list goes on and keeps featuring the words 'kitchen', 'kitchens' or 'home'.

And then, almost three hours in …

I'd sorted Paul out. Promised him an exceptional reference. Gave him my *M* Style Awards goodie bag. Raided the prize cupboard and thrown albums and premiere tickets and t-shirts at him. Promised never to call him Work Experience Paul again.

'Finally,' I told him. 'You are going to reap the rewards of undertaking thankless and barely-paid tasks for London's third-favourite commercial radio endeavour. And you are going to reap those rewards *daily*.'

Then Pippy walked in and told him to fetch her a posh coffee.

I'd been here, on this road, for an hour. Busied myself for a while in the café under the bridge. Read the *Sun* cover to cover. Apparently there'd be an explosive story at the weekend '*set to change all you thought you knew about a major British star – only in this week's super soaraway* Sun on Sunday*!*'

I looked over at the door again. This was one tatty operation. Peeling paint, scratched glass. Faded sky-blue logo not touched since the eighties. Rusty cages protecting cheap double-glazing, ancient curved PC screens.

A woman pushed the door open, bade someone inside goodnight. The wind caught the bag in her hand and she smoothed her jacket down, braving an evening on the turn.

My phone buzzed.

Blocked.

I knew what this was. I could answer; put him off. But I needed time.

No, I should answer.

'Hello?'

'Tom, this is Jo Ward – just checking you're there and your phone's on.'

'Yes, Jo, hi …' I said. 'I'm not at the studio, but I'm on my way.'

'You're …'

'It'll be fine, Jo, speak soon.'

Hang up.

Still no sign of Pia.

I decided I must do this. I could be back at the studio in twenty minutes if the tube was kind. I pushed at the door. It was locked. I pressed the bell. They buzzed me in.

Inside the small office of Mandrake Kitchens and Home Supplies, six desks at odd angles battled for space. It was otherwise empty, save for a short, red-faced woman in the corner. Absolute Radio blathered away in the corner. The woman sat in a navy MKHS sweater below a poster for rivets and joints and MDF.

'Can I help you?' she said, all smiles.

'Hi,' I said. 'Look, this'll sound odd, but does Pia work here?'

Her face lit up.

'Pia Jones?'

When she'd said it that night – 'Don't you want to be normal? Order the same curry every Friday night from the same place you always use? Get an office job, answer the phones, "*Good morning, Kitchen and Home Supplies, Tom speaking* …?"' – I'd thought nothing of it. But it was a little piece of grey reality in a world she wanted to be rainbows.

'Pia … Jones,' I said. 'Yes.'

The woman pointed at a photo, enlarged but faded, tacked to the wall. Staff Christmas Party. All smiles, drunk in a Wetherspoons, holding barley-yellow pints, Pia giggling. It was the first time I'd seen her as really *part* of something.

'Yes, she works here. Well, she did. Well, she does.'

'Did or does?'

'Tomorrow's her last day. It was her leaving do last night.'

Of course it was.

'Who are you, sorry?' said the woman.

I wasn't sure what to say.

'I'm her friend,' I said. 'I'm her best friend.'

She stood.

'Tom!'

She knew about me, this woman. Looked delighted. Said Pia put the show on in the office. Talked about me, proudly. They knew my voice here.

'What time do you have to get up?' she said, moving towards me. 'Do you have to go to bed really early?'

'When it's still dark, and yes,' I said.

'What's Cass like?' she said. 'She sounds lovely. Why didn't you come to the leaving do? Oh, you should have come. You could have brought Cass. All the boys—'

'Listen, I'm so sorry to be rude, but can I ask: where's Pia right now?'

'Have you called her?'

'Yes,' I lied. 'Went straight to voicemail.'

'That girl,' she said, shaking her head and laughing. 'Well, she went home. I gave her an early. No point sticking around when there's nothing to do.'

'And where is home?' I said, slowly, trying my luck.

'Round the corner,' she said, uncertainly. 'Not far. Though if you don't know, I'm not sure I can really tell you. Is everything okay? Did you two have a fight or something?'

'Why?'

'I just thought she'd been doing really well lately. And then all of a sudden she wasn't, and then she said she was thinking about moving back home, and she stopped putting your show on in the mornings, and …'

'Going home?'

'I know. I thought she'd been turning a corner, lately, is all.'

I thought maybe we both were.

For a second I saw the woman's eyes flicker towards something on the wall by the side of her desk – a scrappy piece of A4, corners curled by the sun and Blu-Tacked to peeling paint.

'Well, listen … whatever you do, don't look at that piece of paper. It's our contacts sheet. I'd hate for you to see something you shouldn't. Now, do you want a cup of tea?'

She walked out of the room taking her mug with her. Maureen would be proud.

I looked at the piece of paper. Then at the photo of Pia again.

'Can I ask a question?' I called out, and the woman backed up, poked her head around the door, gave me permission.

'It's just that this place doesn't seem very ... Pia.'

I hoped she didn't find this too rude.

'God, love, no, it's not,' she said. 'I think she wanted to work here because ... well, she wanted to be *close* to things.'

She made a you-understand face.

I nodded, like I did, like I knew what she meant.

But I didn't have a clue.

She saw me the second she walked out, her parka on, hood up, the fur of the hood like a scarf on her shoulders. I watched her as she stood there, outside the battered door of her second floor flat on Eric Street, framed by satellite dishes and St George flags, and she watched me right back.

The kids on the estate were kicking a football against an Astra.

I had my hands in my pockets, not hiding, not trying to go unseen. Our eyes met and though there was a moment of surprise, she understood.

I wasn't here to talk.

I thought of what Andy had told me as Pia and I walked, one after the other, keeping our distance, her leading, me just following, all the way down Eric Street onto the Mile End Road and through the ticket barrier at the station.

We rode the tube together, her three seats away from me, head leaned back against the window, staring up at the lights, neither of us acknowledging the other, nor what was happening here.

Hayley had been right: Pia had known all about her. She knew all about Jeremy. She'd known, and she'd followed me out of CC that day to tell me. She wanted me to know the truth – partly out of kindness, partly because she hated Hayley's pomposity and grand ideas – but when she'd followed me she'd seen something frail in me; something that couldn't cope. And as we locked eyes on the bridge, and I stormed off towards the Tesco, she trailed after me, part of her still wanting to tell me about my girlfriend and her lover, part of her wondering what would happen if she didn't. What if I wasn't strong enough to hear it? What if I could be made to be stronger?

We got out at East Ham. Walked a few hundred feet, waited at the bus stop in silence for what turned out to be a 101, found seats on the same level, but six or seven people apart. Wordless. More jumpers these days, the odd hat too, autumn knocking on the door. No one could guess we knew each other, no one could guess we were going to the same place, no one could see I was just following.

The phone again.

Blocked.

Not here.

Decline.

She stood, now, and glanced behind her to make sure I'd seen, and she pressed the bell and I got up as she climbed off the bus, hands back in her pockets, head down, moving past the other, normal Londoners, heading home to loved ones, or at the very least microwave meals-for-one.

But now I knew where we were going. Now I was sure. The signs, leading us there, just as we'd all go there one day.

Andy had kept schtum about the zoo for a while, breaking only when pressed, but I wanted to see this for myself, and more importantly ...

Pia had to show me.

She stopped by a florist's, waited for me to catch up, went inside.

We left together with white lilacs, her a few steps ahead of me, and moments later were at the small walls and the three short arches of the City of London Cemetery.

*

Pia had lost it all, one day, two Decembers back.

The man she came to London for had been the man her family advised her against. Not just advised. Said would ruin her.

Not because he was a drunk, or a wife-beater, or a stoner. But because he was so very, very normal. He was a nice enough guy, they'd said, he just lacked ambition. He'd drag her down, slow her down, there was 'nothing about him'. He was boring.

But Pia didn't think he was boring.

He was a biologist. He favoured amphibians. She'd just completed her Diploma in the Management of Zoo and Aquarium Animals from Sparsholt. Got her City & Guilds. World at her feet – or if not the world, then at least the animal kingdom.

They'd met two weeks after he'd returned home from China, after a guest lecture at the Royal Society. He'd been out of the country six months, volunteering for the ZSL, studying a Chinese giant salamander project in central and southern China, and he talked of them with enthusiasm and care. The salamander was dying, because the salamander found it hard to adapt to its environment.

They fell for each other, hard. And six months later, Simon Jones and Pia Kosinski had been married, in front of just a few friends, at the zoo.

He wanted to show her the marmosets that day. He said Ash could get them in. He said his best man had to do everything he asked on his wedding day.

But Pia's mother didn't come. It was too quick for her. Her daughter was settling. They were getting married in a *zoo*, for Christ's sake. Cracks widened.

Pia's mother hadn't been the love of her father's life and Pia knew it. He had done the sensible thing when he'd moved here from New York, a man with sad eyes approaching his thirties. He'd opened up one night at Christmas, drunk on the daiquiris his great aunt used to make, and drunk also on memories, and he talked of a girl with eyes that could light up the sky, the daughter of the man who'd become his best friend over a few months in the early 1980s – the man whose work he'd helped spread round the world with his first ever published-work. An essay that eventually made it into the *New Yorker* and now languished, ignored, somewhere deep in the web.

Pia didn't call her mum to beg for her forgiveness. Why should she? This was the man Pia loved. But how could she explain she needed to follow her heart without using her dad as an example? Cracks turned to chasms.

Chasms to an ocean.

I let her walk on her own, the final fifty metres or so.

My phone buzzed in my pocket. I ignored it.

She stooped by a grave. Lay the flowers gently down. Thought something private, for this guy, for her Simon.

Even when he'd gone – the illness short and swift – her mother couldn't bring herself to call.

Instead, just to be a good Christian, Andy said, she'd sent a condolence card.

Blank.

Could Pia really go 'home' after that? Forgive and forget? Maybe one day. She wasn't ready to leave her husband yet. But to live in this city at all she had to work. She'd just have to make life work in the gaps.

'So now you know,' she said, suddenly there, hands pushed deep into parka pockets, but not stopping, not making eye contact.

Pia had less than anyone I knew.

My phone buzzed again. I pulled it out.

Blocked.

I turned, watching her walk away.

This time I answered.

'Matthew?'

'Tom, what the *fuck*?'

His voice urgent, angry.

'I'm sorry. I'm not ready. I don't think I can do this.'

'*What*?' he said. There were voices in the background. A man shouting at another man. 'Tom, don't do this to me. We *have* to do this. I *chose* you. This will be *good* for you.'

'I can't, Matthew,' I said.

'Oh, *Christ*,' he said. 'You were in on this. This was the *plan*. Why are you doing this? We need to do this *tonight*!'

Pia reached the gates. She walked through.

'Matthew,' I said. 'I'm going to give you a number …'

thirty-seven

'I didn't think I'd see you again,' she said, and we watched the steam rise from the mug she gripped so tightly.

We sat in Pia's flat in Eric Street.

It was ex-local authority. One bedroom. Thump-thump-thump of the stereo next door, then quiet.

We let the silence win.

Then the next song … 'Carry On' by Aphra.

We laughed.

'You didn't tell me,' I said, when we'd stopped. 'About your husband. About Simon.'

'If I had, then that's who I would have been to you,' she said. 'That's who I've been to everyone in that office all this time. But I figured it's time to stop being that person. And with you I didn't have to be.'

'It's why you follow,' I said.

'It's like exploring,' she said. 'My dad said Cockroft told him exploring is just another way of saying it's okay to get lost. I wanted to get lost. I used to be different, before all that happened. I was happy. Can you believe that?' – she laughed, shook her head – 'I was the happy-go-lucky one always making light of things. I always had something to do; a new idea. And then one day that all went away, and I thought it would come back but the only thing that stayed was the dark.'

'I know about the dark,' I said.

'I know you do,' she said. 'Amitriptyline. I looked it up.'

'How did you know about that?'

'Why do you think I wanted to dye my hair back at your place? So I could look in your cupboards. I knew you were taking something.'

'You dyed your hair just to get in my bathroom? Why not just say you needed the toilet?'

She shrugged.

'More dramatic,' she said. 'But I could see it in you. That day I first saw you, I was going to tell you all about Hayley – where she'd gone, why, with who.'

'I know.'

'Your life was about to get ripped apart and I didn't want that to happen.'

'You made my life better,' I said. 'Showed me another side of it all.'

'I think this is who you're supposed to be,' she said, gently. 'Or at least, getting close.'

'What about you?'

'I don't know.'

'But if you're exploring, you're looking for something and you might not know what it is. The others – Andy and Jackie and the others – they do it because they're looking for who they could be. You do it because you're looking for who you used to be.'

She stared into her tea.

'You want to come back,' I said. 'You want to be who you were.'

She nodded.

'I do.'

'So what are you going to do?'

She sighed.

'Face up to things. I think I could move back to mum's. We've been talking a little on the phone. You sort of helped with that.'

'Me?'

'You once said, "How hard is it to pick up a phone?" You were banging on about love and you were doing it with such conviction that I thought you had a point. I thought I should follow your example.'

'And what then?'

'Get a job. Sue at Mandrake said she'd give me a reference. Says her brother owns a timber merchants up there, there might be some casual work.'

'You're going to be a lumberjack?' I said.

'*Office* work,' she smiled, and she batted my arm.

I'd miss that.

'What about you?' she said. 'What are you going to do? Go back to Hayley?'

I smiled.

'She's left a few messages,' I said. 'Said she's made up her mind. Wants to move to Bristol. Wants me to take her back. She wants to settle down with me, have a family with me …'

'Do you believe her?'

'For all I know she saw someone say that on *EastEnders* and decided it sounded good. No, I went round there this morning after work. Packed the rest of my stuff. Left her a note.'

'A note? What did it say?'

'It said, "Hayley – *this* is how you leave someone."'

She laughed.

'I'll miss this awful place,' she said.

I looked around.

'Maybe I'll take it,' I said. 'I can't stay in the Holiday Inn forever.'

'They have a wonderful meeting room,' she said. 'Free Wi-Fi.'

I finished my tea, put it down, stood up.

'You used to say I didn't know what I wanted,' she said. 'But I think I'll find it. I think I'll know it when I see it.'

A thought struck me. A memory. Dr Moon's waiting room.

I got my wallet out, opened it.

'What are you doing?' she said. 'You going to give me a book token?'

There, behind my bank cards, that was where I'd put it.

I handed it to her.

'I saw this and thought of you. Think of it as a goodbye present.'

She smiled. Held it in her hands. Thought for a moment.

'I'm Pia,' she said. 'I'm twenty-seven-and-a-third, and my favourite colour is blue too.'

I smiled. She took my hand.

'Goodbye, Tom Ditto.'

thirty-eight

Do you know what?

Leslie James's interview with Matthew Channing had been a *sensation*, in the end.

He'd taken the call that night from Matthew himself, recorded the whole thing down the ISDN line at his house, and gone big on it the next day on Sunrise. The *Sun on Sunday* had to play catch-up. They'd gone huge, though. Front-page splash. Called Matthew a Love Rat. Used the picture of him outside the Randolph, cropped so you could see him and Alice – but not without noticing he had me in a headlock, too.

Leslie had given him exactly what he needed, and exactly what I wouldn't have. A very hard time. 'We're here to report,' Leslie once said. 'Not help.' The audio had been pounced upon and used up and down the country immediately – every news website had it, every Twitter feed seemed to point at it. It was played on *Newsnight* in a debate about press intrusion, it was played on Lorraine in a debate about unfit fathers.

And each time, there I was – unnamed friend in a headlock.

Leslie was asked to do interviews himself. Suddenly, he wasn't the Mad Jam Nazi Rant guy any more. He was the guy with two broken arms and a black eye who'd got the exclusive with the man everyone wanted to hear from. He was the eccentric-looking DJ that *TMZ*, *Deadline* and the *Hollywood Reporter* all at one point or other called 'hard-nosed radio journalist Leslie James'.

He'd been pathetically grateful to me. Six months later, when he was offered drivetime back at Talk London (and he could use his arms again) he let them hang on for a while before saying yes – and asking if I'd join him. This time, though, his agent ensured contractually that Leslie got his own cupboard for jam.

I thought about the offer. Weighed it up against Bristol, and breakfast again. Drivetime meant I'd really have to be up and out of bed by … let me see … 11.15 or so. Plus there was a pay bump. A fixed contract. Something approaching the first hints of respect.

I let him hang on for a while before saying no. I told him I was happy where I was.

Which was lucky, actually, because one month later he was arrested on suspicion of a string of historic sexual harassment offences which took place in the 1970s and early 1980s.

Mike Brundell got drive and couldn't believe his bloody luck.

The piece of paper I'd given Pia. She'd opened it right there in front of me that day, and something had happened in her eyes. Some moment of determination. Like she'd seen a sign. In reality, what she'd seen was a job ad.

She'd applied. Used me as a reference, and Ash, too. They had her in for interview, she'd been nervous but held it together, but they knew her there already. They'd been waiting for her to come back, they said. She had experience. She had her DMZAA. Slowly, she had found her enthusiasm, again.

Maybe she had even finally found herself.

So Pia Jones became a junior keeper at Whipsnade Zoo on twenty-three grand a year plus pension. She said Simon would have loved it.

She bought a small blue car, and had a badge that said Mammal Team. I did not stop making fun of her about this for weeks.

Because although we said goodbye that night on Eric Street, it was only so we could say hello again a fortnight later, somewhere else, when the dust had settled, when we could say hello like it was for the first time.

I'd just turned around – in a Tesco Express – and there she was. Standing at the self-service till behind me, matching me bleep for bleep, beaming up at me in that very same blue parka.

They never did find Binky, now that you ask. I like to think he's still out there. I like to think maybe he found his way to CC, and learned to follow, adapt, blend in, did what Pia always says: 'subscribe to life in a different way.' Maybe he was out there now, finally part of society, no longer an outsider looking for the way in, making friends, having fun, taking lovers, laughing loudly, following. Monkey see, monkey do …

Or maybe he'd been hit by a car.

Ding.

Email.

'Who's it from?' said Pia, resting her head on my shoulder. 'Is it from Cass?'

It was 10am. A bright, clear day. If I had to guess, I'd say highs of nineteen.

We were on the Heathrow Express. We'd been waiting with our bags at Paddington until we'd spotted someone suitable.

It had been seven months, two weeks and a day since I'd left Hayley. Hayley – a girl I'm not sure I'd ever even really had. And finally I was getting my holiday. It was Pia's idea, and that's a pretty big step for flatmates. You spend so much time together, talking about the small things, the big things, arguing, bickering, laughing, that it seems odd to want to do it all together somewhere else for two weeks.

'Not Cass, no,' I said.

'You're lucky,' she said. 'Some girls would kill you for this.'

'I don't think Cass sees you as a direct threat to our relationship, if I'm honest,' I said. 'You're a small woman in a big parka and a panda hat. I look like your carer.'

Dad had come over for Christmas. He loved Cass. Said Mum would have done too. Said he'd never liked Hayley.

'Why?' I said. 'You've never even met her!'

'She didn't remind me of anyone,' he said, thinking about it. 'I know that sounds unusual, Tom, but whenever you talked about her … I could never tell who she was.'

The dog was still around, of course. No happy ending there. I don't think the dog will ever really truly go away. I don't think they do. But it's a smaller breed, now. I think I can hopefully say I've at least found the beginnings of a leash.

Pia had left Eric Street and I'd quite obviously moved out of Wandsworth. There are only so many nights in a row you can eat a Holiday Inn Express Chicken Tikka Masala. We found a small two-bed together in Hackney, above the Hard Wok Café. It had a little balcony. We could sit there, with our tea, legs dangling over the edge, watching people go by, guessing where they were going, following their journeys in our heads.

We both lost people, me and Pia. We both lost ourselves. We almost lost each other.

'It's probably just the usual,' I said, getting my phone out. 'Spam. Or some different spam.'

'Will this work out, do you think?' she said. 'I mean, this guy could be going anywhere.'

She cocked her head and nodded at the man we'd chosen. Baseball cap down low, sunglasses, decent jeans, expensive bag, oblivious.

Los Angeles? Paris? Monaco?

'It'll work out,' I said. 'It'll be an adventure.'

She smiled.

I looked at my phone and my heart sank.

....

FROM: MAUREEN THOMAS
TO: ALL STAFF

All staff PLEASE refrain from PUTTING BISCUIT'S in the
CUPBOARD'S as these CUPBOARD'S are NOT meant for
FOOD.

WILL YOU EVER UNDERSTAND?

....

I stared at it.

Took a breath.

My fingers hovered over the keypad.

'I love you, mate,' said Pia, suddenly.

I turned to her.

'I love you too,' I said.

Someone nearby sneezed.

'But not like that,' she said, turning away again.

'Christ no,' I said, looking back at my email. 'Not like that.'

I hit reply.

The first time I'd done this.

....

FROM: TOM ADOYO
TO: MAUREEN THOMAS

....

I thought about it.

Should I?

Sod it.

....

CC: ALL STAFF

....

What to write?
How to put this?
Ah, yes.

....

UNSUBSCRIBE.

....

I pressed Send, then put my arm around Pia, two friends on a train, wondering what might happen next.

And what happened next was that the man in the hat got his ticket out.

And we held our breath.

Acknowledgements

My first thanks must go to Matt Dyson, one of Britain's finest newsreaders, who unwittingly allowed me to intricately study the minutiae of his work for four hours a day, five days a week, between August 1st 2011 and December 21st 2012, from a distance of less than six feet. *That's* research.

Matt is not Tom Adoyo, but he taught him everything he knows.

At the same time, I should thank Dave Masterman, Andy Ashton, Steve Ferdinando and Simon Fowler, as well as everyone at Global Radio (which is not and never has been SoundHaus...). Also to the confirmed listeners of Xfm – thank you.

Thanks to my editor, Jake Lingwood. To Emily Yau, Gillian Green, Louise Jones, Amelia Harvell and everyone at Ebury.

Thanks to George Cockroft of Canaan, New York.

Thanks to Greta and Elliot, and to mum and dad, who read everything first and always will.

And – of course – thank you to you.

www.dannywallace.com

If you enjoyed *Who is Tom Ditto?*
read on for a sneak peek at

Charlotte Street

also by Danny Wallace

EBURY
PRESS

There's nothin' like the humdrum
Of life and love in London
Chasin' girls out of the sticks
Changing worlds with twelve quick clicks

Girl in a Photo, The Kicks

'*As good things go … she went.*'

Hovis Presley

BEFORE

It happened on a Tuesday.

I suppose the noise it would make in a film would be *boom*, but there was no boom with this.

No boom, no bang, no tap, crack or snap.

Just a flash of glass, a moment in flight, a flicker of shooting star through a history lesson, and all the colder for it.

Things like this aren't supposed to happen on Tuesdays. It's history, then art; it's not *this*.

I shivered the second I saw him, but the strange thing is that I also noticed the weather; this weak, grey veil of rain beyond the chipped old railings, beyond the thin scarred trees.

It was like the moment in a dream where you see something happening, something bad, something that should never be, and your bones become heavy and your feet hard to raise, as whatever warning you try and call out through the fog of it all becomes too slurred and too blurred to be useful.

It would have been better, had it been a dream.

What would you call him? A gunman? Seems dramatic, especially this early in the story, but a gunman he was. There, on the other side of the street, maybe nine storeys up, pleased with his first shot, now cocking the rifle and snapping it back, reloading, finding his aim.

Gunman will do.

'Right. *Up*. Let's go.'

Calm. Short words. Quickly.

'*Now*, please.'

I'm suddenly in the middle of the room. It feels like I can do most good here but really, what *can* I do? I turn and scan the flats again, find him.

He's *laughing*. His mate is, too.

'What? Where to?' said someone, maybe Jaideep, or maybe the one with the hair whose name I could never remember. You know the one – the one the teachers call Superfly. Instinctively I stood in front of him, his paid protector, like he'd made himself a target just by asking sir a question.

'Hall,' was the best I could manage, the back of my neck expecting attack, my faked calm fighting my fight or flight. 'Up.'

'Hey ...' said someone else. 'Hey ...', and I looked at them, and right across their face was the terror I felt, as they struggled to understand what they were seeing, what it meant.

'Okay, *now* please, Anna. Please.'

'Sir ...'

The waver in the voice, the fear; it would spread, and fast.

'Out the DOOR.'

They moved, shocked, and quickly now, as quick as the news spread through the school. As quick as the police arrived, with their own guns, their cars and their dogs, their helmets and shields. The kids found their confidence again then, pressed up against windows, peeping through buckled Venetians, as eight or ten armed coppers made a heavy path up the stairwell of Alma Rose House while the others, tense and furrow-browed, stared the place out, willing our shooter to try something.

The kids applauded as they dragged him out. Applause was the first sign it was over. They applauded the vans, shouted jokes at the coppers and cooed at the chopper ... but the kids hadn't seen what I'd seen.

I was last out of 3Gc, I'd tell Sarah, later. She'd stopped at the offie for an eight-pack of Stella and a bottle of Rioja – the only medicine she had a licence to give – but she'd rushed home to be with me, her arm on mine, her head against my shoulder. The kids had been safe, I told her, and I'd stayed with them while Anna Lincoln and Ben Powell ran to Mrs Abercrombie's office to get help, though Ranjit had already dialled 999 by then, and probably posted on Twitter too.

But I'd stayed in that room just a second or two longer, just to work out whether this could be real, whether he could actually be doing what he was doing, whether I was making a mistake raising this alarm.

And that's when he'd laughed again. And taken aim again.

I'd never felt more alone. Never more aware of myself. What I was, what I wasn't, what I wanted.

And another glimpse of shooting star flit its path inches from my face, to bounce against a wall behind and scutter and scuttle and skip on the floor.

And that, doctor, is when the damage was done.

ONE

Or '(She) Got Me Bad'

I wonder if we should start with the introductions.

I know who you are. You're the person reading this. For whatever reason, and in whatever place, that's you, and soon we'll be friends, and you'll never ever convince me otherwise.

But me?

I'm Jason Priestley.

And I know what you're thinking. You're thinking: Goodness! Are you the same Jason Priestley, born in Canada in 1969, famous for his portrayal of Brandon Walsh, the moral centre of the hit American television series *Beverly Hills 90210*?

And the surprising answer to your very sensible question is no. No, I'm not. I'm the other one. I'm the thirty-two-year-old Jason Priestley who lives on the Caledonian Road, above a videogame shop between a Polish newsagents and that place that everyone *thought* was a brothel, but wasn't. The Jason Priestley who gave up his job as a deputy head of department in a bad North London school to chase a dream of being a journalist after his girlfriend left him but who's ended up single and going to cheap restaurants and awful films so's he can write about them in that free newspaper they give you on the tube which you take but don't read.

Yeah. *That* Jason Priestley.

I'm also the Jason Priestley with a problem.

You see, just in front of me – right here, on this table, just in front of me – is a small plastic box. A small plastic box I've come to regard as a small plastic box that could *change* things. Or, at least, make them *different*.

And right now, I'd take different.

I don't know what's in this small plastic box, and I don't know if I ever will. *That's* the problem. I *could* know; I could have it open within the hour, and I could pore over its contents, and I could know once and for all whether there was any … *hope* in there.

But if I do, and it turns out there *is* hope in there, what if that's all it is? Just a bit of hope? And what if that hope turns to nothing?

Because the one thing I hate about hope – the one thing I *despise* about it, that no one ever seems to *admit* about it – is that suddenly having hope is the easiest route to sudden hope-lessness there is.

And yet that hope is already within me. Somehow, without my inviting it in or expecting it in any way, it's there, and based on what? Nothing. Nothing apart from the glance she gave me and the fleeting glimpse I got of … *something*.

I'd been standing on the corner of Charlotte Street when it happened.

It was maybe six o'clock, and a girl – because yeah, you and I both *knew* there was going to be a girl; there *had* to be a girl; there's *always* a girl – was struggling with the door of the black cab and the packages in her hands. She had a blue coat and nice shoes, and white bags with names I'd never seen before on them, and boxes, and even, I think, a cactus poking out the top of a Heal's bag.

I was ready to walk past, because that's what you do in London, and to be honest, I nearly did … but then she nearly dropped the cactus. And the other packages all shifted about, and she had to stoop to keep them all up, and for a moment there was something sweet and small and helpless about her.

And then she uttered a few choice words I won't tell you here in case your nan comes round and finds this page.

I stifled a smile, and then looked at the cabbie, but he was doing nothing, just listening to TalkSport and smoking, and so – and I don't know why, because like I say, this is *London* – I asked if I could help.

And she smiled at me. This incredible smile. And suddenly I felt all manly and confident, like a handyman who knows *just* which nail to buy, and now I'm holding her packages and some of her bags, and she's shovelling new ones that seem to have appeared from nowhere into the cab, and she's saying, '*Thank* you, this is *so* kind of you,' and then there's that moment. The glance, the fleeting glimpse of that *something* I mentioned. And it felt like a beginning. But the cabbie was impatient and the night air cold, and I suppose we were just too British to say anything else and then it was, '*Thanks,*' and that smile again.

She closed the door, and I watched the cab move off, tail lights fading into the city, hope trailing and clattering on the ground behind it.

And then – just as the moment seemed over – I looked down.

I had something in my hands.

A small plastic box.

I read the words on the front.

Single Use 35mm Disposable Camera.

I wanted to shout at the cab – hold the camera up and make sure she knew she'd left something behind. And for a second I was filled with ideas – maybe when she came running back, I'd suggest a coffee, and then agree when she said what she *really* needed was a huge glass of wine, and then we'd get a bottle, because it made better financial sense to get a bottle, and then we'd agree we shouldn't be eating on empty stomachs, and then we'd jack in our jobs and buy a boat and start making cheese in the country.

But nothing happened.

No screech of car tyre, no pause then crunch of gears, no reverse lights, no running, smiling girl in nice shoes and a blue coat.

Just a new taxi stopping, so a fat man could get out at a cashpoint.

You see what I mean about hope?

'Now, before we go any further whatsoever,' said Dev, holding up the cartridge and tapping it very gently with his finger. 'Let's talk about the name. "Altered Beast".'

I was staring at Dev in what I like to imagine was quite a blank manner. It didn't matter. In all the years I've known him I doubt he's seen many looks from me, other than my blank one. He probably thinks I've looked like this since university.

'Now, it conjures up not only mysticism, of course, but also *intrigue*, meshing as it does both Roman culture *and* Greek mythology.'

I turned and looked at Pawel, who seemed mildly traumatised.

'Now, the interesting thing about the sound effects—' said Dev, and he pressed a button on his keyring and out came a tinny, distorted noise that sounded as if it *might* be trying to say, *'Wise Fwom Your Gwaaave!'.*

I put my hand up.

'Yes, Jase, you've got a question?'

'Why've you got that noise on your keyring?'

Dev sighed, and made quite a show of it. 'Oh, I'm sorry, Jason, but I'm *trying* to tell Pawel here about the early development of Sega Mega Drive games in the late 1980s and early 1990s. I'm sorry we're not covering your personal passion of the work of American musical duo Hall & Oates, but that's not why Pawel is here, is it?'

Pawel just smiled.

Pawel does a lot of smiling when he visits the shop. It's usually to collect money Dev owes him for his lunchtime snacks. I sometimes watch his face as he wanders around the floor, taking in ancient, faded posters of *Sonic 2* or *Out Run*, picking up chipped carts or battered copies of old magazines, flicking through the reviews of long-dead platformers or shoot-em-ups that look like they were drawn by toddlers now. Dev let him borrow a Master System and a copy of *Shinobi* the other day. Turns out you didn't really get many Master Systems in mid-80s Eastern Europe, and even less ninjas. We're not going to let him borrow the Xbox, because Dev says his eyes might explode.

'Anyway,' said Dev. 'The name of this very shop – Power Up! – owes its existence to—'

And I start to realise what Dev's doing. He's trying to *bore* Pawel out of here. Dominate the conversation. Bully him into leaving, the way men with useless knowledge often do. Throw in phrases like, 'Oh, didn't you *know* that?', or, 'Of course, you'll *already* be aware …' in order to patronise and thwart and win.

He can't have enough cash on him for lunch.

'How much does he owe you, Pawel?' I asked, fishing for a fiver in my pocket.

Dev shot me a smile.

I love London.

I love everything about it. I love its palaces and its museums and its galleries, sure. But also, I love its filth, and damp, and stink. Okay, well, I don't mean *love*, exactly. But I don't mind it. Not any more. Not now I'm used to it. You don't mind anything once you're used to it. Not the graffiti you find on your door the week after you painted over it, or the chicken bones and cider cans you have to move before you can sit down for your damp and muddy picnic. Not the everchanging fast food joints – AbraKebabra to Pizza the Action to Really Fried Chicken – and all on a high street that despite its three new names a week never seems to look any different. Its tawdriness can be comforting, its wilfulness inspiring. It's the London I see every day. I mean, tourists: they see the Dorchester. They see Harrods, and they see men in bearskins and Carnaby Street. They very rarely see the Happy Shopper on the Mile End Road, or a drab Peckham disco. They head for Buckingham Palace, and see waving above it the red, white and blue, while the rest of us order dansak from the Tandoori Palace, and see Simply Red, White Lightning, and Duncan from Blue.

But we should be proud of that, too.

Or, at least, get used to it.

You could find a little bit of Poland on one end of the Caledonian Road these days, the way you could find Portugal in Stockwell, or Turkey all through Haringey. Since the shops came, Dev has used his lunchtimes to explore an entirely new culture. He was like that at university when he met a Bolivian girl at Leicester's number one nightclub, Boomboom. I was studying English, and for a month or so, Dev was studying Bolivian. Each night he'd dial-up Internet and wait ten minutes for a single page to load, before printing it off and committing stock Spanish phrases to memory, hoping once again to bump into her, but never, ever managing it.

'Fate!' he'd say. 'Ah, fate.'

Now it was all about Poland. He gorges himself on *Z szynka* cheese, proclaiming it to be the finest cheese he's ever tasted, ignoring the fact it's processed and in little plastic packets and tastes *exactly* like Dairylea. He buys *Krokiety* and *Krupnik* and more cheese, with bright pink synthetic ham pebbledashed across each bland jaundiced slab. Once he bought a beetroot, but he didn't eat it. Plus, if it's the end of the day he'll make sure whatever customer happens to still be there sees him with a couple of *Paczki* and a goblet of *Jezynowka*. And once he's made it obvious enough and they've asked what he on *earth* he's got in his hands, he'll say, 'Oh, they're brilliant. Haven't you ever *had Paczki*?', and then look all international and pleased with himself for a bit.

But he's not doing it to show off. Not really. He's got a good heart, and I think he thinks he's being welcoming and informative. It's still the laziest form of tourism there is, though. No one else I know simply sits there, playing videogames, and waiting for the countries to come to him, with each new wave of what he likes to call the 'Newbies'. He wants to see the world, he'll tell you – but he prefers to see it all from the window of his shop.

Men come from everywhere to shop here. Men trying to recapture their youth, or complete a collection, or find that one game they used to be brilliant at. There's new stuff, sure – but that's just to survive. That's not why people come. And when they do, sometimes they get the Power Up! reference. After that, it's only a matter of moments before Dev mentions Makoto Uchida, and that's usually enough to establish his superiority and scare them off, maybe having bought a £2 copy of *Decap Attack* or *Mr Nutz*, but probably not.

Dev sells next to nothing, but next to nothing seems to be just enough. His dad owns a few restaurants on Brick Lane and keeps the basics paid, and what little extra there is keeps Dev in ham-flecked *Szazinska*, at any rate. Plus he's been good to me, so I shouldn't judge him. I lost a girlfriend and a flat but gained a flatmate and virtually no rent in return for a few afternoon shifts and a weekly supply of *Krokiety*.

Talking of which …

'Right, we've got *Żubr* or *Żywiec* – take your pick!' said Dev, holding up the bottles. I wasn't sure I could pronounce either of them so pointed at the one with the least letters.

'Or I think I've got some *Lech* somewhere,' he said, pronouncing it 'Letch' and then giggling. Dev knows it's pronounced 'Leck', because he asked Pawel, but he prefers saying 'Letch' because it means he can giggle afterwards.

'*Żubr* is fine,' I said – something I'd never said before – and he flipped the lid and passed it over.

I caught sight of myself in the mirror behind him.

I looked tired.

Sometimes I look at myself and think, Is this it?, and then I think, Yes, it is. This is literally the best you will ever look. Tomorrow, you will look just a little bit worse, and this is how it will go, for ever. You should definitely buy some Berocca.

I have the haircut of the mid-thirties man. Until recently, I wore cool, ironic T-shirts, until I realised the real irony was they made me look less cool.

I'm too old to experiment with my hair, see, but too young to have found the style I'll take to the grave. You know the one I mean – the one we're all headed for, if we're lucky enough to have any left by then. Flat and dulled and sitting on every man in an oversized shirt at an all-inclusive holiday resort breakfast buffet, surrounded by unpleasant children and a passive aggressive wife who have worked together in single-minded unity to quash his ambitions the way they have quashed his hairstyle.

I say that like I'm any better, or that my ambitions are heroic and worthy. I am a man between styles, is all, and there are millions of me. I'm at that awkward stage between the man of his twenties and the man of his forties. A stage I have come to call 'the man in his thirties'.

I sometimes wonder what the caption at the bottom of my *Vanity Fair* shoot would say, the day I wrote the cover story and they decided to make a big deal of me:

Hair by Angela at Toni & Guy, near Angel tube, even though her fingers smell of nicotine and she says 'axe' instead of 'ask'.
Smell: Lynx Africa (for men). £2.76, Tesco Metro, Charing Cross.
Watch: Swatch ('It was an impulse buy at Geneva airport,' he confides, laughing lightly, and picking at his salade niçoise. 'Our plane was three hours delayed and I'd already bought a Toblerone!')
Clothes: Model's own (with thanks to Topman VIP 10% discount card, available free to literally everyone in the world).

But I'm not that bad. A Spanish model I met at a Spanish bar on Hanway Street and once even had a passable date with said I looked 'very English', which I took to mean like Errol Flynn, even though later I found out he was Australian.

'What. A. Day,' said Dev, sighing a little too heavily for a man who can't really have had that much of a day. 'You? Yours?'

'Yeah,' I said. 'You know, not bad,' by which I meant the opposite.

It had been bad from the moment I'd got up this morning. The milk had been off, but how's that different from normal, and the postman had slammed and clattered our letterbox, but the real kicker was when, with a grim tightening of my stomach, I'd flicked my laptop on, and headed for Facebook, and even though I *knew* something like this would eventually happen, I saw those words, the words I *knew* would come.

… *is having the time of her life.*

Seven words.

A status update.

And next to it, Sarah's name, so easily clickable.

And so I'd clicked it. And there she was. Having the time of her life.

Stop, I'd thought. Enough now. Get up, have a shower.

So I'd clicked on her photos.

She was in Andorra. With Gary. Having the time of her fucking life.

I'd snapped the laptop shut.

Didn't she care that I'd see this? Didn't she realise that this would go straight to my screen, straight to my stomach? These photos … these snapshots … taken from the point of view and angle *I* used to see her from. But now it's not *me* behind the camera. It's not *me* capturing the moment. These memories aren't *mine*. So I don't want them. I don't *want* to see her, tanned and happy and sleeveless. I don't *want* to see her across a table with a cocktail and a look of joy and love and laughter on her face. I don't *want* to search for and take in the tiny, pointless, hurtful details – they'd shared a Margherita, the curls of her hair had lightened in the sun, she'd stopped wearing the necklace I gave her – I didn't want *any* of it. But I'd opened up the laptop again and I'd looked again anyway, pored over them, took in *everything*. I hadn't been able to help it. Sarah was having the time of her life, and I was … well. What?

I'd looked to see what *my* last update had been.

Jason Priestley is … *eating some soup.*

Jesus. What a catch. Hey, Sarah, I know you're off having the time of your life and all, but let's not forget that only last Wednesday I was eating some soup.

Why didn't I just delete her? Take her out of the equation? Make the Internet safe again? Same reason there was still a picture of her in my wallet. The one of her on her first day at work – all big blue eyes and Louis Vuitton. I'd not been strong enough to rip it up or bin it. It seemed so … final. Like giving up, or something. But here's the thing: deep down, I knew one day *she'd* delete *me*. And then that really would be it, and it wouldn't be my decision, and then I'd be screwed. Part of me hoped that she wouldn't – that somewhere, in that bag of hers, the one full of make-up and *Grazia* and Kleenex, somewhere in that bag would be a photo of *me* …

And yeah, there's that hope again.

But then one day it'll be cruelly and casually crushed and I'll be forgotten, probably just before she decides that her and Gary should move in together, or her and Gary should get hitched, or her and Gary should make another, tiny Gary, which they'll call Gary, and who'll look exactly like bloody Gary.

I'll probably be sitting there, on my own, when she finally deletes me. In a grey room with a Paddington duvet above a videogame shop next to that place that everyone *thought* was a brothel but wasn't. A momentary afterthought, if that. Staring at a screen that informs me I can no longer obsess over her life. That I'm no longer deemed worthy of seeing her photos, seeing who her friends are, finding out when she's hungover, or sleepy, or late for work. That *she's* no longer interested in finding out when *I'm* eating soup.

My life.

Deleted.

Misery.

Still. Could be worse.

We could have run out of *Żubr*.

An hour later, and we'd run out of *Żubr*.

Dev had suggested the Den – a tiny Irish pub next to the tool hire shop, halfway down to King's Cross – and I'd said yeah, why not. You never know. I might have the time of my life.

'Ah, listen,' said Dev, waving one hand in the air. 'Who wants to go to Andorra anyway? What's so good about Andorra?'

The Pogues were on and we were now a little drunk.

'The scenery. The tax free shopping. The fact that it has two heads of State, those being the King of France and a Spanish bishop.'

A pause.

'You've been on Wikipedia, haven't you?'

I nodded.

'*Is* there a King of France?' asked Dev.

'President, then, I can't remember. All I know is it's somewhere you go and have the time of your life. With a man called Gary, just before you have a pride of little Garys – all of whom will look like tiny thuggish babies – and then you buy a boat and make cheese in the country.'

'What are you *talking* about?' said Dev.

'Sarah.'

'Is she having tiny thuggish babies?'

'Probably,' I slurred. 'Probably right now she's just popped another one out. They'll take over the world, her thuggish babies. They'll spread and multiply, like in *Arachnophobia*. They'll stick to people's faces and pound them with their little fists.'

Dev considered my wise words.

'You didn't used to be like this,' he said. 'Where did you go? Who's this grumpy man?'

'It is me,' I said. 'I am Mr Grumpy. I called home last week and Mum was like, "You never come back to Durham, why do you never come home to Durham?".'

'So why do you never go back to Durham?'

'Because it's a reminder, isn't it? Of going backwards. Anyway, Sarah doesn't have that problem. She's gonna have tiny thuggish babies.'

'I don't think she'll have thuggish babies. I thought Gary was, like, an investment banker?'

'Doesn't mean he's not gonna have thuggish babies,' I said, pointing my finger in the air to show I would not accept any form of contradiction on this. 'He's *exactly* the type of man to have a thuggish baby. A little skinhead one. Who's always shouting.'

'But that's just a *baby*,' said Dev.

'Whatever,' I said. 'Just don't feed one of them after midnight.'

There was a brief silence. An AC/DC track came on. My favourite. 'Back In Black' – the finest rock song of its time. I was momentarily cheered.

'Let's have another pint,' I said. 'A *Żubr*! Or a Zyborg!'

But Dev was looking at me, very seriously now.

'You should delete her,' he said, flatly. 'Just delete her. Be done with it. Leave Mr Grumpy behind, because Mr Grumpy is in danger of becoming Mr Dick. I'm no expert, but I'm sure that's what they'd say on *This Morning*, if you phoned up and asked one of those old women who solve problems.'

I nodded.

'I know,' I said, sadly.

'These are 2000 calories!' said Dev. '2000! I read about it in the paper!'

'You read about it in *my* paper,' I said. After several pints in the Den, we'd had the 'one we came for' and stopped at Oz's for a kebab on the way home. 'I'm the one who showed it to you and said, "Read this! It says kebabs are 2000 calories!"'

'Wherever I read it, I'm just saying, 2000 calories is a lot of calories for a kebab. But they're good for you, too.'

'How are they *good* for you?'

'They line your stomach with fat, so that when the apocalypse comes, you are better prepared. We'll survive longer. Tubby people will inherit the earth!'

Dev made a little 'yahoo!' sound, but then started coughing on his chilli sauce. He's a little obsessed with the apocalypse, through years of roaming post-apocalyptic landscapes, scavenging for objects and fighting giant beetles on videogames, which he genuinely regards as his 'important training'.

Right now, he was having trouble getting the key into the door. You'd lose points for that in an apocalypse. You'd also lose points for wearing glasses, but they're an important part of Dev. He has an IQ of around 146 according not just to a psychiatrist when he was four but also to some interactive quiz he did on the telly, which makes me proud of him when I'm drunk, though you'd never think it was anywhere *close* to 146 to speak to him. He has applied for four of the however-many-series of *The Apprentice* there've been, but for some reason they are yet to reply satisfactorily to this part-owner of a very minor second-hand videogame shop on the Caledonian Road, which I would find funny, if I didn't know this actually broke his heart.

It'd be easy to argue that Dev was defined at fourteen. His interests, his way with girls, even his look. See, when Dev was fourteen, his grandfather died, and that had a huge impact on his life. Not because it was emotionally traumatic, though of course it was, but because Dev's dad doesn't like to see money wasted. And the year before, Dev had started to notice he wasn't like the other kids. Just small things – not being able to see a sign, not being able to read a clock, and persistently and with great flair falling out of his bed. He was short-sighted.

His dad is a businessman. His dad thought, why pay for frames, when a pair of frames were clearly so nearly ready and available for no money whatsoever?

And so Dev had been given his granddad's frames. His *granddad's*. Literally three days after the funeral. Re-lensed, obviously, but by his dad's mate, on the Whitechapel Road, and with cheap, scuffable plastic. Dev went through the next four years ridiculed by all and sundry for having a young boy's face and an old man's pair of specs, like a toddler wearing his mum's sunglasses. He tried to grow a moustache to compensate, but that just made him look like a miniature military dictator.

And he'd never bought a new pair. Why should he? He'd found his look. And these days, it was working to his advantage. At university, at least at first, it had been considered odd, these thick black frames on a weird new kid, but they were a comfort blanket in year one, an eccentricity or quirk in year two and, he hoped, a chick magnet in year three.

(They weren't.)

But later, when you added them to the hair he couldn't be bothered to get cut and the T-shirts he either got for free or bought from eBay for a pound and a penny, these glasses screamed confidence. These glasses screamed ... well, they screamed 'Dev'.

Foreign girls, who couldn't understand him but liked bright jackets, thought he looked cool.

'Come on!' he said, finally through the door and slamming the banister with his fist as we stumbled upstairs. 'I know what'll cheer you up.'

In the flat, Dev threw his kebab onto the table and made for the kitchen, where he started to go through cupboards and loudly shift stuff about.

I wandered into my bedroom and picked up my laptop and made a determined face.

Maybe I *should* do it, I thought. Just delete her. Move on. Forget about things. Be the grown-up. It'd be easy. And then I could turn on my computer without that low, dull ache. That anticipation of maybe seeing something bad. I could get on with my life.

I heard Dev shout, 'Aha!', as I fired up the Internet.

'Found it, Jase! Prime bottle of *Jezynowka*! Blackberry brandy! How's about we hook up the N64 and drink *Jezynowka* and play *GoldenEye* 'til dawn?'

But I wasn't listening. Not really. I was only guessing at what he was saying. He could have been knocking over vases and composing racist songs for all I knew, because I was transfixed, and shocked, and I don't know what else, by what I saw on the screen.

One word this time.

One word that kicked me in the teeth and stamped on my hope and made fun of my family.

'Jase?' said Dev, suddenly there, in my doorway. 'D'you want to be James Bond or Natalia?'

But I didn't look round.

My eyes were pricked with tears and I could feel every hair on my body, because all I could see were the words 'Sarah Bennett is …' and then that last one, that killer, that complete and absolute *bastard* of a word.

Also by Danny Wallace:

Charlotte Street

My name is Jason – and I have just met the most incredible woman, on Charlotte Street. Well, I say 'met'. I sort of held her bags for a second. But she smiled at me! And it was this amazing smile.

Of course, I don't know her name, or anything about her at all. But I do happen to have something of hers. She left behind one of those old-school disposable cameras. I've got it. It's here in front of me.

So there are two things I could now do: I could develop the photos. See her again, see her life. Maybe work out a way of finding her. Find that smile. Or I could chuck it in a bin like a grown-up.

I'm fairly sure one of those ideas is a good one. I'm fairly sure the other might be illegal. Look, if you were me... what would you do?

EBURY
PRESS

Awkward Situations for Men

DANNY WALLACE IS A MAN.

And a man is a very tricky thing to be these days.

Trouble is everywhere. Embarrassment follows closely behind.

Whether accidentally insulting a friend's baby, being caught wearing pyjamas by his wife, or inadvertently following a woman down a very dark street, Danny is no stranger to awkward situations.

As we follow a year in Danny's life in which he blunders from one bewildering social situation to the next, it becomes clear that here is a man who struggles even to look after himself properly. And then an even greater responsibility looms on the horizon...

EBURY
PRESS

Also by Danny Wallace:

More Awkward Situations for Men

In the brilliant AWKWARD SITUATIONS FOR MEN, Danny Wallace entertained us with wonderfully funny true stories from his often embarrassing and bewildering everyday life as a man.

Well, Danny is back – and he's even more confused than ever!

A lot has happened to Danny Wallace in the past year. He has had a baby and has been hobnobbing with the powers that be in Hollywood. But that hasn't made him any less awkward.

Being more of a grown up brings its own baffling etiquette and expected social graces, and no-one has told Danny.

Join Danny once again on his very funny stumble through more Awkward Situations. It's not easy being a man!

EBURY
PRESS

Also by Danny Wallace:

Yes Man

'I, Danny Wallace, being of sound mind and body, do hereby write this manifesto for my life. I swear I will be more open to opportunity. I swear I will live my life taking every available chance. I will say Yes to every favour, request, suggestion and invitation. I WILL SWEAR TO SAY YES WHERE ONCE I WOULD SAY NO.'

Danny Wallace had been staying in. Far too much. Having been dumped by his girlfriend, he really wasn't doing the young, free and single thing very well. Instead he was avoiding people. Texting them instead of calling them. Calling them instead of meeting them. That is until one fateful date when a mystery man on a late-night bus told him to 'say yes more'. These three simple words changed Danny's life forever. *Yes Man* is the story of what happened when Danny decided to say YES to everything, in order to make his life more interesting. And boy, did it get more interesting.

Danny's story was made into a hit film starring Jim Carrey.

EBURY
PRESS